RISE OF THE MANŌ

KAIMANA ISLAND BOOK ONE

LEIALOHA HUMPHERYS

This book is a work of fiction. Any references to historical events, real people, or real places are used fictitiously. Other names, characters, places, and events are products of the author's imagination, and any resemblances to actual events or places or persons, living or dead, is entirely coincidental.

First paperback edition January 2022

ISBN (paperback) 978-1-7378074-2-1

ISBN (ebook) 978-1-7378074-3-8

Published by Hokulani Press

Santaquin, Utah

United States of America

www.naturallyaloha.com

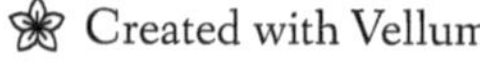

To my sister, Kamele, for cheering me on through every step of this book. The world needs more people like you.

Kaimana Island
KE AO MAKANI ISLAND
HENEKA'I
Hakalau Village
WINDWARD
King Makana
MAUNA KI'E KI'E
KĪPUKA
WOOD OF PURPLE
KĪPUKA
Papaikou Village
The Māku'e
TWIN VOLCANOS
LEEWARD
Waiakea Village
Fortress of King Ekewaka
Olukai
The Hune
Kea'au Village
Huna Bay
The Great White Manō
KIPUKA
Kealakekua Bay
MOANA PĀKĪPIKA
Ghost Village
MAUNA LANI
A
K
H
H
HAUNTED ISLAND
Village at South Point

CHAPTER ONE

Nohea sprinted through the king's garden, a place forbidden to slaves like her. The ferns and leaves brushed against her legs, and the palm trees made rustling noises as the trade winds moved through the area.

A *pueo* flew overhead and a brief shadow crossed Nohea's face. Her bare feet slipped along the mossy garden floor but she caught herself in time to see the owl hovering above, his brown wings tinged with gold. He rarely circled the gardens, but when he did, she felt a strong sense that she needed to honor its presence.

Nohea glanced to the distance towards her destination, then back to the sky, tapping her fingers against her side. She sighed and grabbed hold of the nearest coconut tree, hoisting herself up.

This will be quick, she thought.

Her brown arms pulled her higher and higher until she reached the top, panting as she brushed aside the coconut fronds and scanned the sky. The pueo hooted and landed on the nearest tree.

"It's not much," Nohea said, reaching into the woven *lauhala* bag at her side. Food was hard to come by as a slave, but she'd managed to save some bits of taro for any animal friends she passed along the garden. Of all the animals she crossed, this pueo's visits felt special.

She unwrapped the small chunk of taro from the ti leaves, and held it as far as she could to the owl. He was quite small, with fuzzy feathers and a white belly. He cocked his head to one side, his golden eyes curious.

"It's for you," Nohea said, her fingers shaking both from her sprint and hunger. The owl blinked and hesitated, then hopped closer to grab the chunk from her hand. It tipped its head. A smile crossed Nohea's face and she tipped her head back to it.

Spreading its wings, the owl flew, the taro chunk in its little beak. As Nohea watched him drifting away, her eyes caught the view in the distance: the ocean. At the age of sixteen, Nohea had never seen the ocean up close, not even felt the sticky mist on her skin. Confined to the life of slavery in the king's fortress, Nohea's only hope of seeing the ocean was in climbing. She'd stopped climbing long ago, as the view of the ocean only made her jealous and angry.

And today, the distance between her and the ocean served as one more reminder of her status as a slave. She would never get to see the water up close, hear the waves, or feel the sand.

Sometimes, it felt like the ocean didn't exist beyond the walls of the king's fortress. The tall walls, made of koa trunks, towered over everything, keeping the slaves inside and the villagers out. Whoever built the walls lashed the koa trees so tightly together, that not even a small child could fit through the cracks. Nohea knew, because she tried when she was younger.

There was no way out of the king's fortress, besides a few gates that Nohea never saw.

She wiped some sweat from her forehead. But her status didn't matter, and this was all she knew. She glanced at the earth beneath, scanning the gardens, hoping to see any sort of new plant, herb, or remedy.

No time. Nohea swallowed hard. She let herself down the

coconut trunk and landed softly onto the garden floor. A gentle breeze blew, carrying with it a fresh hint of *maile,* her favorite scent.

Without hesitating to enjoy the smell longer, she darted, again, through the grounds. If she didn't find a cure—any kind of cure—she might lose someone dear to her, a fellow slave. Though not blood related, Kimo felt like family and his wife, Nui, felt like an aunt. Nohea didn't call them "aunty" and "uncle" like her peers, though, because Nohea was more mature than those her age. All the adults even treated her as an equal.

Nohea's hair stood on end, though sweat glistened on her skin, as she thought of the accident. Not many days ago Kimo sliced his leg open, on accident of course, with the *leimanō* while working. It happened frequently among the slaves as they were too tired to use caution. Usually the slaves healed, thanks to Nohea's medicines and herbs. But this time, the injury went so deep, Nohea was at a loss. She tried disinfecting and cauterizing the wound, but Kimo raged with a fever for days.

Frustration welled up in her chest. Why didn't she know more formulas and concoctions for medicine? She splashed through a river, not even pausing to cool off her hands and face. Her mother, Edena, was an accomplished alchemist, and though she said she taught Nohea "everything," as Edena put it, Nohea still wondered if Edena withheld some knowledge.

A humming from the earth beneath made Nohea stop. Again. Though her mind pounded on her to hurry, she respected this sign. She closed her eyes and listened. Whenever the earth moved, the trade winds blew a cool breeze, or the energy around her vibrated, Nohea knew it was the island, Kaimana Island. Not very many people listened to the island, because its signs and messages were quiet, easy to ignore. But some, like Nohea, had learned to quiet their mind and connect with the land. She always trusted the messages from the land, knowing that when she listened and cared for the land, it would care for her.

The ʻōhiʻa tree.

The island had no loud voice, but the impression came so clearly that when Nohea opened her eyes and looked at her surroundings, she knew the island had prompted her. Reaching for the branches of the nearest ʻōhiʻa, she began snipping off its *lehua* blossoms.

Nohea knew how the ʻōhiʻa, and many other plants in the garden, could help people heal. Edena brought Nohea to the king's garden long ago, teaching Nohea the names and uses of every plant, but there was so much more in the garden that Nohea needed to explore. There were more plants than what Edena had taught, and Nohea sighed at all the gaps in her personal knowledge.

Though the slaves called Nohea their alchemist, it did little to help Nohea feel official. Until she found a cure to end all their ailments, she didn't feel like a successful alchemist. She didn't deserve that title.

"Hey sis, what took you so long?"

Nohea jumped, wrapped up in her worries as she plucked the fiery red lehua blossoms. A young man stood before her, his body tipped to one side as he leaned on a bamboo crutch. Nohea folded her arms. It was Likeke, the king's son.

"I could ask you the same question."

The boy smiled, his teeth looking very white against his dark brown skin. His thick midnight hair ran down his back, and his body looked frail in his black skirt. He was a little taller than Nohea, with a wide nose and lips.

Many of the men wore skirts and the *kihei*, a triangular cloth tied over one shoulder and hung over the chest. Meanwhile, the women wore wrap-around dresses or tunics, with simple woven belts made of *ti* leaves or other island plants.

Some women, if they had enough clothes, wore a kihei over the shoulder, like the men. But most slaves didn't have any means to make or trade for clothes, so they made their clothes out of hand-me-downs, whatever *kapa* scraps the king's concubines tossed away.

Nohea wore a light brown tunic today, tied on both shoulders, and it hung to her knees, secured by a braided ti leaf cord around her waist.

"I was hung up with my father," Like said and stopped before her. They kissed one another's cheeks, the island custom. A year older than Nohea, Like paled in size and stature to his older brother, Lopaka. Every slave knew Lopaka, for he sometimes wandered around, like a spoiled, hungry mongoose, making trouble with the slaves. He was tall and strong, a warrior to the king, but Nohea couldn't stand when he came around the little slave village to brawl, gamble, or drink. Though Lopaka had been absent for the last couple of months—busy on the king's missions—Nohea still avoided him anytime she caught a glimpse of him roaming the area.

Like was different. He was kind and understanding, a friend since she started searching the garden alone.

"What happened today?" Nohea asked as she reached into the bag at her side, finding the medicine she made for Like. He'd been born with something that made his joints swell, and it caused him severe pain. Of the king's only two sons, Like was not favored because of his ailments. Rumors spread that the king would've killed Like had he not been a male. But Nohea never believed rumors.

And besides, she thought, *my job isn't about gossip. It's about helping. Like is in pain, so I will help him.* She made medicine every week to help his joints stop swelling and to ease the pain.

"I'm not sure, but my father was very upset this morning when he found out he had another daughter. Anyway, he's going to Waimea today to see how the horses are breeding." Like grimaced. "Did you find something for your friend?"

Nohea shook her head. "I wish. Only some uli and nuts from the kukui tree." She motioned to the "ōhi'a tree beside her. "And some lehua blossoms."

"Can I show you something? I thought of it this morning—it's kind of hidden, but I passed by it the other day and thought of you."

"How far is it?" Nohea knew the garden was bigger than she expected, and it would take days to explore every crack and crevice.

She grabbed a small glass vial from her bag and handed it to Like. "A drop a day should go a long way." He'd given her the little glass vials, relics from the white foreigners who disappeared years ago. After he used up the medicine in one vial, he returned it to her for filling.

Like then opened his own woven bag. "Thanks, and this is for you."

They traded. She made him medicine, and he gave her food: four fried fish, four cooked sweet potatoes, and some sweet coconut pudding squares, all of it wrapped in ti leaves. She carefully placed them in her bag, her stomach growling as she restrained herself from eating that very moment. Nohea needed to save the food to share with her mother and other unfortunate slave families, especially the ill. Maybe if the pueo came around again later she would share with him too.

Like took a drop of medicine, his dark hands trembling so much that Nohea considered helping him. Instead, she looked away, pretending his shaking condition wasn't as bad as it truly was. He already struggled with his confidence and she didn't want to make it worse.

"It's not far from here." He put the medicine into his bag, sighed, then hobbled into the thicker part of the garden. Nohea knew this part, where the banyan trees took up huge amounts of space, their branches hanging so low that they dug into the ground.

Sweat covered Like's thick brows. The sun began to grow warmer and a pang of fear struck Nohea's chest. The other slaves had probably awakened at this point, and were hurrying off to their stations. The slave master, Pulu, kept charge of every slave, noting who went where, and at what times. If any person slacked off or was late, they received a swift punishment. He even reported it to the king's counselor in charge of the slaves, Ano.

Nohea winced at the thought. She'd been late to her post more than a few times, and could still feel the sting of the whip on her back, or the swift blow to her ear.

But Kimo... Her mind kept going back to him. Nohea tried to shake off her impatience with their pace. It wasn't Like's fault that he walked so slowly.

"Here it is." Like moved some thick ferns aside and they stepped into an opening.

"It's beautiful." Nohea gasped. For the many times she explored the garden, she still had so much to see and explore.

A dark pond rippled before them, the air cool. A soft gurgling noise sounded in the distance, but the movement of orange, gold, and red colors in the water caught Nohea's eye. She knelt next to the pond and saw long, thick-bodied fish, with large eyes, fat lips, and mustache-like pieces on the sides of their lips.

"They're called koi," Like said.

The sun barely peeked through the thickness of the banyan tree canopy, but when it did, the koi's scaly bodies reflected beautiful colors on the water's surface.

"These fish are from the foreigners," Like added, but he didn't need to, because Nohea already knew. The king coveted anything of the foreigners, and she wasn't surprised he'd been breeding these fish in secret.

She chuckled, but it came out more as a snort and she gasped at her own unladylike response before speaking. "What other foreigner things does the king hide?"

Like sat next to her and didn't answer as their reflections stared back at them. Nohea blinked at herself. It'd been a long time since she saw herself this clearly: tanned skin, a few freckles across her rosy cheeks and nose, cheeks sunken in from hunger, and long, wavy hair cascading down either side of her face. She brushed her hair back, the sun shining on the bright highlights, a result of hours of labor in the outdoors. Her eyes were the most unique part of her, for her left eye was a light brown, the same warm color of coconut husks, and the other an intense gold, the color of sand—or so she'd been told, as she'd never seen the ocean up close.

Usually unique features, deformities, or disabilities were regarded by the *kahuna*, the priests and sorcerers, as something bad, like a curse or mark of disfavor. But the slave family hardly acknowledged her strange eyes, just as they didn't worry about the fact that Kimo was deaf. The slaves had other things to worry about, like surviving.

"You know what he hides," Like finally answered. "Books, glass... some even rumor there's a shipwreck on the east coast that he's been hiding for years."

Nohea eyed Like. "A shipwreck? Serious?"

"'Ae, Lopaka confirmed it."

She studied him, then broke into a laugh. "You're teasing!"

Like's serious gaze fell apart as he laughed too. "You believed me—"

"Not for long!" She elbowed him, knowing that there were no foreigners on Kaimana Island, nor any of their ships. King Ekewaka and the islanders burned them while the rest of the foreigners escaped, sailing far away, never to be seen again.

Nohea then noticed the koi swimming towards the edge of the pond, trying to get her attention. Their faces broke the surface, curious to see if she'd dropped anything in. Nohea shook her head. *Not today.* She would rather give her food to an owl friend than the king's fat fish. Her smile faded.

The foreigners... they were the ones who introduced diseases to the islanders, wiped them all out. While the foreigners had advanced technology and sophisticated ways of writing and recording, the sickness they brought killed almost every islander. The entire bloodline of the *ali'i*, the true kings and queens of Kaimana island, succumbed to the diseases. A man named Ekewaka, along with his brother Makana, rose up to lead the people, kill or scare off the rest of the foreigners, and restore peace and order to Kaimana Island.

If only I had some sort of cure, Nohea thought. *Then the foreigners wouldn't have killed our people. The cure would have protected us...*

"I have to go," she said quite abruptly, and Like sobered.

"Sorry for taking so much of your time," he said.

"No need to apologize." Nohea used her stone knife to snip more purple-blue uli heads. Various types of ginger grew abundantly on Kaimana island, but Nohea understood the purple ginger, uli, the best. It possessed juices and oils that soothed wounds and eased pain, yet a whiff of it dry could put anyone to sleep.

"Mahalo," she whispered as she bowed her head to the earth and touched the ground beneath the ginger bushes. It was only appropriate to thank the island for its abundance when taking something from it. The island hummed beneath her feet in response.

"Good luck Nohea," Like said before she rushed off.

"Thanks Like." She looked at the sky, knowing if she didn't hurry it would be a whipping for sure. She stood and sprinted out of the garden, her mind already racing on ways to create a cure for Kimo.

CHAPTER TWO

Nohea didn't make it in time to her post. Pulu knocked her head with his thick, calloused hand, making her left ear ring for the rest of the day. But she worked diligently, as usual, alongside Nui.

Nui's eyes were puffy and red from crying the previous night, and Nohea hated it.

"Don't give up hope," she said to Nui as they bent over the water-filled kalo field. The large heart-shaped leaves made the women's skin itchy, and the cold water caused them to shiver. But they had no choice. Their task was to weed a portion of the field, and then harvest another part. Nohea's hands hurt from the wet, hard weeds growing around the large green kalo plants.

"I have to be prepared for the worst," Nui replied, after seeing the slave master occupied with something else.

"I got some uli this morning." Nohea kept glancing at the task master, making sure he didn't see them conversing. "I'm sure it will help—uli almost always soothes aches."

Nui didn't reply. Instead, she stared blankly at her work, her eyes tired, and her expression somber.

. . .

WHEN THE SUN began to set over the horizon, the task master released the slaves. Nohea ran to her mother's hut. Edena, the only privileged slave of the slaves, was given the task to care for the king's library. He claimed to be the only person on the whole island with books, the magical work from the foreigners. Nohea knew, though, that her mother did more than just sit in the library, guarding the books. She studied the books to teach every concept, every strategy, and every bit of knowledge from them to Nohea. And Edena wouldn't be home until the skies grew completely dark.

Nohea sat on the woven mat of her mother's hut and dumped out the things from her bag. Her stomach rumbled at the sight of the food Like gave her earlier, but she ignored it—Kimo needed her help. And now.

She got to work crushing the blue ginger heads on her homemade mortar and pestle, a gray lava slab on the ground, with a long rounded lava rock in her hand. Soon, she found herself in the familiar rhythm of her work, and her mind drifted to all the things her mother taught her: things about plants, medicines, oils, flowers, roots, and bark. And Edena taught Nohea so many languages: the language of the islanders, the foreigners, and even the witch women, called the *meha.*

To Nohea, Edena was the most accomplished alchemist, even if she was the only known alchemist to the slaves, on Kaimana Island. When Nohea started doing alchemy herself, Edena retreated. She no longer wished to practice alchemy, only contributing to help a woman give birth if Nohea asked. Sometimes Nohea felt angry that her mother didn't teach or help her more. But she needed to be grateful for what knowledge her mother did pass on.

At least she taught me many useful things, Nohea thought, *and at least I have a mother.*

When the foreigners came, more than twenty years ago, they brought with them sicknesses and disease. The illnesses exploded like the twin volcanoes, destroying everything in its path. Almost every islander died, leaving behind widows, orphans, and broken families. The culture, language, and customs of the people of Kaimana island were lost for a moment, as the royal ali'i, the true kings and queens of the island, died from the sicknesses.

But there's always hope, Nohea reminded herself, reflecting on the current king. A new leader rose, Ekewaka, a man who reunited the island, restored the customs, traditions, language, and more. He had served the island well, picking up the pieces of a crumbled society and creating a kingdom that thrived. His brother, Makana, was equally as strong of a leader, or so Nohea had been told. His *mana* was powerful, and intimidating.

The brothers started out as true brothers, but something happened, war broke out, and they parted ways, Makana and his followers being outcast to the leeward side of the island, never to be heard of or seen again. Other leaders broke away from the rule of Ekewaka, some retreating to the wood of purple, a dark place, and others fleeing into the heart of the mountains.

Nohea blinked hard, stirring herself from the strange history. Like said that those who fled to the purple forest transformed... at least, their bodies transformed. Their ears changed, as they claimed to be the only ones who could communicate with and truly hear the voice of the island.

Like also said that those who fled to the mountains were of an ancient race of Menehune, dwarf men and women.

"Nohea."

Startled, Nohea turned to the door of the hut, where a young girl stood, rocking on her heels.

"Pua." The young girl often came to Nohea's hut to deliver messages from other slaves.

"I'm sorry to interrupt," Pua said, wringing her hands. She had to be no older than eight years old. "But he's getting worse. Nui asked when you're coming over."

A pang struck Nohea's chest as she looked at the smashed herbs below her. She wasn't even close to a new solution, but she had to try something. Anything. The blue purple goo from the smashed uli plant gave her some confidence. Uli rarely let her down. "Now."

The girl nodded and ran off. The sun set and Nohea made her way to the other side of the slave village.

WHEN NOHEA SET out to Kimo's hut, her body trembled, tired from fatigue and lack of food, but she forced herself to keep moving.

Nui sat beside her husband, tears in her eyes. Other slaves had gathered, crowding the hut, chanting quiet *'oli* of healing.

Kimo laid on the woven mats of the hut, his frail body shaking, his eyes open but vacant.

Nohea knelt beside him, feeling his hot forehead. He gazed straight through Nohea, a look she knew too well. It was the look of one ready to breathe their last *hā,* their last breath.

Nohea and Nui gently elevated Kimo's upper body so Nohea could empty her small coconut bowl of medicine into his mouth. She wanted to cry seeing him like this, but she kept strong, her trembling fingers the only indication of her breaking emotions.

He choked, coughing hard, but swallowed most of it. His graying hair was down, but he usually wore it up. It was as though the mourners had already dressed him for death. His once dark, healthy color now looked pale. Purple half moons rimmed his dark brown eyes.

Nui sat on one side of him, holding his hand, and Nohea on the other, holding his other hand. Their eyes met and Nohea nodded, joining the chanting of those in the room. The Hawaiian words caused chills to run up Nohea's spine:

May healing be yours,
Showered upon you like the rains of the mauna,
Come forth with rushing like the waves of the kai,
Destroy the fiery illness like the lava from below...

The hut fell into a trance. A soft breeze entered from the door of the hut.

Kimo's body calmed down, and he rested, the shakes and shivers gone. Nohea felt his forehead, his temperature decreased.

Letting out a sigh of relief, she nodded to Nui. The medicine had worked, and Nohea was grateful for it.

She closed her eyes for a moment, thanking the island. Uli rarely let her down, and this was no exception. Mixed with the blossoms and juice of the ʻōhiʻa lehua blossom, it had become extra potent.

As Nohea gathered her things, she felt an itch that someone was watching her.

Sure enough, Edena stood at the door frame of the hut, observing the scene. Edena had bright brown eyes, a slender frame, and long black hair. She was a beautiful woman, always with a stern look on her face. Edena glanced from Kimo to Nohea and nodded, then disappeared into the darkness. Edena was not a woman of many words, and Nohea expected that when she arrived home, her mother would ask only a few questions before retiring to sleep.

"I'll return in the morning," Nohea said to Nui as they kissed one another's cheeks. "You should get some rest," she added and Nui nodded, her dark eyes sunken with fatigue.

Before Nohea left the hut, she glanced once more at Kimo. He looked peaceful, and Nui rested next to him, staring at his face. Nohea smiled , grateful for the generosity of the island and the nourishment of its plants. Then she hurried home.

Edena had already delivered half the food to other slave families in need, leaving only two fishes, two sweet potatoes, and one coconut pudding square. Nohea took the large gourd, full of water, sitting by the door frame and opened it to pour water into coconut bowls.

"What did you try for Kimo?" Edena asked, her usual voice tight and distant.

"The uli head with a dash of ʻōhiʻa juice."

Edena nodded, handing Nohea a leaf plate of food. "That was very wise—a good choice. His fever went down?"

Nohea took a drink before saying, "'Ae, very quickly."

Her mother didn't smile, and, instead, began eating her food in silence. Nohea swallowed hard before taking a bite. This was her mother's typical reaction, and it seemed no matter how impressed Nohea felt with herself, Edena never commended her successes.

"Like showed me the koi pond this morning," Nohea added, trying to keep her voice upbeat.

Silence. Then, "Oh... the king owns too many fish."

"They were beautiful." Nohea knew the conversation was over, and her mother would say no more words. Edena didn't even glance at Nohea. She ate her food and looked to the torch that warmed the hut a few feet away from them.

Only a few days ago Edena announced she'd taught Nohea everything from the books in the library. Since then, the words exchanged were fewer than ever before, and Nohea's desire to have *any* conversations were crushed. So they ate in silence, and then Edena laid down to rest, turning so her back faced Nohea. Though this occurred every night, it still sent a pang through Nohea's chest. She and her mother were not close. She'd seen her mother's hidden glances of annoyance, her nose sniffed up in disgust at Nohea. Nohea clearly knew she was an unwanted child, from a man that Edena despised and would not name.

A quiet sigh escaped Nohea before she returned to making more medicine for Kimo. She would wake up long before the sun and check on him. As she crushed the *uli,* the blue purple juices pooled on the oval-shaped stone. *Kimo will be fine...* She could already see him: healthy, happy, making the slaves laugh like he always did. It gave her the strength to complete the medicine before she rested her head to sleep.

. . .

Sleep never came. Something didn't feel right, and she kept hearing a pueo hooting in the distance, probably the one that followed her around. Nohea finally sat up, annoyed, pushing hair out of her face.

Fine, she thought, then grabbed her bag of medicine to check up on Kimo.

The slave village was small, with the huts, made of trunks and thatched roofing, sitting close to one another. A private conversation would never be considered "private" because the walls, built of woven mats and secured by trunks of various woods, and the roofs of thatched grass or ti leaves, were terribly thin. All the huts circled around one main area, where a slave kept watch over the little village and the big campfire.

The slaves started appointing a watch because some of the king's warriors, including the king's son Lopaka, used to sneak into the village to drink and gamble. Since the watch, the *pilikia,* trouble, disappeared.

Kimo and Nui lived on the opposite end of the village, so Nohea made her way around the huts, her bare feet making little noise on the dusty ground.

"Eh Nohea—what you doing up so late?" The slave on watch at the campfire called to her. He was much older than Kimo, a survivor of the diseases, though he'd developed some kind of cough and never fully recovered.

"I'm checking on Kimo," she replied. The watch tipped his head to her and she continued.

As she neared the hut of Kimo and Nui, she felt something was wrong. The sound of sobs broke through the hut walls, though Nohea didn't want to believe it.

And, in spite of herself, she ran. Before Nohea even reached the doorframe, she knew.

As she stood there, looking in, seeing Nui's tear stricken face, Kimo's body peacefully lying there, his eyes closed, Nohea dropped to her knees.

Her medicine hadn't worked after all. She hadn't been able to save Kimo. She couldn't do it. She bowed her head to the ground and wept.

Kimo was gone, and she couldn't save him.

THE FOLLOWING DAY, the slaves worked so hard, their backs burned from the tropical sun, and they each walked at a painstakingly slow pace to their homes at the end of the shift. The king was having a grand celebration for the birth of his daughter and invited the greatest from the island to join. Nohea rubbed her sunburnt neck as she walked with the others. Her body and skin hurt, but her heart hurt more. Anger welled up in her chest.

It had always been unfair to be a slave, but today felt especially infuriating. Not only did the life of a slave cause her uncle to lose his life, but the other slaves could not even take the time to grieve him like other islanders. They had to return straight away to hard physical labour... *all while the king prepares for his lavish parties,* Nohea thought, curling her fists.

She didn't usually get angry at the king, but his position and power stung her today.

To add to her already broken and confused feelings, halfway through the day it felt like something crushed her leg so hard, she fell to the ground. She'd been standing in the kalo field, and Nui grabbed her. The task master scolded Nohea for acting so dramatically, but she limped the rest of the day. She hated when moments like this randomly occurred in her life: a tingling in the fingers, air knocked out of the stomach, the feeling of burning skin, a ringing ear. But she ignored it, because she already had so many other things to worry about.

That night, the slaves carried Kimo's body to the distant *heiau* within the fortress, a designated heiau for the slaves, where they gathered wood and burned the body. As Nohea stared at the flames, something in her grew. She didn't need her mother's graces, though she'd always be grateful for the knowledge. But she would not become cold like her mother—she would keep using her gifts and knowledge for good.

She would find a cure to help the slaves. She'd lost too many brothers, sisters, uncles, and aunts to diseases, fatigue, and childbirth... but no, Kimo would be the last one.

And maybe the cure would gain the slaves their freedom. *Nobody should* ever *be a slave,* she thought.

She watched as Nui trembled and cried, held by the other slave women for support.

Nohea glanced up and noticed Edena staring at her. The flames danced in Edena's eyes, her lips turned downward, her eyebrows creased, and Nohea felt a strong sense of anger directed right at herself. The moment passed, as Edena turned and disappeared in the shadows of the night.

Nohea decided: No matter what it cost, she would find a cure for the people of the island. There would no longer be a ghost generation lost to foreigners' diseases, no longer be unnecessary deaths amongst the slaves, and the entire island would all be healthy. *Healthiness leads to happiness,* she thought and nodded, her mind set.

Edena had no courage or strength to do it, but Nohea did.

She would do all she could to learn and find the cure for the suffering people of the island, no matter the cost.

CHAPTER THREE

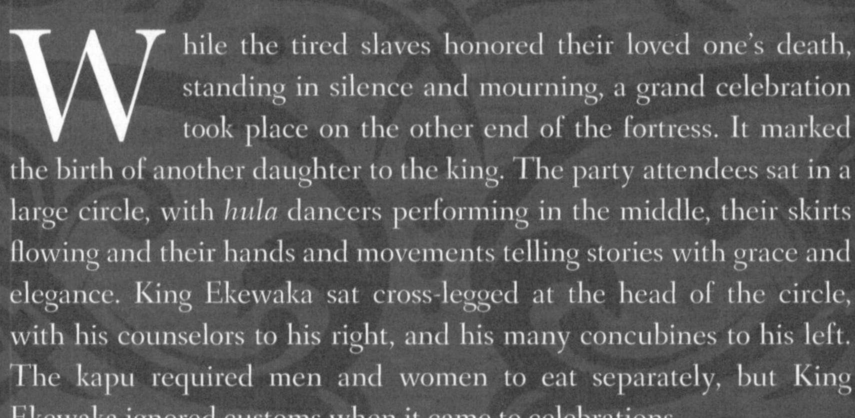

While the tired slaves honored their loved one's death, standing in silence and mourning, a grand celebration took place on the other end of the fortress. It marked the birth of another daughter to the king. The party attendees sat in a large circle, with *hula* dancers performing in the middle, their skirts flowing and their hands and movements telling stories with grace and elegance. King Ekewaka sat cross-legged at the head of the circle, with his counselors to his right, and his many concubines to his left. The kapu required men and women to eat separately, but King Ekewaka ignored customs when it came to celebrations.

A young counselor sat a few places away from the king, and he tried to keep a troubled look from his face. His name was Olukai, and he observed the king's mood change from grumpy—grumpy from the day's happenings, and grumpy to have yet another daughter— to delighted by the entertainment. Olukai folded his arms and tried to focus: this was not a moment to watch the king. It was a moment to keep on his mask, the mask that hid his true identity.

At the age of nineteen, Olukai had seen the entire island, and the king needed him because of that. Olukai started going on the king's missions at the age of sixteen and began leading the king's armies and warriors at the age of seventeen.

By the age of nineteen, Olukai was more than just a captain to the king. He earned his place on the council. As the islanders said, Olukai was the "best fire dancer" on Kaimana, and King Ekewaka appointed Olukai to teach the islanders the ancient art of fire dancing, taken from their ancestors before they left Samoa. After the foreigners destroyed more than half of the islanders, Ekewaka made the wise decision to bring back ancient customs and arts, and Olukai gladly stepped up to the plate.

As the next group of hula dancers stood up to perform, King Ekewaka tapped Olukai's shoulder. "See that one there? That is Haunani. I've heard the rumors about you two." Olukai followed the direction of the king's gaze to a beautiful young woman. She had to be about sixteen years old, with thick black hair that fell past her waist. She had a heart shaped face, skin the golden brown color of sand at sunset, and dark brown eyes. She moved with expression, from the way she pointed her toes, the graceful movements of her hands and arms, and the emotion on her face. Her ti leaf skirt swayed perfectly with her every movement and Olukai nodded, impressed. She was, indeed, a beautiful young woman and hula dancer.

Olukai had met her once before. Rumors had spread through the kingdom, like the heavy flow of lava, that Olukai and Haunani were meant for one another, because he was known as the island's greatest fire knife dancer, and she the island's greatest hula dancer. But when he met her, it was because Olukai needed the help of her *hānai* brother, not her.

Po, Haunani's hānai brother, was Olukai's messenger. As Olukai sat in the circle with the others, he felt a strangeness in the air that he would need Po that very night. The island seemed disturbed, an unnerving tension in the ground, but Olukai couldn't make out the message amidst the drums, laughter, and talk.

Though Haunani kept smiling at him, Olukai's attention turned to the distant horizon, the ocean. The celebration spot was on the highest hill in the king's fortress, affording Olukai such a view of the moonlight sparkling on the waves. Only in this place could someone look out to see the ocean from the fortress, unless they climbed a tree.

Olukai rubbed his right wrist, covered with a black kapa cloth. A few months ago, the great white manō revealed a mark on Olukai's skin. It had started on his wrist but slowly grew up his forearm, the tribal symbols coming together to reveal the shape of a manō. It was the mark of the island's true ali'i. Olukai fidgeted with the kapa cloth, tired of how long he'd worn this. He feigned a burn from his fire knife, and everyone believed him so far, but it was only a matter of time before the symbol spread up his shoulders, then possibly to his neck and chest. What then? There would be no hiding his true identity, but was he good enough to be an ali'i? Olukai glanced at King Ekewaka.

Ekewaka, who was not truly from the line of the great ali'i, seemed a better ruler than Olukai. When the foreigners came, their diseases killed the entire line of the ali'i, or so everyone thought, but the island had forgotten about an ali'i princess who had been cast out years before the foreigners arrived. That was Olukai's mother, Kehau. She married for love, and because of her disobedience was despised by her family. But Olukai's heart melted each time he thought of his mother: she had been so beautiful, so thoughtful, and compassionate, compared to the stiffness and coldness of his father.

As the foreigners' sicknesses took the islanders one by one, Ekewaka, once a good man, rose and gathered the people together. He cast out the foreigners, sent the rest of the infected to exile on the Haunted Island, and established himself the new king of Kaimana island.

Olukai wondered: Did he have as much courage as, if not more than, Ekewaka, to reunite the island once more? Many people didn't agree with Ekewaka's ways, and they branched off: the Māku'e went to the dark forest, the Hune dug into the mountains, and Makana fled to the northern side of the island. How could Olukai live up to his role? A headache started coming on.

"Come eat, Olukai! You are distracted!" the king boomed, his eyes merry as he drank from a large gourd. Olukai immediately brightened up, putting on a smile, though he felt distant from the facade he wore. His face was charming, and the king's daughters across the way erupted in giggles, blushes, and laughter. Olukai ignored them. He ignored all of the girls, as they all fantasized about him, making him uncomfortable. The king's daughters weren't the only ones eyeing him out. The hula dancers kept batting their eyes, throwing him smiles, and winking.

Olukai had never wanted this life, especially since he was only a poor fisherman before this. He never expected to get this much attention, and now that he knew his true identity, it made his head spin. With his fingers, he took a bite of the purple poi to calm his thoughts.

But the poi only sent a pang through his chest, reminding him of his mother. She made the best poi. Olukai could still remember when he was seven, and the king's warriors went through each household on the island, checking for any markings of disease. He could almost feel the relief flooding through him as he and both of his parents were cleared. They had no sign of disease. But his relief was short-lived, as a year later, somehow his mother caught the sickness. She passed away when Olukai was eight.

"They are good, no?" King Ekewaka asked, leaning over Kahiko, another trusted counselor and kahuna to the king, to address Olukai. The king's dark eyes watched the performers. The king always enjoyed small talk with Olukai, as opposed to Kahiko.

Olukai nodded, trying to stay present. "'Ae, I am impressed."

"You will perform for us tonight?" the king asked.

"If it pleases the king," Olukai bowed his head.

King Ekewaka laughed, drunk with pride and power. "'Ae! It does please me!"

Kahiko's dark black eyes glared at Olukai. A perpetual power struggle always existed between Kahiko, the king's other counselor, a kahuna, and Olukai.

Olukai simply smirked at Kahiko, then looked towards the

performers. The king had been very displeased earlier that day when he tried to ride one of the island's best horses from Waimea. King Ekewaka was so large and intimidating, the horse panicked and kicked him between the knee and shin. The impact was so hard, the king's bones nearly snapped. The king ordered all the horses executed, but Olukai helped him calm down and, afterwards, reassured the caretakers that they would not return to kill the horses.

The king had quite the temper, but now he was in a good mood, drinking the magical island juice, called soran, from his gourd and watching the dancers. His leg was neatly wrapped in kapa cloth.

Olukai took another bite of his food. Haunani caught his eye from across the circle and she smiled, a lovely smile. He smiled back, but his thoughts kept returning to the ocean. He had no intention of marriage right now, and no time for courtship.

Olukai had his heart set on his mission: a duty to honor his ancestors, and to obey the wishes of the island. And because of his experience with the great white manō, he had much more clarity now.

He had been called, and one of his ancestors, in the form of the great white manō, reminded him of that. The island beneath urged him again, clearly impressing on his mind, this time prompting louder than the drums: *Reveal yourself as the manō, destroy the soran, take your rightful place as king of Kaimana Island.*

But Olukai couldn't. He wasn't good enough to rule. Who would believe him anyway? He swallowed hard.

Before he could ponder more on this, he noticed two of the king's warriors hurrying around the circle of celebrators, towards him. These warriors stood tall, muscled, and thick like the king. Black tattoos covered their arms and chests, signifying their rank as the king's highest, most esteemed and trained warriors. They usually kept guard around the king, and drank the same magical island juice, but these two had probably come from another part of the fortress, where they'd been assigned to keep watch.

Right away, Olukai could tell the men looked unnerved, like

they'd seen a ghost. The warriors hesitated in the shadows, glancing from the king to Olukai.

That's odd, Olukai thought, standing to approach them.

"What are you doing?" he asked. Akamu, one of the king's top warriors, frowned.

"The king will be very displeased," he said. The drums, chanting, and drunken laughter drowned out his voice so the king, distracted, wouldn't hear or notice.

"What happened?"

"The king's slave... she burned his library."

"What?" It was so random that Olukai let out a laugh. The warriors glanced at one another and Olukai realized it was no joke. He sobered. "Who—why?"

"Her name is Edena—we caught her before she could get away. The books though... they're all gone."

Olukai's eyes went wide. He knew the king's intense love for the works of the foreigners, and how he coveted the books in his library. Nobody in the whole island had books, and these were *special* books. These books were preserved after the "doctor" of the foreigners, along with many others who bore unknown diseases, were banished to the Haunted island. These books contained information about the medicine, methods, and ways of the foreigners. The king couldn't read them—nobody on the island could, because it was the language of the foreigners—but they were deeply precious.

"Why?"

"We don't know sir..." Akamu and the other warrior glanced at one another, then to Olukai. "Will you tell the king... or is it better not to at this time?"

Olukai looked back at the king, sitting on his soft woven mats. King Ekewaka's eyes were filled with merriment, his hands latched onto the large gourd of soran.

"We have to tell him."

The warriors nodded and waited. Olukai left the shadows to bear the news to the king. He knew it would not bode well.

CHAPTER FOUR

As Olukai went to discuss matters with the king, a lonely figure approached the outskirts of the fortress. The figure blended in with the night, wearing a black kihei, cape, and long skirt. A hood covered his golden hair as he waited in the darkness of the trees.

He looked up to the moon while stroking his horse's mane. Surely the island led him here, and it never led him astray. A light breeze made him shiver, as though confirming his thoughts.

"Po, is that you?" A quiet voice whispered from the brush behind him.

"Depends who's asking." The young man, Po, smirked, recognizing the other voice in the night. He slipped off his dark brown horse, Kūpa'a, and waited for the figure to approach, his hand on the spear at his back, in case it was a trick.

As an older man came to view, Po smiled and greeted him with a brotherly hug. Then they touched foreheads and breathed one another's hā.

"It is good to see you Haku," Po said, placing his hand on the man's shoulder.

"I felt the tension in the wind a day ago, and left for Olukai's house as fast as I could," Haku said. His deep cheekbones seemed emphasized in the light of the moon. Po and Haku had been friends for a few years, especially when Po started delivering messages throughout the island for Olukai.

They were part of a cause, a rebellion of sorts, because Kaimana needed the true line of the ali'i to rule. Though Ekewaka had done much good for the island, he was not the true ruler. The royal blood did not course through his veins, and it was deeply important and symbolic for the Hawaiian people to have a ruler with ali'i blood. It was said that the ali'i descended, long ago, from the gods. Therefore, they were endowed with the power to rule. They had special mana.

And Po knew Olukai was the man, the true ruler of Kaimana Island, and a descendant of the great ali'i. The first great ali'i of Kaimana Island took the form of a great white shark after his death, and this great king was Olukai's 'aumakua. Olukai was gifted the name of the "manō" by his 'aumakua. So instead of calling Olukai by his real name, as Olukai walked a fine line by serving the current king, Po and Haku simply called him the manō.

Not many years ago, the island guided Olukai to Po's village, where they met. As Po and Olukai spoke, the ground beneath Po's feet tremored, confirming the truthfulness of Olukai's words. Olukai was the true king of the island, and Po needed to be his messenger. Po accepted his calling, maybe even selfishly, for he wanted nothing more than to leave his childhood home.

"Olukai wasn't there, so I followed the signs, and here I am," Haku smiled. The "signs" meant anything that the nature of Kaimana Island would use to warn, guide, and inspire, like a whisper in the wind, a humming beneath the feet, tension in the energy, and other strange, yet natural occurrences. These signs came to those who lived pono, with integrity and honesty. It was a huge reason Po tried to be a good, moral person. If he went off balance in any way, he knew he would lose the aid of the natural world around him, the earth that sent quiet signs to direct him where to go next.

"Do you think we should go in? Is the manō in trouble?" Haku asked and the two men stepped closer to the edge of the thick forest, studying the walls of the king's fortress.

"It doesn't feel that way," Po replied. "I'm sure we will find out soon enough."

"If it isn't urgent," Haku said, "I would like to visit my sister."

"Well we don't know what's going on yet." Po folded his arms, adding playfully, "I'm sure your sister can wait."

Haku scoffed. "You haven't changed one bit."

"Perhaps not," Po smiled. "But you've gotten older, that's for sure." Haku laughed and punched Po's shoulder.

"Edena–is that her name?" Po asked. He and Haku had few missions together, but Po liked to remember details about others. His attention to detail won him many friends along his missions for Olukai, and most times, he had a warm hut to sleep in. It was rare that he camped alone in the island's thick forests.

On one mission for Olukai a few years ago, Po and Haku traveled south to speak with the villagers and share the message that there was a descendant of the ali'i who would rise up soon. It was the first time they traveled together, and Po learned much from Haku: about his family, the value of *ho'okipa,* and how to earn the trust and loyalty of the island people.

Haku had three young daughters and a generous wife, and they lived in Kea'au. Haku was a farmer who grew up with four blood brothers and one blood sister, as well as a hānai sister, Edena.

"'Ae, Edena, my hānai sister. I worry about her, and the wellbeing of her daughter."

It was through the concept of hānai that Po felt a connection to Haku. Po had been hānai at a very young age because his father left.

Po could hardly remember his father. His father's white hair, strange language, and habits reminded Po that his father was not a native to Kaimana Island. He didn't even know his father's name, and nor did his hānai parents. The thing that Po remembered most, though, was his father leaving him. He'd only been five when a native couple, Sina and Tua, came to his home and took him with them. They never spoke of it, but Po had been left alone for two days, waiting for his father to return.

His childhood consisted of building canoes with Tua. Po longed to go out to sea, but Tua and Sina, his hānai parents, refused him.

At this memory, Po frowned. He hated his childhood, mostly the oppression he felt by his gossipy, loud hānai mother and his strict hānai father. They hardly let him go by the ocean, but one day he'd prove them all wrong, and show them that he truly belonged at sea.

Haunani, his hānai sister, had always been full of talent, and she was the only one in his hānai family that he didn't mind. Graceful and coordinated, sassy yet kind, Haunani had taught Po many things about the island and dance. Though, Po was never a good dancer. He left his hānai family three years ago, when she was thirteen and he was sixteen.

And he never looked back, for his purpose now was to serve the manō, Olukai, and relay any messages he needed.

"Maybe you'll have a moment," Po shrugged, returning his attention to the conversation. "I'm just wondering what all this is about."

"I agree—I've never felt such trouble in the wind."

"Looks like there's a celebration." Po pointed to a high point within the fortress, where a fire burned, and the shadows of dancers glided down the hillside.

"Perhaps another child," Haku said, rubbing his chin.

"I say we wait." Po sat back and placed his elbows on his knees.

"Agreed." Haku sat back too. They watched the celebration on top of the hill, wondering, waiting, and ready to do anything the manō asked of them.

Time passed slowly, so they reminisced about their recent whereabouts. "So where have you been lately?" Haku asked. Po shrugged. "I was in the Hakalau village talking to some people. They say the great white shark is moving in closer to the island."

"Closer?" Haku frowned in the darkness.

"Ae, it was spotted closer to the reef than it's ever been. The fishermen said even the mermaids seem to be migrating to safer places."

"So what does it mean?"

Po shrugged. "The way I see it, we're running out of time... or... the manō is running out of time."

Silence sat between them as both men evaluated the situation. The great white manō, larger than any shark in the history of the islands, circled Kaimana island. It was distinct from any other great white due to its terrifying size, as well as the tribal markings across its body. It was an ʻaumakua of someone, and every islander knew it must be an aliʻi's ʻaumakua. But Po knew that aliʻi was Olukai.

Olukai, a fisherman turned greatest fire dancer in the island, had royal blood from his mother. His ancestor, now in the form of the shark, would not let the islanders leave, nor let any foreigners close.

While on his many missions for the king, Olukai discovered that the king paid the mermaids soran to keep the islanders from getting too close to the shark's territories. But with Po's recent discovery of the mermaids moving around, migrating to different places around the island for safety, it felt that nobody was safe in the water. Not until the shark got what it wanted, and as far as Po knew, it wanted Olukai to re-establish his line—the true line—as the king of the island. And not only that, but the island demanded the destruction of soran, a powerful, addictive drink.

Hence the reason for Po's work. As a messenger, he went about the island sharing the message that the great white was the ancestor of the aliʻi, and it's descendant would soon rise. He also shared the dangers of soran. Many people warmly welcomed his message, as they began to tire of King Ekewaka's dictatorship. Some, especially those who lived closer to the fortress, feared for their lives, hoping the king wouldn't begin recruiting people to find soran again.

"Did you see your family while you were out there?" Haku asked, cutting off Po's thoughts.

He wrinkled his nose. "No."

"Why not? You were right there—"

"I didn't have time, alright?" Po snapped.

Haku whistled low.

Po rolled his eyes. "Look, it's better when I don't see them."

Haku paused before saying. "You know, hānai family is still family."

Po shook his head. He hated when Haku asked about his hānai family. Life was always better when he didn't see them, though he choked the feeling that he did miss talking to Haunani, the only person who seemed to understand him and withhold judgment.

But his hānai parents... he could stay away from them for a lifetime... for all they did to him, confining him to the life of a canoe builder—a *canoe builder!* He frowned at the thought. At least as a messenger people respected him. Olukai, a real ali'i, even respected him. And when Olukai became king of the island, Po would take a canoe and sail far, *far* away from here, a place where he didn't belong, where his family didn't honor his wishes to sail and navigate. Yes, as soon as Olukai became king, Po would never look back.

"Did you see Milo when you went?" Haku asked, changing the subject.

"Ae, I did. He's crazy as ever." Po chuckled, thinking of the fishermen on the outskirts of Hakalau, the place he grew up. It was mostly a fishing village, with many sailors.

Except me, Po thought, still salty as ever about his upbringing.

The night wore on as the men spoke of their common friends. Haku, a messenger like Po, knew many of the same people so they frequently caught each other up on their recent visits to the islanders. Haku became a messenger around the same time as Po. Similar to Po's experience, Olukai had been led by the island to speak with Haku, a humble kalo farmer.

The tension thinned as Po began cracking jokes and Haku's more reserved demeanor turned into a state of humor. They were like two drunken fools, but not drunk on the kava they saw being so freely given to the party attendees on the hill. They laughed and spoke with a sincere concern for one another's wellbeing and the goodness of the island.

As the night faded into a dark morning, a figure appeared from the gates of the fortress. He was tall, well-built, and walked with confidence.

Both Po and Haku stood. Olukai, also known as the manō, the true king of the island, was finally approaching.

CHAPTER FIVE

Nohea ducked behind a ti leaf bush. The guards didn't usually come into these parts of the garden. In fact, they almost never came around, but for some ridiculous reason, they were here. Today. The lush greenery and flora blinded her from their view.

Two tall, bulky men walked past, not even glancing her way. The native birds were too loud anyways for them to hear her breathing. The men wore the attire of the king's elite warrior: a black skirt, and a black kihei with the king's symbol, stacked triangles, printed on them in red. Tattoos lined their necks, chests, and arms. Some of them even had tattoos wrapping up their legs. They held long spears and their bare feet hardly made a sound on the mossy rock path as they passed. They weren't ordinary guards, but warriors, and everything about them made that fact obvious. Long ago, these kinds of warriors were known as the koa, but, for some reason, the king's elite warriors had no distinguishing name.

Meanwhile, ordinary guards and soldiers were small, sloppy, and untrained. But the king's warriors had the stealth of eels and the strength of mountains.

After they passed, Nohoea crouched towards the plant she'd come to find in the garden: the red gingers.

She sniffed it, each petal pointing upward and forming a beautiful comb head. It didn't smell like anything, but she was eager to break it down, learn more about it, and discover how this plant could help her slave family. This morning, after the funeral, she traveled deeper than she'd ever gone into the king's garden.

Strangely, her mother had not been at the hut after the ceremony for Kimo. Normally Nohea would have worried, but on random evenings, her mother had been out late into the nights, so Nohea went to sleep alone, eager to wake up early the next morning.

A pueo hooted at her, louder than she'd ever heard it. Nohea looked up, covering her eyes from the sun. The brown bird, with its big, golden eyes, winked at her. It was a sign.

Time to go, she thought, and began making her way back to the slave village. She usually spent more time in the garden, but today she felt pressured to return and study the plants before going to her daily duties. Her mind echoed her failure:

No matter what I tried, I couldn't save him.

If only she'd studied more plants, tried new recipes, and came up with new ideas...

The pueo let out a shrill cry, one she hadn't heard before, and she ducked again, her skin crawling as she wondered why there were so many guards at this early morning hour, and in the garden of all places. She'd always been alone in the garden but this... this was new.

A few more guards rushed past, spears in hand. They *ran.* Nohea waited patiently behind the tall ferns.

With the garden seemingly empty again, Nohea made her way out, staying close to the path, but not on it. She limped and sometimes hunched over because her right knee and shin hurt so badly from whatever happened to it the previous day.

As she hobbled out of the garden, the sun shone on her full body, warming her skin after the shaded canopy of the trees.

She was surprised to not have seen Likeke that morning, as he usually showed up towards the end of her time in the garden. Since she started giving him her newest formula, he had been doing better, even if his hands shook the previous day. His overall color and health seemed to improve with the new medicine she recently tried with him.

Nohea followed the red dirt road towards the little village of slaves. The tall grass, on either side of the path, blew softly in the wind. It was a beautiful morning, and when Nohea finished her tasks for the day, she had every intention of experimenting with the newly collected plants in her bag.

She ran through her chores of the day: launder the concubine's clothes, spend a couple of hours in the fields, and then tend to the pigs. If a slave was found doing any other work besides service for the king during the daylight, they were punished with a club.

The voices of the birds dimmed in the background behind Nohea, and a calm seemed to envelope the air around her. The slaves were probably awake, finding something to eat before leaving to their assigned tasks. The sun rose over the horizon.

"Nohea!" The voice of her friend interrupted Nohea's thoughts.

Nohea paused and waited for Nui to approach. Beads of sweat dripped down Nui's forehead and wide nose.

"Nui?" Nohea asked as they kissed one another's cheeks.

"You must go—I've gathered your things." Nui's deep voice rang through the morning air. Nohea then noticed the bag, her own bag, around Nui's shoulder. "I've packed as many of your things as I could, but you must leave now!"

"What's going on? Why?" Nohea asked, surprised as Nui offloaded the bag and swung it over Nohea's shoulder. It was heavier than she thought, and she realized Nui must have packed, quite literally, almost everything that Nohea owned, which included random alchemist things like mortal and pestle, fermenting brews, strange clays, and so forth. A heavy gourd, full of water, swung from one side of the bag, attached with woven leaf cords.

"Your mother... they took her." Nui was out of breath.

"My mother? Who? Where?" Nohea began to make a move towards the village—they were so close anyways. What was Nui talking about? But Nui was taller and stronger, and she grabbed Nohea's arm with such force, Nohea nearly fell backwards.

"Kahiko took her."

"Kahiko?" Nohea's mouth dropped.

Kahiko, the king's trusted counselor, a kahuna, sorcerer, a priest, and keeper of secrets. Nobody would dare mess with Kahiko. It was said he could kill a person with even one word from his lips, for he delved into dark magic, of things better left unspoken.

"Why?"

"Something about... she burned the king's books."

"Why did she burn—"

"Nohea there is no time," Nui said, flustered. "You must leave. The guards are looking for you now. A messenger came to warn us—he has eyes the color of the sea. He said Haku will meet you at the edge of the garden and the messenger will take you to safety—you must turn back now and find your uncle!"

"My mother..." Nohea tried to step forward but Nui's firm grip on her arm stopped her.

"Nohea... there is nothing you can do for her." Nui's eyes watered , most likely stinging from the loss of her husband, and the loss that Nohea would now experience.

Nohea's eyebrows creased as she processed: Edena burned the king's books, so they would kill Nohea's mother... if they hadn't already. Then the story twisted: Edena burned the king's books, so they would kill Nohea. Unexpected anger welled up inside Nohea. Her mother abandoned her, set her up... of course she would. *Edena always hated me,* Nohea thought, the truth finally surfacing. It still sent a pang through her heart.

"Promise you will be safe," Nui said.

"I will—and you too," Nohea said.

"Now hurry, go!" Nui pushed Nohea. "I'll stall them!"

"Don't mess with Kahiko—" Nohea began to say, but Nui looked frustrated and impatient.

"Go Nohea!"

Nohea nodded again, her heart pumping, legs trembling. She limped back towards the garden, moving even slower because of her belongings. The heaviest things in her bag from Nui, though, were the bombs.

When rumor spread that a fellow slave got killed on the spot by Kahiko years ago, Nohea started making little bombs that the slaves could fit in a hidden pocket on the inside of their skirts. The bombs were made of uli, the powerful ginger that could make any person fall asleep with one whiff. Most slaves hid the bombs in their huts, while very few others carried them, in the secret pocket, to work.

As Nohea stepped into the garden, the honeycreepers and pueo chirped so loudly, Nohea knew she was being closely followed. The tall trees shaded the way, leaving only pockets of sunshine.

"Nohea!" She recognized the voice.

"Like!" Nohea rushed to the prince's arms. His long black hair was down today, and his eyes were wide.

"I've been looking all over for you—you have to leave," he said, resting on his crutches, yet still able to hold her shoulders. He looked better today than yesterday.

"Like, I don't have any more medicine for you. I'm so sorry, I—"

He shook his head. "You must run, and hurry."

"I have to find my uncle. Nui said he'd be at the edge of the garden. I don't know where—"

"Head that way," Like said, pointing down the path he came from. "Many of the villagers enter the garden through that way."

Like and Nohea kissed one another's cheeks. "Good luck," said Like but before she passed him, he gently touched her arm. "Nohea, don't come back," he added.

Her hair stood on end, but she nodded, and then hurried as fast as she could limp.

Uncle Haku was surely close.

. . .

FAMILIAR SCENES of the garden passed her view: so many places she'd trimmed or clipped plants to try new remedies, so many places she once sat and chatted with Like, learning about the outside world or complaining about her circumstances as a slave, listening to his life as a prince.

The ferns, gingers, flowers, and bushes grew in abundance on either side of the garden. She couldn't believe she was leaving this.

And so soon.

The brown owl flew across Nohea's path, close enough to her face that she could've kissed its fluffy feathers.

A warning.

She dove off to the side bushes and waited. Guards approached from the direction she was going and her skin crawled.

Kahiko.

There he was, the sorcerer, with his hair, black as the night, falling down his wide back. His eyes were dark as lava rock, and his shoulders, arms, and chest were covered in heavy black tribal tattoos. He wore a black skirt, as well as a kihei across one shoulder, like the guards, but he carried a long, green ti leaf in one hand, and a leimanō in the other. The wooden knife had white shark teeth tied all around it; a lethal weapon. A wooden staff hung across his back.

"Wait." Kahiko stopped a few steps away from Nohea. She held perfectly still, sure that the large plants blinded her from view.

Kahiko took a step towards her. Nohea shut her eyes, her palms sweating. He took another step. The honeycreepers and owl started making loud noises in the tall trees above. If they didn't give her away, she didn't know what would.

She held her breath. If she had stood, Nohea was sure she would've been face to face with Kahiko, though he was significantly taller.

"Someone's over there," said a guard, but his voice wasn't in her direction.

Like! she thought, hope rising in her.

"I hear it too," said another guard. Kahiko took a step away and grunted.

Nohea held still until she heard their footsteps fade away. Then she let out a quiet breath, her heart pumping. She owed Like big time.

She then continued limping along the path. It seemed to wind on forever, and for all the times she'd walked down these paths, they had never seemed this long.

After what felt like a lifetime, Nohea could see the sunlight shining brightly onto the path, the forest garden clearing into nearby fields. She didn't know that people from the village could get in this way. How long she'd felt trapped here, and there was a way out of the garden after all!

A tall figure moved from the shadows and, for the first time that day, Nohea was greeted by a big white smile.

"Uncle Haku!" she exclaimed and they embraced, kissing one another's cheeks.

"You made it!" Uncle Haku laughed. He grabbed her bags from her and offered his arm. "We must hurry! We can't keep the messenger waiting."

Uncle Haku had deep brown eyes, full of wisdom. His black, curly hair was pulled up into a bun, and he wore the clothes of a commoner, a red kihei with a light blue skirt. He had deep cheekbones and a wide nose. His whole body was full of muscles, with a tattoo of an 'apapane on his shoulder. He looked nothing like Edena, his sister, because they were only hānai, adopted, siblings. Nohea knew nothing of her mother's heritage, for her mother grew angry when Nohea asked any questions. Uncle Haku respected his sister's wishes and gave Nohea no answers either.

"What happened to your leg?" he asked as she hobbled off the path and into a thick forest of guava trees. A chilly breeze made Nohea shiver.

"I'm not sure. I was in the kalo field yesterday and then it felt like something just..." Nohea shrugged and slashed the air with her hand. "Smashed my leg. I'm not sure..."

"That's strange," was all Uncle Haku said, his eyes alert. His shoulders were tense, and he held Nohea's hand with a fierceness she'd never felt in him before.

"It's around here somewhere...." he said, looking about.

"What are we looking for?"

"The *paniana* trees." The banyan trees.

"That way," Nohea pointed into the distance, proud of knowing the in's and out's of most of the garden. Though, she was still mind blown that there was an exit to the village from here. "What's there?"

"Our way out." He smiled again.

"How did you know about my mother?"

"I'll explain all later. We must get you to safety first."

They stepped over a slow moving waterfall, which soaked their sandals. The screeching of the birds ahead sent a chill down Nohea's spine.

"The birds—" Nohea said and ducked, but Uncle Haku didn't get the cue, too distracted on the task at hand to notice messages and warnings from the island.

"I see someone!" A voice shouted in the distance.

"Run!" Uncle Haku sprinted, and Nohea felt like she was being dragged.

"Careful with that bag!" she exclaimed, seeing it clank against his side as they bolted through the forest. She'd only tried out one bomb before, and it created a small explosion. She would wrap the powder, usually uli, in ti leaves, tie it with woven cord, and pressure cook it in an imu. After letting them cool, she threw one against the tree and marveled at the plume of uli powder that came from it. So she made the bombs bigger, but she'd never actually tried one of the new bombs.

Nohea could only imagine, with horror, one of the uli bombs exploding out of the bag slung across Uncle Haku's shoulder, putting them to sleep. What a sight that'd be for the guards and Kahiko!

The large banyan trees loomed before them, with a maze of branches and trunks. The canopy above created a cool, shady area. Meanwhile, the branches hung so low, some of them looked like they became roots growing into the ground.

"It's around here..." Uncle Haku let go of Nohea to start knocking on the tree.

"What are you—"

"No ask, just knock." His voice was calm but stern. Nohea knocked on the tree, aware that at any moment the guards could show up.

"They're here! By the tree!" The guard's voice was close... too close.

"Come on Po!" Uncle Haku pounded on the tree, letting his anger out. He ran around to the thickest and widest parts of the trunk, where the branches were so fat, they were the size of his torso.

Nohea bit her lip as she also ran around the tree, copying Uncle Haku, and banging her fists on the thick, windy, hanging branches.

As she rounded a corner, she bumped right into a tall figure with sun-kissed skin. He held her shoulders and their eyes met. Nohea gasped.

She'd never, not once in her whole life, seen eyes the color of the ocean, nor seen hair so golden, she was sure it had to be the true color of sand. It was pulled up, but she gaped at imagining it down. His hair had to look like rays of sunshine.

"You made it!" The young man smiled. A strange feeling fluttered in Nohea's stomach and heat rushed to her cheeks. She swallowed and looked behind him. Somehow, some way, the young man had parted a few branches and stepped out of a black hole in the tree.

"Hurry!" Uncle Haku shoved Nohea into the young man's arms and the boy pulled her into the hole. Then Uncle Haku jumped in and closed the branches behind them. They were left in complete darkness.

"Shhhh..." Uncle Haku said before Nohea could ask questions.

The young man held her arms, and he pulled her back into the blackness. The air, chilly and wet, smelled muggy.

The footsteps of the guards sounded around the tree above.

"Did you see where they went?" one guard asked, baffled.

"You fools, they found a way to the lava tubes below. Come on." Kahiko's voice. Nohea knew he was smart enough not to waste his time looking for the entrance from the tree.

"He's going to meet us at the exit," the young man whispered.

"We can't take on Kahiko," Nohea shivered.

"Shhhh.... Let's keep moving," said Uncle Haku.

And they did. The young man let go of Nohea and offered her his arm, though he had to tell her because it was too dark to see anything.

Nohea reached out, feeling his muscled shoulder, then held his arm.

"These are the old lava tubes," he said, adding, "It gets darker than this." His voice sounded cool and confident. He kept his other hand on her hand to hold her steady as she stumbled in the dark. He seemed to know exactly where to go though.

They climbed deeper into the earth, even crawling at some parts, and the soil drenched Nohea's arms, tunic, and hair. The old caves smelled of dirt and water, a musty smell.

They really hadn't talked much until their feet touched solid ground again, and they stood straight.

"Where are we now?" asked Nohea, shivering into the coolness around her.

"Under the earth," said the young man.

"Nohea, this is Pōmaika'i," said Uncle Haku, reaching out to touch her shoulder.

"You can call me Po for short though."

Nohea could feel that he was smiling in the darkness.

"Pleased to meet you Nohea," he added.

"'Ae," said Nohea. "A pleasure. Thank you for rescuing me." The thought of his blue eyes made her stomach flip again, and she was glad he couldn't see her face in the darkness, for a blush started at her cheeks again. The realization settled over her that the strange feelings were *attraction.* Nohea frowned to herself, pushing it out of her mind. There was no time for that, and she didn't even know him.

"No problem," Po said, adding, "Although it's not much of a rescue until we're out of these lava dungeons."

"Lava dungeons?" Nohea's foot splashed in cold water and she gasped in surprise.

Po tsked. "'Ae, that was the pool of blood of some dead soul."

"What?"

"The king sends all his prisoners and unwanteds down here, and they either starve to death or kill themselves."

Nohea let out a groan, squeezing her eyes shut, her skin crawling at the thought of her feet being soaked with blood.

"Po, that's not funny," Uncle Haku cut in. Po chuckled and Nohea rubbed her forehead, confused. "He likes to tease," Uncle Haku said. "If there were some light I'd give one to your head Po," he added.

Po laughed. "I'm joking, don't take it so seriously." But Nohea let go of his arm and stood still.

"I need some light," she said, fresh anger in her voice. She didn't usually have a temper, but Po's ego was getting on her nerves.

Uncle Haku, who walked behind, bumped into her.

"It's a joke—" Po started but Nohea cut in.

"It's not funny."

"Alright, sorry..."

"Hang on... " Uncle Haku said. "I'm pretty sure they're not following and Nohea is right. Let's get some light."

Nohea let out a sigh of relief. Within a few minutes, Uncle Haku started a small fire using hibiscus twigs from his own bag. In the light of the little flame, Po pulled a small torch from the bag around his own shoulder. These men were prepared. As the light began illuminating the area, Nohea noticed that Po wore a black skirt and kihei like the king's guards.

"Do you work for the king?" Nohea asked, not trusting him.

"Oh... no." He glanced at her. "What makes you think that?"

"You're wearing the color of the guard."

"I'm a messenger. I wear black to blend in with the night, and, from a distance, to look like a guard."

"Who are you a messenger for?"

"The manō." He held the torch up and the world around them turned a warm golden color. Nohea looked about. All the uneven rock walls around her were solid black, and the "ceiling" seemed to go up forever. Roots dangled from above, some of them even reaching the ground and holding tight below.

She shivered. "The manō? That is a legend."

Every family had an ʻaumakua, a guardian spirit, or spirit animal. And everyone on Kaimana island knew that the aliʻi, true royalty, had an ʻaumakua in the form of the great white shark. But unfortunately, that line died when the foreigners came. Ekewaka claimed to be a lost descendant of the royal family, and the islanders believed him because he had all the attributes of a leader. He brought the people together to kill the foreigners, and chase the rest off the island, never to be seen again.

This all happened before Nohea was born, but there was another terrible battle for the throne between Ekewaka and his brother, Makana, as they both wanted to be the aliʻi.

Ekewaka won the bloody battles and pronounced himself king of the island, while his brother was outcast into the northern part of the island and either died, or continued to live in hiding. Another branch of people, unhappy with the new king, broke off into the mountain forests becoming the Mākuʻe, the dark tribe, and yet another people went into the mountains becoming the dwarf people, the Hune.

"The great white manō's line is still alive and well," said Po. "We call the rightful king of the island the manō, and he will restore balance to the island."

"Oh I know now..." Nohea said, following closely behind the tall young man. "Like told me about this. They're nothing more than a group of rebels, bound to destruction like all the rest that rose up against Ekewaka—"

"No." Po stopped in his tracks and Nohea bumped into him. She blushed.

"So that is what the slaves believe?" Po asked. He rolled his eyes. Nohea frowned, her dislike of Po growing with each passing conversation. She hated being called a slave, but she kept her mouth shut.

"Nohea," Uncle Haku cut in. "The blood of the ali'i runs in a man... Nobody knew about it until now. Ekewaka never had the true blood of the ali'i. He has deceived us all, and now the island is in danger. The manō is our only hope to restore peace throughout the island."

"How do you know that?" Nohea's head burned with questions, while she trembled in the cold of the cave.

"Because the great white manō revealed it. The true ali'i of Kaimana Island have always had distinguishing marks on their bodies." Uncle Haku replied. "You will meet the true king of the island... we are taking you to him now."

Nohea paused and met her uncle's serious gaze. She had no reason to distrust Uncle Haku, and he'd rescued her, while her own mother set her up.

"I trust you Uncle Haku," she finally said. "If you believe there is a man with the blood of the ali'i, I believe you."

Uncle Haku smiled . "You are strong," he said. "Like your mother."

She cringed. *My mother was weak,* she thought but didn't say it.

The cave began to smell rotten, and Nohea wrinkled her nose.

"What is that?" she asked.

Po laughed. "What do you think it is?"

She frowned at his back. He laughed and said, "It's probably from the old vents around here. This is a very old lava tube. Lava doesn't flow through here. I mean, it's so old, even the plants dug their roots through."

His eyes teased when he looked back at her. She still couldn't believe his eyes were blue. In the light of the torch she could see he had a handsome face, with a soft pointed nose, and dimples. She figured he had to be about eighteen years old. But the initial fascination she had for him had quickly faded with his terrible jokes and dark sense of humor.

"Who are your parents?" she asked, realizing too late that it was probably rude. After all, it was completely unnatural for an islander to have an appearance like Po. Was he a foreigner? Was he a descendant of a foreigner? Because any descendants of foreigners were killed or banished to the Haunted island, where, one could assume, they died. Or maybe he was a Hawaiian with fair skin and light colored hair, someone with albinism.

Po chuckled. "You don't want to know..."

"Why not?"

"It doesn't matter." His voice went flat.

"Are you a foreigner—"

"Listen, I know you think I'm handsome—"

"I do not—"

"But that's the wrong way to go about flirting with someone."

She pushed his arm. "I'm not flirting."

"That was flirting," he chuckled as she pushed him again.

Nohea, beyond annoyed at his behavior let out a groan and stepped beside her uncle.

"He's just kidding," Uncle Haku said, amused. But a strange silence had settled over Po, and Nohea decided to let her question about his lineage rest.

After a while of only hearing their footsteps in the water, and the dripping from the cave ceiling, Po stood still and Nohea bumped into him.

Again, she thought, rolling her eyes.

"Do you hear that?" Po looked at Uncle Haku. They all stood still, listening.

And then Nohea heard it. Faint echoes, like whispers in the

wind, bounced through the cave. The island had to be warning them of danger at the end of the tube.

"We're getting close to the end, and they're waiting for us." Po pulled the spear hanging from his back.

"How does Kahiko know about this?" Nohea asked, her skin crawling as she thought about Kahiko. The reality of everything still hadn't sunk in yet: that the guards were chasing her, and even Kahiko had been searching for her.

"Everyone knows there are old lava tubes under the fortress... well, under the whole island," said Po. "The king knows of it. But he didn't know we dug a hole to get into his garden." He laughed then spoke to Uncle Haku. "We're almost there. They're waiting for us at the entrance... and if not, they're definitely on their way."

"You come here often?" Nohea asked.

"'Ae... It's easy to get lost here. It's like a maze. I've only bumped into a few ghosts down here." He said it so casually, it sent a shiver down Nohea's spine.

"A few ghosts?" Any ghosts on the island were bad news. She'd heard tales of ghosts doing terrible things to people, scarring them emotionally and mentally for life.

"Ae, many people die down here."

Nohea wrinkled her nose. She was so sick of death: dead mothers in childbirth, slaves succumbing to diseases, a slave giving up the will to live and lying on the side of the hut to die in the sun, and, of course, Kimo. Her eyes watered at the thought of her failure.

"He's kidding..." Uncle Haku said. "Again. That's quite enough Po."

Po chuckled and Nohea groaned again, annoyed. She *definitely* didn't like him.

"Not many people use these caves because they don't know how to navigate them," Uncle Haku continued. "Except Po. Po knows how to navigate these tunnels better than anyone else."

"How?"

"The island," Po answered, his playful voice now serious.

Nohea didn't need to ask anymore questions, for she caught his meaning. The island bestowed goodness on those who were good. While she felt quite annoyed with him, Nohea also felt a connection. The island trusted Po with its knowledge and promptings, so he must be *somewhat* good.

The island guided him through the tunnels, whispering where to turn. Nohea nodded to herself, as it made sense. But just because the island trusted Po, didn't mean Nohea had to trust him. Not yet, at least.

They began climbing up some steep parts of the cave, and Nohea winced when she skinned her knee against the lava rock. "You alright?" Po asked, pausing to check on her. His tone was gentle, but Nohea looked at him, crossed. How could he go from incredibly annoying to friendly so quickly? He smirked and she rolled her eyes. "I'm fine."

As they climbed more, Po finally broke the silence. "Do you feel that?" he asked. The air grew warmer, and, finally, the light of the torch dimmed in comparison to a pocket of sunlight around the corner. Po stopped both Nohea and Uncle Haku before turning a corner, where the light poured in.

"Hang on," he said. "There are at least two guards out there waiting for us. There might be more." He rubbed his eyes. "I'll go first. Let your eyes adjust and then head straight for the horses."

Nohea squinted at the light. It felt like it burned through her head, but her eyes adjusted. Po nodded to Uncle Haku. "We'll do what we must," Po said. Uncle Haku and Po grasped one another's arms for a moment, a bond of brotherhood, then Po smiled at Nohea.

"See you again soon, my friend."

"Friend?" Nohea began to add more, feeling irritated at his assumption. Sure, he helped rescue her, but his personality and "funny" lies were no words of a friend.

Before she could reply, Po crept towards the light and disappeared.

"Attack!" It was the voice of the king's warriors.

The guards had been waiting. Nohea glanced around the corner to see Po fighting. His speed and agility with the spear impressed her, but she covered her mouth and hid her face when she spotted blood.

"Hurry, now!" Po yelled from outside, though he fought. Uncle Haku grabbed Nohea's hand and rushed past Po, who was busy fighting a guard at least twice his size. Po's spear and tooth-dagger had been tossed to the side, so he held up his fists.

Two horses, a gray and a brown, tied to a nearby tree, looked uneasy. Uncle Haku helped Nohea onto the gray horse, untied the braided cord from the tree, then jumped up behind her.

"Get out of here!" said Uncle Haku to Po, and Nohea saw what her uncle saw. More guards approached, from a distance, on horses, and Kahiko rode at the front.

Po knocked his head against the bigger man, leaving Po's blue eyes rolling for a bit. Without thinking about it, Nohea grabbed something from the bag at Uncle Haku's side and threw it at the guard's face, her aim surprisingly spot on. When it hit Po's attacker, blue powder exploded into the air. It was so loud, a ringing sensation filled Nohea's ears for a moment. The large man fell to the ground, and Po grinned at her.

"Thanks! Now go!" He rushed to their horse and smacked its flank, launching it forward. Nohea leaned over to get a glimpse of him as they rode away into a tall, grassy plain. He saluted her then jumped on his brown horse, riding in the opposite direction. For all of his annoying behavior, she couldn't help her lips from turning upward at his confidence, so bold and proud. Maybe they would be friends one day.

The approaching guards split up. Four of them, including Kahiko, followed Nohea and Uncle Haku, and four followed Po.

"Don't lean like that. You make it hard for the horse," said Uncle Haku, gently pushing her shoulder to sit straight.

"Keep your head as low as you can," he continued. "They might have spears." So Nohea put her head as close to the horse's mane as possible. She was so close, the smell of sweat filled her nose. Her teeth chattered each time the horse moved forward, and her back began to ache. She'd never ridden a horse before.

The five men on horseback caught up, as their horses were bigger and only carrying one person each.

"Come on!" Uncle Haku said to their own horse, nudging it faster. It galloped through the fields, towards the dark mountain in the distance. But what amazed Nohea the most was the darkness of the forest looming ahead of them.

This was the first time she'd been outside of the king's fortress. She could see the tall walls of the fortress in the distance, proving how far the three had walked through the lava tunnels below the earth. The sun shone high above them, an afternoon sun. They had probably been in the cave for several hours.

She fixed her attention to the dark forest before them. It sat like a wall of green and brown colors, thick with moss-covered banyan trees. The more she stared at it, the more the colors blended to give the appearance of purple woods.

The guards were getting so close, Nohea could hear the heavy breathing of their horses.

"Duck!" she yelled to Uncle Haku, as one of the guards threw a spear. He did so, and it whizzed past his back. "Hold on," Uncle Haku said and turned the horse to take a sharp right.

The guards turned their horses too, but it gave Nohea and Uncle Haku more distance. "Almost there..." he said, staring into the forest straight ahead.

Prince Like once told Nohea about these woods, the wood of purple. It was said to be haunted by the dead, and, in the deepest part lived the Māku'e, the dark tribe, who broke off from King Ekewaka after the foreigners left. They stuck to themselves, hoarding their soran, a mythical source of healing, coveting their pure waterfalls, and drinking their days away.

Like said they wore all white, and didn't like others. Because of their isolation and the lack of sunlight, their bodies changed. Their ears mutated, because, as Like put it, "They claim to be the only people that hear the island the best." The Māku'e thought themselves superior to others. The outsiders were too poor, careless, and greedy. Nohea imagined that it would be a once-in-a-lifetime experience to see a member of the Māku'e, or the place they inhabited.

As they got closer to the edge of the woods, the air changed. It grew cold, heavy, and damp. The gray horse whined and started slowing down, but Uncle Haku pushed it forward. It started trotting, and Nohea looked at Uncle Haku.

"Let's run," he said, bringing the horse to a full stop before sliding off. Nohea's bag clanked against his side and she cringed as she slid off the horse.

Please don't explode, she thought. It was an amusing thought if the bombs in the bag exploded earlier, but after seeing Po's fight and the blood across the ground, as well as this intense horse chase, Nohea was far from amused.

The guards, not far behind, slowed their whiney, unhappy horses to a stop so they could dismount. Kahiko slowed down at the back of the group, making eye contact with Nohea. A shiver ran down her spine.

Uncle Haku sprinted and Nohea lagged behind him. As she slipped through the branches of a thick banyan tree, stepping into the mossy woods, an uneasy feeling churned through her stomach. The sunlight slipped away behind her, and the whole world grew shadowed.

"Come on Nohea," said Uncle Haku. It was so dark, he looked nothing more than a black figure. She reached for his hand and held it tightly as they ran ahead.

"Stop there!" The warriors followed, but, for some reason, they moved slowly.

A spear whizzed past Nohea's face, but before she could say "duck," it struck Uncle Haku right in the shoulder. He fell to the ground, shocked.

"It's alright, it's alright," Nohea heard herself saying. She'd helped many people with wounds, but she couldn't keep her hands from trembling as she grabbed the spear handle and yanked. Uncle Haku cried out in pain, beads of sweat the only thing reflecting light on his body.

"We've got you surrounded," said a guard, approaching them, and panting. Kahiko stood there too, breathing heavily and folding his arms.

Nohea held the spear and stood up. Her uncle had protected her this far, and now she had to protect him.

The guards laughed, all four of them getting close to her with their different weapons: leimanōs, spears, and clubs.

"Kill the man, take her alive," said Kahiko, his voice cool. Nohea reached into her pouch, feeling for the bombs, like the one she'd used earlier. She had filled bombs with random plants, so she wasn't sure what all the bombs in her bag did, except the blue ones full of uli, the sleeping powder.

The men charged.

Nohea threw the bombs at their feet, some of the bombs exploding with blue powder, some with fire, and some with red powder. One of the guards fell to the ground, asleep, and the others fell back, shocked. But they weren't discouraged. They charged again, and Nohea threw more bombs. They launched their spears but Nohea ducked, a spear still in one hand.

"What are you doing, fools? Get her!" screamed Kahiko, furious.

She threw whatever bombs she had left, sending one more guard to sleep with the intoxicating blue powder.

But one guard pounced on her, holding her down. He yanked the spear from her hand and easily pulled her hands together.

"Let go of me!" Nohea struggled against his grasp, her legs kicking in the air, but he twisted her hands behind her back.

The man fell to the side, falling to a scuffle on the ground with Uncle Haku. Another guard grabbed Nohea's arm before she could pick up the nearest spear. She yanked herself free, but fell backwards, falling to the ground and hitting her head so hard, everything turned white for a moment.

She stared up at the thick branches of the forest, disoriented. Then a face appeared over hers, one so unique and handsome, she believed, for a moment, that she'd died. The young man brushed some loose hair from her face, touched her cheek, and turned his face to observe Uncle Haku.

And then she saw them. His ears were... a little pointed. He was from the dark tribe. Her instinct was to protect Uncle Haku, so she began to prop herself up on her elbows while staring at this young man. He stared back at her, both of them curious in this quiet moment amidst the chaos. He looked up, but too late, and Nohea felt a swift blow on the right side of her face.

A guard had kneed and tripped over her while attempting to attack the young man with pointed ears. A stinging sensation filled her head, turning everything green as she fell back to the ground. The young man, with his bare hands, twisted the guard's head, making the loudest cracking noise she'd ever heard. She covered her eyes, afraid, every sound now muffling out.

If the guards didn't kill her and Uncle Haku, surely the Māku'e, like this young man, would.

Kahiko's voice mumbled strange words in the darkness, and then a girl, wearing white, stepped in front of Nohea's view. A bright light glowed from the tip of the spear in her hand.

The last thing Nohea heard was Kahiko's loud scream as the light from the girl's spear grew and blinded everything.

And then all went dark.

CHAPTER SIX

Olukai walked through the rows of his young men in training while Lopaka barked orders.

“Ekahi!” Lopaka called, counting. Each time he said a number, the men changed their stance. Sweat glistened on the mens' bodies as they swung their various weapons in unison. Ripples of nervousness went through the men each time Olukai passed by them, he could feel it. This was a new group of recruits, young men who were old enough to be trained and serve the king. Eventually, when these men were trained enough, they would go on missions for the king too. Some of the young men were previously slaves, but most were from the poorest parts of the island, those wishing for a better life, and would risk anything for improved living conditions, even if it meant going on death missions.

“Elua!” Lopaka called, and the men changed their stance with a loud “hah!” Olukai stopped by a young boy who couldn't be older than twelve. The boy glanced at Olukai and stiffened. “Relax,” Olukai said, placing a hand on the boy's sweaty shoulder. These sessions were intense, with Olukai demonstrating and teaching the men how to use the knife, and then Lopaka, the king's oldest son, making the men repeat, over and over, the routines. They took a few breaks throughout the day but then spent most of the time sparring and practicing by dueling one on one.

"Ekolu!" The men did the next move and Olukai stood clear before their fourth movement: the twirling of the knife, for those who held knives, and the throwing of the clubs, spears, and leimanōs at some koa trunk targets off to the side.

"Ehā!" Lopaka's voice rang out loud and clear. The men each took a step away from each other and started to twirl the knives, making them look like mere circles from the front. The others ran into position and threw their weapons. Most of them hit the trunk and stayed. Olukai nodded, pleased. Under his mentorship, the men learned quickly. This is why the king admired and trusted Olukai. Olukai was good at what he did, and his results were almost always successful.

"Take a break!" Lopaka said, and the men stopped circling their knives so they could drink water. The others yanked their weapons out of the tree and returned them to a weapon stand made of koa. Lopaka leaned against it as he watched the men put their weapons back, respectfully and in an organized way.

"Well done," Lopaka said to the boys as he chewed on a piece of grass. He glanced at Olukai.

"You look bored," he said.

Olukai took a knife from the stand and circled it around his hand. "I'm not bored, just... thinking."

Lopaka grinned. "About that girl last night?"

Olukai had forgotten all about Haunani. He snorted and Lopaka raised an eyebrow. "Apparently even the finest dancer in all of Kaimana island isn't good enough for you?"

Or maybe Olukai wasn't good enough for anyone else. He tossed the long metal knife into the air and caught it without looking. Lopaka rolled his eyes. "Show off," he muttered.

"No, it's not that. Maybe it's that everyone's been rumoring our marriage for so long that it might be fun to prove everyone wrong."

Lopaka laughed. "Always the rebel."

Olukai picked up another knife and held it out. As Lopaka took it, he nodded to Olukai's forearm, covered in black kapa. "Still not healed?" he asked.

Olukai shrugged. "It's taking a while." They walked to a large sand pit. Olukai and Lopaka trained the men within the king's fortress. Great measures had been made to keep the training grounds in pristine condition. The weapons were sharpened every night. Fresh sand was brought in for the sand pits once a week. Koa trees were chopped down for target practice at least once a month.

The young men naturally formed a circle around Olukai and Lopaka. They watched, fascinated, with eagerness to become like the two warriors before them. Olukai dipped the end of his knife in oil and held it up to a nearby torch. Flames engulfed the blade, warming up his face and hand. Lopaka did the same and stood at the other end of the sand pit.

Olukai smiled as Lopaka swung his fire knife single-handedly. That was an easy trick, but that's all it was: a trick. Olukai knew the true art of fire dancing, and his love for dancing with the fire knife extended into fighting with it. Beads of sweat dripped down Olukai's dark forehead as he circled around Lopaka. Both of their heavy bodies sank with each step in the white sand. The salty air made their hair stick to their faces.

The onlookers watched with anticipation, each of the young men leaning forward to get a better look.

"Come on Lopaka," said Olukai, standing straight and swinging his fire knife around his hand. The flames created a perfect, effortless circle.

Lopaka laughed and jumped forward to attack. They sparred back and forth, the flames causing overwhelming heat to permeate the air as their blades collided. Olukai tripped Lopaka by kicking the back of his knee, but Lopaka rolled to the side, just in time to block Olukai's blade.

The men continued to laugh, *ooh*, and *ah* as Lopaka and Olukai continued to battle it out. Finally, Olukai blocked one of Lopaka's blows, then reached out and grabbed the handle of Lopaka's knife with his other hand. Surprised, Lopaka tried to step back, but, instead, fell backwards as Olukai yanked the knife free.

The soldiers laughed as Olukai let out a loud, "cheeehoo!" and swung both knives, one around each hand. He threw them both into the air. They created a beautiful display of flames in the setting sun, and landed flawlessly back into Olukai's hands. He stopped swinging them to point both ends of the knives at Lopaka's neck.

Fear flashed across Lopaka's eyes for a moment, then he laughed, letting his head rest in the sand.

Olukai shifted both knives to one hand and helped Lopaka up. "Good match!" he exclaimed and dipped the knives into a barrel of water. The soldiers clapped and cheered, drowning out the steamy noise the blades made.

"I almost had you," Lopaka said, wiping his forehead, black strands of hair falling from his bun. His long, flat nose and large lips looked similar to his father Ekewaka, the king. His eyes were such a dark brown, they almost looked black. He grabbed his kihei to cover his chest, as did Olukai.

Many thought that Olukai and Lopaka were brothers, because they were the same age and build. Both were nineteen years old, tall, strong, and brave... although the whole kingdom knew Olukai to be the best fire dancer of them all, and Lopaka to be the island's next king after Ekewaka.

"Better luck next time," said Olukai, tying his black kihei over one shoulder.

"I'll keep practicing." Lopaka stretched his shoulder, wincing. They returned their attention to the young men.

"Get your weapons," Olukai said as he checked that the kapa cloth still covered his forearm. "Let's get to work!"

The little boy he'd seen earlier reached for his weapon, but Olukai stopped him. Darkness rimmed the young boy's face and he looked pale. These were intense sessions, and compassion filled

Olukai's heart. He knew exactly where that compassion came from, and it sent a wave of sadness through his heart.

"You're done for today," Olukai said. The boy looked up, wide eyed.

"Am I in trouble?" he asked, the panic visibly sinking in.

Olukai laughed. "No, not at all. You look exhausted. Go to your quarters and get some rest. Come back tomorrow."

Lopaka watched the exchange and snorted once the boy disappeared. "You're too nice. When I was training you didn't let us off the hook like that."

"Maybe you didn't deserve it," Olukai joked. Lopaka shook his head, leaving Olukai to start yelling orders at the men again.

"Sir."

One of the king's messengers, a familiar face, as this young man came often to deliver messages to Olukai at his home, bowed to Olukai. "The king has requested your attendance tomorrow morning at his council." He glanced at Lopaka, who was already giving orders. "He wishes Prince Lopaka to attend as well. Will you pass the message?"

"'Ae," Olukai nodded, adding, "What is the council about?"

"A new mission, sir, for you and Prince Lopaka." Olukai tried not to groan aloud. He already had much to worry about, including his hope that Po and Haku got the alchemist out of the fortress alive. But he only thanked the messenger before returning to his men. How long would he carry on this charade?

WHEN OLUKAI RODE to his home outside the walls of the fortress, he stopped to take in the view. His home, made of koa wood, ropes, and a thatched roof, was built on top of a hill, overlooking a sandy beach. Olukai loved it here.

He'd been born near here, to a poor father, a fisherman, to be exact. After Kehau, his mother, passed, Olukai's father, Sio, was never the same.

As Olukai led his horse up the sandy hill to his home, he saw his servants tidying up and lighting torches to illuminate his way. Olukai smiled. The loyalty of his servants was unmatched.

"Sir," said the oldest servant, Lala, the cook and maid of the home, "Your food is ready. Will you eat now?"

Olukai smiled at the woman, darkened from the sun and years of her service. Lala once worked for one of the kingdom's wealthy landowners. Olukai frequently went to feasts of the wealthy people, because everyone wanted to be friends with the "best fire dancer." But Olukai had caught Lala being beaten, and the next day he purchased her freedom.

Lala refused "freedom" and instead chose to work for Olukai the rest of her life. Two of her sons also worked on the grounds of Olukai's home.

"I think I'll clean first," he replied. She nodded, hobbling away with her frail body, but turned around once to say, "Your bathwater is ready in the back sir."

Olukai had a total of eight servants, something he never dared to dream of throughout his youth. Only the wealthy had servants, and it seemed impossible that he, once a poor farm boy, could one day attain so many.

But he'd done it... all alone.

As Olukai walked into his washroom and closed the door, he saw himself in the mirror. Only the wealthiest had mirrors, a coveted prize of the rich. He was tall, with a wide and muscular build. Scars lined his chest, arms, and shoulders, a direct result from years of training, practicing, and finally perfecting the art of fire dancing. He had brown eyes and a strong jawline. He wore his dark hair down, and it fell in waves to his shoulders.

He knew his mother would be proud of him...

If only she could see me now, thought Olukai, a small smile on his lips, though the smile was short lived. Maybe it was better he never saw his mother again. After all, he failed Sio.

On his thirteenth birthday, Olukai recalled going to the village square with his father. Olukai had wanted so badly to learn fire dancing. He'd seen many others doing it, and the king paid a handsome price for any who learned the skill in order to teach it.

Olukai still remembered the stirring in his blood: fire dancing could be the way out of poverty for him and his father.

The image of Olukai's father came to mind. Sio was tall and dark, yet so frail and skinny. His hair dangled about his sides, unkempt since his wife's passing. Olukai and his father walked side by side, with eight months of saved earnings stashed in the pouch his father held. As a gift to Olukai, his father wanted to buy a fire knife.

But it was bad timing though, and neither of them thought to be in danger.

As they neared the village square, a tall, dark man spoke loudly, a man whom Olukai would later know personally as Kahiko.

"We seek twelve volunteers to aid the king's army in search of soran. Their return is not guaranteed. The volunteers will be paid a handsome price of fifteen gold coins." The crowd gasped and looked about.

Kahiko's dark eyes scanned the crowd. "Any volunteers?"

Silence. Most of the people knew, by now, that anyone who joined the king's army never returned. He sent them on daunting tasks to get eaten alive or singed by moʻo, to try to make peace with the dark tribe, to risk walking across the lava plains, to deal with the seductive mermaids, or wander the mazes of the Hune.

"We only need twelve volunteers," repeated Kahiko. He stood on a large stone in the middle of the square. Some people began inching away, disappearing in the alleys between the huts and shops.

Olukai looked at Sio. As a farmer, Sio only made twelve silver coins a year, and twelve silver coins equaled one gold coin. This could mean fifteen years of stability. The foreigners had introduced the system of coinage, and many of the villagers still didn't grasp its importance, preferring to trade goods for goods. But the king accepted and traded coins for goods, and Olukai knew that meant the king might trade coins for food or wood, or even a plot of land.

"Father," said Olukai, "I can go."

"No son." Sio placed his hand on Olukai's shoulder but continued looking forward to Kahiko. Olukai knew then, right then, that he might never see his father again. In many ways, Olukai's father had died when his mother died. Sio had no motivation. He drank kava in the nights, hardly took the time to catch fish, so Olukai went out fishing everyday. Olukai even started spearfishing to provide enough food to sell or barter and feed his family. Sio, as a father, was nothing more than a ghost.

When no one volunteered, Kahiko ordered his guards to grab random folks, mostly the old, the withered, those who would die anyways.

And they took Sio, but he did not resist. Olukai pleaded with his father, and Kahiko, saying he would go instead.

But it was too late. His father disappeared that very day and never returned. All Olukai had left in his life that day was a handsome sum of money, and a thirst for revenge. But over the years, his mother's love filled him, and revenge all but faded away. Until the great white shark reminded Olukai of his true identity and kuleana.

Someone knocked on the door and Olukai blinked out of his memory.

"'Ae?"

"Sir, there is a messenger here for you."

"I'll be out in a minute." Olukai bathed in a hurry. He wished every day to make his mother proud and prove that his father's sacrifice (or more so, his forced labor) was not in vain. He wanted to honor his mother and her kindness.

Since his thirteenth birthday, Olukai took the fifteen gold coins and multiplied them. He practiced fire dancing everyday, teaching himself new techniques and hiring stone workers to refine the blades and the long handles. He bought land and hired servants, and, by the age of fifteen, he caught the attention of the king.

At age sixteen, the king called Olukai a "natural alaka'i" and Olukai led armies to find soran himself. He'd been to the highest parts of Kaimana's mountains, where snow blizzards killed many, and sailed all around the island, where he braved the highest waves.

He met members of the Māku'e in the deep woods of the islands, Hune in the hot volcanic mountains, and saw the colorful tempting eyes of mermaids in the deepest oceans... all by the age of nineteen.

And he did it to honor his father's death, a needless sacrifice for the king's obsession, and for the people.

Now King Ekewaka trusted Olukai. He would not even give a second thought on who to ask questions to, or who to send on missions. It was always Olukai. And, though the king didn't say a word about what happened with Edena, Olukai knew it was only a matter of time before the king spilled his secrets.

Olukai brushed his hair and ran some coconut oil through the ends. His servants knew his deep secret, that he was a double player, but they were deathly loyal to them, for he was a kind and wise master. And Olukai had a plan in his mind, for the great white manō confirmed Olukai's leadership.

He could still remember the moment that the great white manō, the largest shark in these waters, spoke to him.

Olukai shivered as he put on a fresh light cream tunic and tied a cord around his waist. He smiled in the mirror, eager to hear the news.

This "messenger" came from the resistance, not the king. And Olukai hoped he brought help with him—but not just any help... an alchemist.

Po STOOD on Olukai's balcony overlooking the ocean. His golden hair looked wind-swept, and his tall frame leaned over the edge, tired. The waves beat down on the shore, a constant, peaceful hum of the sea.

"Welcome friend," Olukai said and clapped Po's hand. "You've come alone?" Olukai looked back into his large living space.

Po nodded. "Kahiko and some guards chased us. We separated. Haku and the alchemist are in the wood of purple."

Olukai rubbed his chin. "I was hoping she'd be here now... I'm going on a mission tomorrow."

Po folded his arms. "How long?"

"A week or two, not longer."

"I plan to go back and get them, though I trust Haku knows his way out," Po said.

Olukai looked out to the ocean, feeling annoyed. This complicated his plans, as he expected Nohea to be here. He needed her help, and now. The sooner she helped him, the sooner he could establish himself as ali'i. Or so he persuaded himself.

Olukai sighed. "Let's hope Kahiko didn't get them first."

CHAPTER SEVEN

There seemed to be no motion around her, so Nohea sat up, feeling pain on the right side of her face. She winced as she gently touched her cheek. Her ear rang with each breath and she squeezed her eyes shut, trying to ignore the tenderness of the area.

I could use some herbs, she thought reaching for her bag. Nui had somehow fit everything: a spare tunic, bombs, herbs, old kapa cloth with the ancient language of the meha, the witch women, that her mother taught her, and so forth.

Uncle Haku rested to her left, and both of them were on a patch of soft grass. A gurgling stream sounded nearby, and Nohea marvelled that the trees above were thin enough to let soft sunlight into the woods. It certainly felt different than the forest they stepped into the previous day.

Nohea frowned. Had it been a day? Her head spun as she tried to process everything: Edena had burned the books, Kahiko was looking for her, Uncle Haku and Po rescued her, they fled to the wood of purple, some members of the Māku'e saved her and Uncle Haku, and here they were.

There was no sign of life around her—people, at least. It was only her and Uncle Haku. She looked over his wound where the spear had pierced, noticing it had neat little stitches. She marvelled. Who knew the art of stitching as well as she? Her mother, Edena, taught her to stitch up wounds using the purest hairs of the banana leaf. How her mother knew so many things always filled Nohea with wonder, but whenever she asked, her mother glared or ignored her.

Nohea wondered if the Māku'e had done that.

And where are they now? she began questioning herself, looking about the clearing. The handsome young man who'd saved her yesterday, was he real? Or had it all been a dream? *Did I really see a Māku'e?*

She gently shook Uncle Haku awake. He bolted up, almost hitting his head against Nohea's. "Calm down," she said, chuckling at his surprise.

"Are we safe?" he asked, surveying their surroundings. His dark brown eyes looked tired, and Nohea felt sorry he had to be doing this, not that he was terribly old. But he should've been at home, with his family, not in the middle of nowhere. "'Ae."

"They must have recognized me," he said, rubbing his forehead. Nohea reached into her bag and pulled out some dried herbs. She rubbed them with her hand and then moved his hand to place her own on his forehead. "Po must have warned my family," said Uncle Haku, taking a breath.

Nohea had never met his wife or children, but based on his rare but tender visits, she had no doubt he was a devoted father. She nodded, feeling his concern for their safety.

"What happened?" Nohea asked. "Did you see the Māku'e?"

"Ae, I did. I spoke with one of them—the girl... but she put uli to my nose, and I knocked out."

Uli. Of course.

"What did she say? How many Māku'e were there?"

"Two. They were siblings. They fought off the guards, but she wouldn't tell me their names. She recommended we leave the woods as soon as we can…" He sighed. "We need to find Po and get you to the manō."

"Why?" Nohea asked, watching his eyes and feeling his pulse to monitor his pain. Holding the herb to his forehead was helping, she could tell, as his body relaxed.

"I cannot tell you everything now, my niece." He closed his eyes. "But for now, we are safe. Kahiko and the guards are far away. They will come back for us… eventually. The sooner we leave these woods, the sooner we can get you to complete safety."

"There is no such thing as complete safety," Nohea said with no tone or emotion in her voice.

Uncle Haku opened his eyes and frowned . "That is the reason we need the true heir of the manō. Only a true aliʻi of Kaimana can guarantee health and safety for his people."

"The manō is a legend," Nohea said, annoyed. She had been willing to listen in the lava cave, but now, in the light of day, she felt her head clearing up, though she knew her body still processed the shock of everything. The manō was nothing more than tales told by the old folks as the slaves sat around a night fire.

"Edena didn't believe in the old tales, the old prophecies?" Uncle Haku asked, gently taking Nohea's hand off his forehead.

"No, *I* don't believe those old wise tales," Nohea said. "They are nothing more than folklore. The only thing we can believe in is ourselves, and our own wit and knowledge to get through. And trust that if we are good, the island is good to us." At that, her stomach gurgled.

Standing, she added, "I can find something to eat. I know what plants are safe." Blood rushed from her head and she leaned against the nearest tree to steady herself.

Uncle Haku paused for a moment, thinking about what she said. So she added, "I believe we choose our fate, not some mystic animal or ghost story. We are what we make of ourselves."

"And so you would have chosen to be a slave forever?" His eyes looked up at her, tenderly, as a father would look at his child.

"No. I was going to discover something... something that would cure all, and it would be the means to free all the slaves." She sighed. "I know I can do it... I just need more time—"

"And the manō can give you that time."

"I don't want to hear about the manō," Nohea rolled her eyes. "That's a legend—"

"Listen," Uncle Haku stood and placed his hands on her shoulders. Nohea looked up at him. "There is a man who sailed to many islands, even those far beyond our shores. He leads a devoted group of warriors, all experts with the fire knife. On one voyage, they *all* saw the great white manō—"

"The great white manō that never haunts these shores..." Nohea interrupted. Uncle Haku paused, his eyes sad, and she sighed, "I'm sorry... continue."

"It came from the deep, it's fin taller than the sail on the canoe, with ancient markings on its long body... it came and surrounded them. No one could deny the mana. The power was there. And then the shark bumped the canoe and all the men fell off."

Nohea raised her eyebrows.

"The men frantically swam towards the canoe. The great white manō weaved around the men. They were terrified, except one."

Nohea swallowed. She'd never seen a manō but some of the women, whose husbands were far away fishing in the sea, wore manō tooth necklaces. And the leiomanō, which the men used as weapons and tools, were incredibly sharp. Edena once drew a picture with a piece of charcoal and described the manō to Nohea: long, sharp teeth, strong bodies, and a fearful look.

"Their leader called his men. Told them to stay calm, lower their weapons..."

"Lower their weapons?" Nohea tried not to frown.

"The men were too afraid, panicking. They held their weapons around them, but their leader had no fear."

No fear? That phrase picked Nohea's interest. The very thought made her want to stand taller. How could someone be so fearless?

Her own fears lurked below her determined confidence: fear of failure, fear of death, fear of never being able to help others.

"He dove under the water and made eye contact with the great white manō. It swam straight towards the leader, who held out his hand and touched the great white manō's head. Have you heard stories of 'aumakua or the ali'i of Kaimana Island before?"

Nohea shivered. "'Ae, but very few. Most 'aumakua never show themselves to their descendents." Every family had an 'aumakua, including her own, but she never met hers.

"You are right, Nohea. But the great white manō revealed the lineage of this young leader. The great shark left a mark on the man's arm, the mark of the manō. It means he comes from the true blood line of the ali'i. The island led me to this man, and I know for a fact that he is the island's true king."

"Because of the mark?"

"'Ae."

"Who is he?"

"We do not speak his name. We only call him manō, until the time comes for his rise as ruler of the island."

"But you know him?" Nohea raised her eyebrows again.

"You don't believe me?"

"It doesn't sound real. Who has no fears?"

Uncle Haku let his hands off her shoulders. "You are not the same girl I remember," he said softly.

"I'm not a little girl anymore." She frowned. "I've seen enough death and hardship to not believe in old men's tales. We don't need anymore foolish magic or legends—we need answers. I'm going to find the cure to end all diseases, and then we are safe."

Her stomach growled again. "Thank you for the tale Uncle, but let's find something to eat."

"We will stick together," Uncle Haku replied, clutching his right shoulder in pain as they started walking. His countenance had dropped, and Nohea felt genuinely sorry that she didn't believe his story.

After seeing so many deaths, and even knowing about all those who died in the ghost generation, all the generations before who died from the foreigners' diseases, she knew that myths were nothing more than that. The people of the island needed true, hard facts to survive.

Though, she couldn't help the nagging feeling inside of her. *The island has been good to me...* The numerous times the birds had warned and comforted her kept coming to mind. If she felt a connection to the island and the birds, would it be so far-fetched to believe that the great white manō would connect with the mind of a man?

There was a rumor that circulated, not long ago, that there was a great white shark circling the island, and it was the reason the islanders couldn't leave, and foreigners couldn't enter. But what did it matter? It was probably the best thing for the island, as any contact with foreigners would mean more foreign diseases. The islanders had no immunity for such a situation again.

Nohea shook her head. King Ekewaka didn't seem like such a bad king, but if there was one thing she wanted to change, it was that of the slaves. Nobody deserved to be a slave.

After a minute, Uncle Haku laughed , and Nohea looked back, amused.

"What's so funny?" she asked.

"We're both broken... I'm slowing you down." He paused, taking a deep breath. Nohea offered him her arm but he shook his head. "You walk ahead—just don't go too far."

Nohea nodded and walked towards a fallen tree. Moss grew all over the sides, and some mushrooms poked up from beneath the trunk. She didn't like mushrooms, but, since they weren't the poisonous type, and her stomach rumbled like thunder, she grabbed a few.

If she could get close to the stream, she knew she could find berries, maybe even some banana trees, guava, or a safe watercress.

Uncle Haku lagged behind her.

Anthuriums and ferns grew in abundance but there really wasn't much fruit or edible leaves.

As Nohea looked at the vibrant red colors of the anthuriums, her heart sank. These were her mother's favorite flowers. Up until now, Nohea hadn't been able to grieve. The shock still hadn't truly processed.

Edena was probably killed by now. And for what? What secrets did her mother hide from her? Why could she not ever tell her own daughter? Why did she burn the books?

And now Nohea knew she might never see her mother again. She would never know. Though she wasn't close to her mother, and she committed to never be like her, it was still a loss.

"Edena's favorite." Uncle Haku put an arm on her shoulder. "We cannot let her death be in vain Nohea."

"You know why they took her?" Nohea took his arm to support him. "Why did she burn the books??"

"She burned the books in the library..." Uncle Haku mused. "The only books and tools left behind from the sailors long ago."

"I know... but why?"

Uncle Haku shrugged. "My guess is as good as yours." Nohea continued to stare.

"Your mother... she had many secrets," he added. "And I'm sorry to say that I know none of them. She has never revealed any to me, which is why I came out to take care of you."

"And for that I am grateful." Nohea kissed his cheek. "Now I must take care of you. Come on, we're getting closer to the stream."

Along the way, Nohea picked some long green ti leaves, the perfect way to wrap food later. She brushed her hands against the soft ferns as they walked through the dense forest. Though light filtered through the tall trees, the forest floor was a maze of plants. She loved being in this, and, in some strange way, the mysterious forest felt comforting and familiar.

"I need a rest," said Uncle Haku, sitting on the grass. Nohea followed after, helping him lean back against the mossy tree behind him. It was a thick, sturdy koa tree, and the roots sat perfectly on either side of him to rest his arms. She put her hand on his forearm.

"I can get you some water," she said, untying her gourd from the bag. It had been full when Nui gave it to her, but now it was empty, and she wondered if the Māku'e had used it to clean their wounds. So Nohea glanced at the direction of the moving water.

"Call if you need me," Uncle Haku said, sighing. He looked tired, pale even, for being such a dark person. Nohea figured it was from the loss of blood. She needed to restore his health, and if she could find some nutritious watercress by the river, that would help too.

"I'll be back." She hurried off.

The soft flowing of the stream made the air around it feel peaceful. The water stretched wide and shallow, with many large ferns and bushes hanging along its sides. Nohea searched for footing amongst the dense greenery growing about the side walls.

As she stepped down the steep side, hoping she wouldn't fall and slip into the stream, she held onto some fern bushes and took a step at a time, the mud already starting to cake on the bottom of her sandals.

There was a large dry rock sitting outside of the stream and Nohea hoped to step on that. She hated getting her sandals wet, which made them uncomfortable and loud to walk in.

As she took a step down, her foot slid over the mud and the fern she held onto ripped from the ground. Nohea fell into the stream, bottom first.

Ouch! With the bottom of her tunic and bag now soaking wet, she stood up and rubbed her back. Glancing around to make sure nobody saw, she frowned and squeezed the water from her tunic.

With her sandals wet, she decided to scrub off the mud. They'd be loud now, no doubt. She sat on the rock and dipped her hand to put some cold water onto the right side of her face. She winced again at the tingling sensation. The water moved too rapidly for her to see her reflection, but she was sure it was purple and bruised from the soldier who tripped over her in the darkness.

"You left your old man already?"

Nohea looked up, alarmed. A girl stood on the bank across from her, folding her arms. Nohea had never seen anyone quite like this young woman: she wore a white tunic, with black hair falling down her back, complemented with a few braids. In her right ear was a big red hibiscus, and she wore a bright red lei around her neck. With light brown skin, large hazel eyes, and plump dark lips, the girl intimidated Nohea. In many ways, Nohea felt ugly next to this girl.

Nohea blinked. "Excuse me?"

"Your old man... you left him?" The girl stepped down the bank and her feet lightly stepped into the stream. She wore thick sandals with long, complicated straps around her calves. She had some kind of strap across her chest too, with a long spear attached to her back.

"No, I'm getting water for him. Who are you?" She crouched down again to continue filling the gourd.

"We rescued you folks yesterday... a thanks would do," the girl said smugly. Nohea recalled the girl with the light coming out of her spear.

"Well.. thank you." Nohea continued filling the water then stood. "Who are you?"

"I'd like to know who you are first. Those guards are going to be back any time now, and we need to decide if it's worth our time to help you or not."

"We?" Nohea asked but in that moment was startled as a figure walked around from behind her, the same young man who had rescued her the day before. The same one who twisted the guard's head, resulting in that loud snapping noise. Nohea cringed. He nodded to her and stood by the girl.

He was handsome, with the same features as the girl in white: light brown skin, tall, but with amber eyes. Instead of black hair, like the girls, his was a dark brown with beautiful golden highlights, probably a result of his being in the sun. Unlike most men, his hair was cut short, not growing past his ears. He had angular cheekbones and skin as smooth as the ti leaf. He wore a green lei around his neck, a white skirt and kihei, and similar thick sandals with complicated ties.

Nohea noticed two large scars on his body. One went from his right shoulder to his middle finger, and the other from the left side of his mouth to his cheek. Her stomach fluttered and she realized the same feeling when she met Po. *Attraction.* She blinked hard and turned her attention to the girl, though she began to feel self conscious of her own soaking tunic and mottled purple face.

"I'm Nohea."

"Your old man?" The girl folded her arms.

"Uncle Haku."

"Why were those king men following you?"

"They killed my mother, and they wanted to kill me too. My uncle rescued me."

The young man and lady exchanged glances. He frowned , concerned.

"Why did they kill your mother—" the girl started asking.

"I don't have time for this," Nohea interrupted, knowing full well that they had weapons and she didn't. But they'd also saved her life, so she didn't feel too worried about them hurting her. "Thank you for helping us yesterday, but I will be on my way." She had filled up the gourd with water by this time and started walking towards the ferny bank, more embarrassment sinking in as they no doubt saw her wet tunic.

"Your uncle is gone."

Nohea whirled around. "What?"

"Never leave one another's sight. Have you not heard of these woods? They're infested with old spirits..."

"The *Kupua*?" Nohea asked, her mind recalling, once more, the tales told round those fires, her young eyes full of wander. She had stopped believing in those superstitions. *Kupua* were old spirits that could take the form of whatever they wanted, sometimes leaf bodies, flower bodies, bird bodies, or tree bodies.

The girl nodded. "You won't be able to save him alone."

"You're lying." Nohea shook her head and left them standing behind her.

She rushed through the thick brush, her sandals making a *squish* noise every time she stepped.

"Uncle Haku!" The stream hadn't been far from where he sat to rest.

She stopped as she reached the soft patch of grass. One of her bags sat on the ground, the one she'd been carrying before Nui brought her other belongings in a separate bag.

But Uncle Haku was gone, as well as the tree he'd been resting against.

CHAPTER EIGHT

Olukai walked through the king's fortress, passing the many huts of the counselors. Their wives sat outside gossiping with the king's many concubines, fanning their fat faces and giving Olukai the stink eye. They used to holler at him, vying for his attention as each wanted him to marry their daughters. After being overly polite for years, Olukai finally put his foot down, expressing his disinterest, and since then, the king's many concubines glared at him.

As Olukai continued through the fortress, passing the concubine's huts, guest huts, the warrior's huts, and more, he felt grateful to have his own private home outside the fortress. Olukai and Kahiko were the only two of the king's counselors to live outside the fortress. Olukai was wealthy enough to live outside the gates, and Kahiko preferred his privacy, the typical way of a sorcerer. The other counselors pretended to be helpful to the king, but really indulged the king in order to live within the walls and get paid to eat, drink, and gossip.

The king built a great wall around his little village of "royalty."

Regular townspeople would never be seen within the gates, only those on the king's errand like slaves, soldiers, and tax collectors.

The slaves lived on the northwestern end, in a secluded village, by the garden and fields. Thinking of the slaves made Olukai send out a silent call to the island to keep Po, Nohea, and Haku safe. The previous night Po had stopped by. He looked tired, worried, yet energized.

Po's words sounded in Olukai's ears: "She really is beautiful," Po had said. "But her eyes..."

"What about her eyes?" Olukai and Po were like brothers, Po being eighteen, a year younger.

"One was golden..."

Olukai couldn't stop thinking about it. It didn't sit right with him. Was it a curse? Was she a descendant of a dark spirit? Or was it simply an abnormality?

Any abnormalities on the island were treated as a mark of disfavor, and, therefore, people treated any person with abnormalities as "different." From being crippled, lame, deaf, or mute... these people were usually cast out, or given the hardest tasks as slaves.

Or maybe, deep down, Olukai wondered if the golden eye bothered him because the king, himself, had one golden eye.

"Olukai!" The young man slowed down so Lopaka could catch up.

"You're not going to like this mission," Lopaka said. Olukai raised his eyebrows, and Lopaka added, "Just know I gave you a fair warning."

They approached the king's council hut, with a thatched roof so tall, it shaded the many palm trees around it. The warriors in front of the opening stood much taller and larger than Olukai and Lopaka, and their dark countenance gave off an intimidating energy. The king had about twenty large warriors, around the hut, always there to protect him should anything happen. They were not mere soldiers, they were warriors, trained to kill, drinkers of soran. Their tattoos, along with their large size, distinguished them from normal soldiers.

The warriors glanced at Olukai and Lopaka then moved their spears aside so that the two young men could enter. Once inside, Olukai and Lopaka removed their sandals and both knelt on one knee, their faces down.

"My sons," said the king at the head of the hall. He raised his hands, fingers facing them, palms toward the ceiling, a symbol of peace. "Enter."

Both young men stepped forward. The rest of the council was already settled in, their overweight bodies sweating as they fanned themselves.

Olukai sat cross legged on the mat at the king's left. Lopaka sat next to him. Kahiko's black eyes glared at Olukai from the other side of the king.

It had always been a game to win the king's favor for Olukai and Kahiko. Neither were named the king's official first counselor. They had always been his top two, "most trusted" counselors.

"Let us start our council," said the king, and the slaves, kneeling behind him, left in silence to bring back drinks.

"Our island is a beautiful place," said the king, "and our people are even more beautiful." The king had a deep, loud voice, as he was a very big man. Muscled, with brown skin tough as weathered lava rock, King Ekewaka was the face of intimidation. Everything about him was big: his voice, his body, his energy.

Even his dark black hair looked big and wavy, in a braid down his back. He stood much taller than Olukai, with legs as wide as tree trunks and shoulders the size of the drums used to dance hula.

"We cannot lose our people again," the king said. "We need to discover a cure... and the only other known potion makers on this island... are the meha."

The whole room fell silent. The men stopped fanning themselves. Just the word made every person's hair stand on end.

Olukai had his fair share of dealings with the meha, the witch women, who lived in different kīpuka, the lush forests growing in the middle of old lava fields. People told horror stories about the meha, like how they wore veils over their faces to hide their deformities and dark markings, or how they spoke strange words to curse people. Their magic ways and dark rituals scared away any person.

No counselor had the guts to ask why, so Olukai did. "How would this benefit the island?" he asked. Kahiko's death glare started bothering Olukai so he made eye contact, and Kahiko looked away.

Of all the magical creatures on the island, the meha were the ones Olukai wanted to avoid the most. He served many missions for the king, including those that passed the kīpuka of meha.

On one expedition, Olukai heard them howling in the night, the light of their fire burning into the sky. He'd seen them in the day too, with brown kapa cloths covering their faces. They were like the living dead.

"They can create a cure like soran," said the king, "Or discover how to source soran. There are no other magic-makers, alchemists, or herbalogists who can do such a thing."

"Or sorcerers?" Olukai asked, egging it on. Kahiko looked like he'd kill Olukai at that moment.

"No," said the king. His golden eye beamed brightly in the light. A slave bowed to him, holding a tray with a glass ball. The inside swirled with a purple liquid, the magical island juice, soran.

Soran was the island's most coveted possession, possibly the cure to all diseases, and the reason the king was so large and lived so long. It could heal any wound, remove a disease, and, the king believed, even save those on the brink of death. It seemed absurd, but Olukai knew soran was no legend, no myth, no folktale.

It was real, for he'd gone on many missions to retrieve it for the king. He'd seen all the creatures of the island, from people of the dark tribe, to the old kupua, the night marchers, the luring eyes of mermaids, the water spirits, the moʻo, and, of course, the manō, the shark. He'd climbed the highest peaks of the island, where blizzards abounded, and nearly suffocated in the darkest lava tubes. He'd seen and felt the searing heat of flowing lava up close and personal.

He had seen and experienced all of the island... for the king's love of soran. It was an addiction, and Olukai knew that Kaimana Island wanted it gone. The great white manō would continue to circle the island until soran was destroyed. It was too powerful for any race.

King Ekewaka picked up the glass ball and took a sip of the purple liquid. A slave knelt and bowed to Olukai as she handed him an opened coconut. The refreshing smell of coconut water filled his nose as he held the ball in his hands.

"Sorcerers will do us no good this time," said the king, nodding to Kahiko, as if to acknowledge that Kahiko was a sorcerer, and the king meant no harm. "Kahiko has done well, going on as many expeditions as yourself, Olukai. You both know the island and the creatures better than any others. But there are no persons on the island as expert as the meha... they can find the way to reproduce soran from the walls of my home itself."

Olukai nodded, "That is a wise idea, your majesty. Who will find the meha?"

"You and Lopaka will go. Kahiko has a different assignment." The king sipped more of the soran. His eyes dilated every time he caught a whiff of it.

Olukai knew exactly what the soran smelled like, though he'd never dared to taste it himself. It smelled musty, like fermented coconut water. He saw, firsthand, what it did to the king, and he didn't want to follow those footsteps.

This soran was the cause of so much grief, the true reason Sio, his father, was killed. This soran was the cure and the bane of the island.

"If I may be so bold, your highness," said Olukai, bowing to the king, "May I ask the whereabouts of Kahiko's mission?"

"Why must a fire dancer know what a sorcerer is up to?" Kahiko blurted, his thick lips curled up in a snarl.

The king looked to the other counselors, and waved his hand. "Leave."

The fat men stood, piling out in haste, a surprising feat for their size and health. Those counselors were in charge of slaves, taxes and the collectors, and other organizations in the kingdom.

Lopaka stayed put, as he always did. Olukai considered Lopaka a sort of sidekick. Whatever Olukai knew about the king's whereabouts, he told Lopaka. And whatever Lopaka knew, he told Olukai. They'd gone on too many missions together to leave out any details of the king's mysterious intentions.

It was strange that Lopaka was the king's son, the next in line to the throne, but King Ekewaka never acknowledged that. In some dark way, it seemed to Olukai that King Ekewaka expected that Lopaka would never rule. And, strangely enough, Lopaka hardly appeared bothered by this. He had always preferred to follow Olukai, or be told what to do.

Once the counselors were gone, and the slaves excused themselves to the furthest corners of the room, where they could hear nothing, the king rolled his eyes.

"We have lost the slave girl. Her mother, Edena, is in prison. We discovered she has been hiding secrets."

Olukai frowned.

"For one," continued Ekewaka, "Edena knows the ways of the island—the plants, their purposes, medicine. She might understand the ways of soran... but we must kill her. She is too dangerous." The king took another drink of his soran.

So she's not dead, Olukai thought.

"Has she done more harm... besides burning the books in your library?" asked Olukai. For all the questions he asked, the king never seemed to get annoyed. After all the successful missions he'd gone on, Olukai had earned the king's trust and patience.

"She is a sorceress," the king said, "and a very, *very* powerful one. She can put a curse on anyone. And because of that..." He paused, thinking, then changed his tone. "She will be executed in the morning."

Olukai nodded and bowed his head. "I understand. And what of her daughter?" Maybe he couldn't save the mother, Edena, in time, but the island urged him to save Nohea. He needed her. Desperately. She was his only hope of carrying out his plans to become the island's ali'i. She could discover how to destroy soran, once and for all.

"I will go with Kahiko to the dark wood." King Ekewaka's eyes narrowed. "And we will find her. I must find some answers for myself." He glared into the distance.

Olukai opened his mouth to ask, *What answers?* But thought better of it. He'd already asked too many questions and didn't want to test his luck. "That is a good plan, your majesty."

"The rumors of the manō seem to have circulated throughout this island." The king changed the subject, while glancing at the kapa cloth covering Olukai's forearm. "Have you heard of them?"

Olukai nodded. "'Ae, but I don't believe them to be true. *You* are the heir, and the only heir, to the bloodline of the great white manō. There is none other." He bowed his head to the ground.

That's a lie. Take your rightful throne. The island vibrated angrily beneath him, as though his 'aumakua, deep in the water, was speaking straight to Olukai. The quiet fear gnawed inside Olukai's chest. He knew it was time to reveal himself, but he couldn't. He wasn't ready. Or so he told himself.

The king rolled his eyes, "Except my brother."

King Ekewaka's brother, Makana, was as aggressive and violent in nature as Ekewaka. After the foreigners came and a whole generation of islanders were killed from the diseases, the island desperately needed a leader. Ekewaka and Makana started out as brotherly leaders, uniting the island against the foreigners, driving them out, striking up deals with mermaids to keep them out. They helped the people pick up from their desolation.

But then power and greed entered their eyes, and the brothers fought. The people fought. Until, finally, Makana took his followers and migrated to the northern part of the island, the driest parts. Rumor said that Makana and his people starved to death out there, for they had not waged battle for many years.

But every person knew better, especially Olukai. He'd seen Makana's kingdom: an enclosed city with a well of soran next to it.

Olukai had never told Ekewaka, for Olukai wanted to avoid battle at any cost. But Makana was still out there, and Olukai had no doubt he was alive and well, thanks to the soran.

"Your brother is dead," Kahiko said, his low voice echoing through the hall.

"I would like to see for myself," scoffed the king. "After I find this girl and get the meha, I want to visit the leeward side." His nose flared. "If he is not dead, I will see to it."

Both Kahiko and Olukai bowed their heads. "'Ae, that is wise," said Kahiko for himself and Olukai.

The king took a breath, as if to calm himself down. His black and gold eyes seemed to return to their normal size. He stood up, but almost fell, and both Kahiko and Olukai jumped to his aid.

"Stop!" the king exclaimed, catching himself. His leg still looked swollen from the horse that bucked him. Though King Ekewaka had dark brown skin, the purple-green bruises showed up.

"I want the whole tribe of meha," the king said to Olukai, grunting. "Don't leave one behind. Bring the whole tribe."

Olukai bowed his head. "Of course, your majesty." He held up his palm to the king. "And I hope you find the answers you seek in the dark wood."

The king nodded, then began to leave the room, with Kahiko and a slave on either side to help the king walk.

"Wait, father!"

The men turned to see Like approaching from the end of the hall. Lopaka groaned to himself. Like, the weaker, lesser, younger brother of Lopaka, hobbled in.

"Father, you cannot kill Edena." Like's face was pale, as though he'd exerted a great effort to hurry into the hall.

The king glared at his son. "What do you want?" He rolled his eyes. "And how dare you enter without permission!"

Like ignored his father's complaints. "She told me herself. If you kill her, the curse will not be lifted."

The curse? Olukai looked from Like to the king, whose face turned red in anger. The king had mentioned Edena was a sorceress, and she could curse anyone... but did that mean something more?

"Stupid boy! Get out of here!"

Like flinched, and Olukai felt sorry for him. Olukai had never known Like well, because Like was too weak to go on any of the king's missions. Lopaka shook his head, as if to warn his younger brother.

"The meha in the nearest kīpuka cannot remove the curse. Only Edena or—"

"*Now!*" the king screamed, his veins jutting from his forehead and neck. Lopaka rubbed his forehead, as though bracing himself to step in between Like and the king.

Like nodded and quickly turned around, running out.

"Leave." The king was in his anger, and both Olukai and Lopaka bowed before rushing out of the throne room.

But Olukai kept wondering to himself... *What curse?*

CHAPTER NINE

Nohea grabbed her bag and patted the soft grass. "Uncle Haku?" She felt the panic as she stood up. "Uncle Haku!"

The young man and woman stood behind Nohea, a look of sorrow in both of their eyes.

"We can help you," said the girl.

"You did this to him!" Nohea stood face to face with the girl. "Where is he?" The girl didn't flinch, and, instead, pointed into the distance, where the woods grew more shaded and darker.

"The old spirits take their feasts there. We have some time." She pulled the spear from her back. "But first we want to know who you *really* are... Not anyone has eyes like yours."

It had been a long time since anyone mentioned Nohea's different eye colors. She fidgeted, looking from the darkness to Kiani. She had no choice. "I'm Nohea." Her cheeks began to burn as she added, "I am a daughter of a slave, nothing more."

A lie. Deep down Nohea was an alchemist and maker of medicines. But they didn't need to know that, not now, at least.

The two met one another's eyes and the young man nodded.

"Perhaps there is more to your story," said the girl, "something that you do not yet know. We will help you find your uncle, and then we will leave you in peace."

Nohea swallowed and looked into the darkness. Every minute away from her uncle was a minute that he could be tortured, or worse...

"We know many of the kupua here," said the girl. "They have become familiar spirits and don't bother us anymore. Only new blood that comes in here, like you."

The boy retrieved his own spear from his back and then reached for a small gourd hanging from a strap on the girl's shoulder.

"The only way you can scare away a kupua is with pure white light," said the girl. "This water is from the highest mountain on the island, Mauna Ki'eki'e. It is said a white god came down many years ago, and he blessed the people and this island. We traveled to get this pure water, because when it strikes any darkness, it lets out a great light. That light scares darkness away."

"That's what you used against the kahuna?" Nohea asked, putting her extra bag around her shoulder, feeling inside to ensure her bombs remained in place. When her hand brushed against the outside coating of the ti leaf, a hint of relief touched her shoulders. At least she had *some* kind of weapon.

"'Ae. Kahiko is a dark man—"

"So you know Kahiko?" Nohea interrupted.

"We know many of your people," she said. "But we are wanderers." She dipped her own spear into the gourd and then the young man shut it.

"What are your names?" Nohea asked as she played with her fingers, quickly walking towards the darkness.

"I am Kiani, and this is my younger brother, Wena." Nohea met Wena's eyes, and he nodded to her.

"He is the one who stitched your uncle's wound," said Kiani. "He has been blessed with steady hands, and a straight aim. He never misses a target."

Nohea's fingers instinctively went to the tender side of her face, wondering if it looked as bad as she imagined it.

She then realized, up until that moment, that the young man hadn't said one word. "How old are you?" she asked him.

"Eighteen," replied Kiani.

Nohea nodded, too nervous to find her uncle to think about why Wena didn't say anything. They pushed forward into the darkness, the tree canopy above them growing thicker and thicker, until everything looked like shadows again. Wena stopped and Kiani stood next to him as he knelt by the ground and touched the moss and ferns.

The ferns looked discolored, and when Wena touched them and lifted his palm to show them girls, Nohea noticed the crimson color of blood. He sniffed his palm and nodded to Kiani, making a sign with his hand, then pointing with all his fingers to their right.

Kiani and Wena's eyes met one another, as though they communicated without words, though Kiani spoke. "Is it the old kupua Lapa'au?" she asked. Wena nodded and then began making signals with his hands, while mouthing words.

Nohea stared. She'd seen this very behavior before, and she began to understand what Wena was saying.

He must have her uncle bound up in his branches. He won't go to the shaded part—he'll take her uncle to the thickness of the ferns. We can use our spears to break the light and free her uncle. If her uncle is high in the tree, we'll need to somehow catch him...

His hands moved fast, as she'd seen before, and she remembered the many signs she used to make to communicate with Kimo.

This wasn't any mind reading game. Wena was signing and communicating with his sister.

Wena was deaf.

Nohea's skin crawled, but she didn't know why.

Kiani nodded, "I'll catch him. I'm strong enough. You have a better aim than me so you get old Lapa'au and I'll catch her uncle." She tipped her head towards Nohea, "With her help."

Wena looked up at Nohea and his cheeks turned pink. He then

stared at his spear as he stood. Nohea smiled shyly and signed back to him when their eyes met again. *That is a great plan.*

Both Kiani and Wena froze. Kiani's jaw dropped but she caught herself and frowned. Nohea shrugged. " "A man I knew was deaf. He was like family." She didn't want to think about Kimo, and how she let him down so she turned and started walking again. But not before catching the young man smile, the first in their brief encounter. He had a charming smile, with nice teeth. Nohea's cheeks warmed as she walked faster so they wouldn't see her face.

Kiani laughed, following after Nohea. "Well, I guess she knows what's going on. Let's hurry, before the old spirit decides he's hungry now."

They ran, and Nohea's tender ear began ringing. She held it with one hand and couldn't help but catch quick glances at Wena. What were these two siblings doing in the middle of the woods? They were clearly members of the dark tribe, but why did Kiani call them "wanderers?"

She studied their pointy ears when they weren't watching. *How strange,* she thought. *If only Like could see this, for he did not exaggerate the odd features of these people at all.*

The air grew colder as they hiked up steep hills covered in ferns and long blades of grass. The trees loomed together, thicker, blocking out the sunlight. Blowing through the wood, the wind sounded like a man breathing deeply.

Nohea shivered and held her shoulders, the tender side of her face feeling swollen from the blood rushing through her body. The siblings readied their spears.

"Almost there," Kiani whispered to Nohea. "You can't miss old Lapa'au. He's the biggest tree around—quite a beauty, but also a pest. We've had our fair share of bouts with Lapa'au..."

Nohea looked at Wena only to notice he'd been watching her, and they both looked away.

The ground grew softer, to the point that Nohea's sandals made a loud *squish* noise with every step. Kiani glared at her. "Can you be any quieter?"

"I'm sorry. These are the only ones I—"

Wena motioned for her to silence and duck. He pointed with his fingers into the distance and nodded.

All three crouched behind a thick bunch of dark ferns, but when Nohea peeked over the hedge to see what Wena saw, her mouth dropped.

Indeed, the old kupua was quite the beauty. He was an old koa tree, and so large that his trunk had to be at least five times the size of Nohea around. He stood tall, his branches shading the entire area of ferns and greenery beneath him. Nohea squinted into the branches and found Uncle Haku caught up there, a large branch wrapped around his waist.

She couldn't tell if he was awake—or even alive. Smaller branches covered his mouth.

"Change of plans," Kiani said to Nohea. "Wena and I will get your uncle. You stay here."

"What?" Nohea glanced from Kiani to Wena. "I must do something."

Kiani bit her lower lip, but shook her head. "You're not strong enough. These forest spirits are rough, and you don't know anything about them."

Not strong enough? Anger immediately fumed through Nohea. How dare Kiani make such an assumption! *She wouldn't survive one day in the life of a slave...*

"But I—"

Wena interrupted Nohea by tapping her arm, then mouthed and signed, *I'm sorry. You'll have to trust us.*

His eyes truly looked sorry, and Nohea's instant reaction to roll her eyes melted away.

"Fine," she whispered, "but if anything happens I'll think of something." She already thought of the few bombs in her bag, and what might work... though she had no idea if an old spirit, in the form of a tree, would react to the bombs.

Wena and Kiani crawled out of the ferns, crouching low, spears in hand. Compared to the size of the tree, the two looked like mere ants. With spear in hand, they moved through the brush, making no more noise than the wind blowing.

The tree shifted , and a large crackling sound echoed through the clearing as his trunk twisted to face them.

"You can't hide from me!"

Nohea's skin crawled. She'd never felt such darkness, such a disturbance in the energy around her. The life within the tree felt... *unnatural.* The voice, a raspy, old, annoyed voice, came from the tree, like a hiss.

Wena stood, and the tree shook, making a terrible noise, the leaves trembling in a frenzy, and the trunk twisting with a loud *snap* to face the young man.

Nohea could now see the old spirit's face, a pudgy nose, dark brown eyes, and a hollowed mouth. He looked ancient. This was, who Wena and Kiani called, Lapa'au.

Without hesitation, Wena raised his spear and launched it straight between the old spirit's eyes. As soon as the spear left his fingers, he ran to the side of the tree, ready to catch Uncle Haku, though Nohea didn't see him moving because a bright white light flooded the entire area, blinding her for a few seconds.

"Again!" she heard Kiani yell. Nohea's eyes adjusted and grew wide as the tree straightened out to scream, letting out a roar that blew her hair straight back. Panic overwhelmed her as she realized Uncle Haku was still in the tree.

The white light didn't shock Lapa'au enough to drop Uncle Haku. The tree's face turned to Kiani and Wena, his roots rising from the ground and grabbing Wena's leg. It looked like Kiani had tried to throw her spear to Wena, but the tree's roots caught it midair.

Without thinking, Nohea bolted into the clearing and threw an uli bomb straight at the old spirit's big nose. Blue powder exploded into the air, painting his face and eyes. He sniffed and then started to sneeze.

"Ah..." he tried to catch himself. "Ahh..."

Nohea ran to help Wena pull the roots off his legs, though both of them made no difference as they yanked at the tightly gripped roots. Kiani managed to free her spear from the roots, but before she could aim, Lapa'au let out the largest sneeze Nohea had ever heard. It came with such great force, it blew all of them into the air.

All his roots and branches went loose for a brief moment, enough time to set Uncle Haku free. He went flying into the air with the huge gust of the wind.

All four landed in the distant ferns, and the old spirit looked about, confused. "Run," said Kiani, grabbing Uncle Haku's arm and pulling him to run. Wena grabbed Nohea's hand and pulled her to her feet.

"Nooooo..." the tree howled, the wind from his cries pushing them further and faster.

Nohea felt a sudden tug at her foot and she tripped. Wena whirled around and jumped to grab her arms, but it was too late, as the roots of the old spirit dragged her backwards. She clawed at the ground, then was lifted into the air, face to face with Lapa'au.

"I know who you are," he breathed. "You are one of them."

"Let me go!" She tried to wriggle free, but the roots circled around her arms and legs, feeling like coarse dirt rubbing her skin raw.

"I will let you go, but leave me more uli," the tree said, eyeing her, seeming more awake now than before. "I have not had that for a very long time..." Nohea scanned the forest floor and was surprised to realize, for the first time, that the blue purple gingers didn't grow here. Why did the tree want uli? This wasn't the time to ponder the question.

He loosened his grip to free her hands, keeping her legs bound. Wena ran up to the tree, spear in hand. Uncle Haku and Kiani stopped at the edge of the clearing.

"Wait!" Nohea called to Wena, holding up her palms to stop him from launching the next spear. He paused, his eyes intent on her, trusting her deeper than Nohea felt comfortable. She dug into the bag at her side. "Don't bother us anymore... or anyone."

"Our kind used to be friends," said the old tree. Nohea blinked at the strange feeling that came over her. She'd been afraid of this *thing*, this unnatural spirit. And now, she couldn't help but pity it.

"What do you mean we're friends? I've never met you." She held out the bombs. Though Nohea had more in her bag, she didn't dare give it all up.

"The times have changed. Leave your uli and I will leave you."

"You were once friends with humans?"

"*I* was once a human, punished to this form by the island because of the darkness inside of me." He let her down onto the ground and Wena stood beside her, taking her arm, his calloused hands warm. "Your kind used to help set us free, break the curse. I eagerly waited for my turn."

The roots and branches took the bombs from her hands. She'd never heard this about the kupua before. How did a human get into this form? Had Lapaʻau been cursed by someone? Wena slipped his hand into hers, squeezing it to warn her they needed to leave. But Nohea ignored him.

"Who cursed you?" she asked. Her right cheek began hurting, sending the ringing back into her ear. She held it with her free hand.

"That is not a discussion for today," Lapaʻau said.

"Then why do you like uli?" She persisted.

Wena took a step back, pulling her hand gently, but Nohea continued to stand firm.

"It is an old treat from old friends," Lapaʻau said. "Perhaps it may make me sneeze, but I will take the risk for the comfort of good memories. Your kind never visits these parts anymore. The Mākuʻe have darkened these woods with their greed, and we are left alone. Punished and cursed, as the island wishes it."

Nohea took a breath to ask another question but the tree closed his eyes. "Goodbye." The roots disappeared beneath the ground, and the tree turned its face to the side, disappearing.

Come on, Wena signed to her and stepped back.

Nohea stared at the tree, trying to think why it *did, indeed,* feel familiar. She felt something strange within her, like Lapa'au knew more about herself than she did. What did he mean by her "kind?" Her mind wouldn't let it go.

"Let's go!" Kiani exclaimed, and Nohea allowed Wena to hold her hand as they ran off, away from the old spirit Lapa'au and his crazy, ancient, words.

CHAPTER TEN

Nohea's thoughts swam in confusion. What did Lapa'au know that she didn't? Something about this encounter felt important, but frustration welled up that she didn't know why. As they broke into a fresh clearing, Wena slipped his fingers from Nohea's. She blushed, realizing she'd been squeezing his hand the entire time.

"Sorry," she mumbled as she wiped her hand on her tunic, also realizing, to her own embarrassment, that while her mind wandered in anxiety and confusion, her hands had become sweaty. Wena simply tipped his head to her, unbothered by it, and then took the lead.

Both Kiani and Nohea walked on either side of Uncle Haku, his breaths shallow and tired. When they reached a soft waterfall, the girls helped Uncle Haku sit. Scratches and scrapes lined his body and face, and a bloody patch covered his knee. When Nohea sat beside him, she noticed similar red scuffs all over her body. The tree's rough roots had scraped her skin raw and bloody in some places, like her shoulders, shins, and calves.

Taking a shaky breath, Nohea dug into her bag for a small gourd of salve. Nohea always had this salve on hand, made from a few of her favorite herbs, including uli, along with gel from aloe. She took a generous heaping into her hand and passed the gourd to Uncle Haku.

Wena washed his hands in the stream while Kiani watched, curious. Nohea placed the salve on her raw skin and let out a breath of relief as the burning and itching soothed. She didn't want to put it on her face, knowing that her face needed a cold compress, not the salve.

"That feels great," said Uncle Haku as he placed the salve on his own wounds. Nohea noticed Wena's raw skin around his ankle, as the roots had grabbed him earlier too.

"Here," she passed the gourd to him, but he hesitated, glancing at his sister. Kiani shrugged and he took it.

"Where did you get all of those things in your bag?" asked Kiani, folding her arms.

"I borrowed them," Nohea said, not sure how much of the truth she was willing to share. Technically she'd stolen them from the garden and made them all herself, but she justified stealing because the servants paid it back with their labor. Kiani blinked, not believing Nohea for one minute. But she didn't say anything, and, instead, bent over to wash her hands in the water.

Wena handed the gourd back to Nohea and she glanced at his ankle. He hadn't used the salve. "You didn't use it," she said, for some reason feeling offended. She reasoned with herself: She didn't even know these people. Even though they helped save Uncle Haku, they were still strangers. But why did he look at her with such... trust, when she spoke with Lapa'au? And maybe she was feeling offended because they held hands and that seemed deeply personal.... Yet he didn't use her remedy.

It has uli in it, he signed. What was wrong with uli? And how did he know? It was one of Nohea's favorite and most dependable plants.

Before she could say something, Kiani cut in. "Are you a kahuna?"

"No," Nohea replied too quickly, and Kiani raised her eyebrows, suspicious.

"Then you are a meha?"

"No, I'm just a slave." Nohea avoided Kiani by tending to Uncle Haku. He rubbed his forehead, as though a headache had come on.

"I don't believe that." Kiani knelt on the ground and eyed Nohea. "Then how did you make these remedies or those bombs?"

Nohea and Uncle Haku's eyes met. "Are you alright Uncle Haku?" Nohea placed her hand on his back, hoping to ignore Kiani's question. Kiani waited, but Nohea still didn't answer as she ripped some kapa cloth off the end of her tunic to help his wounds.

"Where are we?" he asked. "What happened to me?" Nohea grasped the opportunity to change the subject, and Kiani glared at her, still suspicious. Wena disappeared and by the time he came back with some food, Nohea finished the story of how Uncle Haku got carried away by a kupua. Kiani stayed with them, sitting cross-legged and interjecting Nohea's story to add more details, much to Nohea's chagrin.

"I'm glad you came," Uncle Haku chuckled. "Who knew a place to rest would be so dangerous?"

"These woods are full of kupua," said Kiani. "We can escort you out if you'd like."

"We must stay here until our messenger arrives," said Uncle Haku.

"Your messenger won't be able to find you here. It's too deep." Kiani paused. "Unless you are in a place where he *can* find you..."

Wena shook his head, and Kiani bit her lip. "We can take you to a place where he can find you, but we cannot enter."

"Where is it?" Uncle Haku asked.

"The Māku'e."

Silence.

Nohea met Uncle Haku's eyes, feeling there was more to Wena shaking his head than she knew. "Maybe it is better if we leave the woods," she said. "He can probably find us if we hide at the outskirts."

Uncle Haku rubbed his chin, his hands looking oily from the

salve. "If we hide on the outskirts, we'll be too easy for the king to find."

"Why are you running from the king?" Kiani asked. Nohea tried to conceal her glare. Why did Kiani have so many questions? She reasoned with herself again: they were all strangers, and, for some reason, it seemed like Kiani *wanted* something to do. She *wanted* to help. While Nohea had been annoyed and petty about Kiani's questions, a sense of admiration filled her.

Uncle Haku waved his hand. "I can explain later." He rubbed his chin again. "For now, perhaps it *is* time we visited the dark tribe." Uncle Haku looked up to the sky. "They must know the truth of what is coming. Neither Po nor myself have visited them to spread the message. It's long overdue."

All three young people looked at him, waiting for some explanation.

"I mean the manō," said Uncle Haku. "They must know."

"The manō?" Kiani leaned forward. "No." She laughed, the first Nohea had seen her smile. A pang of jealousy and self consciousness came over Nohea. Kiani was so pretty. Kiani continued. "You mean... the true ali'i of the island? *That* manō?"

Uncle Haku nodded, smiling too. An electric energy filled the air at the mention of the manō, the true king. Even Nohea, weirded out as she was by the whole concept of a "true king of Kaimana Island," couldn't deny the feeling.

Kiani and Wena exchanged looks and Wena, who never smiled, let the corner of his lip turn up. Nohea's stomach fluttered and she focused instead on the lines of dirt streaking her hands.

"We've heard of those rumors circulating through the island." Kiani's eyes flashed curious, then dark. "The Māku'e will not believe you," she continued, "Unless the manō himself comes to them."

. . .

"He cannot come at this time," Uncle Haku sat up straighter, smoothing his aging hair back with his brown hand. "Yes, we must go to the dark tribe. Our messenger can find us there."

"So the manō is real." Kiani pulled a small guava from her bag and began eating, then realized her error in the ways of hospitality and handed one each to Nohea and Uncle Haku. Wena didn't want one. Nohea ate in haste, realizing how hungry she felt. Wena had brought food earlier, but Nohea was still hungry and the sweetness of this was so unlike any other fruit she had. She caught Wena watching her and blushed at her lack of manners.

"'Ae, he is real." Uncle Haku bit his guava slowly, thinking.

"You've met him?" Kiani leaned in again.

"Ae, he is a true ali'i." Uncle Haku's eyes filled with wonder. "He is everything our island needs. He will bring peace and when he takes his place as king, the great white shark will open the waters to sail again."

"Is it true that he bears the marking of the shark?" Kiani asked.

Uncle Haku nodded.

Both Kiani and Wena stared at Uncle Haku, then Kiani sighed. "Then we must do everything we can to help him. It will take about four days to get to the dark tribe. The Māku'e are in the deep parts of the wood. We can take you there, and scout for your messenger friend to guide him there as well."

Wena signed to Kiani and she added, "We cannot go in, but we will lead you as far as we can."

"Why can't you go in?" Nohea asked, then took another bite of the sweet, juicy fruit. She opened her mouth too big to bite causing right ear to ring again. She paused to squeeze her eyes shut at the pain and held her ear.

Kiani held her hands together, as though preparing to share a long story. At this, Wena turned his back to them and began cleaning his hands, arms, and face in the stream nearby. Kiani folded her arms. "The dark tribe is exactly what they call themselves: dark. They are vain, proud, and full of deceit. They pretend to be bold, mighty, and beautiful, but their spirits are dark. They have forgotten the light. They hide in the deep woods, hoarding their treasures and goods, and pretending that the outside world doesn't exist."

"And what of you? You are... outcasts?" Uncle Haku tried to sound sympathetic, but Nohea felt like it came out rude.

Kiani folded her arms again and shook her head. "I was six years old when Wena was born. They knew something was wrong, but they couldn't figure it out. They had a sorcerer, an evil man, do things to him as an infant." Kiani paused and glanced at her brother. His back faced them. "He still bears those scars."

Nohea's heart dropped. That explained the scars on his face and body. She wanted to give the young man a hug.

"When they discovered he couldn't hear anything, they decided to leave him in the deepest parts of the woods to die." Kiani cleared her throat. "I would not let that happen. I took my little brother as my own, and was exiled because of it. I have never been back since."

"You've been here in the woods... since you were six?" Uncle Haku sat up and folded his arms. "What family would do that to their own?"

"They are not family. We do not have parents." Kiani almost seemed to spit the words. "It is just Wena and I, wanderers. We've traveled all over the island, exploring the beauty of our world. We've seen the plight of the slaves," she nodded to Nohea, "and the wealth and power of the kings."

"Kings?" Nohea asked, confused.

"Makana is still alive." Kiani rolled her eyes. "I know they've told you otherwise."

Nohea's jaw dropped. All the stories said he died on the leeward side of the island. This was news indeed, and she worried that if King Ekewaka knew, it might mean war. Would he send the slaves to war? She reminded herself she was no longer a slave, but she still worried for the others. The tales of Makana and Ekewaka's wars were always full of gore and horror. Nohea covered her mouth, not wanting to recall the terrible and inhumane ways they tortured one anothers followers.

"She's right," Uncle Haku nodded to Nohea, then looked back at Kiani. "I am so sorry for your hardships."

Kiani shrugged. "I see it as a blessing.I am not stuck in that awful place, with people I don't like, coveting things and pretending to be something I am not. No... this life in exile is much better."

At that, Wena turned around and met Nohea's eyes. A moment of sympathy crossed between the two. Here was Wena, the outcast, the one who they meant to leave for dead, and his warrior sister, who chose exile to save a life. Nohea could see no people more brave or honorable than them both. While she'd felt jealous of Kiani's beauty, and sorry for Wena's disability, she now felt ashamed of herself. She'd judged them, and she had to make it right. The island hummed beneath her feet, accepting her repentant heart and desire to not judge others so quickly.

Kiani now looked even more beautiful to Nohea, and a deep sense of admiration filled Nohea. Wena, too, never looked more strong and Nohea wished with all her heart that the two would find what they were looking for in life. Nohea turned to Uncle Haku. "And you want to go to the Māku'e? After hearing what they did to these two?"

"The manō needs all the help he can get."

Nohea frowned. "For what?"

"Nohea, we can speak more of this later. I promise." He was looking at the sky, evaluating the time. "We should get ready for the night."

Nohea wanted to roll her eyes at all the unanswered questions. How could she possibly believe that the descendent of the great white manō was anyone but King Ekewaka? After the foreigners and their diseases nearly wiped out the whole population, *he* united the island when it desperately needed a ruler.

And now, this rumor of the "true manō" made Nohea's head hurt. It also made her annoyed. How could anyone claim such a title when

King Ekewaka was *the* actual king? If people started doing things like that, and others believed, it could mean chaos for the island.

Nohea glanced at Uncle Haku, wondering, for a moment, how he believed such things about a new leader, a "true" leader. How could he and Po go about spreading messages about this unidentified man? It seemed cowardly that this so-called ali'i sent others instead of going about the island himself. The question lingered in Nohea's mind: Did she even want to join this manō person? Kiani and Wena believed Uncle Haku without any hesitation. Was something wrong with them or her?

"You seem like honest people," said Kiani, cutting Nohea's thoughts short. "Or else we wouldn't have helped you. We felt a change in the woods when you entered, which is why we were drawn to you."

"That is good of you," said Uncle Haku. "It sounds like you listen to the island too. We are not perfect, but we strive to heed the signs all around us. We want to use our skills and strengths for the freedom of every person on this island."

Kiani smiled . "That's a nice thought."

"You don't believe such a place could exist?" Uncle Haku seemed offended.

"Men are weak." She stood up, ending the conversation. "We can camp here for the night. It's a safe place. You both need your rest. The journey to the dark tribe is... difficult."

Uncle Haku glanced from Kiani to Nohea, and Nohea realized his judgment on them. Her generation didn't believe or trust as easily as his. Things had changed.

While Uncle Haku started building a fire, Kiani and Wena left to forage for more food. Grateful for the privacy, Nohea decided to confront her uncle. She gently pressed a cool, wet kapa cloth to her face as she watched Uncle Haku.

"I still don't really believe the great white manō has a long lost descendant," said Nohea as she pulled out some hibiscus twigs from her bag with her free hand. It was always a handy thing to carry for starting fires. "I mean, King Ekewaka was the one to unify the island after the ali'i all died from the diseases. Not just anyone can do something like that."

"You have a point," replied Uncle Haku. "But I have met the manō myself." He dug a pit in the pebbly ground. The waterfall next to them played a soothing melody in the background. "If you could only meet him, you would know he is the island's true ali'i. He is disguised right now, which is why I cannot speak too much of him. But he is a good man."

"Is it Po?"

"No. Po is the messenger, the son of ghosts. His parents were exiled to the Haunted island because of their diseases. Po is a good man too, but he is not the manō."

So that's what happened to Po's parents, Nohea thought. She could almost feel, again, the awkwardness of Po's silence when she asked the question about his parents. Barely south of Kaimana Island sat a long stretch of land, hardly an island, but rumored to be full of ghosts. Years ago, King Ekewaka exiled the people with diseases to the small island for life.

"Why would the manō need the help of the dark tribe?"

"The manō wants to unite all the islanders, rule the island, and rid it of soran. Nohea, this is why we need you." Uncle Haku leaned small twigs against one another in the middle of the little pit. "You are the only knowledgeable and gifted alchemist on the whole island. You are possibly the only one that can learn how to destroy soran."

Soran. She had heard of it, the magical island juice. Like told her how the king sent out his warriors to find soran. He said they usually took all the soran from the pools and scoured every part of the island to find more and more. Supposedly it healed anything, but she didn't believe it. Like also mentioned that the king gave soran to mermaids, the fish-women, but for what purpose, neither Like nor Nohea knew.

"There is no other person that reads and understands plants and herbs as you do. You are not a sorcerer or a witch—you rely on the science—"

"Science?"

"It's a study of foreigners, the topic of the books your mother burned. As I've reflected on Edena's deeds, I've come to believe that your mother learned all she could from those books, taught them to you, and, when she felt you knew it all, burned those books so that nobody else on the island has the knowledge you possess."

Nohea sat back, stunned. "So my mother really did set me up?" The confirmation stung more than the thought.

"Not set up. Prepared. I've said it before, and I'll say it again. I don't understand all your mother's secrets. I don't know why she did all she did." He sounded pleading. "But I know that she *hated* the king. And if there was any way she could get back at him for all the hatred she possessed, then that was probably her way."

So Edena *did* set Nohea up. She set Nohea up to destroy the king's favorite drink, soran. *Wonderful.* Nohea restrained herself, again, from rolling her eyes.

"Why did she hate the king so much?" Nohea recalled her mother's intense anger towards the king, but she figured it was because Edena hated being a slave. *Nobody* wanted to be a slave.

Uncle Haku stared into the distance. The skies began to darken, and the evening sun cast hues of pink and purple in the patches of light shining through the wooded area. The fresh smell of the waterfall filled the air, and a cool breeze brushed Nohea's hair into her face. She pulled it up into a high bun, tired of the strands itching her cheeks and the tender right side of her face.

"Perhaps it was because she was a slave," Uncle Haku finally said. "One can only imagine the horror of bringing a child into the world as a slave."

He gently took the hibiscus twigs from Nohea's hand to start the fire. "And," he added,"The king will stop at nothing to get soran. Maybe something happened to your mother that made her want revenge towards him."

Nohea sat back and thought about it. Perhaps she'd be angry at life too, if her only child was not born free. And if the king only cared about soran, not the health and happiness of his subjects. She would probably feel a sense of anger too.

I should be angry about that now. After all, she *was* a slave, and the king did nothing to benefit her own life. The anger and unfairness of not being able to mourn Kimo returned to her chest. Perhaps she *did* want revenge, and soran might be the perfect thing. King Ekewaka deprived her life of freedom and dignity, so she could deprive his life of a silly island liquid.

"I know nothing of soran," she said bluntly. Uncle Haku glanced at her. "The manō can tell you all about it. He knows where to find it, unlike anyone else."

"The manō drinks soran too?"

"No, not at all," Uncle Haku answered. "He wants to destroy it. But we need your help."

Kiani and Wena approached, and the two fell silent. Nohea thought about her mother. No matter what Uncle Haku said, Nohea still felt resentment toward Edena. Maybe she wouldn't have felt so angry if her mother had said something.

But no, concluded Nohea. *She was too consumed in herself to care about others.* Nohea remembered her vow as she watched Kimo in the flames: *I will find something to help this island. I am stronger and smarter than Edena.*

As Kiani placed a variety of fresh fruits and flowers onto the ground beside the fire, Wena knelt by the river and peeled the sweet potatoes. In that moment, Nohea could only imagine the horror of *not being wanted at all.* She couldn't help but pity Wena. At least Edena raised and taught her things, while Wena's parents would've left him for dead... if not for his sister.

But Nohea cut her thoughts short: Wena did not need pitying. He was more of a person than anyone else. How could one be so in tune with the world around them, yet not be able to hear a thing?

Nohea folded her arms and looked up at the tree tops, wondering how she fit into all of this. Uncle Haku had a point. *He's probably right.* She was the only alchemist on the island–not a perfect alchemist, but a good one.

Perhaps, if the manō needed her help, she would oblige. The king, after all, couldn't prove himself of the line of the manō, and, in some ways, Nohea pitied her mother, with all her complicated emotions, secrets, and anger. In the end, it was the king who ordered Edena captured by Kahiko, right? And by now, Edena was probably dead.

Nohea looked down at the fire, now burning and providing warmth. She felt a tinge of anger growing within her. *Yes,* she concluded. *Uncle Haku is right.* Even though she didn't always understand her mother, she couldn't let her mother's death be in vain. And even though she hadn't met the manō, she had to trust Uncle Haku's judgment. After all, he won her freedom from slavery, and she owed him.

CHAPTER ELEVEN

"I honestly have no idea," said Lopaka to Olukai. They stood in the king's large stable, readying their horses as Olukai wondered aloud why the king wanted meha, witch women, within the walls of his own fortress.

The two were set to leave the next morning, as the meha lived in the kīpuka north of the fortress. Various groups of meha lived throughout the island, but Olukai and Lopaka planned to capture this specific tribe, the biggest one, a tribe that didn't travel around like others. This group of meha would be easy to find.

It would take a couple days to get there, and Olukai had every intention of going on horseback. They planned to take a small band of twelve men that Olukai had handpicked. Olukai taught these specific twelve fighters all he knew, helping them become experts with the fire knife. He trusted them and their skills, as each man proved well on every one of the king's missions to get soran.

Deep down he felt that they knew his secret, as they'd been present when the great manō appeared and Olukai connected with it. But they never spoke of the experience. Lopaka hadn't been with Olukai on that expedition, and Olukai felt secretly grateful for that. If

Lopaka had witnessed the sighting of the great white manō, there was no doubt Lopaka would know Olukai was the rightful king of the island.

Lopaka cleared his throat. "I wouldn't ask the king about it either." He looked nervous. "You saw how he spoke to Like. If there's some sort of curse floating around these parts, he probably wants those meha to help break it."

Olukai stroked his horse's mane. "'Ae. Do you know anything about that curse?"

Lopaka shook his head. Silence fell between them, Olukai's thoughts still distracted by the weight of his secret. He considered telling Lopaka a few times. After all, Lopaka was like a brother. But Olukai always found an excuse *not* to tell the truth: Lopaka was Ekewaka's son and would turn against Olukai, Lopaka wouldn't believe him, or Lopaka would be jealous. But all of those were petty, and Olukai knew it. Even the island hummed beneath his feet, getting impatient with his justifications.

"I'm eager to get this over with," Lopaka finally said.

"Why, so you can make trouble with the slaves?" Olukai teased.

Lopaka glared. "Hey, I haven't been there for a while now, alright?" Lopaka's notoriety for troublemaking had grown over the last few years.

"You know, there are plenty of eligible women *for marriage* across the island," Olukai added.

"I wouldn't stoop to the level of the slaves," Lopaka scoffed. "I just go there for some kava and gambling, since my father doesn't allow gambling. He says it's a low sport. And he only brings out the kava at celebrations."

"Drinking is—"

"I know, I know. You've said it before. Drinking is for fools. I get it alright?"

Olukai smirked. "But you win at gambling?"

"I always lose. I'm terrible at it," Lopaka laughed, beginning to blush. It was Lopaka's weakness, almost an addiction, and though

Olukai had tried helping and intervening in the past, it made no difference. Lopaka had to overcome it himself. He had to *choose* to overcome it. The quiet between them grew so thick that Olukai spoke up.

"Why haven't you been over there lately?"

"Cause we've been busy, remember? If I'm busy, then I stay away from it. I don't know what I'm going to do once I become king though," Lopaka sighed. "It seems all my father does is sit around all day, doing nothing. I would go crazy."

They'd talked about this before, how Lopaka itched to be anything but king. And Olukai didn't blame him. Ekewaka didn't have much of an exciting life. He wasted his days away drinking soran and sleeping with his concubines. He never left the fortress, and when he did, it was on some secret mission that nobody knew about.

But Lopaka won't become king, Olukai reminded himself. *I will.* His skin chilled with betrayal, but he knew it wasn't so much betrayal as it was a lack of trust. Lopaka trusted him, yet Olukai kept his guard.

Tell Lopaka, the island urged, but Olukai ignored it.

"I guess you'll cross that bridge when you get there," Olukai said, though he spoke quietly, knowing that probably the best way he could help his friend and brother was by asking for help as the true king.

"Hey, we better get going. Tomorrow's a big day," Lopaka ended their conversation. He ran his fingers through his horse's mane then turned to Olukai. "See you later." They clasped hands and hugged with a hard pat on the back, then Lopaka left the stable.

Olukai stood there a moment, his confidence draining. The more he kept his cover, the more disconnected from everything he felt, even disconnected from good friends like Lopaka. He stroked his horse's mane and shook his head, concentrating.

The curse.

Olukai wondered about Like, Lopaka's sickly younger brother. If

Like had a word with the alchemist's mother, perhaps Like knew more than anyone thought.

And if the king was cursed, Olukai wanted to know about it immediately. Soran made the king invincible, but if there was something else that weakened the effects of soran, perhaps Olukai needed to know, in case Ekewaka chose to fight, instead of supporting Olukai as king.

"I brought something for you." Startled, Olukai turned to see one of the king's daughters, Api, standing at the door of the stable. It was late for her to be out, as the king's many daughters had strict rules. Api was about seventeen years of age, and she always followed Olukai at any chance she got.

He tried to be gracious though, thinking to himself that if anyone were to ruin his good favors with the king, it would be one of the king's daughters, specifically, Api.

"Hello Api," he said, doing nothing to sound cheerful, as he loathed her awkward advances. She hurried in to stand next to him. Her dark skin glowed in the light of the stable torches, revealing the coarseness across her cheeks. She hadn't been blessed with much beauty, but she was probably a nice girl.

Just too needy, Olukai thought, trying to be gracious.

She held up a big green ti leaf lei and Olukai bent over so she could place it on him and kiss his cheek. "Thank you," he said, then continued to groom his horse.

She stood there so he added, "I will be sure to wear it when we leave tomorrow."

She stayed put, smiling, her hands clasped together. He looked at her again, nodded, and bowed his head. "Thank you, princess."

"I heard you're going to see the meha," she blurted, forcing a conversation. Olukai cleared his throat. "'Ae."

"That's very brave of you. I hope they will help my father."

"'Ae, me too." He bowed his head again to her, as if to excuse her. But she didn't budge.

"Don't you think you're old enough to marry?" Her voice cracked. Olukai almost felt sorry for her nervousness.

"I have plenty of time to get married."

"I am of age." She added, "Perhaps my father will pick your bride."

Olukai looked at her and blinked, wondering if her father would consider Api's proposal. King Ekewaka showed little affection for any of his children, and much less so to his wives. They were all like pawns in his game, and Olukai felt sorry for each one of them. Even sadder was the fact that King Ekewaka grew incredibly grumpy when he had plenty of daughters and only two sons. He didn't treat his daughters with the honor and respect they deserved.

But he doesn't treat his sons well either, he reminded himself. Ekewaka showed little to no affection or care for Like or Lopaka. If anything, he treated Olukai with more respect than he did Lopaka. It often made Olukai feel guilty, yet Lopaka held no resentment towards Olukai. That alone should have been reason enough for Olukai to trust Lopaka. But he didn't.

Olukai cleared his throat. "Your father trusts my judgment on the matter. Besides, I have many missions left to do. A wife might distract me, and the king needs my full attention."

Api looked down, disappointed. "Well, I will talk to my father." Before Olukai could reply, she ran out.

Olukai sighed and shook his head.

On top of all the things to worry about, now he had to think about an excuse to *not* marry the king's daughter.

If you revealed yourself as the manō, the island scolded beneath his feet, *then you will get to choose your bride.* Olukai rolled his eyes and ignored it.

The next morning, Olukai woke up before sunrise. He had a ritual before going on the king's missions. No matter how many he'd gone on, or how confident he seemed, the king's missions always made Olukai nervous, and especially this one. Memories of the meha still haunted him.

He put on his short palekoki and walked along the shore. The waves crashed down, sounding like thunder in the distance. The sea spray misted the air, filling it with the smell of salt and brine.

Olukai loved the ocean, and though he ignored the voices of Kaimana Island lately, he still needed this. He still needed the guidance of his ancestors. It was moments like these where he felt connected with the great white manō, his ancestor, his ʻaumakua. He still remembered the moment of sheer panic, when the great white manō flipped the canoe, sending all the men into the water. He still remembered how monster-like the manō looked as it wove between the men.

Fear.

It felt so strong in the energy of that moment, it seemed to choke all the life out of the men. And Olukai embraced it at that moment. He accepted what is, and what was. He accepted his last moment, in the middle of the ocean, the place he loved the most.

But yet, it was when he overcame his fear that he was able to help others. He had complete control of his mind and body. He called to them, gave them enough courage to calm down, pay respects to the king of the ocean, and to let go of the fear. One by one, the men stopped panicking and accepted their fate.

That was when the great white manō approached him, and they stared into one another's eyes. As Olukai's hand rested on the manō's head, the mark burned into his skin.

Olukai changed. A new courage and purpose entered into him. The great white manō communicated with his mind, telling him exactly what he needed to do next.

"I have chosen you, a descendant of my line, an aliʻi. Go. Free this island of the darkness that ails it. Cleanse the island and destroy the unnatural soran. Rule the people well." Olukai knew it was true. His mother, Kehau, was a princess, the daughter of the true aliʻi, the family that was killed by the foreigners' diseases. She never revealed her status to anyone, and the markings on her arm began to fade away. Though Olukai remembered all the ways she carried herself as a royal. She was kind and fair to all, never impatient, and walked with the grace of a dancer.

A light breeze misted Olukai with salty water. He stood at the edge of the water, remembering, feeling, becoming one with the world around him. Olukai glanced down at the mark on his arm, slipping off the kapa cloth and revealing the image of a tribal designed manō. The mark was turning darker and darker, and spreading closer to his elbow. He had to get a bigger piece of cloth to cover this growing symbol.

Olukai sighed. He had received his calling, and now he had to do it. But the doubts always began creeping in.

I'm not fit to be king. How do I dethrone Ekewaka? Will people support me?

He felt the presence of the great white manō and looked to the ocean, seeing the large fin moving in the distance. Olukai felt a pang of shame. He had learned of his true identity months ago, and he still hadn't done anything.

But Nohea will help me, he thought. *The alchemist will know how to destroy soran and we'll start there.* But he couldn't get rid of the nagging feeling that Nohea wasn't the only answer. He had to act. But he didn't know how... or so he believed.

The morning light painted the sky in a deep shade of purple as Olukai and Lopaka got on their horses. They wore their armor, made by skilled artisans, of koa wood. Meanwhile, their little band of twelve men sat on horses behind them, also wearing armor. All of the men held knives, meant to be lit with fire while in combat, and a few had spears strapped to their backs. Their helmets, made from gourds, had large cutouts in the front so the men could see.

Olukai and Lopaka wore the helmets of the leaders, made of koa. Unlike the ill-fitting gourds, Olukai and Lopaka's helmets fit nicely around their heads and had a mohawk style of feathers that ran down their backs. The feathers were plucked from the black birds in the mountains, black being the king's colors.

Around Olukai's neck lay the thick green lei that Api gave him. She stood, with her many sisters, on the side of the gates to watch them leave. Many of the women held ti leaves and waved them, to wish them luck.

Kahiko approached with a ti leaf and bowl of water. After dipping the leaf into the water, he sprinkled Olukai, Lopaka, and the band of men.

"Good luck," Kahiko said grimly to Olukai and stood back. The king was absent, as he didn't have a need to be awake that early.

Olukai smiled smugly back at Kahiko. "Thanks, you too."

Then he nudged his horse forward. The women cheered and clapped as the men left the king's gates and headed northeast, towards Mauna Ki'eki'e, towards the old lava fields, towards the meha.

CHAPTER TWELVE

Nohea woke up with a throb in her leg. She massaged it, wondering if it still hurt from her limp the other day, or if the roots of Lapaʻau had damaged the muscles within. She rubbed her eyes, feeling quite broken: tenderness on the right side of her face, scratches all over her skin, and throbbing in her leg. *Can it get any worse?* she wondered.

Uncle Haku was fast asleep, as well as Kiani, while Wena sat watch by the river's edge. A sudden longing filled Nohea's chest and she found herself standing and approaching the young man. She worried that, because he was deaf, he couldn't hear her approaching, but he turned his head and nodded to her.

She signed to him. *How did you know I was coming?*

He signed and mouthed back, *I cannot hear, but I can listen.*

Nohea sat and pondered his words. Here was a young man who could hear nothing, yet he listened. How was that so?

How did you survive all these years? she asked, quickly signing an apology if she seemed rude. He shook his head.

My sister knows survival best. She was destined to be one of the dark tribe's greatest warriors. They saw her ability from a very young age.

So you both survived all on your own? Nohea still couldn't believe that a six year old girl could raise a baby all by herself.

Wena brought his knees to his chest and rested his arms on them. He smelled like fresh maile, and Nohea tried not to get a good whiff of him. It was her favorite scent, after all. Then he turned and signed to her, *You wouldn't understand. Kiani said you don't even believe in the manō.*

Warmth spread through Nohea's cheeks. *I have no reason to. I can only trust in myself and the island.*

If you trust the island, then you would know that there really is a giant shark patrolling the borders, and it's an ancestor of the ali'i. He looked almost scolding when he replied and though she hated the way it felt, she knew he was right. If she really listened to the island, as she claimed, then she would *know*.

Silence settled between them, and Wena sighed. *I'm sorry, I don't mean to be rude. It's just that Kiani and I have hoped for a true king our whole lives, someone who would stop the nonsense of these corrupt leaders and traditions.*

It's alright, Nohea signed. *I understand.* They both sat side by side, arms almost touching, staring at the torch light reflecting on the quiet river in front of them.

If I told you what miracles spared our lives in these woods, Wena said to her, *You wouldn't believe it.*

Try me.

Wena shrugged. *Maybe you can ask Kiani.*

Nohea brought her own knees to her chest and hugged them. Perhaps Wena was right. Perhaps she was too skeptical. But she couldn't help it. Old tales had never saved a person's life, only the herbs and medicines she created. Folklore and legends had never served any good except to spook the children into obeying their parents and keeping out of trouble in the night.

She glanced back at her Uncle Haku. Good Uncle Haku.

She nudged Wena and signed to him, *My Uncle Haku is a good man. You both were right to trust him.*

Is he your hānai uncle? Wena asked. Nohea nodded. She couldn't help smiling, remembering how kind Uncle Haku had always been to her. Nohea always wondered what "normal" people did in the town, and her uncle was the only person to provide that picture for her.

He used to bring me new clothes, and sandals, Nohea signed. Wena let a small smile fall on his lips as she told him stories of her life as a slave, and the joy Uncle Haku brought.

He couldn't come all the time, Nohea signed. *Many moons would pass before he visited. He smuggled in food from the town, and he told us about the king's many celebrations. My mother was very grateful for him.*

Who were your mother's parents? Wena asked.

Nohea bit her lower lip. *She was ashamed of her heritage, and would not tell me. She only told me that Uncle Haku's parents took her in as their own.*

Wena watched her face carefully, so Nohea avoided eye contact, her face feeling warm, but she continued signing. *He has been good to me. I've never met his wife or children, because it's too risky to bring them all to the slave's quarters, but I know he is a good father.*

And he is loyal to a good cause, said Wena. *He wants to bring the message of the manō to the Māku'e. Don't judge the dark tribe too harshly. Every person has their own problems, and they are not unique. I do not judge my parents. Especially since they are of higher ranking, it was expected of them to be perfect. Every member of the dark tribe strives for perfection, and if it is not attained, they would rather die than live in humiliation because of their lack.*

Wena ran his fingers through his soft hair, and it parted gently to the other side of his face. *I think your uncle is right to go to the dark tribe. If there is a true descendant of the great white manō, then he deserves to be ali'i of Kaimana Island. Everyone should know.* He tipped his head, adding, *And King Ekewaka should be dethroned.*

King Ekewaka? Why is everyone so against him? Nohea asked. *My only thing against him is that he has slaves.*

He is obsessed with soran, Wena replied. *He will stop at nothing to get it. He has killed many innocent people to get it.*

Nohea frowned. Soran. Again. She had never heard so much about the island's magical juice in her life. Is that what the outside world worried about?

She sat up when she heard a bird chirp in the distance. Both her and Wena looked at each other, both mouthing at the same time, *The honeycreeper.*

Kiani, behind them, already sat up straight. She shook Uncle Haku awake.

"A bird calls," she whispered to him. "It warns of danger. We must move." Uncle Haku sat up too, rubbing his eyes.

Wena touched Nohea's arm to get her attention again. *We'll continue this discussion later?* he asked. Nohea nodded, her heart feeling a sense of calm. She had felt so awkward around him earlier, after holding his hand, eyeing him out, so finally connecting personally with him made the weird tension between them somewhat disappear. When they started cleaning the camp, Kiani eyed them both, making Nohea's cheeks warm, even though she and Wena hadn't been doing anything inappropriate.

It didn't take the four very long to hide any evidence of being there, and continue forward. Nohea walked next to Uncle Haku, letting him lean on her when he needed it.

Wena took the lead, and Kiani walked behind, making sure they left no tracks.

"If you see any shadows move," she said to them, "It's probably a kupua. Keep your eyes open. We don't want any surprises."

"I thought you said you knew them?" Nohea asked, "Or you're familiar with them?"

"Familiar," said Kiani. "We've wandered these woods for many years. Many of them don't bother us anymore, but it doesn't hurt to be careful."

"Kiani," said Nohea, looking back, "Wena wouldn't tell me how you both survived for so long in these woods, especially when you were only six."

"Do not underestimate the tender age of young ones," Kiani snapped back. "Just because I was *only six* doesn't mean I didn't have more wisdom than those much older than me."

"I'm sorry," Nohea swallowed. "I didn't mean to—"

"It's alright," Kiani cut in. "I don't think it's fair to judge someone because of their age."

Nohea nodded, and they walked in silence for a moment, the only loud sound being Uncle Haku's heavy breathing, and Nohea's squishy sandals.

"But if you must know," Kiani finally said, "We had a lot of help. The island was gracious with us, merciful... tender, even. We left in the night, because our parents vowed to make Wena 'disappear' the next morning. I wrapped him in the white cloth worn by all in the dark tribe, and left the safety of the Māku'e. I wandered with him until the next night, where he cried until he could not cry any longer. I found food and water."

Nohea could only imagine the fear, yet the courage, of young Kiani to save the baby's life.

"I knew my fate," Kiani said. "I knew that we might not survive long. But the thought of dying together was better than leaving him to die alone."

Wena glanced back at the crew, his tousled hair looking strikingly handsome. Nohea stared ahead at a koa tree, distracting herself.

"We had help, of course," Kiani went on. "I don't think any child could do it on their own. We should have died, but kind strangers helped us... I do not wish to speak their names, for they are sacred to us. Our gratitude and debt to them will go on for eternity. Perhaps their kindness has inspired us to help wanderers, like yourselves."

Nohea looked at Uncle Haku, who managed a smile. "And you have inspired us," he added. "Perhaps one day we will be able to pay our debt to you."

"We require no payment from you," Kiani replied. "A simple thanks would do."

Nohea smiled to herself, remembering Kiani saying that the first time they met.

They walked on in silence the rest of the day, breaking only for food and to relieve themselves. Nohea stuck close to Uncle Haku, but a part of her felt like the two siblings were growing on her. Their story was so sad, yet so courageous.

Without hesitation, they believed Uncle Haku about the manō, and Nohea began to wonder if she, too, had the courage—or the knowledge, even—to help the manō on his mission.

CHAPTER THIRTEEN

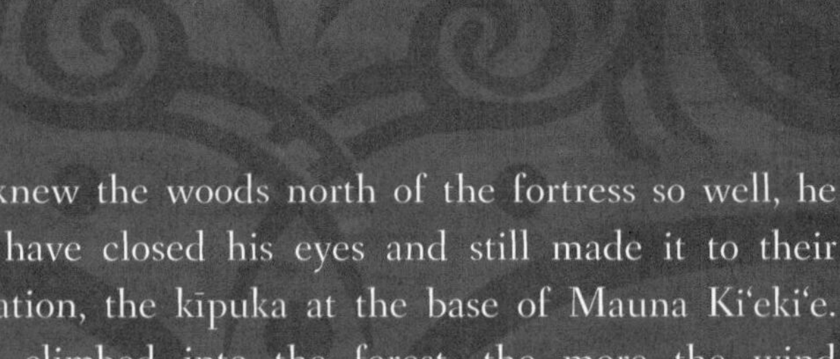

Olukai knew the woods north of the fortress so well, he could have closed his eyes and still made it to their destination, the kīpuka at the base of Mauna Ki'eki'e. The higher they climbed into the forest, the more the wind moaned through the 'ōhi'a trees. The red apapane birds above chirped aloud to one another, and nēnē geese honked in the distance.

Olukai used this route many times before, passing this same group of meha. There were meha but this was the largest and most well known. None of the groups of women had names to distinguish themselves, so they were all collectively known as meha.

Olukai shuddered at the memories, particularly one: chilled to the bone with his group of men, trying to hurry to the northern part of the old lava field, choosing this route because it was the fastest. They had to find a new pool of soran, as soon as possible, as the king was running out, but their only way through was closest to the meha.

Olukai remembered their cries in the night, and the figures coming out of the kīpuka to scare the little band of men away. He had been so frightened, like never before. He ordered his men to run, because he didn't know if the women would curse them with their masked faces.

"Olukai?"

Olukai blinked into the mist, now realizing he'd been daydreaming. It had started drizzling, and Olukai's face, hair, and cape dripped with water. One of his warriors, Ioane, a young man of seventeen years, rode next to him.

"'Ae?" Olukai swiped the water off his forehead.

"Did you see that?"

Olukai looked about. A fog had settled around them, blocking Olukai's view of the men in the back. "What was it?"

"A white pueo. It flew in front of us."

Olukai frowned and Ioane looked about, his dark brown face tense. White pueo usually meant good luck, but when it flew in front of them, it was a bad omen.

"Who saw it?" Olukai asked.

"Only me... just now. The men are too cold and tired to notice, and you didn't seem to be..." Ioane paused.

"Paying attention?" Olukai finished, hinting at humor. Ioane nodded, obviously meaning no disrespect.

"Thank you for your observation, Ioane." The young man nodded and fell back, allowing Olukai the full lead again.

He glanced back at his shivering warriors. Even Lopaka, equal in strength, size, and courage to Olukai, looked down at his horse's mane.

But Olukai knew they couldn't rest until the daylight faded away. They had a mission, and he wanted it over as soon as possible.

And I won't tell the men about the white owl, he thought. It would only exacerbate their fears.

After riding a full day, Olukai and his men stopped to camp, every man chilled to the bone. These were cold woods, because of the altitude, and the men held their black capes closely round them as they huddled by their fires. Wind howled through the trees like the roaring of waves. Most of the men tossed and turned, unable to sleep.

It was easy—too easy—to get spooked by the meha. Even Olukai, who had seen the entire island and traveled to the Haunted Island, looking for soran, felt his hairs standing on end at the very mention of the meha.

People believed in superstitions too easily, and that made Olukai wonder if it was easier than he thought to reveal himself as the true king. He had royal blood from his mother, and the mark on his arm was proof. Every ali'i, including his mother, had those markings, and it showed as long as they accepted their place. His mother's mark began to fade overtime, making it easier for her to blend in with the other islanders.

But Olukai wasn't meant to blend in. He was supposed to rule the island. Would the islanders support him, or simply call him a mad man? He chuckled.

"What?" Lopaka asked from the other side of the fire. He sat on his side, drawing something on a large green leaf with a piece of charcoal.

"Superstitions," Olukai muttered. Lopaka grinned and continued drawing. Lopaka did this every night they went on missions, probably his way of coping with his fear and anxiety. Olukai didn't blame him, as he, himself, was still unnerved about the white pueo flying across their path. If it had flown over them, or behind them, that would have been good luck.

But it wasn't so, Olukai thought and sighed.

Olukai stared into the fire, musing on where the alchemist and her uncle might be at this moment. Did Po find them? How long would it take? How long until he heard back from the messenger?

He had it all pictured in his mind: Po would find the alchemist and her uncle, deliver them safely to Olukai's home, and Olukai would transform one of his large guest rooms to the girl's experiments and tests. He would steal some soran from the king (or another of the many wells on the island) and let her experiment. If she could discover the way to destroy it, they had a chance of making things right. Olukai would become the true ali'i of Kaimana island, and he, with the alchemist's help, would destroy all the soran. There would be no more slaves, division, and contention amongst the island races.

Restore balance to the island, he thought as the great white manō's wise eyes came to mind. The shark would not let anyone in or out until the soran was destroyed.

Olukai's thoughts turned to the other island races. Because he had been amiable with all of them on his missions for the king, why wouldn't they side with him? Surely they would acknowledge his mark and therefore, Olukai as king.

From the queen of the dark tribe, to the dwarf Hune in the volcanoes, the mermaids in the ocean, the mo'o in their secret places, and, of course, the meha, he'd met and seen them all. Although, he had to admit, he didn't really "meet" the meha, more like ran from them. While he felt it was realistic and even possible to unite all creatures under one king on the island, the only people that didn't fit were the meha.

He couldn't imagine how to unite with the witches... they were the very epitome of darkness. It troubled him. He had a vision of one people, with skills of many kinds, contributors to society. Olukai even wished to unite with the people of Makana, the king's brother.

But the meha... It gnawed at him over and over again. Did the great white manō mean to unite with the dark women? They seemed like demons born of the shadows.

I guess we'll find out more tomorrow, he thought to himself. He and Lopaka had devised the plan of how they would capture the witches.

Since the women didn't sleep at night, Olukai assumed they could attack during the day. The men brought large fishing nets, as well as bamboo cages on wheels to bring the women back to the king.

It looked barbaric, but, to Olukai, these women were barbaric. He needed to complete this mission to stay in the king's favor, to keep up his mask as a friend of the king's.

I'm so close, he thought, eager to get back to his home, eager to meet the alchemist and discover how to destroy the wicked liquid soran.

Then I will reveal myself and rule the island, he thought, despite the irritating feeling that he was simply stalling.

For this moment, he decided he needed to keep face with King Ekewaka until the timing was right.

"If superstitions are true," Lopaka said, disrupting Olukai's thoughts, "Then I sure hope we can bind those meha's mouths before they curse us."

Olukai shuddered and glanced at the men. Some were listening, and Olukai had no doubt every single one of them had the same hope as Lopaka.

CHAPTER FOURTEEN

The days flew by for Nohea, for each step brought new scenery, from lush green ferns surrounding roaring waterfalls, to tall koa trees surrounded by long bladed grass and mossy floors. The forest smelled lovely, of fresh flowers and leaves that grew in abundance. Though, every whiff of maile drew her attention to Wena.

Each time she found herself staring or watching him, Nohea silently scolded herself. She pushed the fluttering out of her stomach and, instead, did her best to focus on her love of being free.

For a lifetime of slavery, Nohea felt that being out with Uncle Haku, with nobody to beat her if she disobeyed, gave her a spiritual breath of fresh air.

It was a feeling she'd never had before. Yet, her thoughts often went back to her slave family: *Are they alright? Did Nui make it back safely, without being beaten? Were the other slaves alright for hiding and helping her?*

If the manō was a true leader, would he free the slaves? Would he *really* do good for the island?

Nohea held her thoughts close to her heart, staring ahead at

Wena's sun-kisssed hair, lean muscled back, and shoulders. When he caught her eyes on him, she pretended to study the trees and grass around them.

On one of the nights, Wena disappeared for a while, foraging for food. Kiani wasn't worried at the length of his absence, but Nohea wondered if something happened to him. He finally reappeared with a spear in hand, and gave it to Nohea.

I made this for you, he said, holding back a smile. *Now you can feel more protected... even though you have a bag of bombs.* They laughed .

Nohea held the spear in her hands, the handle made from a smooth, cleaned guava tree trunk, and the spearhead made from a polished rock.

Now we are all armed, in case something happens, Wena said, proud as Nohea endlessly complimented his work.

At night, Nohea found herself awake, staring at the tree tops, wondering about her mother, the manō, and her place in all of it. She then tossed and turned, feeling guilty that Wena stayed awake keeping watch. But he and Kiani switched places part way through the night, and it eased Nohea's worries about him.

After a few nights of tossing and turning, however, Nohea finally sat up and inched towards Wena, who kept watch not far from the group.

He sat with his knees close to his chest, and his back hunched over as he braided something. Nohea stepped closer, noticing that he wove a fresh ti leaf lei. He and Kiani always wore fresh lei, and one or the other could be found weaving and braiding new leis at their leisure. His wavy hair fell down the sides of his forehead as he focused.

As Nohea inched closer, Wena looked up at her, and his eyebrows creased. *Shouldn't you be sleeping?*

Surprised by his grumpy reaction, when he'd been so amiable the last time, Nohea sniffed and signed. *I couldn't sleep so...* She shrugged. When Wena made no invitation for her to sit next to him, she plopped herself beside him anyway. He blinked, looked back to the sleeping forms of Uncle Haku and Kiani, and then focused on his work again, or at least it seemed he was trying to.

Why must you wear fresh lei everyday? Nohea asked, as she wrapped her uncle's cloak tightly around her. The forest wasn't too cold at night, but the light breeze did make her shiver.

It is the custom, he signed to her, then continued to weave the fresh flowers into the two twisted ti leaves. One side of the lei he held between two of his toes, and the other he continued adding ti leaves and flowers, making a full, bright lei. When he didn't say anything else, Nohea rested her chin on top of her knees. The gurgling river nearby always sounded so refreshing. Was the dark forest really that dangerous? It felt so magical in certain places. She could live here.

Nohea sensed Wena's eyes on her and when she made eye contact, he looked away, his shoulders sinking. The frown was gone, replaced by a sigh before he signed to her. *Perhaps it is the vanity of the Māku'e that we wear these everyday. But Kiani and I believe it is for our own health. There's something about wearing the beauty of the earth that shows our appreciation for the island.*

She continued to watch him, wondering why he hadn't appreciated her initially. That tension wore off fast enough though.

His answer to her question was thoughtful, and Nohea wondered how she showed her own appreciation for the island. She would always say "mahalo" as she snipped a plant or flower from the king's garden. She gave food to the birds when she could. Was that enough?

Whenever the flowers and leaves of the leis finally started wilting, Wena and Kiani placed their fresh flower leis, crowns, and bracelets into the waterfall or river. They watched their flower arrangements floating along until they disappeared around the river bend.

Why do you put them in water when you're done with them? Nohea asked. He returned his attention to her, studying her face, but mainly focusing on her lips. Blood rushed to her cheeks, self consciousness overwhelming her senses. She knew Wena was only reading her lips, as Kimo always did so he could read what she said. But with Wena, it felt... different. Nohea couldn't point out why, but it just did.

Water symbolizes many things, Wena signed. *But for us, it's a symbol of trying again. We are not perfect, and, at the end of each day, we ask the island's forgiveness for our shortcomings. We release any negative energy and let it down the river with our lei. It's all washed away, and the island grants us a fresh start the next day.* He paused and smiled at Nohea. Her heart skipped a beat.

She'd never been friends with boys besides younger ones who were slaves until about the age of ten, and then the king took them to be trained and join his army. But now, she felt something deep inside, perhaps friendship.

This is for you. Wena held up the head lei he made. In the moonlight, the orchids on it shone beautiful hues of blue, purple, and pink. The ferns and small buds complimented the flowers. As he placed it on her head, Nohea felt like a princess. Not because of the crown, but because of the way it made her feel. She'd never felt beautiful. No person had complimented her looks, besides a word of validation here and there from Nui. Perhaps she wasn't actually beautiful, but wearing this head lei made her *feel* beautiful.

She looked into the reflection of the slow moving river next to them. For the first time, she smiled at herself. Then she noticed Wena looking at her, and her cheeks burned once more. *Mahalo.* She kissed his cheek and sat back, pleased.

When this wilts, I will let the river take it home, she signed to him. *I've made too many mistakes. But I will wash away any bad mana and become new.*

Wena smiled and nodded, his eyes lingering on her for longer than felt natural. Then he looked into the distance and said no more.

As THE DAYS WORE ON, Nohea began to realize that Wena might know as much, if not more, about the island and plants than she did.

When she heard Uncle Haku sound asleep, and Kiani breathing steadily, Nohea sat up and settled next to Wena, who kept watch again.

You should get rest, he said, though he smiled.

I can't sleep, Nohea replied, but she was sure she could if she wanted. *I was thinking about soran.* But she lied. She had been waiting all day to talk to Wena privately. Throughout the day she wanted to steal a moment with him, without the influence of his sister or Uncle Haku, but they stuck as a group. *What do you know of it?*

Wena kept his eyes forward, staring into the darkness of the forest ahead of them. The river next to them, which they followed for days, gurgled softly.

It's not good, Wena finally signed, then ran his fingers through his hair. *It corrupts the mind, makes it think of nothing else.*

"Like an addiction?" Nohea whispered, thinking of the slave men who did anything in their power to obtain kava, the depressant drink of the island. They would do anything to get it, even to the point of abusing their wives and families. Nohea shuddered. She knew addictions all too well.

Wena nodded. They sat in silence.

Even one drop of that is poison, he finally signed. *The kahuna of the Māku'e tried to use soran on me.* Wena's hands clenched . *It made my mind sick, but Kiani got me help. Most don't recall memories of their infant days.* He rubbed his forehead, looking tired. *But I recall the pain of withdrawal from the soran... in dreams, visions, and around certain plants.*

Which plants?

Mostly around uli.

Nohea touched his shoulder. She wanted to say something about his story, even "I'm sorry," but she'd said it so many times already. The world had mistreated him, when he'd done no wrong.

You should get some rest, she signed. *I'll keep watch.*

He shook his head. *I'm alright—*

But Nohea squeezed his arm. *No. Please. Go rest.*

He looked down at her, a curious gleam in his eye. She tried to look confident, firm. His eyes flicked to her hand on his arm, and he touched it. Nohea swallowed, but he only removed it gently, placing her hand on her lap. Then he nodded and walked to the fire, lying in the spot she'd been resting earlier.

As she stared into the forest, Nohea tried to listen to herself, the wind, and the earth around her. Would it let her know her path?

The night remained silent.

Uncle Haku stirred. "Nohea?"

He approached and sat beside her, his eyes looking sad.

Nohea put her hand on his back. "Are you alright?"

"I worry about my family." He let out a quiet sigh. Nohea's heart dropped.

"I'm sure they miss you."

"It feels like I've been gone from them for so long, but it has only been a few days."

"After we meet the dark tribe, we should go straight to them," Nohea said, but Uncle Haku shook his head.

"They're long gone... I hope. I assume Po already warned them. They've gone to the hiding place at south point."

"There's a hiding place?"

"'Ae, for the supporters of the manō. You could call it a resistance fort, a base, whatever you wish. It is hidden though, not very easy to find."

Nohea took her uncle's arm and rested her head on his shoulder. "What else is there you need to tell me about the manō?"

Uncle Haku sighed and smoothed his hair back. "Probably that he is one of the only people on this island that I trust besides my own wife."

"Would you do anything he asks you?"

"'Ae, I would."

Nohea sat up. "You know... I've been thinking, uncle. I trust you, and I've learned to trust these good people we're with. Now I am beginning to see that I might have a place in all of this." Uncle Haku faced her, amused.

"I think I would do anything the manō asks of me too," Nohea finally said.

Uncle Haku's smile couldn't have grown any wider. "You would?"

"Yes... I mean, that is my choice now." She quickly added, "It could change."

Uncle Haku gave her a big hug. "I think that is a wise choice. I do believe our choices can change, but hopefully when they change, it's for the better."

Nohea smiled and nodded. This was *her* decision, not something imposed by anyone else. And if she should learn anything about the manō that she didn't like or agree with, then she knew, deep down in her heart, that she had full permission to change her mind anytime she wanted.

CHAPTER FIFTEEN

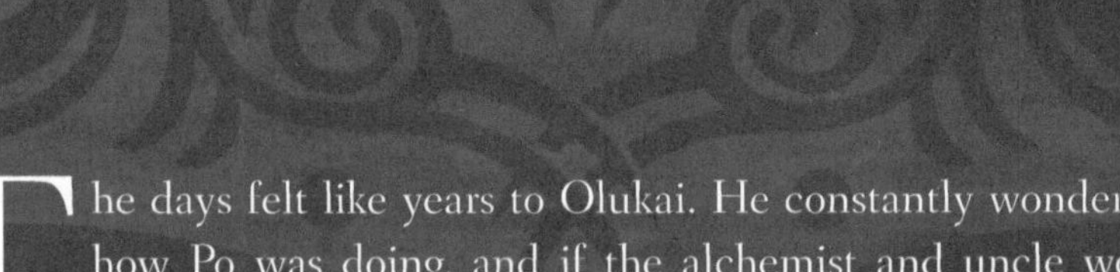

The days felt like years to Olukai. He constantly wondered how Po was doing, and if the alchemist and uncle were found. He wondered if he or his men would get cursed by the meha, or if the mission would go smoother than expected.

They traveled on the dry lava plains for days, the horses beginning to whine because the lava ate at their feet. The horses didn't mind the *pahoehoe* lava, the long, billowy waves of dried black rock. But they whined endlessly when they had to walk across the *a'a* lava,the short, rough, clinky black rock that crumbled at parts and wore out the horse's hooves.

So they made a decision to leave the horses and four men at a smaller kīpuka, while the rest continued by foot. The worst parts of the day were midday, as the sun shone directly above, heating the dry lava and casting a harsh glare on all those walking upon it.

The men walked for two days without their horses, and that worried Olukai, for it meant they'd be walking two days back with the meha. He'd rather have them in the cages, pulled by the horses, but the horses were in too much pain to endure the rocks.

As the sun lingered at the edge of the horizon, Olukai knew they were close. He felt the change in the wind, and could even smell the fresh forested kīpuka in the distance. He ordered the men to set up for the night, and they would evaluate the kīpuka when the sun set.

The men didn't set up campfires though, hoping for the element of surprise the following morning. Meanwhile, Olukai chose a couple of his men, including Lopaka, to accompany him in surveying the size of the kīpuka. These were brave young men, who'd been with Olukai through many of his missions. But this was different because they had to deal with the witches.

THE MEN WALKED IN SILENCE, each holding onto a long piece of braided ti leaf—not only for good luck, but to stick together in the darkness. The bits of moonlight that shone through the clouds landed on the lava rock, creating a path so the men wouldn't fall or slip into any ditches and get hurt. The large kīpuka loomed ahead of them.

Olukai took the lead, Lopaka behind him, and two of their men, Ioane and Kehua, specifically chosen by Olukai, took the back. He trusted their skills, agility, and judgment, as these two were the stealthiest of his trained warriors.

Soon, a soft warm glow lit up the sky ahead, a light dancing amidst the blackness of trees.

The meha. Olukai's heart raced and sweat poured down his brow. It was a chilly night in the mountains, mist covering the lava field, but Olukai felt more hot from fear than anything.

"Getting close," he whispered to his men, the whites of their eyes the only thing he could see of them in the overcast moonlight.

As they walked closer to the edge of the kīpuka, they could make out the tops of the trees, the outlines of ferns, and then feel the soft, thick grass beneath their feet. Olukai stopped at the edge, listening.

The wind rustled through the kīpuka forest, like a person breathing deeply.

Olukai took a deep breath, knowing that one step onto the meha's territory had warned the women. Whenever strangers got close to his own home on the beach, he felt a shift in the energy, so it didn't seem strange if the witches suspected new blood on their territory,

They know we're here. He motioned for his men to move away from the soft grassy edge of the kīpuka. *We need distance.*

As if in response to Olukai's thought, a loud howling noise rang out in the dead quiet. The men froze in place, chills running down their backs. Other howling noises joined and the kīpuka rang with the cries of the meha.

It wasn't a loud, angry howl, but that of mourning with a mix of ancient ʻoli and chants that Olukai had never heard before. He shivered and continued leading his men around the edge of the forest. He only needed to survey how big it was, so they could figure out some plan of action.

As they moved in the shadows, they kept their eyes and ears vigilant. At one point, they could see the burning bonfire, with figures howling and dancing around it, looking like shadows on cave walls.

"There they are," Olukai said, watching through the ferns.

"It's so... unnatural," Lopaka managed to say through gulps. Olukai glanced at his men, their eyes wide, their jaws dropped, pure terror on their faces.

"Come on." Olukai led his men on, feeling a sense of relief that the kīpuka wasn't as large as he remembered it, making it easier to surround and catch the meha the following day.

When they returned to the other men at camp, the sounds of howling became mere echoes behind them. Olukai and the three others slumped on the ground, overwhelmed.

But Olukai straightened out first, trying to set an example. "The good news is the kīpuka isn't as big as I thought," he told them. "We go at the break of dawn."

. . .

Olukai couldn't rest for even a minute that night. He lay awake, staring at the stars, wondering if this mission was his last, and perhaps he'd failed as the great white manō's choice.

But I have a choice, he thought. *I can turn back with my men now, and just say we couldn't get the meha. The king couldn't be mad at that, because he'd have to come out here himself... which he'd never do.*

His mind swarmed with options, the same nagging feeling returning: *I should tell my men who I really am. They would gladly serve the manō.* But Olukai kept ignoring the thought until Lopaka began waking the other men.

"It's time," Lopaka whispered, though they were far enough from the meha that he could speak normally.

Olukai felt something from the island, a whisper in the wind. He *needed* to do this, even though it was a mission for the king. Even though an owl had crossed his path, even though every omen said it was bad luck, the island itself needed Olukai to kidnap these meha. With that new message and confirmation, he sat up and stretched before pulling his long dark hair into a bun on top of his head.

"Are you ready?" Lopaka asked Olukai. Lopaka looked like he hadn't gotten any sleep either. Similar purple bags rimmed the eyes of all the men.

Olukai nodded and stood before his men. "My friends," he said, "Let's do this quick and clean—you know the plan." He made eye contact with each one. "Let's go."

He was too tired for a speech, but also too anxious. He wanted this to be over with.

The men held their nets ready and watched each of their steps on the lava rock. They wanted to be as silent as possible, and sometimes stepping on broken lava made a crinkling noise, like glass. As the group neared the kīpuka, it looked peaceful. A mist settled over the black field and sat in the treetops. Drops of dew rested on the grass and leaves. The smell of rain and lava rock filled the air.

The lush green trees and bushes were a pleasant and welcome

sight in the midst of the black rocks. Birds could be heard chirping above, and Olukai secretly hoped the birds weren't communicating with the witches.

He had no idea of how the meha slept, or if they slept at all, but the plan was to surround the women on all sides, so they had nowhere to run, and cast the nets. If that failed, then it would be utter chaos of catching each meha, one by one. But each man carried extra woven ropes on their shoulders to chase and tie up the meha in case that happened.

Olukai signaled with his hand, pointing with all fingers to direct each man to his station. He crept around the corner to a large fern plant, net in hand, making sure he could see the other men hidden on either side of him, and across from him. They also held nets in their own hands, glancing from Olukai to the direction ahead of them.

Olukai nodded, giving them the signal to start walking towards the center of the kīpuka. The men did so, creeping so softly, even a raindrop fell louder than their steps. Because the air was so cold, each breath lingered in the air, nipping at the men's noses, and making them shiver.

As they crept closer, Olukai could now see each one of his men, their nets ready. He kept scanning the area, but saw no meha.

They were getting closer to the area where the women burned their fire the night before... perhaps they slept around the fire.

As Olukai moved the ferns and made his way to the clearing, the hairs on his skin rose like never before, and chills ran down his back.

There were at least eight meha, standing in a circle around the dead fire. They wore light brown kapa cloths over their faces and hair, and dresses that covered their entire bodies, except their hands. The witch women held one another's hands to form a circle and each of them faced outward.

They're expecting us, Olukai thought. The men crept closer, but the meha didn't move. As Olukai stepped from the brush into the clearing, one of the meha turned and faced directly at him. She was the only meha with a strange black charcoal line on the cloth covering her whole head.

Fear flashed through his mind. *She's going to curse me!*

"Now!" he yelled, and as he did, the meha raised their hands to the skies and screamed.

It was so unearthly that Olukai almost tripped and fell, wanting to cover his ears. But he kept running and cast his net over them. The other men did too, and the women fell, howling and struggling beneath the nets.

It seemed too easy to Olukai. The women put up no fight besides screaming, which was quite terrifying but did nothing to protect them.

"Grab them before they can speak any words!" Olukai said, jumping over the nets to place his hand over the mouth of a meha, hoping she wouldn't bite.

If they have normal faces and mouths, he thought. The other men did the same and soon there were only muffled cries from the women as Olukai and his men pulled each one out, binding the women's hands with cords behind their backs.

Soon, each meha had a tightly wrapped gag around her mouth, though none of the men could see their faces through the long veils covering their faces.

Olukai counted the meha: twelve.

"You three, check the surrounding area," said Olukai to his men. "See if we missed any." He held the rope that tied all the meha together in a row. They stood still, gagged heads down, a row of solitary figures.

Lopaka stood at the end of the row of women.

"We found this," said a soldier, returning with some old kapa cloth, black charcoal symbols drawn all over it. "And this," said another soldier, holding up a yellowed, old human skull.

Olukai shuddered as he glanced back at the meha. Not only were they witches and crazy, but they were murderers.

"Get rid of that," he said to the soldier with the skull and motioned to his men. "Let's go."

As they marched away, the women following in a long row, Olukai couldn't stop looking behind, checking that all of them were perfectly gagged up. He couldn't risk getting cursed while his back faced them.

CHAPTER SIXTEEN

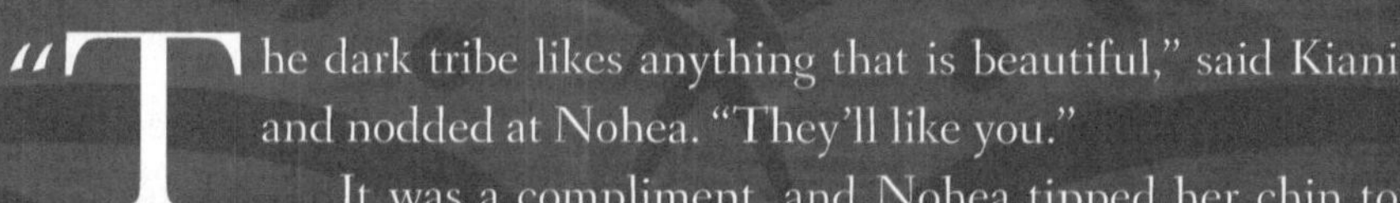

"The dark tribe likes anything that is beautiful," said Kiani and nodded at Nohea. "They'll like you."

It was a compliment, and Nohea tipped her chin to Kiani.

"If it spares our lives, then it is a gift," she said, though Nohea never really felt beautiful. She remembered a couple nights before, wearing the lei poʻo that Wena made. She had felt beautiful and alive the entire time she wore it. Then she watched it float down the river and felt that it had all been a dream. She hadn't actually been beautiful.

Living as a slave had taught her that she wasn't worth it to anyone if she didn't make a contribution... if she didn't make more medicine, come up with remedy for common colds, help deliver a baby... if she didn't do all her slave tasks, from working in the fields to laundering the concubine's many clothes... If she didn't do *something* to help others, then she was worthless.

Nohea swallowed the feelings, trying to drown them out by assuring herself that she would soon be needed, by the manō, if he was who he said he was.

Curiosity got the best of her and she glanced at Wena, curious to know if he reacted to Kiani's compliment. He seemed lost in his own thoughts.

"Who is the current chief of the Māku'e?" asked Uncle Haku to Kiani, though he knew the answer. Over the last day, as they got closer, Uncle Haku asked similar questions about the Māku'e.

"A queen," said Kiani, brushing her fingers through her long dark hair and adjusting her flower crown. "Queen Awa. You outsiders rarely hear about the dark tribe because they try to keep their government a secret. It's become corrupted over the years, marred by vanity and deceit."

While Uncle Haku asked repeat questions, Kiani chatted nonstop the closer they got to the dark tribe. To Nohea, the repetitive conversations grew annoying, so she stopped interacting, whereas Uncle Haku gratefully took any information and knowledge he could from Kiani.

Today Kiani wore an especially colorful flower crown, her hair flowing down, and Wena wore a simple green lei. Wena had stopped talking entirely the last day, only nodding or bowing when Nohea said something to him.

She couldn't imagine their pain—going close to a place that had rejected them, cast them out, *tried to kill them*. She felt sorry for them, only because she could see her slave family rejoicing in seeing her. This was completely different.

"Nohea," Uncle Haku slowed down to walk with Nohea, who lagged behind. "We are arriving at the dark tribe soon, I can sense it... remember what we talked about?"

Nohea nodded, "Ae. I made a promise, and I don't break them."

Uncle Haku nodded, "Thank you."

The previous night, when they found out how close they were to the dark tribe, Uncle Haku and Nohea had a talk... not a simple talk, but a deep one.

"We must present the manō to them in a way that they believe me," said Uncle Haku. "I've come to realize that not everyone believes in the royal line... because of King Ekewaka and Makana. They claimed to be descendants of the ali'i, but they lied. We must give the Māku'e hope that the island will have a true leader, from the bloodline of the ali'i, and the oceans will be open for sailing again. We are wayfinders, after all."

He continued, "And we must not say any word of soran, not until we discover where they stand. Promise you will let me do the talking here?"

And Nohea nodded, "I promise." She didn't know what to say anyways. The fact that he didn't want to mention soran also confused her. Why didn't he want to talk about it if the manō clearly wanted to destroy it? It had been late though, and she dozed off to sleep. She wanted to stay up so she could talk with Wena, but continuous nights with no sleep left her exhausted.

Wena suddenly held out his hand to stop the three walking behind him. Both he and Kiani grabbed the spears off their backs, prepared to attack.

"Calm down, we're not going to hurt you," said a smooth voice. From the shadows in front of them appeared a young man, tall as Wena, with brown eyes and golden skin. He was clean shaven with a flared nose and smug lips. His long, wavy hair fell to his shoulders, his ears pointed. A few men and women walked behind him, some older and some younger.

"Kawika," Kiani said, a raspiness in her voice that Nohea hadn't heard before. "Your guard is out farther than usual." She sounded genuinely surprised, and worried, which worried Nohea.

"Lower your weapons," Kawika ordered, a spear in hand. The people behind him held their own spears, Nohea noticed, as opposed to leiamanō or clubs. It made sense though, as the dark tribe lived in the woods, so how would they have access to finding shark teeth for weapons? In many ways, the Māku'e people looked sophisticated and elegant with their spears.

"She doesn't mean harm," said Uncle Haku, stepping forward,

palms up. "They were just guiding us here. We come in peace, and have a message for your highness, the great queen of the woods."

Kawika raised an eyebrow and glanced from Uncle Haku to Nohea, looking her up and down. Her throat went dry and she hugged her arms close to her. His right lip curled up.

"Pity," he said, and though he didn't say why, he stared straight at Nohea's odd colored eyes. He thought her ugly, and it made Nohea's cheeks warm with embarrassment. In front of them, Wena's grip tightened on his spear.

"Leave them alone," said Kiani, stepping in front of Nohea. "They ask one favor of the queen, not you. Take them to the queen—"

"Don't give me orders, you outcast," Kawika snapped. "Give us your weapons, now."

"We won't go any farther," said Kiani. To Nohea, Kiani kept surprisingly calm, considering Kawika's loud tone. "Let them through and we will leave."

Kawika nodded to his guards, who pointed their spears at Nohea and Uncle Haku. Nohea gasped, throwing up her hands in innocence.

"We come in peace," Uncle Haku said over and over. Wena glanced at his sister and nodded, then lowered his spear. A dark tribe woman yanked the spear from his hands. Kiani rolled her eyes and handed her spear to Kawika.

"You too," Kawika said to Uncle Haku and Nohea. Nohea took the spear off her back and Uncle Haku turned in his shark tooth knife.

Some of the other dark tribe members stepped forward and bound Uncle Haku and Nohea's hands. Without warning, a few other tribe members jumped on Wena, grabbing his hair and tackling him to the ground. Nohea gasped. "Stop it!" she cried. "Let him go!" She ran towards him but someone else grabbed her wrist and twisted it behind her back. She screamed and Wena made eye contact with her, sensing her pain. As he turned to protect her, Kawika delivered a swift blow to Wena's eye.

"Wena!" Nohea exclaimed, her entire body shaking. Wena fell back, but he scrambled up, ready to fight, a red crescent shape forming below his eye. Kiani jumped in. "Stop it! All of you!"

She stood face to face with Kawika, both of them breathing heavily. "Wena and I will take our leave now. This is unnecessary."

Kawika scoffed. "Oh you're not going anywhere. The queen will be *so* happy to see you." He snapped his fingers and his guards tackled both Kiani and Wena, who was now getting bloodier, as the tribe people delivered blows to his face and stomach.

Nohea and Uncle Haku watched in horror, screaming protests. Wena put up a fight, but there were so many people ganging up on him, that they finally piled up on him until he laid on the ground, almost unconscious. Meanwhile, Kiani put up her own fight but some women pulled on her hair and Kiani fell to the ground, where they tied her hands and placed a gag over her mouth.

She lunged towards Kawika, though she could say no words. A tribe woman held Kiani's tied hands back so she couldn't touch the young man, but Kiani's eyes alone looked like they could kill him.

"Let them go!" Nohea cried the entire time, screaming and kicking as she watched her friends being tortured. "They didn't do anything—they don't even want to go in! Let them go!"

Uncle Haku repeated her pleas, adding, "We will do anything but please, let them go!"

"They should have died years ago," Kawika spat and turned around, ignoring their cries. The men and women pulled Nohea by a cord connected to her wrists,and she walked forward, looking back to the unconscious figure of Wena. A large member of the Māku'e, who was so broad, tall, and muscular he didn't look like he fit in with the rest of the group, tossed Wena over his shoulder and they all followed Kawika.

. . .

Not long after the scuffle, the dark tribe members placed a covering over Nohea's head and she walked blindly. She figured it was because the dark tribe wanted their home to remain a secret. From what she could tell, they walked over soft grass and through some itchy vines. She heard a loud, rumbling waterfall as they climbed up many soft wooden stairs. Finally, someone removed the kapa cloth from their faces.

Nohea blinked in confusion, as the brightness and colors around her weren't what she expected. When she thought of the "dark tribe" she thought of a dark place. But it wasn't that dark, especially because they stood high above the ground. The air smelled like flowers and a cool breeze felt fresh against Nohea's skin.

A woman sat before them, on a throne made of bent bamboo trunks. The bamboo looked like the design of a peacock, the back of the chair high above her head. Her hands sat comfortably on the armrests at either side of her. She was adorned in fresh flowers, from the flower crown on her head, to the lei around her neck, and the flower bracelets around her wrists and ankles. Her black hair fell in soft waves to her stomach, and she wore a long white dress, so long that it flowed below her cozy bamboo throne.

To Nohea, this woman was beautiful in a terrifying way, with dark piercing brown eyes, a pointed chin, high arched eyebrows, and full pink lips. At the bottom of her pointed ears hung hand-carved bamboo earrings. A few freckles graced her nose and cheeks. Her bronze skin looked smoother than a polished coconut.

Nohea noticed Uncle Haku standing to her left then Kiani and Wena to her right. Wena was now completely unconscious, his eye purple and dry blood hanging below his nose, the corners of his lips, and below his eye.

Kawika stood to the side, along with his entourage that had bound them earlier.

"How dare you come back..." The woman before them spoke directly to Kiani. Her voice sounded smooth, yet loud. "You are outcasts, exiled! And *how dare* you bring others?!" She pointed at Uncle Haku and Nohea. Nohea flinched.

"We had no intention of coming back," Kiani snapped back, "Only guiding them to this awful place."

"You have disobeyed your orders, and now you will be punished... by death," said the woman.

"No!" Both Uncle Haku and Nohea exclaimed. The woman turned her head, glaring at Nohea. She almost leaped out of her seat.

"What did you say?"

"Your majesty," Uncle Haku interrupted. "Please listen to us. I am your humble servant, Haku, and this is my niece, Nohea. We are seeking refuge until our messenger can find us."

"Your messenger?"

"'Ae, we had trouble with the king's counselor, Kahiko."

"Kahiko," she scoffed. "That old sorcerer? He is weak. He couldn't tell a spell from a chant." Kawika and the others laughed at that. The woman tipped her head to the side and stared at Nohea. "Do you know who I am?" she asked.

"'Ae, you are the queen..." Nohea mumbled.

"What? Speak louder."

"You are the queen." Nohea wet her lips and looked down. She glanced at Uncle Haku, remembering her promise. But the queen had addressed her, not him, so Nohea only felt like it was appropriate to reply. She could feel the queen's intense emotions, and it vaguely reminded Nohea of her own mother: always so angry, uncomfortable, and demanding. And while her mother kept her anger to herself, this woman let it explode into the energy around her.

"'Ae," replied the queen, her eyes narrowing. "I am Awa, queen of the Māku'e, the dark woods, the purple woods that you fled to. I know all the whereabouts of this forest, including where these—" she pointed at Kiani and Wena, "are."

Nohea tried not to frown. She didn't like people being referenced to as "things" or "these." Kiani and Wena were people too, but she bit her tongue. The slave masters used to call slaves "things" and "these." It made her blood boil.

"We mean no trouble," Uncle Haku cut in.

"Silence!" the queen screamed, her voice echoing through the leaves and branches surrounding them. Only then Nohea realized that they were standing on a platform high above the ground. In the distance behind them was a white flowing waterfall, with a large pool of water below it. The whole area grew thick with tall koa trees and an abundance of flowers.

"Why are you here?" Queen Awa asked Nohea. "You, with those strange eyes..."

Nohea glanced at Uncle Haku again and he nodded, as if giving her permission to break the promise. The queen's anger and impatience fumed, and Nohea knew this conversation could make or break their safety.

"We are seeking refuge, a place where our messenger can find us." She repeated Uncle Haku's words from earlier. How many times did they need to tell the queen until she understood?

"And who does your messenger work for?"

"Our business is our own," replied Nohea, looking directly into the queen's eyes. Queen Awa's eyebrows creased, not convinced.

"Who are you seeking refuge from?"

"The king, Kahiko, and the king's men."

"What wrong have they done towards you?"

"They killed my mother. I was a slave."

"Your mother?" the queen folded her arms. "And what did *she* do wrong?"

"She burned the king's books." The queen didn't look impressed. She raised her eyebrows.

"I am an alchemist," Nohea blurted. All eyes turned on her. Kawika's mouth dropped. Kiani even shot a glance at Nohea. All this time they'd hidden Nohea's identity, and now Kiani looked completely cross about it.

"An... alchemist?" The queen paused, her brown eyes darkening as she looked past Nohea at the waterfall. "What do you know of alchemy?"

"I can create medicine. I understand plants—I can break them down, see what they're made of, and how they can be used to help." Nohea spoke in haste, noticing the queen thinking about it. "I learned science from the books my mother burned."

"Science—like the work of foreigners?"

"'Ae."

The queen frowned and shook her head. "You're lying."

"I'm not—I've helped deliver many babies safely, I've created remedies for burns and cuts, salves to tend to itchy bites..."

"You understand the properties of liquids too?"

"'Ae, I can find things to purify water so that people don't get sick from drinking it. I've studied blood to see what's in it—"

"I have an offer," the queen interrupted, her fingers drumming the arm rest. Her high arched eyebrows never ceased to frown, intimidating and unkind. "There is a sickness that ails my people. If you can find a cure for it during your stay, I will protect you until your messenger arrives. And I will let you *and* your friends leave in peace." She pointed to the three beside Nohea. The queen's long fingers, adorned with bamboo rings, made clicking sounds anytime she moved them.

"What is the sickness?"

"That I will not tell you *until* we have an agreement."

"That's not fair—"

"Do you wish to live or not?" Queen Awa leaned forward, daring Nohea to test her boundaries.

Nohea frowned. "How long do I have?"

"Two weeks."

"And you won't hurt me, my uncle, Kiani, Wena, *or* the messenger?" Nohea's fists began to clench as she made perfect eye contact with the queen. Uncle Haku glanced down at Nohea, worried, but Nohea focused.

Queen Awa pursed her lips. "I will not."

"One more condition: I need a place to work—somewhere quiet, with glass vials, tools, and basic herbs."

"My kahuna will share his space for the time," Queen Awa said. "Do we have a deal, young slave?"

"My name is Nohea." It came out so fast and aggressively, that even Uncle Haku cringed. The queen's eyes narrowed.

"Fine. Do we have a deal, Nohea, or not?"

"We have a deal."

The queen smiled. "Good, now take these two away—"

"You said you wouldn't hurt them!" Nohea exclaimed.

"I said *I* wouldn't hurt them," Queen Awa snarled as the guards grabbed Nohea and Uncle Haku, taking them in the opposite direction of Kiani and Wena.

"You said you wouldn't hurt them! You lied!" Nohea screamed again and again as she and Kiani cast worried glances at one another. The guards dragged Nohea away, kicking and whining.

Nohea's anger rose as she and the queen death-stared at one another.

If she wants to play like that... fine. I'll play like that, Nohea thought as the guard pulled her down the staircase, breaking the fiery eye contact.

CHAPTER SEVENTEEN

Not far from the outskirts of the dark forest was Waiakea village, the same village Olukai saw the last glimpse of his father. The dusty streets bustled with people and craftsmen, soldiers and slaves. This was the closest village to the king's fortress, so the soldiers walked around, bored, watching for trouble, but finding nothing.

A lonely figure walked casually through the shadows, observing the people, checking that things looked normal.

He came to the village by foot, which was usually only a couple hours from Olukai's home by the shore. However, it had taken the young man much longer to get to the village because of the king's guards, endlessly searching for him.

He needed to find a friend in the village, someone willing to loan a horse. He left his favorite horse at Olukai's home, knowing that switching things up kept the soldiers confused.

Consistency is a messenger's bane, he thought, remembering how many times he learned that lesson. He constantly changed routes, plans, and appearance to keep himself aloof from the guards.

"Psst..." A woman's voice came from the shadows behind the young man.

"Aunty, there you are." The young man smiled, keeping his golden hair covered with a bandana. He changed from his black garments to the colors of the villagers: blue skirt and red kihei.

A large woman grabbed the tall young man's face and kissed both his cheeks. "Come on inside Po, or they'll see you."

This was normal for Po. As a messenger he hid in many of the villager's homes. They knew him—and they knew he was constantly in danger, but most shared a dislike for the king, and a desire for the true ali'i to rise again. Many considered Po family, like this woman whom he'd talked to on many occasions.

As they stepped inside the hut, the woman motioned for Po to sit in the corner. "What you need?" she asked, already making him a leaf plate with sweet potatoes and fish. The woman was Aunty Hea, and, after handing him the food, she wiped her glossy forehead and nose.

"I'm in a hurry aunty," Po said as shoved the food into his mouth. After traveling the last few days practically running, he didn't realize how hungry he was. "I need a horse."

"Uncle Onekaha will help you get one. Eat up, I'll be back." She hurried out of the house, leaving Po alone. The food tasted so good, he didn't notice Aunty Hea's baby lying on her stomach in the corner of the hut, until she cooed.

Po paused, mid bite, and smiled.

"Hey there." He stepped into the corner and stroked the girl's black hair. Her big brown eyes blinked up at him. Compassion filled his heart as he scooped her into his arms and rocked her. "You're so cute," he said, touching her nose and making her laugh. They played this game for a while, and the baby's laughs made his heart melt.

"Oh she likes you." Aunty Hea had returned, and watched. When he handed the baby to Aunty Hea, a strange longing filled his heart as he watched her kiss and snuggle the baby.

He blinked. "I better get going. Mahalo for the food Aunty Hea."

"No worries, Po," she said, kissing his cheek. "Hang tight. I'll pack you some food and then you go to the lodge on the outskirts of town."

Po nodded, already bending to help her pack the food, as she held the cute baby in her arms.

He'd already wasted too much time, and who knew where Nohea and Haku were at this point? On his way to Olukai's house, he stopped at Kea'au village to warn Haku's wife and daughters to flee to the south. Then he had to take too many detours to get to Olukai's home. He'd never seen so many guards in the land, which told him how serious this situation really was.

After catching up with Olukai and resting, Po left Olukai's house, hiding and waiting as the guards flocked through the wooded areas and fields he usually ran through. His shortcuts had been exhausted, and he had to hide in trees and bushes to avoid the guards. He avoided the lava tubes, since he figured the king's guards would be searching for him down there too.

So a few days had passed until he finally reached this village, eager to get a horse and move to the dark forest. He had no idea how to find Haku and Nohea, but he felt confident there would be help, either from the island, kind travelers, or some other way. The people of Kaimana island, he learned over and over again, were good people.

Aunty Hea wiped sweat from her forehead before wrapping another ti leaf pack of food. So many of the women were large and sweaty, like Aunty Hea... *And Sina,* Po thought of his hānai mother. Irritation crossed his chest and he took a breath to ignore it.

Hea's short, chubby brown body bounced with every step she took. Her little children rushed into the house, and she shooed them away too.

"Not right now!"

"Mama, I'm hungry—"

"Just one moment, alright?" Aunty Hea wrapped up Po's food in ti leaves and handed it to him. He felt guilty, as the children glared at him, but there was still plenty of food left. He placed the wrapped food in his side bag, kissed Aunty Hea's sweaty cheek, and left.

The people of the island had always been so kind to him. He wouldn't be able to pay any of them back but by being a messenger, he could do his part for them.

When the manō becomes the island's leader, he thought, *There will be balance, from the mountain to the sea. They won't have to sacrifice family members for the king's addiction to soran...*

It didn't take long for Po to reach the lodge at the outskirts. A few boys tended to some horses nearby. Seeing that there were no soldiers in sight, Po approached. "Where's your father?" he asked one of the older boys. Most of the older kids and teenagers in the villages at least recognized Po as their parents' friend.

"Take the gray one," said an older man approaching. Po touched foreheads with the older man and breathed in his hā.

"Mahalo uncle. I will bring him back if I can."

As he rode away, Po immediately focused on getting to the dark forest. He needed to hurry. Olukai needed the alchemist as soon as possible. And who knew if she and her uncle were safe... or even alive at this point?

CHAPTER EIGHTEEN

"It was too easy," Olukai said to Lopaka. Both stood by their horses, glancing back nervously at the meha. After two days of walking, they finally made it to the horses and got the meha into the bamboo cages. The women hadn't put up any fight, not even tried to break out in the nighttime. They sat there, in silence, during the nights, and walked during the day.

The soldiers hitched the cages to their horses, all working in an eerie silence.

"Let's count our blessings, 'ae?" Lopaka replied, wiping some sweat off his bushy brows and getting on his horse. Olukai wiped sweat off his own forehead.

It didn't add up. Perhaps the witches had literally *no way of defending themselves,* besides scaring others, and their cry, while holding hands, was their last attempt to scare others away. *But why would they just give up?* Olukai wondered. Perhaps it was better to not fight and live?

The women, sitting in the cages, faces covered, with gags around their mouths, were a sorry and sad sight. They leaned against one another, almost as though they'd given up the fight before it even started. The men had bound their hands behind their backs, making it difficult for the women to remove the gags.

Olukai got on his horse and started forward, but he couldn't help glancing back at the women, especially the one who had turned and looked at him earlier. She was easy to distinguish because of the black charcoal mark across the veil on her face.

She faced forward, and, though he couldn't see her eyes beneath the veil, he had a feeling she kept staring at him. It made him nervous, uneasy. He kept glancing back at her, finding that she hadn't moved one bit.

Finally, he had Lopaka take the lead, and Olukai took the rear.

To no surprise, the meha with the charcoal mark turned around to stare straight at him again.

"Hold!" he called to his men, dismounting his horse to approach the caged meha. "Why are you staring at me?" he asked. He didn't want to get too close, worried that she might try something.

Silence. He didn't dare take the gag off, for fear she'd curse him. He and the meha gazed at one another, though he couldn't see her eyes through the veil.

"Stop staring at me," he finally said. He looked up to find all the men watching. Olukai didn't want to look uneasy, so he shrugged and returned to his horse.

But the entire day, he couldn't shake the nagging feeling of being watched. Because, indeed, each time he looked at the meha with the charcoal mark, her gaze, though hidden, was directly on him.

THAT NIGHT, Olukai decided they needed to feed the women. "The king ordered us to bring all of the meha, and he specifically said alive," he told Lopaka.

"I'm worried," Lopaka said, rubbing his head. "I don't know how we'll convince the soldiers to take off those gags. They're spooked." Lopaka laughed. "*I'm* nervous."

Olukai watched his men as they sat around their campfire. They made a fire for the women too, and placed the four cages around. The soldiers couldn't stop glancing at the cages though, afraid that at any moment the witches would rise and kill them all.

"Fine, I'll feed them," Olukai said. Lopaka made a face then shrugged. "Your choice brother."

Olukai took some of the food from the soldiers. They always made plenty, and he'd ordered them to make extras, even though the men resisted at first. They had a fine meal of fish, sweet potatoes, fruit, and *luau* stew.

He knelt before the meha with the charcoal across her veil. "I am going to remove your gag," said Olukai. "I expect that you will not curse me."

Silence passed, then she slowly bowed her head.

Olukai reached his hand into the cage and removed her gag. He instinctively yanked his hand out in haste, as though afraid she might grab it or try something, anything.

Silence, again.

"Here is some food for you—"

"We do not eat fish," said the woman, her voice low and flat. Olukai had been expecting a raspy voice, like the screaming meha he'd heard in the past.

"Well, you can have this." He placed the other food, fruit and vegetables in the cage with her. "Is it safe for me to remove their gags so they can eat? Or should I wait for you all to eat, one at a time?"

The woman tipped her face to the side. "Do you think we are animals?"

"I... don't know what you are," Olukai replied, feeling a blush in his cheeks.

"We are humans, just like you. We are different. Is that so bad?" A tinge of sadness in her voice.

Olukai didn't know what to say.

"I know who you are," she continued. "I know your mission, your purpose, and we have sacrificed ourselves for you."

Olukai glimpsed behind him at the men, but they sat too far to hear the conversation. Lopaka, however, stood not far off, knife in hand.

"Olukai... you alright?" Lopaka asked.

"I'm fine, thanks!" Olukai called back. "What do you mean?" he asked, then pushed the food forward. "Please... eat."

"We do not eat in front of men."

Olukai raised his eyebrows, "Alright..."

"We know you are the heir of the great white manō, the last descendant of the true ali'i on Kaimana island." Olukai shivered. *How did she know?*

"We have seen you in visions, in the stars, in the air. We have felt the great white manō's presence around the island, and we know what he wants. Ekewaka and Makana have ruined the island, imposters claiming royal blood. The great shark, the first great ali'i of the island, will not let anyone in or out until this island be cleansed and united."

Olukai shivered again. The woman continued. "Take us to the king. We know what he wants." She sat forward , smelling of smoke. "He wants us to duplicate his soran, or make an everlasting well of it. *We* will give you the time you need. We will stall. But we do not know the answer. There is only one meha, one who became a wanderer, who knows how to create *and* destroy soran."

"Who is it?" Olukai glanced behind him again, but the men were too busy warming up their hands and feet by the distant fire.

"She is dead, or will soon be, the island has told us."

Olukai frowned.

"But do not give up hope," she said. "She prepared another after her with all the answers..."

Olukai's face seemed to press against the cage. As much as he hated the idea of it, the meha were actually helping him!

"Who did she prepare?"

"Her daughter."

"Who? Where?"

"You already know the answer to that," said the meha, sitting against the back of the cage, her veiled face falling into the shadows.

"Wait..." Olukai shook his head, realization sinking in. "The alchemist? Her mother was a meha?" It began to make sense. If Edena was a sorceress, surely she had to be a meha, because women as kahuna, like Kahiko, were hardly heard of on the island, besides the infamous lady of the lava.

"Not of our tribe, but a meha nonetheless, and one of the most powerful on the island. She could wield magic of light and dark unlike any other. She understood the mana of the island more deeply than any kahuna, even more so than the lady of the lava."

More than the lady of the lava? Olukai knew the tales of her far too well, but he'd never crossed paths with her on his many missions. Probably a good thing. The lady of the lava was a beautiful old woman who lived in the mountains by the volcano, a woman who loved the lava, whose eyes lit up like fire. She was known as the most powerful kahuna on the island, far more powerful than Kahiko. Rumors spread that she could control the lava.

But was there someone more powerful than the lady of the lava? Could the alchemist be that powerful? The idea intimidated Olukai.

"We must find her immediately," said Olukai, trying to think. Where was Po? Did he find the alchemist and her uncle yet? It had been more than several days now...

"She is the only one who knows the answer," said the meha. "We don't understand the ways of soran. It is too deep for us. We are simple witches, lovers of nature, keepers of the earth."

"I thought—"

"You thought we cast spells to curse people? You thought we are murderers? It is all a facade." She chuckled, her voice deep and tired. "We are the caretakers of this island, taking in young sisters who need refuge or who exhibit special abilities. We do not live only in kīpuka only. We travel. We care for the wandering souls, the orphaned children, and the weary. Our safety is in our reputation. As long as we are known as evil, as dark, as fearful, as hideous to behold... we are safe from the grasps of men."

"You... are not cursed?" Olukai asked, baffled.

The woman lifted her veil, and Olukai almost shielded his eyes, afraid of what he'd see. But before him sat a stunningly beautiful woman, with copper skin, full lips, thick eyebrows, and brown eyes. She couldn't have been much older than Haku.

"I am the leader of this tribe. I am Hopohopo, but you can call me Hopo."

"We are friends," Olukai said, bowing his head to her. She bowed back.

"Yes, but we must pretend that we are not. As I said before, Olukai, we will stall as long as we can... but our hope rests in you and the alchemist."

Olukai nodded. "We won't let you down."

Then he commenced to remove all the gags from the women, placed the food in their cages, and hurried back to the campfire with the soldiers.

"It looked like you were talking to her," said Lopaka, rubbing the chicken skin on his arms. Olukai nodded, "'Ae, she promised not to curse us if we feed them everyday."

"We better keep them fed then," said Ioane, who sat by the fire and overheard the conversation.

Olukai tried not to smile. "'Ae, let's make sure they don't starve or we'll all be done for..." But his thoughts kept distracting him, going back to the same question: Where was Nohea, the alchemist, the daughter of one of the most powerful kahuna on the island? He needed her help.... Now.

CHAPTER NINETEEN

After seizing Nohea and Uncle Haku, the guards took them to a simple hut on the forest floor. As they walked, Nohea looked around at the home of the Māku'e. The tribe lived in a lush forest, with koa trees so tall, and branches so thick, they shaded the floor from the sun. Little wooden steps were hammered into chiseled holes in the tree trunks. These make-shift stairs led up to huts in the treetops, and when Nohea glanced behind her, she marveled at the large size of the queen's own tree. It was the largest koa tree in the entire wooded area.

The Māku'e people walked past Nohea and the guards, staring. The peoples' dark skin and eyes had a strangely haunted look to them. They wore white, walked barefoot, and flowers and leaves adorned their heads, necks, wrists, and ankles.

All of them were so beautiful, with their vibrant adornments, but there was also a sense of emptiness. They whispered to one another, pointing at Nohea and Uncle Haku. Most of them trailed behind, nosy to see the commotion and excitement of the guards dragging around two outsiders.

The company passed a huge clearing, most likely the public

square. A few vendors set up shops around the square, selling fruit, white kapa cloth, and jewelry. Nohea had never seen so much jewelry in her life. She paused by a vendor, admiring the rings and headpieces. She noticed that the Māku‘e woman selling the items wore jewelry on her ears.

Nohea paused and stared for a moment, for now she knew what earrings looked like: the queen had worn them, and now this woman. Jewelry was hardly spoken of in the slave family—for they didn't know what it looked like, or even how to wear it.

"Come along," said the guard, pulling her arm forward.

In the center of the courtyard was a smaller tree, with woven ropes hanging down the branches. It looked so out of place, for there were no other trees like it in the area. The large, perfect field of grass, like a village square, seemed awkward with one tree in the middle of it.

"What is that?" Nohea asked the guard. He paused this time, and Nohea now noticed the swarm of people that had formed behind them. They inched back when her gaze fell on them.

"It's the Hahau tree."

"The Hahau tree?"

"Come on…" the guard continued, but Nohea persisted. "What does that mean?"

"Each night a member of the Māku‘e must go beyond the waterfall and retrieve the sacred water. If they are unsuccessful, they are tied to the tree and whipped."

"And they are successful, right?" Nohea's eyebrows creased in concern.

The guard was quiet, glancing at the other guard who held Uncle Haku's arm.

"Don't talk to her," said the other guard.

"‘Ae sir." Nohea's guard didn't say another word until they reached the hut.

"This is where you're staying." He looked nervous. "Someone will come to show you the kahuna's hut." The two guards hurried off, squishing through the thick crowd of Māku'e people that formed outside of the guest hut.

Nohea and Uncle Haku stood there, staring for a moment at the crowd.

Uncle Haku cleared his throat then nodded before going in to look around. Nohea hesitated. The look on the people's faces was familiar: tired, anxious, nervous... Realization settled over her. She saw these expressions before, in the faces of her slave brothers and sisters.

Something was not right.

Most of those in the curious group were children, and they stared at her ears. Nohea tucked a strand of hair behind her ear. "What are your names?" she asked the children, but they didn't reply, nor did they move.

Nohea crouched on the ground and the children inched backwards. So she stood again and tried to read the peoples' faces for any emotion. But she only met the familiar gazes of exhaustion.

"Have any of you tried to get the sacred water?" she asked. Most of the teenagers and adults nodded, hesitant. "Were you successful?"

They looked at one another.

"Come on..." said a teenage boy, grabbing a little girl's hand and pulling her away. The crowd slowly turned around and dispersed, except for one person. An older woman, with a pleasant face, dark brown eyes, and graying hair, stared at Nohea. She wore a red flower lei, and a big vibrant hibiscus in her ear. Bamboo bracelets lined her arms, as well as bamboo earrings, giving her the appearance of a person of status. The woman looked vaguely familiar, but Nohea couldn't quite put a finger on why.

"You are an alchemist?" the woman asked and tipped her head, curious.

"'Ae," Nohea replied, noticing Uncle Haku watching from behind.

"You must forgive the people. They are not used to visitors. Many of them have forgotten the light. There is only darkness here now."

Uncle Haku stepped forward and rubbed his chin.

"Who are you?" Nohea asked.

"I am Kawena," the woman bowed her head. "Rumors spread fast around here and you have brought much hope to the people. If you need anything, please let us know." She turned around to leave, but Nohea blurted out.

"What about the Hahau tree?"

"It is the only way she survives." The woman bowed and walked away.

Nohea met Uncle Haku's eyes.

"There's something strange going on here," he said, but he didn't need to, because Nohea already had a feeling in her stomach that something was definitely off and she'd find out soon what it was all about.

A GUARD DIDN'T VISIT them later that night to show Nohea the kahuna's hut. Instead, servants brought food and filled up a large, polished lava tub with water. They placed hot stones around the base to heat up the tub. Nohea had never seen anything like it, but when she got inside, she felt like she could never leave it. She scrubbed her body with the pikake soap and dipped her head over and over again in the warm water, feeling lovely, refreshed, clean.

A pang struck her heart. What about Wena and Kiani? Why couldn't they get to experience this too? Why did the Māku'e hate them so much? They were the most honorable people Nohea knew besides Uncle Haku.

When she got out, she wiped herself dry with the Māku'e's thick kapa cloths that felt cozy and soft. She wrapped a fresh white kapa tunic around her body, tying a ti leaf sash around her waist. A comb sat on a little table to the side, and she eagerly brushed her hair. It felt like decades since she last bathed and brushed her hair, as the slaves didn't have time to do so everyday.

Uncle Haku waited his turn, patiently, in another room of the hut. He sat cross legged on the floor, staring into the fire pit, the centerpiece of the wooded shack.

"Are you alright?" Nohea asked, sitting next to him, placing a hand on his shoulder.

"You did your best." He smiled at her, obviously thinking about their conversation with the queen.

"Not exactly. Thanks to my poor negotiations, Wena and Kiani are in prison right now, while we're here in this fancy hut."

"But you had no other choice. That queen was..." he sighed. "She was full of anger. I think you saved our lives." He touched her hand. "Thank you, niece. The manō will be grateful for your bravery."

"Do you think the manō would want the Māku'e a part of his kingdom?"

Uncle Haku nodded. "'Ae, he needs all the help he can get. King Ekewaka is... he's nearly invincible."

"Why? It's not like he has huge armies, right?"

"No. He doesn't need grand armies when he drinks soran. He and his warriors, a group of them, drink soran. It makes them powerful, unnatural, stronger, invincible."

For some reason, Nohea thought of the man who picked up Wena earlier. He seemed so unlike the rest of the dark tribe members, who were lean and petite.

A thought crossed Nohea's mind. "Why doesn't everyone on the island drink soran?" She remembered her little talk with Wena, when he mentioned the king killed many innocent lives to obtain soran. And, more so, she thought of her commitment to never be like Edena. Unlike Edena, Nohea would help the islanders, not hide her gift or the useful resources of the island.

"It's addictive. Every person would tear out their neighbor's throat to get it. Trust me, we don't want everyone to drink soran."

"But wouldn't it help protect us from sickness?" Nohea's thoughts drifted to Kimo, lying there, dead, Nui sobbing above him. If only she had soran at that moment, maybe Kimo would still be alive, still cracking jokes, still telling stories...

"'Ae, it would." He sighed again, and it made Nohea want to sigh too. "But death is a natural part of life."

Silence passed between them, the fire crackling in the hut, sending warmth through Nohea's body. She brought her knees to her chest and held them. "I think the manō might have a hard time getting the queen's help, don't you think?"

Uncle Haku smiled. "You'd be surprised... he is a natural alaka'i." A natural leader. Nohea opened her mouth to ask more about the manō when a scream from outside made her jump.

"What was that?" she asked.

The screams continued, painful, a woman's scream, yet it sounded familiar. Uncle Haku rushed out the door, grabbing the torch, as they didn't have any sharp weapons to defend themselves. Nohea had no idea where the guards had taken their weapons after they'd been found in the forest, but she secretly hoped she'd get her spear back. After all, Wena had made it for her.

When the guards brought Uncle Haku and Nohea to the hut, they also checked Nohea's bags. Having no idea what the bombs were, and after Nohea convinced them that they were bundles of herbs, they let her keep *all* of them. She grabbed her bag and hurried after Uncle Haku, knowing that the bombs would work as weapons.

Other people stood by the door of their huts, looking towards the large clearing, the "town square," as Nohea figured it might be. A girl screamed again and Nohea could hear such bitter pain.

It came from the hauhau tree.

"Kiani!" Both Uncle Haku and Nohea cried at the same time, rushing forward. Her wrists were bound to the tree, her back exposed, with red slashes glaring in the light of the torches. Her hair hung down the sides of her face. A guard stood behind her, a long black whip in his hand.

"What are you doing?" Nohea exclaimed as Uncle Haku charged the guard, pinning him to the ground. Nohea ran to Kiani's bound wrists, already untying them.

Someone grabbed Nohea's waist and pulled her back.

"This is by order of her majesty!"

"Let go of me!" Nohea kicked and screamed, even bit into the guard's arm. Uncle Haku struggled against the guards too, until he and Nohea stood side by side, in front of Kiani's limp body.

"You cannot do this to her," Uncle Haku said, holding his torch as if to attack the guards. Nohea grasped the bomb in her bag, ready to throw should the guards charge at them. The guards wore white tunics, their hair in high buns, spears in hand. The one holding the whip had tiny splatters of blood, most likely Kiani's, on his kihei.

"You don't understand," said one of the guards, stepping forward, the one who let a few things slip to Nohea earlier. He looked sorry, his dark eyes shifting from Nohea to Uncle Haku when she glared at him. "She has failed to retrieve the queen's treasure from the moʻo tonight, so she receives twenty lashes as punishment."

"What treasure?" Uncle Haku asked. "Speak!"

"We are not to speak of it. This prisoner has only five lashes to go." The guard looked at the other guards, and, for a moment, Nohea could've sworn she saw guilt on their faces. Did they even *want* to do this?

"Nohea—" Kiani spoke hoarsely. Nohea rushed to her, lifting her face and brushing the sticky, wet hair back. "I know you don't understand," Kiani said. "But you have to let them finish... if you don't, the queen..." Nohea frowned. "The queen will kill them." Kiani let her head hang, though Nohea helped it drop gently. She looked back at the guards, anger fuming in her.

"No," said Uncle Haku. "You will not finish the lashes. She's coming with us." His quiet anger and firmness mirrored Nohea's emotions.

"She can't," said the guard with the whip, though he looked at the other guards, nervous.

"Is there a problem here?"

Nohea recognized the snarly voice before she even saw Kawika's face. He folded his arms as he approached, and then Nohea noticed a group of people gather in the distance, watching.

"Kiani is coming with us." Nohea stood her ground in front of Kiani again, feeling like fumes came out of her head. Her fingers pressed against the soft ti leaf shell of the bombs in her pouch, no doubt it would explode if she squeezed any harder.

"By order of the queen, when we have prisoners, they are sent to retrieve the treasure in the cave," Kawika said, pushing the other guards aside. "And, well, we have two new prisoners." He flashed Nohea a grin. "It gives the people a little break."

"You're not going to hurt her anymore," Uncle Haku reaffirmed. "Or Wena."

"You have no control over that." Kawika sounded bored. "If she doesn't receive the last lashes, then I'm afraid that *these,*" he motioned to the three guards standing there, "will be killed." The young one that held Nohea earlier gulped. *These.* Nohea hated the word. Guards, servants, slaves... they were people, not *these*....

"Just finish it!" Kiani growled. Now Nohea understood. She *completely* understood Kiani. If Nohea had to receive a couple of lashes to save some fellow slaves' lives, she would do it. And, in that moment, Nohea looked up to the largest tree, a grand hut lit up by torches in the night time, the queen's luxurious hut, realizing: *The Māku'e are nothing more than slaves.*

"She has to do it," Nohea pulled Uncle Haku aside, his eyes shocked as he looked down at her.

"What?" Uncle Haku didn't budge.

"She's going back to the prison after this," Kawika told the guards, loud enough for Uncle Haku and Nohea to hear. Uncle Haku let Nohea pull him away this time.

"Oh." Kawika wanted their attention again. "And don't think that little incapable boy is getting out of this tomorrow night. The queen orders it. And what she orders, she gets."

Nohea's hands balled into fists, not around the bombs this time though, her nails driving into her palms. Uncle Haku stood stiff, his muscles tensed.

Kawika glanced from Nohea's face to the guards and then Kiani.

His nose wrinkled, then he shoved the guard holding the whip. "Give that to me—I'll finish it." And he did: quick, as hard as he could, with Kiani screaming each time. Nohea jumped and looked away each time she heard the crack and the scream. It brought back memories, too many painful memories because of petty things: late to the tasks, talking back, rolling her eyes...

"Get back to your huts!" Kawika growled at Nohea, Haku, and the other people who had inched closer and closer to witness the drama.

The guards untied Kiani and dragged her away. Nohea's mouth felt dry, anger surging through her whole body.

"Hurry up!" Kawika screamed again. The people scurried like ants. But Nohea watched Kiani's body, limp, like a doll, as the guards pulled her into the darkness, towards the prison, wherever those were. Then she met Kawika's eyes, and she glared. He smiled and swiped some blood off his face.

"You better get a move on," he said. "Or you won't last one night here."

Uncle Haku took Nohea's shoulders and pulled her away. But she couldn't help feeling the rage inside: burning, like molten lava, moving slow, yet destroying everything in its path.

"I am Noa, the great kahuna of the dark woods." Nohea stood alone before a man not much taller than herself. He had skin as dark as the damp soil, with large eyes, a round face, and thick white hair that ran down his wrinkled back. His white kihei complimented his hair, and the many lei he wore showed his status, like the Queen. He smelled strange, like he used too many oils on his skin. It was morning, as Nohea hardly slept the entire night, worried about Kiani and Wena, and the smell made her nauseous.

She bowed her head. "I am Nohea, the alchemist." A guard escorted Nohea to the kahuna's hut that morning, while Uncle Haku requested to see Kiani and Wena, taking some of Nohea's salve and a pouch of food. As they split ways, Nohea longed to go with Uncle Haku, but she knew they all depended on her for their safety and freedom.

"Consider this space yours," said Noa, moving aside. His flower lei rustled when he moved, his long white skirt dragging on the ground.

The hut was bigger than Nohea expected, built against a large cliff, the same one that the waterfall fell from not far away. The hut smelled of incense, but Nohea figured the smell would be gone soon, as a comfortable breeze wafted through the large cut-out windows. Dry herbs hung from strings across the thatched ceiling. A large koa table sat in the center of the room, with a counter on the side, built of koa wood as well. Glass balls and vials laid about the room, along with rock slabs, mortar, and pestle.

"Will you be here often?" Nohea asked.

"I do work here, along with my apprentice, Makoa. But if you prefer your privacy, I can work from my hut," he said, bowing his head.

"I prefer to work alone."

"Of course." He bowed again. They stood there awkwardly, Nohea waiting for him to leave. Noa cleared his throat. "May I show you where things are around here?"

"I am happy to look through it myself," Nohea answered, her impatience growing.

The man bowed. "May I ask... have you cured many diseases before?"

Nohea didn't know what Noa was getting at. Was he curious? Or nosy?

Perhaps he just wants to feel better than me, she thought and folded her arms. "I've helped ease the pain of many sicknesses. I wouldn't say I've 'cured' something."

"But you've mixed different plants together to create a... concoction?"

"'Ae. Why?"

Noa tipped his head. "I have lived and worked here many years, but I have not been able to solve the queen's mystery. Would you mind if I checked in every once in a while? I am curious to learn from you." His fingers, full of bamboo rings, fidgeted nervously.

She felt sorry for him: an old man, of high status, with a lack of skills to create the queen's remedy. She heard herself say, "Yes, but if you are a bother, I will ask you to leave."

"Of course, of course," the kahuna said, bowing again.

She cleared her throat, and the old man finally got the hint. "'Ae, 'ae.... I'll leave you to it... Alchemist..." He muttered things to himself as he left.

Nohea sighed and looked about. Surely the kahuna had everything she needed. *How did I get us into this mess?* she thought.

In her mind, she imagined that any other slave would be content right now. She and Uncle Haku stayed in a nice little hut with all the luxuries Nohea ever dreamed of: multiple clean tunics, kiheis and wraparound dresses to wear, warm water baths, soaps made of the finest materials, and food in abundance. Some servants even visited that morning with fresh lei and crowns to wear.

The Māku'e lived in such a beautiful place, yet... last night. She couldn't get the image out of her head, the gashes on Kiani's back, the serpent-like face of Kawika, the inability to do *anything*...

She opened cabinets and looked in cubbies, examining the kahuna's materials, her feet making no noise as she moved about. The wooded area was so clean, and the grass so soft, even Nohea took her sandals off to walk around barefoot.

After what felt like ages, Uncle Haku approached from the path nearby. Out of the hut's large window openings, Nohea had a grand view of the path. Beyond the path stood the forest of tall trees, where the Māku'e's houses were built on the trees or in the shaded area below.

"Do you know your assignment yet?" Uncle Haku asked, as he stepped in, then leaned against the thick koa table, across from Nohea. She shook her head.

"No, but I met Noa. He's the kahuna around here." She folded her arms. "Are they alright?" She could hardly ask the question, filled with guilt for her lack of specifying the agreement with the queen. Her heart still raged within her at the queen's dishonesty and unfairness.

"'Ae, they are. But you might want to visit later. Wena's face got a good beating, and I thought maybe the salve you gave wasn't enough for both of them."

"They are... in prison?" A lump formed in Nohea's throat.

Uncle Haku nodded. "I don't like this at all. We must figure something out. An escape..."

Nohea swallowed then looked out the window past Uncle Haku. "Look. The queen approaches." Finally. *Finally* Nohea would receive her assignment.

Queen Awa took big steps, with a trail of guards and servants behind her. The queen entered the kahuna's hut, and the servant behind her carried a wood tray with a white cloth covering it.

"I have a problem, alchemist," said the queen, not even bothering with pleasantries. She wore so many yellow plumeria leis, she could have been naked underneath and nobody knew. Her flower crown was so thick too, that it covered her entire forehead. "I expect you to find a solution within two weeks." She nodded to the servant, who unveiled the tray.

On it sat a clear glass ball of something Nohea had never seen before. It was purple, shiny, and thin. Uncle Haku rubbed his chin.

"What is this?" Nohea asked, taking the ball and holding it up to the light.

"It doesn't matter what it is," said the queen. "I simply need you to find a way to reproduce it. A mo'o has decided to move into our waterfall, cutting our supply of this liquid short. I need you to find a formula to make more of it. Figure out what is in it, what ingredients we need, and how we can make it ourselves... understood?"

This was the queen's treasure behind the waterfall. Nohea nodded, "'Ae."

The queen held up two fingers, her nostrils flared. "Two weeks," she said, then whirled around to leave.

"Wait—" Nohea could hardly breathe, her nose and throat getting choked by the strong fragrance of the plumerias.

"What?" Queen Awa folded her arms, tapping her foot.

"My friends... you can't hurt them like that. Kiani got twenty lashings last night—"

"Your 'friends' were once part of the Māku'e, before they became outcasts. It's about time they took a turn in that waterfall."

"How can you do that?" Nohea stared into the queen's face, hatred building up inside all over again. "I refuse to find a formula for this if you keep hurting my friends." She placed the glass ball down hard, yet gentle enough to not break it.

"You wish to break our deal?" Queen Awa's dark eyes widened.

"No, I want you to keep your part of the deal—*you* promised safety. Sending my friends into the cave and then whipping them is *not* safe." This time Nohea folded her arms.

The queen's eyebrows creased. "That worthless Wena will take his turn tonight."

Nohea opened her mouth to say something but the queen interrupted, "And if he doesn't succeed, he *will* receive his whippings. It is the way of our tribe."

"But—"

"By taking their turns, they contribute their part to this society. Understand?"

Nohea frowned, a lump in her throat. "No. Absolutely not. Let them stay with us, not in the prison."

"I can't risk that." The queen rolled her eyes as Nohea kept her arms folded, not budging. Queen Awa continued. "I'm already letting that girl go free tonight... to find the messenger, so you should be grateful."

Nohea and the queen stared at one another, a wall of hatred growing thicker between them by the moment.

"Anymore questions?"

"If you're letting Kiani go, then let Wena go too."

"I'll think about it."

Nohea opened her mouth to protest but the queen whirled around, ignoring her.

"You lied," Nohea said to Queen Awa's back. The queen paused, but only for a moment. Then she left the hut.

Once she and the entourage disappeared, Nohea clenched her fists. "Ugh, I could just..." She held up her hands, exasperated.

"You did your best," Uncle Haku said again, putting his hand on her shoulder. He motioned to the glass ball. "You don't know what this is?" It was more of a statement than a question. Nohea shook her head.

"It's soran."

Nohea's stomach dropped. Soran. This magical liquid that everyone seemed to be highly interested in: King Ekewaka, the manō, and Queen Awa. Who else had an opinion about this?

Uncle Haku sat on a stool and rubbed his temples. "Of course she would..." He sighed and placed his face in his palms. Nohea sat next to him, realization sinking in.

The people *weren't* sick... the queen was sick! She wanted the soran for herself, so she sent people to the cave each night to retrieve it. But if they failed... The image of Kiani flashed in her mind and she shuddered. There was no way she could let the queen have that soran. No, she needed to help these people.

"Uncle, I have an idea..."

He glanced at her.

"There's a mo'o in the waterfall..."

"And?"

"The queen doesn't know me," she continued, her heart rate rising. "She doesn't know what I'm capable of..."

Uncle Haku looked up at her. "What do you mean?"

"Can you trust me on this one?" Nohea asked. They stared into one another's eyes for a moment.

Uncle Haku stood. "Alright, what do you need?"

CHAPTER TWENTY

Po woke, startled. He rubbed his eyes, sitting up, a cool breeze flowing through the woods around. Pulling his black cloak tighter around him, he rolled his eyes at the fact he'd let the fire die. He'd fallen into a deep sleep, a dangerous thing to do in the dark woods. He began rebuilding the campfire, leaning small twigs against one another and sticking tinder in the center.

Po yawned as he rubbed hibiscus sticks together. Smoke wisped from the rubbing place between the twigs and Po blew. The smoke turned into a flame and Po used it to light the tinder of his campfire.

The tree canopy allowed small pockets of starlight to shine through, but Po was too exhausted to lie down and admire the stars. He had scouted the outskirts of the forest for the last couple of days, hoping that at some point he'd bump into Nohea and Haku.

But it had been a futile and disappointing day.

He had been so confident in relying on the island for any sort of help, but no help came, and he had no idea where to go. He couldn't even feel a tension in the wind to give him any direction. He kept asking, throughout the day, "Have I done something wrong? Please tell me now..."

But the island remained quiet: no wind, humming, voices, nothing.

And to make matters worse, he had a nightmare, the same one that made him never want to close his eyes. It pulled at every heart string, thrusting him into a sea of self doubt. *I'll never be a sailor. I'll never get out to sea,* he thought. He'd never satisfy the yearnings of his heart.

Ever since he was a young boy, Po dreamed of sailing. But he never got to sail, only when he and his friends tried a few times in the night. Of course, they always got in trouble—no thanks to a tattle tale named Kamu—but Po still did whatever he could to get into the ocean.

His hānai father, Tua, built wa'a, and raised Po to do the same. Po knew everything about building canoes, from chopping the trees in the forest, to carving, weaving, and preparing the boats for sailing, but he never got to sail. Tua had his reasons: Po was too young, inexperienced, not a strong enough swimmer, and—the worst of the excuses—Po's place was in building the canoes, not sailing them.

It always felt so disappointing, and infuriating.

No wonder I left as soon as I had the chance, he thought, remembering how he randomly met sixteen year old Olukai on a road by the shore. Olukai had been alone, taking a break from training the village men to use the fire knife. At that point, Olukai had already gone on several missions for the king, and though he was only sixteen, he had the maturity of a kupuna. Their conversation came easily, and then Olukai, after looking out to sea for a brief minute, told Po the truth.

Olukai was the manō. He was a true descendant of the ali'i, and his ancestor, the great white shark patrolling the shores, confirmed that Olukai needed Po's help. Since then, Po became Olukai's messenger, going to various villages around the island, sharing the message that there was a descendant of the true ali'i still alive, and it certainly wasn't Ekewaka and Makana. Po's hānai parents didn't understand exactly what he did, and Po refused to share all the details. But they were kind enough to give him their blessing before he left.

And though many around the island believed Po's message, and serving the manō gave Po a sense of purpose, it did not satisfy his desire to be at sea.

No, he'd been on land for years. While Olukai sailed on the king's many missions, Po stayed on the island. Sometimes it felt defeating, but Po tried to stay optimistic. *Eventually,* thought Po. Eventually, when Olukai restored balance to the island and united all the people, Po would sail far away... he would leave this island forever, find an island and place of his own.

But that was never a guarantee, and as Po sat on the cold, grassy floor of the dark forest, he frowned.

He frowned because his recurring nightmare egged on the belief that Po would never go out to sea. He would never man a wa'a or be a sailor.

In his nightmare, the angles and perspectives always changed, but the story line remained the same:

Po stood at the back of a large wa'a—his very own wa'a—with cream sails and a smooth koa wood deck. He held the hoe uli, the steering paddle, and confidently guided the boat to his next destination. There was no island in sight. It was only a man and the sea. Po's hands were rough, his skin dark and tanned, his hair windswept and kissed by the sun, like he'd been out at sea for years. This was the dream.

And then something always went wrong.

Po rubbed his eyes again. He always hated this part, the part that ruined everything. He heard a voice, the same voice who spoke to his mind when he fell into a cave at the age of eight.

Always getting into trouble, Po and his friends found the cave of a mo'o, the large lizard creatures of the island, similar to what foreigners called "dragons." The villagers rumored a black mo'o lived in the forest near the village, but nobody wanted to take any chances. To the villagers, ignorance had always been bliss.

But not for Po. Even at the young age of eight, he connived his friends to join him in finding the black moʻo. Haunani, his hānai sister, had stumbled behind the group of boys, not yet graceful and coordinated as a dancer then. She protested multiple times, finally shutting her mouth when Po threatened to throw her into the cave first.

Po only intended to find the cave, but his curiosity peaked and he couldn't resist *going in.* The blackness, the density of the forest, the hot air coming from the inside... it drew him in. But just as he convinced himself that it was probably a bad idea, the rock beneath him broke and he tumbled below, into the blackness of the cave.

"Po!"

Even now, in the darkness of the woods, Po rubbed his head, remembering his friends calling after him, panicked. But the panic turned into jests and then, to be funny, his friends pushed Kamu into the cave. Kamu, the annoying, tattle-tale, rat of a person. Kamu's skeleton-frame shook violently, like he always did, never making eye contact, always fidgeting with his fingers.

"Are you alright?" Haunani screamed down, her voice thick with worry. "We'll get a rope and help you get out!" Then they were gone.

Kamu held his arms around his knees, and Po rolled his eyes, figuring that since they were stuck down here he might as well explore the cave. He lit up a torch from the pouch at his side and stepped into the darkness. He'd not gone three steps when he heard the breathing.

Something was definitely in the cave. And it was alive.

Po took a few more steps, surprised to see that the cave ended, though the wall before him looked like a glittery wall of black. He touched the wall, warmth seeping into his fingers, his heart beat rising.

It wasn't a wall... it was the moʻo. Po stepped back, his foot crunching on something. Bones. Bones. Everywhere, all around the cave. He was going to die.

Kamu saw it too. He buried his head in his knees, covering his neck with his skinny arms.

"Cl—climb..." Po muttered to Kamu as he stepped backwards, though he knew Kamu couldn't hear.

The moʻo's breathing stopped, and a large yellow eye opened right where Po had touched. The eye itself was as tall as Po. He couldn't imagine how big it meant the moʻo was.

Kamu, still quiet, rocked back and forth on his heels, still hunched over. And then Po heard the voice.... But not an actual voice. It was in his head.

Weak humans... I suppose an easy meal wouldn't hurt...

Po reached out with his mind and said, at the same time, "No! Wait!"

The moʻo sat up, and Po hid a gasp, seeing how large the cave was and how tall the moʻo's neck went. The moʻo turned his face to look closer at Po. *Did you just... speak to me?* It asked.

Po nodded. *ʻAe.* This time he sent the message straight from his own mind to the dragon.

The moʻo smiled, revealing rows of sharp white teeth. *Interesting.*

AT THIS MEMORY Po shook his head, standing up. He didn't want to relive the conversation with the moʻo. It had been absolutely terrifying. He and Kamu were lucky to still be alive. The moʻo let them go, stepping back into the cave and watching them climb out. He told Po if he ever returned, he better bring real food. Po gulped, hoping he wouldn't have to face those large yellow eyes again.

But the last words of the moʻo always bothered Po. They were the same words that echoed in his nightmares:

The island must perish, or all the humans will perish.

Po didn't know what it meant. In the dream, as Po sailed, those words floated through his head whenever the same moment occurred —the moment that always went wrong:

. . .

In the dream, the setting sun shone over the horizon, and three lonely figures appeared. Their look and behavior were not like the wa'a. These were foreigner ships, with large, white sails and wooden bodies like loaded, oversized bananas.

As they got closer, Po began to steer his canoe to the right, hoping to avoid them. But they turned too, and he knew this was a confrontation. At that moment, there were always yells and cheers, and when he turned around to see where they came from, he was surprised to find islanders, like him, on their canoes.

Except these islanders he did not know. They were not from the towns and villages he passed through on Kaimana Island. They were the elite warriors of King Ekewaka, those thick, soran-drinking warriors with huge bodies, black tattoos, heaps of muscle, and skin of rock. They were invincible. They threw their fire-pointed spears at the foreigner's ships. Some of the warriors swam to the foreigners' ships and climbed, killing all aboard, a blood bath. The foreigners were no match for the king and his warriors.

And then the King noticed Po. He jumped onto Po's wa'a, a fight immediately ensuing. Po resisted, defending himself with his fire knife, the same way Olukai had once taught him. But he had never been as quick or skilled with the knife as Olukai. The king grabbed the knife with his bare hands, and, much to Po's surprise, the knife did not cut the king's hand. Ekewaka tossed the knife into the sea. And then, the king grabbed Po's head and snapped it.

Po massaged his neck, hating that moment of the nightmare. An owl hooted nearby and a frog started croaking, as if to remind of Po's location in the dark forest.

"That's it," Po murmured and sat against a large tree. He wouldn't sleep the rest of the night. So he stared into the fire, kindling other thoughts besides this endless nightmare. He imagined what he might say when he saw Nohea and Haku again. Nohea had been so beautiful, unlike any girl he'd ever seen. When she first bumped into him, he remembered how shocked and intrigued she'd stared into his eyes. She probably didn't like him—he'd been too annoying in the lava tubes—but he secretly wondered if maybe he had a chance in the future. The thoughts distracted him, but only vaguely. The moʻo's words continued to haunt him: *The island must perish, or all the humans will perish...*

CHAPTER TWENTY-ONE

Nohea followed the guard to the prison. They walked through bushes, pushed through vine walls, and finally, climbed up windy stairs around an old, ancient koa tree. Nohea's leg felt like limp seaweed by the time they reached the top.

While she checked on Wena and *maybe* Kiani, Uncle Haku sat at dinner with the queen's counselors, wanting to gauge the politics of the dark tribe, and maybe even ask about the Māku'e's belief in the line of the true ali'i. Uncle Haku suggested she attend with him, but Nohea couldn't wait any longer. She needed to make sure Wena and Kiani were alright, and, though she would miss a meal, she had no other time in the day to visit. They'd already been at the Māku'e for four days. *Four days.*

And all her time she spent in the kahuna's little hut, mixing ingredients, feverishly preparing to carry out her plans. Plans that nobody else knew about, not even Uncle Haku.

She knew Wena had probably already got his whippings, as the queen wished, and she worried about him: his health, the wounds, and just *him* in general.

At the top of the tree, she stood on a large platform that rested on the strong, old branches. Several bamboo cages sat in a row at the edges of the platform. Shaped like cones, with only a few open spots to peer in, the cages looked claustrophobic and tight.

"Wena? Kiani?" Nohea looked through the cages.

The guard on watch rolled his eyes. "At the end."

Nohea hurried to the end of the row, her fingers trembling, heart racing. She could imagine them in their cages, sick, not being able to eat for days.

All the cages were empty, except the last one. A tall figure stood up as she approached. She wanted to hug him, just to know that he was alright. But all she could do was lean over to peer through the little hole, where two bamboo poles had been pulled apart, barely enough to squeeze a hand through.

"Wena?" She squinted to see inside the cage, wondering how they even got the prisoners in there. But then she saw a small bamboo door and a lock made of wood to hold it snug. Wena crouched down so she could see his face. He tried to smile, but it wasn't real.

Are you alright? She signed and mouthed. He watched her lips, like he always did.

He nodded, signing back, *Are you?*

She nodded, and they stared at one another. Nohea didn't know what to say. *What* in the world was she to say to this young man who protected her? Who risked his life to bring her here and... and she had him locked up? Unintentionally, of course, but still.

I'm so sorry. She felt awkward, hunched over the little hole, knowing that he, too, awkwardly crouched. He shrugged. *It's not your fault. You did what you could.*

Where's Kiani?

They let her go... to find the messenger. She was badly wounded from the whippings, worse than me. He frowned and shook his head.

Nohea held the bridge of her nose. *This is all my fault.*

It's not. We chose to come here.

Nohea felt a twinge of hurt, a moment of realization that he might hate her. And he had every reason to.

I will get us out of this, she signed to him. *I promise.*

Wena eyed her and Nohea's cheeks went warm. He signed, *Your uncle visited but I wasn't able to understand what's happening.* Wena continued to study Nohea. *Are you alright?*

How could he be worried about her, when he was locked up in a cage?

Nohea dipped her head, making sure the warden didn't see her signing. *I have a plan... it's too much to explain now, but I promise we'll get out of here.*

She reached into her pouch, pulling out the small gourd of salve. *This is for you...* In the darkness of the bamboo cage, Wena's face looked a little swollen. She wondered what his back looked like, her stomach knotting at the thought. He took it. *Thank you.*

Wena opened and smelled it.

"There's no uli in it, if that's what you're wondering," Nohea said aloud, as though offended he didn't trust her.

He glanced up at her and smiled. A real smile. *It's good to see you.* He mouthed the words, not even bothering to sign them. Nohea smiled back, a sense of calm filling her heart. How she wished to be more like Wena! He always seemed so put together, calm, and calculated, while she constantly felt frazzled, confused, and distressed.

Please be safe, he signed, as though to let her know there wasn't much else to discuss through that tiny, awkward hole.

She nodded. *You too.*

But she felt silly as she signed it, wanting to bang her head against the wall. Of course he couldn't do anything in that cage. Of course he'd "be safe." Her cheeks started burning so she nodded before hurrying off, not even murmuring a "bye" or "see you later."

Every part of her body felt ashamed: she got them into this mess. And while Wena quickly forgave and kept a cool head, Nohea knew she couldn't be like him now. She was mad at everything that had happened, starting with Queen Awa. Wena was quick to forgive, but Nohea was not. Nohea's hatred for Queen Awa burned more fervently now than ever before at seeing Wena's circumstances.

I'm going to get us out of this mess, came the reassuring voice in her head. The island below trembled in agreement. She nodded. Yes. She would get them out of here safely, and Queen Awa would have nothing to say about it.

Nohea wrote all her notes in the ancient language of the meha, a skill her mother taught her. She couldn't risk doing diagrams and symbols for fear that it would be too easy to decipher. The meha had a very complex writing system, and it would take days for anyone to decode her work.

Uncle Haku went about exploring the Māku'e, finding the exits, noting where they kept the horses, and planning a means of escape. On one evening, the woman, Kawena, stopped by the hut, bringing a beautiful array of fruits and warm sweet potatoes. Though Haku and Nohea had been given plenty to eat, Nohea smiled politely as Kawena stepped inside with her tray.

"Our majesty probably gives you plenty of food," Kawena said as she placed the tray on the large koa table. "But our people sense something different about you..."

Nohea bowed. "Thank you for your kindness."

"You will reproduce the soran?" Kawena's eyes looked hopeful.

"I will, and..." Nohea began to add more, but then cut herself short. "I will." Nohea couldn't trust anyone here, except Uncle Haku.

"We hope you will. The queen..." Kawena's warm brown eyes, so similar to Wena and Kiani's eyes, seemed to sparkle. "She has made it hard for our people. But if you can do it, we will sing praises of your name forever."

Nohea blushed. She never imagined people singing songs and chants about her. "Oh... no, it's not a problem."

"Was there anything you needed from the people?" The woman opened her palms. A light breeze pushed wisps of Nohea's hair into her face. She brushed it back.

"Maybe..." Would the woman be offended? "I have a friend in the cages. Could you take this tray to him?"

Kawena's eyebrows creased. "If you want to give this food to those outcasts, you can take it yourself."

Immediate tension filled the room, matching the woman's sudden change of tone. Nohea paused in her work. "Why are you all so against them? They didn't do anything to you."

"That boy is deformed," the woman spat back. "I will have nothing to do with them." She folded her arms, a defiant look on her face.

Nohea could see Kiani's nose, the tan color of Wena's skin, the long fingers."Those are your children, aren't they?"

Kawena lifted her chin. "They are a disgrace to our family. A shame. Ugly. Deformed. We should have killed them a long time ago." Her finger tapped against her arm.

Disgust welled up in Nohea's stomach. She wanted to flip the tray of food, scream at the woman to leave. How could the Māku'e live like this? How could they even *wish* to kill their children? But she took a calm, cool breath. "Please leave."

Kawena glanced at her, a look of surprise on her face. The anger rose within Nohea, her heart rate rising, her hands beginning to sweat as she bunched them into fists. Kawena nodded, and turned to leave, but Nohea added, "And take that tray with you."

A look of shame crossed the woman's eyes but then she frowned, picked up the tray, and walked out with haste. When her white kihei disappeared into the darkness of the night, Nohea slammed her fist onto the table. She hadn't felt so angry in a long time... not since... not since Kimo died. And then finding out that her mother set her up. And then Queen Awa lying right to Nohea's face.

But this... this stirred something deep within her. It almost felt like a desire for Wena—a longing to help him feel loved and accepted. She had a slave family, but his family—his *own mother*—despised him. She didn't want to treat Wena kindly because of pity though. She looked down at her notes, only seeing scribbles across the pages, but recommitted to her work. She would definitely get them out of here, and Awa *and* Kawena would have nothing to say about it.

Not much later that day, a knock startled Nohea and she looked up to see a young woman standing at the door of the hut. The young woman looked vaguely familiar, yet... Nohea was sure they hadn't met before. Nohea rubbed her forehead.

"Can I help you?"

The girl tipped her head. "May I come in?"

Nohea covered her notes with a slab of lava rock and nodded. The girl was tall, like Kiani. Her black hair was pulled into a thick braid, and her brown skin was the warm color of coconut fibers. She stepped in, eyeing Nohea's herbs, notes, and the glass ball of soran on the koa table.

"I wanted to introduce myself," the young woman said, brushing her long fingers across the koa wood table. "I'm Kukui, Kiani and Wena's cousin."

Oh great. More of their family. Nohea tried not to let the sour feelings from Kawena resurface, but she couldn't help making a face.

Kukui chuckled. "You met Kawena, didn't you?" Kukui had to be in her mid twenties, probably not much older than Kiani. Most girls around that age were already married off by their parents and bearing children of their own, at least that's what Nohea had been told about the customs outside of the king's fortress. Growing up a slave was different. A slave woman either found a slave man or a guard to marry, or they didn't marry at all.

But Nohea didn't want to pry. After all, the Māku'e tribe was coming off as more and more vain and annoying to her with their selfish customs and wicked traditions.

Kukui glanced around the room, as if to check that nobody else was around, then leaned in and whispered so softly that Nohea leaned in too. "You have to disobey the queen," she said.

Nohea's skin stood on end. "What do you mean?" she asked, not wanting to give away her plan, not trusting anyone around here, but especially anyone from Wena and Kiani's family.

Kukui's eyes were as dark and midnight as her hair, and the corner of her lip turned upward as she leaned back and folded her arms. "She is a very, *very* wicked woman."

"Why are you here?" Nohea cut in, tired of the riddles and games that people tried to play with her.

"Because I want to set my cousin free. And if you don't have a plan to dupe the queen, I'm getting Wena out of here myself."

Nohea blinked. "What?"

Kukui rolled her eyes, and in that motion looked so much like Kiani. "Tell me, do you have a plan to save him or not? Who's side are you on?"

"Not on the queens if that's what you're wondering." In spite of feeling slightly offended by Kukui's boldness, Nohea liked the girl. She shared similarities with Kiani, and Nohea wondered if they grew up together, until Kiani left.

Kukui eyed Nohea, and then they both smiled. "You've got something planned, I can tell," Kukui said. "I want in."

Nohea didn't trust people, but something about Kukui's confidence and boldness was different. The island breeze swept through the room, confirming to Nohea that Kukui was true. She would be a loyal friend.

Nohea glanced around before leaning in. "I haven't told Uncle Haku all the plans and I won't tell you either, but if you want to help, start collecting and hiding food in the hut we're staying at."

A wicked grin crossed Kukui's face. "Deal."

THAT NIGHT, after contemplating the complicated family members of Kiani and Wena's life, Nohea decided to visit Wena. Though tired from a long day of pressure cooking her "secret plans," Nohea left Uncle Haku sleeping in the guest hut and took food to Wena.

When she reached the cages, she shook the guard awake.

He grumbled. "What the—"

"Open Wena's cage," Nohea demanded, all of her patience gone.

"I'm not—"

"Open it now or you will regret it." She hadn't ever heard her voice so firm, confident, and commanding. She hated that it sounded like Queen Awa.

"What, so he can run away?"

"So he can stretch and get a decent meal. Open it now."

"If he tries anything, I'll kill you both." The guard, with his graying hairs, fat body, and lumpy nose, Nohea calculated, was no match for Wena.

He opened the cage, and she watched, fascinated, as the wooden key unlocked the pad. Before he could move out of the way, Nohea swung the bamboo door open and pulled Wena out by his wrists. He stood up, surprised, though relieved as he stretched his neck and his arms. Nohea watched, her mouth open, trying not to stare at all his muscles. He smiled and pulled her into a hug.

Their first hug. She wrapped her arms around his stomach and rested her head on his chest. Her hands felt the scars on his back, and she cringed. He felt warm, and she felt her anger—anger at Kawena, at this horrible situation she put everyone in, and her own confusion about her loyalty to the manō—lessen. Before it got too awkward, she gently pushed him away.

"I brought food. Please eat." She didn't bother to sign, knowing he could read her lips—or possibly *listen* to her voice through the wind, vibrations, and echoes. Pulling out food from her pouch, she passed him sweet potatoes, fish, and fruit, now feeling too embarrassed to look at him. She'd been so annoyed with everyone and everything, and now she felt silly. The guard stood not too far, grumbling, as he watched.

"I met your mother." Nohea shook her head as she spoke. "I was so mad at her...I had to see you." She sat cross legged on the floor, and Wena joined her, leaning against the bamboo cage door, his legs stretched out. He ate the food willingly, the purple bruise on his left eye looking less swollen, and green marks across his skin revealing the healing his body went through.

She handed him her gourd of water and he drank. He wiped his mouth and signed, *Why were you mad?*

Nohea blushed, looking away. "I can't believe that a parent would want to kill their own child." As she said it, a sting hit her heart. The truth that someone felt that way towards a child hadn't exactly angered Nohea because of her pity for Wena's situation, though it bothered her deeply.

But it angered her because of what Edena had done.

While it was true that Edena didn't leave Nohea for dead as an infant, Edena did leave Nohea for dead when she decided to burn the books. Edena had set her daughter up. Bitterness crawled through Nohea's stomach.

"Have you met her?" Nohea asked, glancing towards the guard. The guard could probably care less about their conversation, but he still watched, mumbling to himself that men and women shouldn't eat together.

Wena swallowed his food and nodded, his jaw tensing. *We met them in the woods when I was six. It was an accident—we stumbled into the wrong part. They chased us, threatening to kill us. But they didn't.*

Nohea's jaw dropped. "How can you be so calm about this?" Wena shrugged as he chewed on a banana.

Sometimes you have to accept what is and then let things go. He took another gulp of her water and placed his hand on her knee. It felt too intimate and Nohea's head began pounding.

Thank you for the food Nohea. And thank you for visiting me. He smiled, that *real,* charming smile that she was beginning to hate—and love at the same time.

Don't worry about my mother, or about me. Please, just focus on yourself. Kiani and I will be fine. We always have been fine. Nohea opened her mouth to say something but he shook his head. *Promise you won't feel angry about this anymore?*

He knelt on one knee and rested his elbow on the other, leaning towards her. Without thinking, she moved a wavy piece of his sun-kissed hair from his face. Then she swallowed hard and nodded.

He signed, *Let's get out of here as soon as we can, alright?*

She nodded again, but didn't have the strength inside her to say anything. Being so close to her, Wena had taken her breath away.

CHAPTER TWENTY-TWO

The king's fortress felt like a ghost town. Not even Kahiko stood smugly at the gate, waiting to hear of any kind of failure on Olukai's part. Some of the concubines and their daughters watched from a distance. Olukai saw Api among the crowd and she waved eagerly. He waved back, but kept the horse moving forward: getting the meha to the prison was his main goal.

"It's good to see you back," said one of the king's counselors, Ano, a fat man, a taskmaster over the slaves. A few male slaves stood behind him, carrying bundles of kapa.

"What's going on around here?" Olukai asked while motioning his men to take the women to the prison.

"That woman..." Ano leaned in closer, his breath smelling of fish. "She was supposed to be executed, but they put it off." Olukai realized Ano referred to Edena.

"Why did they put it off?"

Ano shrugged. "She got away."

"What?" Olukai looked at the meha walking behind him, slowly, none of them bothering to glance at him. "Does the king know?"

Ano shook his head, his frizzy black curls moving in unison. "We hope to get her before he comes back. He'll be very mad if he finds out."

Olukai nodded. "I thought the king ordered her executed immediately after the council—"

"It was delayed til after he left."

"How long has she been gone?"

"Three days now."

Olukai looked towards the garden in the distance. She could be anywhere at this point.

"We've checked the entire fortress," continued Ano, "and I've already sent a few warriors to spread out around the fortress."

"Did anyone help her escape?"

"I knew you'd ask," Ano said, a sly smile coming to his lips. "Walk with me." He brushed his slaves aside, and they hurried ahead of him.

Olukai glanced at his soldiers and the meha, making their way to the prison. They'd be fine.

He followed Ano to the remote eastern part of the fortress, where no huts had been built yet. The large koa walls loomed in the distance, and a group of slaves carried trunks to a pile in the field. The same slaves that carried the big bundles behind Ano joined the others slaves in the field. Olukai wondered what they were building out there, but he returned his attention back to Ano.

"She was locked up in the prison," said Ano, watching the slaves in the distance. "It was night time, and the guards have no recollection of what happened. They said their last memories were a loud noise, like thunder. Then they woke up, as if from a dream in the morning, and she was gone. But we found this." He pulled a bundle of cloth from his pouch and opened it.

Olukai frowned. Inside was blue powder, along with shredded ti leaves. "What is it?"

"I don't know, nobody knows!" Ano laughed. "But this blue powder was all over the prison huts... like magic."

"You think it was a kahuna?"

"I don't know what, or who, it was, but I've never seen anything like this."

Olukai folded his arms. He'd never seen anything like it either. In all of his travels, he'd not seen blue powder scattered everywhere. And then his hands dropped, a memory surfacing. Po had mentioned blue powder.

She threw it at the guards and it exploded. It couldn't have been *her, Nohea,* though. She was in the dark woods, hopefully with Po not far behind. So who could it have been? And then his thoughts started racing. It had to be another slave. No doubt the alchemist made more blue powder bombs and gave it to others. Perhaps the slaves had been successful in rescuing Edena. Perhaps he'd be able to find Edena, the most powerful sorceress on the island, if not Nohea, to get her help in destroying soran.

"Any ideas?" Ano watched Olukai's face.

"I'm thinking but nothing comes to mind," Olukai lied as he folded his arms again. "What are they building out there?" The slaves used stone machetes to cut back the weeds, and others continued to carry more supplies.

"Oh yes. It's the hut for the alchemist."

"For the alchemist?"

"King Ekewaka fully expects her to help him," Ano said, smiling. "Her skills will be much needed." Ano didn't need to say anything else. Olukai knew exactly that the king intended on Nohea to find a formula for soran. But Olukai also depended on Nohea, even though they'd never met. Worry filled his chest, but he shoved it down. Nohea would obviously choose to side with the manō, especially because the manō would have no slaves and was the true ali'i. Right?

"I appreciate his optimism," Olukai said, returning the smile, the facade he always put on.

"Even if she doesn't agree, the king plans on bringing her here, but you know that." Ano sounded pleasant, though Olukai knew it meant the king would use force.

But Po will get to her first, Olukai kept reassuring himself.

"If you will excuse me," he said to Ano. "I think I will investigate this case further. I'm sure we can find this woman. She can't have gone too far."

"'Ae, 'ae, that would be wise," Ano said. He nodded to Olukai then walked towards the slaves in the distance. Olukai wondered if Nohea ever knew Ano, but he brushed the thought aside. He needed to find Edena. If she was still alive, there might be a chance she could help him sooner than Nohea.

As he walked through the fortress, he passed Lopaka, speaking roughly to Like.

"Are you an idiot?" Lopaka shoved Like. Like, not having much balance to begin with, fell against the hut.

"He's going to kill you—" Lopaka started to say, grabbing Like's tunic and shaking him roughly. He pushed him to the ground.

"What's going on here?" Olukai interrupted.

Lopaka rolled his eyes. "Like is going to get himself killed *for real* this time."

"If you don't kill him first," Olukai joked, then reached out his hand to help Like. But Like pushed it aside, angry.

"She knows how to destroy soran," Like said.

"Edena?" Olukai asked, though he knew this already. Like looked at his older brother, frowning, and then nodded. "Where did she go?" Olukai continued.

"I don't know," Like started but Lopaka moved to shove him again. Olukai held Lopaka back.

"He's lying—father is going to kill you," Lopaka said, irritation tensing his body.

"Did you help her escape?" Olukai cut in.

"No, of course not!" Like said, stepping away, as if expecting a hit from Lopaka at any second. A pang struck Olukai's chest as he watched Like lean on his crutch. "I don't know what happened to her, but I do know she's the only person with the knowledge about soran."

"Because you spoke to her?" Olukai's jaw tensed, and Like

nodded. "Leave him be." He let go of Lopaka and stepped back. Like, the weaker, terrified, younger brother of Lopaka had never been much use. Olukai wanted to ask about "the curse," but he didn't dare push any more questions. They would be suspicious of him.

"I have an idea of where she went though," Like muttered as Lopaka and Olukai turned to leave.

"Alright, I'm going to—" Lopaka started, turning around to punch Like, but Olukai blocked it. It was as if Lopaka saved all his irritation to take out on Like, and Olukai found himself stepping between them when he could.

"Where is she?" Olukai asked calmly. "If we don't find her before your father gets back, he will kill anyone that's a suspect."

Like sighed and pointed towards the garden. "She doesn't know how to get out of the fortress—none of the slaves do. She's probably in the garden."

Olukai opened his mouth to ask how Like was sure of that, but he changed his mind. It was a good thing Po and Haku knew how to help Nohea out of the garden. And they would bring her back. That's all that mattered.

"Come on," Olukai said to Lopaka. "We need to find her. Let's get our warriors together. There's no time to rest. She can be anywhere in that garden..."

AND, unfortunately, they did find her in the garden. Dead.

It looked as though she'd succumbed to fatigue, her skin pale, no signs of struggle. No bites, no scratches or bruises, not even blood, just purple rimmed eyes, sunken cheeks, and terribly white skin. She had probably died of dehydration, though Olukai didn't understand why she didn't drink water in the garden.

Unless she'd been too crazy to understand her own situation.

Lopaka held his breath, looking disgusted as Olukai searched the body. But there was nothing to be found. No pouches. No belongings. Her brown eyes looked up at the sky, crazy, wild. He closed them, disappointed.

He motioned for one of his warriors to carry the body. No words passed between any of the men, an eerie, silent night as they walked through the garden with the dead body.

But Olukai's mind raced. Now he truly had to rely on only one person to discover how to destroy soran: Nohea. And he sure hoped she wasn't dead by now.

CHAPTER TWENTY-THREE

A few days after visiting Wena, Nohea worked busily in the hut, smashing herbs, boiling water, ready to put more ingredients under pressure to make bombs. She still hadn't revealed her plan to Uncle Haku, but she wanted to soon. A servant of the queen entered the kahuna's hut and bowed deeply to Nohea, which felt strange as the usual custom of the island was to kiss one another's cheeks.

"I come with a message from the queen," said the servant. She wore a white tunic with a sash around her waist, and a long white cape that fell to her calves. Flower leis adorned her neck. "She wishes to invite you to the celebration of the full moon tomorrow night."

"What is that?" asked Nohea as she used a stone mortar and pestle to break down some herbs.

The servant girl blushed . "Why... it is the celebration of the full moon." An obvious answer. "Do you not celebrate that?"

"I was once a slave," said Nohea, looking up from her work. "Like you. And we didn't get to join in any celebrations... if we could pull something together for one another then that was great... but we didn't really celebrate anything..."

The girl cleared her throat. "We do not use the word 'slave' here. It is an honor to serve the queen. I am her humble servant."

Nohea didn't believe the girl. "Do you get to attend the celebrations then?" she asked. The pretty girl shook her head. "No, but it is an honor to serve."

Brainwashed, Nohea thought to herself. But then Nohea wondered if she, herself, had been brainwashed as a slave.

No... She remembered the many moments of anger, the unguarded thoughts that made her want to shove the task master, or scream to start a rebellion. *I was definitely* not *brainwashed,* she confirmed to herself.

"Would you be interested in attending?" the girl asked, fidgeting her colorful lei.

"Well... sure, I don't see why not."

"The servants will deliver flowers for you to wear," said the servant and bowed before leaving, her white cape trailing behind her.

THE NEXT NIGHT, Nohea put on the white dress, which actually had a sleeve on her left arm, and her white kihei she tied on the other arm. She fumbled, the white fabric slipping through her fingers as she kept thinking about Wena. Was he alright? After their last encounter, she'd left him, feeling awkward, yet giddy, like she was a little girl anticipating some special event.

"You seem distracted," Uncle Haku said when she stepped into the main area of the hut. He approached with fresh flower leis, and Nohea hoped her ears hadn't turned red.

"We need to get out of here," she muttered, trying to think of something to say besides bringing up her conversation with Wena.

"Yes, I know." Uncle Haku helped tie her white kihei, as her fingers trembled. That very day she'd created the biggest bombs she'd ever made. She designed them carefully so they blew up with the slightest bit of fire. And, she carefully hid them in the trunk of a tree behind the kahuna's house. Her plan was going to work. "When are you going to tell me this plan of yours?" It was as if Uncle Haku could read her thoughts.

He wore a long, white palekoki, with a white kihei across his shoulder. He helped Nohea put on the heavy lei and flower crown, made of large hibiscuses, and her wristbands and anklets made of red ti leaves. Uncle Haku wore a vibrant green ti leaf lei, his hair pulled up into a bun on top of his head.

She glanced around and motioned for Uncle Haku to get closer to her. Then she cupped her hand and whispered into his ear. "I'm going to wake the moʻo."

His eyes widened, then he laughed. "If only I had half the wit and courage you had..." Then he laughed again, a lightness in his eyes. She knew he'd been worried the entire week, scrambling around to find the exits, planning their escape in quiet tones. But this had to work. When the moʻo awoke, furious, the people would scatter like ants, and the moʻo would destroy the hahau tree.

She could see the plan unraveling in his mind. For the last couple of nights she asked Uncle Haku to hide extra food, but never explained why. Extra food appeared in their hut, no doubt dropped off by Kukui. When the timing was right, Nohea wanted to stuff all of the food into the tree, attracting the moʻo when it awoke.

Nohea tried to hide her smile, knowing she'd pleased her uncle. The queen asked for her to find a way to get more soran, and that was Nohea's exact intention. *Move the moʻo,* she thought, *get more flow of soran... that's what the queen asked.*

What the moʻo did after waking was not their problem. Maybe he'd crawl back into the cave. Maybe he'd find a new home. But by that point, Nohea hoped that she, Wena, Uncle Haku, and Kiani would be long gone.

Uncle Haku laughed. "It's brilliant. No wonder you've had me collecting food. I'll keep doing that, and find a way to free Wena." Her heart leaped at the mention of Wena's name.

. . .

Anxiety filled Nohea's stomach. She'd never attended large celebrations, as the slaves rarely had the means to hold something like this. Furthermore, in the back of her head, she worried about Po, Kiani, and mostly Wena. Why didn't he get to come? It wasn't fair.

As she and Uncle Haku left their little hut, she blinked into the moonlight. It cast a misty glow on the trees and ground. By now she understood the layout of the wooded kingdom, so full of tall koa trees, where many of the people had built stairs to their homes high above. Others lived in huts on the mossy forest floor, but in the midst of it all was the large clearing, with the hauhau tree and grass as soft as clouds.

There was no need to wear sandals anywhere in the wooded kingdom, because everything was so soft to walk on. Even before they left their hut, Uncle Haku and Nohea heard the drums coming from the clearing, as well as cheers, whoops of laughter, and chanting.

As the chanting grew louder the closer they got, Nohea had no doubt there would be hula dancing. Her stomach fluttered in nervousness, like something was slowly flying up her throat, as they approached. She held Uncle Haku's arm, and he leaned over to her. "One day, we will have many celebrations like this, where everyone can come and participate."

Nohea nodded, though she began to wonder if she'd even *enjoy* this celebration. She never learned to dance, as a slave, and she didn't know the first thing about socializing at parties. As they neared the crowd, Uncle Haku's words filled her mind: *One day... everyone can come and participate.* She could almost see the faces of her slave family in the faces of those dancing and celebrating.

"It's beautiful," she said. The moon above was so big and bright, it almost hurt to look at it.

They stood to the side, watching the commotion. As the drums played and echoed through the night, a longing went through Nohea's heart. Watching every person there, with their joyous expressions, their pleasure in dancing, and having fun made her want to jump in.

But she couldn't. It wasn't fair to participate while Wena was in prison, or while Kiani wandered the forest alone, looking for Po. Furthermore, Nohea felt like an outcast. She caught sight of Queen Awa sitting on her throne, a glass ball in her hand. Each time the moonlight fell onto the liquid, the color purple glinted within. Nohea frowned.

As if feeling Nohea's negative vibe, the queen made eye contact, raised an eyebrow, and shifted to one side. Then, her lips turned upward, like she knew something Nohea didn't. Though Nohea wanted to return a cold smile, because Nohea held her own secrets from the queen, she only glared and looked away.

"You must be Haku."

Amidst all the chaos, Nohea turned to see Kukui had approached them. A new song started and all the people cheered, every person joining in, including all the bystanders around Nohea and Uncle Haku. A wave of claustrophobia overcame Nohea as bodies pressed and danced in unison all around her. She stepped closer to Uncle Haku, the noise and movement making her head start to hurt.

Kukui yelled so they could hear her above the noise. "I'm Kukui, Kiani and Wena's cousin," she said to Uncle Haku and they kissed one another's cheeks. Kukui glanced at the queen, making sure her attention was elsewhere, which it was.

The queen openly flirted with a large man who looked to be one of her guards, as he, like other men his size, wore exotic green leis. The man was tall and bulky, like the one who carried Wena on the day they came to the dark tribe. As Kukui and Uncle Haku yelled to hear one another over the commotion, Nohea stared at the men around the queen.

It was unusual, unnatural even, to see such large men. Their bones, muscles, and bodies seemed... massive. And they looked strangely youthful so that they couldn't be much older than their mid twenties. What made it stranger to Nohea was that these men, around the queen, were the *only* ones in the whole Māku'e who were so large. When Nohea glanced at the tribe members, they looked normal. Sure there were some tall folks, but not as tall and bulky. The queen's guards though... What made them all so similar in shape and size? And how did they look so young?

As she stared, trying to focus on something other than the chaos around her, someone grabbed her hand and yanked her through the crowds. Amidst the commotion, she'd been separated from Uncle Haku and Kukui quite a ways. Disoriented by the faces of people she didn't know, Nohea panicked and looked to the hand that grabbed hers.

Her stomach twisted in knots as she realized it was Kawika.

"Let go of me!" she cried, trying to resist, but he held onto her so tightly, that her wrist burned. He pulled her out of the crowd, and into darkness. Then she was surrounded: surrounded by a group of boys, slightly older than her, no doubt Kawika's friends.

She tried to wriggle her hand free from Kawika's grasp, but his fingernails dug into her skin as he squeezed her wrist even tighter.

"This is the alchemist," he told his friends. "I was the one who found her—isn't she a sight?" He turned around to stroke her cheek. His friends laughed.

One of them belted. "Kawika said you both kissed, but we don't believe him."

"What?" Nohea's face turned bright red. "I would never—"

"Come on Kawika! Prove it!"

Nohea violently began to free her hand as Kawika grabbed her face. She reached to push his face away, but he only caught her other wrist and she panicked.

"Leave me alone—help!"

The boys laughed even louder. Kawika leaned in but just as he was about to close on her mouth with his thin lips, he lurched back, holding his head.

"Leave her alone, all of you!" A tall girl, with two long braids, stood there holding Kawika's hair.

"Ouch, let go!" Kawika yelped, and the girl tossed him aside, his face being whipped in a weird direction. "Go!" she said, and the boys scurried away, laughing.

"Are you alright?" she asked Nohea. Nohea hadn't realized she'd been crying as she rubbed her bloody wrists. She nodded. "I'm fine. Thank you."

"If Kawika ever bothers you again, let me know." She motioned with her head so that her braids fell behind her back, then started to walk away.

"Wait—" Nohea said, now curious to know how this girl found and saved her. Her soft pointed nose looked familiar. "What is your name?" Nohea asked.

"Maka."

"Do I know you from somewhere?" Nohea had never asked that question before, but it felt right at that moment.

The girl sighed. "Not really. My twin is Wena, and my older sister is Kiani though."

Nohea froze. She didn't know that Wena had a twin. Did he and Kiani have a lot of siblings and family? Did that cause a lot of pain for him, or for Kiani?

"Oh," was all that came out.

The girl shrugged. "We live over there." She pointed to a hut built on one of the large koa trees. "My mother seems to dislike you, but the rest of us are grateful you're here." She folded her arms. "If you need anything, please let us know." Then she disappeared into the crowd.

"Nohea!" Uncle Haku and Kukui appeared. "Are you alright?" they both asked. Kukui gasped at Nohea's bloody wrists.

"Who did that?" she demanded.

"I'm fine." Nohea allowed Uncle Haku to wrap his kihei, then his arm around her shoulders.

"Sorry we lost sight of you," he said. "That was irresponsible. Let's leave. I'm done. This is no celebration." Nohea hadn't heard such anger in Uncle Haku's voice before. She eyed him.

"Look," was all he said and raised his eyebrows, motioning above them.

For the first time that night, Nohea noticed frames of bamboo cages, so high they were easy to miss, hanging from the koa trees above. And there were people in them, watching.

Her heart sank. Wena was in one of the cages. He looked down at the crowd, a loneliness in his eyes, yet holding his pride. He would never be able to join them, because they did not accept them. He would always be the outcast to them, no matter how good of a person he was, no matter how well he listened and understood others.

And then the people below celebrated, so unaware of the broken hearts above them, of the loneliness, the abuse those had suffered at their own hands.

"The queen will pay for this," Kukui said, her fists clenched, adding, "So will his awful parents."

While Nohea didn't know the whole family situation, she felt grateful for Kukui's bravery, so much like Kiani.

Nohea nodded to Uncle Haku. "Yes, let's get out of here. I have work to do." Kukui escorted them back to their guest hut, talking about all the queen's frivolous celebrations and activities, like this moon festival.

"She acts as though she is the perfect alaka'i," she said, adding, "And the people believed in her, forgetting all about the hauhau tree." Her pace quickened.

"But not me," Kukui continued. "I refuse to be under the rule of a dictator, and I'm so grateful the manō will take his place." At some point, Kukui had visited Kiani and they talked about the manō, which proved once more to Nohea that people really did believe he was a true ali'i.

Kukui's words were lost on Nohea's ears as a flame began to burn again within Nohea. Not only had she been treated poorly as a slave, but there were others on the island whose hearts hurt, who were broken, hurting, because they would not be accepted, no matter what.

She began to finally believe they needed the manō. They needed a new ruler to cleanse and unite the island.

The next couple of days, Nohea made several more bombs, digging a small imu in the back of the kahuna's hut. Noa and Makoa, his apprentice, came by a few times but she shooed them away, saying she needed her privacy.

She used some of the plants she found in the area, including plenty of uli. She crushed lehua blossoms, and collected moss to keep some of her ingredients moist, like the ti leaves used to wrap the bombs.

She wondered about the moʻo, knowing that each night someone risked their life by going into the cave. Yet, they always failed, and someone got whipped at the hauhau tree. She thought that maybe the loud drums from the celebration would stir the moʻo, but he was clearly fast asleep. She spent some time hiking around the falls, and one day, while Uncle Haku took food to Wena, decided to peek behind the waterfalls and see the moʻo herself.

The water fell gently as she walked along a narrow ridge to the cave entrance. This was a nice, hidden spot, a perfect place for a moʻo. She'd never seen one in real life, but heard stories of how they enjoyed hidden caves, especially by waterfalls.

As she walked along the narrow ridge, she tried not to look down at how far the cliff fell. Nohea wondered, too, if seeing the pool of soran would give her an idea of how to help the manō destroy it.

When she peeked into the cave, the light reflected on the moʻo's scaly green body, casting beautiful rays across the cave walls. His wings lay flat out to the side, translucent white with hints of rainbow colors. He was a beautiful moʻo, and so large, he could probably swallow her whole. She didn't see his face, but his body was large enough that she could guess at the size of his head.

Crouching on the ground, Nohea tried to catch a glimpse of a soran pool beneath the dragon, but saw nothing. No pool of soran, not even a hint of purple liquid anywhere. Heat escaped the cave, making her sweat. She wiped her forehead, realizing it was the moʻo's hot breath. How could he sleep in this heat?

After she examined his cave, she went back to Noa's hut. Uncle Haku was already back, a look of panic on his face.

"Did they see you?" he asked eagerly. "I've been looking for you all morning—did they see you?"

She shook her head. "Who?"

"The king."

Her jaw dropped. "The king?"

"They're here—they're all here... Ekewaka, Kahiko, and a band of his warriors."

"And the queen let them in?" Nohea rushed to the windows to look out, but Uncle Haku pulled her back. "We must go now," he said. "Before they find you. They *know* you're here."

"Why would the queen let them in?" Nohea's eyes went wide. "She lied, again. She said she would protect us. She lied!"

"Grab your things, hurry!" Uncle Haku grabbed her papers and important belongings.

"Uncle Haku..." Nohea felt her face going pale now. The queen's servant was approaching the hut.

She did the only thing she could think of. "You must hide."

"We go together!" he said, but there was no way out the back of the hut besides the front door and windows, because the hut was placed against the mountain.

"Please uncle, trust me," said Nohea. She threw a kapa blanket over him in the corner of the room. The servant burst into the door, breathless. She bowed deeply, though rushed.

"Alchemist," she said, "I bring news from the queen."

"ʻAe?"

"King Ekewaka has come with an offer for you, but the queen has promised your protection. She wishes to know if you would like to speak with him."

"No..."

The servant girl made a face. "No offense, but are you sure? He has a great band of warriors, and... the negotiations may not be that bright if you don't speak with him."

"The queen said she would protect me. Is she not confident about that offer now?"

The servant girl blinked. "She is confident. But the king seems like he is ready to negotiate aggressively if not given an audience with you."

"So the queen's people are in danger?"

No answer, only a stare.

"Fine, I'll speak with him, only if he promises no harm to me or this people." The servant girl nodded and rushed off.

As soon as she left the hut, Uncle Haku threw the blanket off. "That's it," he said. "We must leave. *Now!*"

"Wait..." said Nohea, taking his arm. "I think I have an idea."

"No, not now—"

"Listen... I cannot use this old kahuna's things to create a bane for soran. I'm sure the king has much more resources. I'm sure I could—"

"And the manō does too. He is wealthy, so wealthy he could find and buy you anything you need. You don't need to risk your life in the king's fortress to figure out how to destroy soran. We *must* go!" Uncle Haku started for the door.

For all the time they'd been fleeing in the forest, Nohea realized that she'd been fearing—fearing for her life, Wena's life, Kiani's life, and Uncle Haku's life. As a slave, that had been natural. Slaves never knew what day would be their last. But now, after all the injustices she'd seen, she thought maybe, *maybe* she could use the king to discover how to destroy soran.

"I am sure we can negotiate something," she calmly told Uncle Haku.

"Please... he is not who you think he is." Uncle Haku still stood by the door, looking out and then back to Nohea.

"I would like you to hide," Nohea said. "Get yourself out of here if you can. Free Wena and find the messenger. I will do what I can to destroy the soran..."

At that, the queen's entourage started down the path to the kahuna's hut. Uncle Haku let out a cry. He placed his hands on her shoulders. "We must run—"

"No, *you* must run. Hurry!"

His eyes were pained and panicked. "You stubborn girl—"

"Don't worry about me, just *go!*" Nohea shooed Uncle Haku away. He dashed out the front door and into the forest before anyone could see him.

Nohea waited calmly, cooly, watching as the queen led Kahiko, the king, and the band of warriors.

She'd never seen the king up close. He was very tall, so tall that he loomed over the queen, and even her unnaturally large guards. His body was massive and bulky, as though made of rock. His band of warriors and Kahiko also looked equally as big. The queen stood at the door of the hut.

"You have spoken, and the king will speak to you. He has asked for privacy, so we will stand a distance," Queen Awa said, her chin up to Nohea.

Nohea didn't bother to bow her head, nor did she bother to say thank you. So she folded her arms and waited.

The entourage stepped back a ways, and the king entered, bending over because the doorway was too small. Up close she could see the details of black tribal tattoos on his dark brown arms, and his face clearly. With a pudgy, wide nose and thick lips, he looked like an ancient islander, the ones spoken of in legends and folktales. It was no wonder people thought him an aliʻi.

His dark hair was pulled back into a thick braid, and oil glistened on his huge forehead. He towered over her, like a giant. She couldn't recall ever seeing anyone that large.

Of all his intimidating features, she couldn't stop staring up at his eyes. One eye was golden, and the other a dark brown, almost black.

How did they *both* have a golden eye? Her interest peaked, though she didn't show it.

"I have waited for this moment to meet you," said King Ekewaka, his voice booming. Nohea could tell he tried to be quiet, but his voice was too deep and it rumbled through the hut.

"Why is that?" she asked. She tried to sound disinterested, but it had become obvious that she was a valuable asset to *both* Queen Awa and King Ekewaka. They both wanted and needed her, and Nohea told herself to keep using that to her advantage. She kept her breaths steady, even though everything about the king felt quite frightening, even more intimidating than Queen Awa.

He smiled, revealing his white teeth. "I've heard many things about you... and the most important is that you are an alchemist, the only one on this island."

He pulled a stool and sat on it so she didn't have to look up at him. The stool made a noise, like it might break under his weight. He had so many muscles, and he was at least three times as wide and round as Nohea. She sniffed and folded her arms.

"We have so much in common," he continued. She cringed at that statement. "You've been creating cures and medicines for the slaves, which I commend you for. And I've been trying to find the cure for every disease this island may face."

Nohea started mashing some herbs in her mortar and pestle, more of something to look at besides his strange eyes. She wondered if that's why people looked at her weird. In a way, it was disorienting and she wanted to stare. But that would be rude.

"You weren't born when the foreigners came," he said, looking past Nohea into the distance. "They brought all of their strange goods, many of which we rejoiced in. They brought their knowledge, their science, their weapons, their complicated systems of communication, all of which we needed. But they also brought their diseases... and those diseases killed almost every person on the island." He paused. "Those diseases killed my parents, and there was nothing—*nothing*—anyone could do. We could only watch in horror as the bodies filled the waters, the fields, the streets, the huts."

He sighed, and their eyes met. Nohea knew it all too well: the ghost generation. It was why so many didn't know their parents and grandparents. It was why there were plenty of young people, and hardly any kupuna.

"I had to do something, so I rose up to lead the people... and it worked. Until my brother, Makana, rose up against me. He was selfish, wanting the island for himself, wanting to let the foreigners back in *even though* he had witnessed the devastation himself. He wanted their goods, their weapons, the accolades of it all. So I had to do what I could to protect our island..."

He looked at Nohea. "Do you know what I did?" She shook her head, the herbs making crunching noises as she mixed.

"I made an agreement with the mermaids... to keep *all* foreigners off our island. I would pay them with soran, this precious liquid." He reached for the glass ball of purple liquid and swished it around. "I have paid them ever since, and I will continue to pay them until I find a remedy, something to protect our people from the diseases of the outside world, something that would make us immune to the ailments of life, to preserve our blood, our heritage."

So that was the deal with the mermaids. Did the king know about the rumored great shark circling the island, and that it was now the reason nobody could go out or come in?

Ekewaka put the glass ball back down on the table. "And then I realized... the remedy *is* soran. I have tried it myself. I feel stronger, healthier, alive..." He looked down at his long, thick, brown fingers. "But my problem is that I'm running out of soran... I wish to distribute it to all the people, but I can barely keep up with paying the mermaids for the safety of our island."

"So you want me to learn how to reproduce it?" Nohea asked, folding her arms again. "I'm not sure if you know, but that's exactly what Queen Awa wants from me."

The king nodded. "'Ae, I understand that's what she wants. But she only wants it for *her* people. I want it for the entire island. If we can mass produce this precious liquid, we can save our people, open trade to the outside world, keep advancing, learning, and growing, all while preserving our precious bloodlines."

Nohea raised her eyebrows. "Why is the bloodline important?"

"Because I've seen too much death and suffering, and half the island wiped out, to help me realize that if we do not protect ourselves, nobody else will. The outsiders will take and take from us, killing us off with their infectious diseases. But if we have something... something to protect us, like this soran, we have nothing to fear. We can let our canoes set sail to other islands. We can let the outsiders back in. Can you see it, Nohea?"

As much as she hated to admit it, she did see it. Everything he said would make the island better. It made complete sense: create more soran and open the island back up for trade, knowledge, and the latest tools and resources. She could also only imagine the wisdom from the outside world. If her mother taught Nohea a fraction of what she learned from those books in the king's library, then Nohea felt that there was so much more to learn.

"If you come with me to the fortress and find a way to mass produce soran," King Ekewaka said, leaning forward. "If you can use whatever natural ingredients and resources from the island, I'll have a place for you on my personal council. He added, "And I will unify Kaimana island with soran remedy for all."

Nohea bit her lip. This vision... it was exactly what *she* wanted. She wanted a remedy for all diseases, and more knowledge from the outside world. Soran answered all of these questions.

But the manō... her mind spun in circles, questioning her allegiance to her dear, sweet uncle, and her trust that he served the right leader. The entire time she hadn't said it aloud to Uncle Haku, but she thought the manō a coward. Why didn't he rescue her himself? Why didn't he reveal himself?

Because he's a fraud. The idea struck her so suddenly that she blinked hard. The manō couldn't have been real. As much as she loved and admired Uncle Haku, there was something totally wrong about the manō. Maybe all these people had been deceived, including Wena and Kiani, who looked so hopeful when they heard of the great white manō rising again, reminding its heir of his rightful place.

But King Ekewaka was the heir, the rightful heir. Why else would the island allow him to rule so long? And how else could he have risen up to rule?

She cleared her throat, her consciousness eating at her. "I have conditions," she said.

"Yes, anything."

"You must convince the queen to free Wena."

The king bowed his head. "I am sure I could arrange that." He held out his hand. "Do we have a deal?" Nohea glanced at his hand, confused.

"Oh, it is the foreigner's way of doing business... you shake it," he laughed .

"Why?"

"It's a symbol of sealing the agreement."

She hesitated, thinking about all the people who would think of her as a traitor, the most important person being her uncle. And, possibly, Wena. Then other faces flashed into her mind: Nui, Kimo, her slave family, and even Like, the king's own son.

And her mother, Edena. Uncle Haku's words came to mind: *Don't let your mother's death be in vain...*

Nohea shook her head. "No deal... you killed my mother."

"Ah..." King Ekewaka nodded, a sadness in his eyes. "Yes. She did a terrible thing to you, Nohea. She is still alive, but she must be executed as soon as I return, if it hasn't been done already."

"What do you mean?"

The king sighed and touched his forehead. "I did not want to tell you until the time was right... but I will do it now." His countenance looked heavy as he met Nohea's eyes. "I am your father."

CHAPTER TWENTY-FOUR

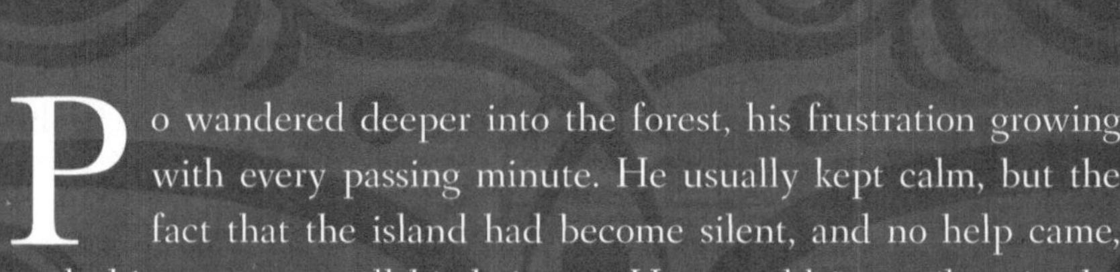

Po wandered deeper into the forest, his frustration growing with every passing minute. He usually kept calm, but the fact that the island had become silent, and no help came, made him want to pull his hair out. How could it go silent in the moment he needed it the most?

What did I do wrong? He kept thinking, over and over.

He didn't want to admit it, but he was hopelessly lost. He'd wandered so far into the woods that he only knew heading east, where the sun rose, could possibly get him out of here. Although, it was still hard to tell where the sun shone. The canopy of the trees intertwined high above him, allowing only hints of sunlight onto the forest floor.

He missed the light of day. The forest air was muggy, making his skirt and kihei stick to his skin. The air grew more humid the deeper he went. It seemed to press around him, a claustrophobic effect that made Po nauseous.

But he kept going, passing old kupua who groaned, yet didn't try to attack, as Po gave them warning glances. He passed plenty of rivers and waterfalls. But there was no sign of life.

Finally, after wandering a few days in the woods, he sat to take a break, swiping away sweat and resting his head against an old koa tree. A gurgling river passed by his left, casting a coolness in the air, a refreshing break from the sticky humidity of the forest. At this point, maybe he'd try calling Nohea and Haku. They might they'd hear him.

Or maybe someone else would hear and hunt him down. He scooped water from his hands and washed his face. The coolness eased Po's anger. He ran his wet fingers through his golden hair and studied the ground, always looking for hints of footprints, life, anything.

But there was nothing. He doubted any footprints could be found around here anyway. The forest most likely changed shape, color, and texture everyday.

I should get back, he thought, his shoulders slumping, defeat overcoming him. He was pretty sure he'd scoured the entire woods. Where could Nohea and Haku possibly be? At this point, they probably left the woods.

Or they're with the Māku'e. The thought had passed his mind many times, but he had no idea where to find those people. He only knew they lived deep in the woods, hence his determination to go deeper and deeper.

A twig snapped in the distance behind him. He readied his knife, sensing a presence. Standing, he glanced around, prepared to attack. The tall, thick foliage and ferns covered everything, making it difficult to see into the distance.

The leaves rustled in the bushes before him, the ground crunching with light footsteps. It was definitely a person. A pig would've run faster through the foliage, devastating everything in its path.

A hand came out first through the ferns, and then a face—a girl! Immediately he noticed her hair was too dark to be Nohea, and a wave of disappointment overcame Po.

"Stop right there," he said, his knife ready. The girl looked up, relief crossing her face.

"You must be Po," she said, stepping through, ignoring his warning. She stood at the same height as Po, her slender body revealing toned arms and legs. Her brown eyes carried a certain warmth, and her tanned skin looked like the color of coconut husk fiber. She wore a white tunic, though it had smears of mud, dirt, and tiny splatters of... *blood.*

"Are you alright?" Po asked, letting his guard down a moment. Then he straightened out. "Who are you?"

She walked past him to the river, scooping up water and drinking. Po scrunched his face. "Your back!" When she splashed the cold water on her face, her dark hair fell on either side of her, revealing a torn, bloody tunic and plenty of lashes, some still looking fresh, across her back.

"That looks really bad. We need a salve."

"I have a salve." She reached into the pouch at her side and pulled out a little gourd. "It's from Nohea."

Just the mention of Nohea's name made Po want to jump. Maybe he didn't fail on this mission after all. "You found her? Where is she? And Haku?"

The girl smiled sadly and raised her palm as if to slow him down. "They're both fine. They're with the Māku'e. My brother and I guided them."

"And... what are they doing there?" Po reached into his own pouch to offer her some food. She shook her head, touching her forehead and sitting down on the grassy floor. Then she opened the gourd, full of salve, and began to reach her arms awkwardly behind her to put it on her back.

"Do you need help?"

"No." She sounded almost annoyed. "You were close, you know," she added. "The Māku'e are not far from here. You would've reached them, or been spotted by a scout soon enough."

What a relief. Po let out a sigh, his feelings of stupidity dissolving. "So who are you again?"

"Kiani." She closed the salve and placed it back into her pouch. "My brother and I were taken prisoners, but they released me to find you. Nohea has been tasked by the queen to make soran."

Soran. Po frowned. The queen wanted soran, and that was already a bad sign. She was no better than Ekewaka.

"And you're escorting me to the Māku'e?"

She nodded. "If that is what you desire. I assume it is. Haku said you were the messenger for the manō."

So she knew about the manō. Po rubbed his chin. If Haku trusted her with that information, then she had to be a friend. Po asked, "So you believe in the manō?"

She nodded, "Of course. I believed Haku's words the minute he said them. It feels right. A true ali'i wouldn't kill people to obtain soran. We've waited for a true ali'i, a true king or queen of the island to rise all our lives. With the great white shark back in these waters, I'm confident he's asked his true descendant to rise."

Po smiled, the first one in their interaction, relaxing his shoulders. "So when can we go? I really need to get those two out of here."

"You will take them to the manō?" Kiani asked, her eyes lighting up.

"'Ae."

"If I take you back to the Māku'e, can I meet the manō too?" Even in their brief interaction, Po couldn't help feeling sorry for the girl. With all the scars on her back and the desperate look in her eyes, he couldn't say no. It felt right. She should meet the manō.

"'Ae," he said. The girl swallowed hard, lifting her chin, as if remembering to not display any emotions.

"We can leave in the morning," she told him. "It gets dark fast in these woods, and it's better to camp for the night than risk getting lost."

Po nodded, already pulling out his twigs to start fire. His spirits rose again, even though he still couldn't feel the whispers of the island. Perhaps, in a way, it had been listening, but waited for the perfect moment to send help.

Kiani found some branches to build the campfire. She was so quick, Po wondered if she'd done this her whole life. She even had coconut fibers in her bag to use as tinder. As the fibers caught fire, Po felt a flame in his heart. They were going to find Nohea and Haku. They were finally, *finally* taking the alchemist to meet the manō.

As the two warmed up by the fire, Po piped up, eager to know about this young woman. Kiani shared her story, a tale of being an outcast with her brother, Wena. Po marvelled as she talked about their many adventures throughout the island, all the places they'd gone.

"But nothing would be so incredible as meeting the manō," she finished, then glanced at Po.

"Where are you from?"

"Hakalau village."

"Ah, so you are a sailor?"

Po tried to keep from frowning, but it was inevitable. Kiani noticed. "Something is wrong?" she asked.

"No, it's just... I'm not a sailor. I built canoes with my hānai father." Before she could ask about his hānai family, he added. "I plan on sailing though."

"Sailing... where?"

"Anywhere," he muttered. "Anywhere but here."

Kiani studied him, then rested on one elbow as she said, "You can't sail away from your problems, you know. It's better to face the storm head on."

Po glared. Kiani knew nothing of his oppression, nor of his painful abandonment. *She does know,* his thoughts nagged at him. Wena had been abandoned but she saved him, becoming an outcast herself. There was truth to her words, but he didn't want to listen. "But if you can avoid a storm then that's probably the best thing," he said.

Kiani shrugged. “Maybe. Point is, sailing away won’t solve your problems.”

Po leaned against the tree, closing his eyes, pretending to be tired. He didn’t want to hear Kiani’s counsel anymore. What did she know about his situation?

The island whispered, the first he’d heard since entering the dark woods. *Enough.*

CHAPTER TWENTY-FIVE

The room spun in circles around Nohea. She tried to swallow, but a lump filled her throat. "My father?" Was it true? How?

"As you may know... Edena hated me. I'm not sure if you know her history—do you?"

Nohea shook her head, slumping down on the stool across the king.

"She was homeless."

Homeless? It didn't sit right with Nohea. Edena had been a part of Uncle Haku's family. How could she have possibly been homeless?

But Nohea didn't interrupt, only listened.

"I wedded her," the king continued, "changing her life completely. It was a difficult adjustment for her. She felt angry, mostly at me and my other wives, because she could not fit in. Though she was very smart in here," he pointed to his head, "she also had much anger in here." He pointed to his heart.

"Anger at her family line, her circumstances, and that manifest itself in anger against others. It reached the point that she could not function in the fortress with the other wives. She would lash out in violence and hurt them... and myself."

He sighed. "So I did what I could. I sent her to live with the slaves, and she seemed to do much better. It was a pity..."

Nohea blinked hard. Her mother was... crazy? It made sense, but also saddened her. Her mother held such great resentment in her heart. Nohea had never seen Edena lash out, but sometimes people kept things inside, like the pressure she used to build her bombs. Perhaps her mother had been doing that, until she burned the books. Perhaps that was her mother's breaking point.

"At some point in her life, she learned the ways of the meha, the witch women," said Ekewaka. "She put a curse on her only daughter —you—and me. Whatever pain I feel, you feel. Whatever pain you feel, I feel..." He grew quiet.

A curse? Things began making sense: the random feelings of a punch to her gut, a pain in her limb, a stinging sensation across the cheek, and so much more.

"So if I die..." Nohea trailed off and the king nodded.

"We are tied. It was the final sealing of your mother's eternal hatred towards us both."

"That's why our eyes..." Nohea pointed to her golden eye while looking into the king's golden eye. He nodded again. "Yes, it all makes sense now, doesn't it?"

Nohea rubbed her head. It was a lot to take in.

He turned towards her, the stool groaning under his weight. "This is why you must come to the fortress. We must discover how to save our island, and how to save ourselves. I am an old man."

Nohea eyed him. He didn't look *that* old.

"If I died," he said, "It would break my heart to take my daughter with me."

Nohea blinked. *My daughter?* She sort of hated the sound of the king saying it. She had been a slave, a mother's daughter, and an alchemist. Not the king's daughter. Her stomach churned once more.

"Together we can change the course of the island. We can unify our people. Together we can change the future history of our island, make it a better place for future generations. With soran, we can gift our people immunity, and open the waters for foreigners."

He paused, his eyes directed towards the waterfall outside. "This is such a beautiful place. Shouldn't it be shared by all?"

Nohea silently agreed. Why did the Māku'e hoard the forest like some selfish pigs? It really was a grand thing to unify the island under one king, so every person was free to roam about, so every person got to enjoy the beauty and abundance of the island.

He turned back to her. "What do you think?"

Nohea tipped her head forward. "I think it all sounds great." Deep down her stomach felt sick. Was it too good to be true?

No, it has to be true, she thought over and over. It just made sense: reproduce soran, immunize the island, have one king of the island, and make it possible for islanders to roam wherever they wanted. And, in her heart, she desired to learn from the foreigners. They would teach her so much more than she knew now. The island people could thrive as they learned new technology and ways of life.

She tried to listen to her heart and mind. The logic was there, but her heart wasn't.

"What about the slaves?

"Ah yes, I'm not perfect. If you desire it, I will free them."

"I do. There's no deal until you free them."

The king studied her, and she wanted to shrink under the intense gaze.

"How about an agreement? If you discover the formula to create more soran, I'll free all the slaves."

Nohea rubbed her chin.

"Do we have a deal?" King Ekewaka asked again, his voice still loud, but calm.

Nohea took a deep breath, running through the options again, but it all came back to reproducing soran for all. She swallowed and nodded, her gut twisting as she replied, "I'm in."

The king stood, clapped his hands, and then reached out his hand. Nohea shook it.

"I will negotiate with the queen," said Ekewaka. "I'm sure she will not be happy, but I will make it work."

"Well, actually," Nohea said, "I *do* have a plan to help the queen get more soran. I mean, she did ask me to find a way to get more."

The king smiled. "Oh? What did you have in mind?"

THE KING DISTRACTED the queen all day, giving Nohea enough time to pack and destroy any remnants of her alchemy in Noa's little kahuna hut. She knew that Uncle Haku couldn't be hiding very far... and maybe, if everyone was so occupied, he might've escaped the place.

As she went back to the guest hut to collect her clothes, Uncle Haku appeared, ducking under the windows.

"You said yes?" His eyebrows creased, and his mouth hung wide. "How could you do that Nohea? How could you turn against the manō?"

"It just... it just made sense," Nohea said, a heaviness in her heart. A part of her had wished Haku fled, so she wouldn't have to confront him. She took a breath. "You must learn to trust me, uncle. I will not put my hope in a man who has no courage to show his true face as a true aliʻi. Whoever this man is... he is a coward."

"He is doing it to protect you!" Uncle Haku exclaimed, throwing his hands up. "Don't you understand? The manō hasn't revealed himself because he..." Uncle Haku paused, growing silent.

"He what?"

"I cannot tell you who he truly is." Uncle Haku sighed, his shoulders sinking. "You are now a traitor. I am sorry, niece. So, *so* sorry." He put his hand on her shoulder. "I have loved you as my own child, since the day you were born... but this... this is not what I expected. We part ways here."

A drop in Nohea's stomach made her blink hard. She placed her hand on his. "I hope you can trust me."

He nodded and kissed her forehead. "I do not know now... but one day, when we meet again..." Frustration welled up inside of her. Why didn't he understand? It made complete sense to follow King Ekewaka, plus he had more resources than Noa's little hut. She could do all the experiments that she needed to do, and it would benefit everyone.

"Where will you go?" she asked, instead of picking an argument with her uncle. He wouldn't understand her point of view anyways.

"I heard you are in the process of freeing Wena already," he said. "So I will disappear. Pretend you have not seen me, and that you do not know me. Farewell, my niece." He kissed her forehead then made his way out of the door opening.

Nohea's eyes grew watery as she watched him leave. Half of her wanted to call after him, saying that she changed her mind and was ready to flee. But the other part of her simply couldn't believe in a legend.

You betrayed him, she thought to herself, guilt sinking in. Did she truly part ways with her uncle, the man she trusted since childhood, for the king, a person she hardly knew? Not to mention Uncle Haku risked his life to save her.

I don't have time to think about this, she confirmed, wiping her eyes and hurrying to pack all her things. She didn't want to follow a coward, some fake aliʻi, a man hiding in secret, just like her mother.

She cursed me. Nohea slammed her clothes and extra sandals into her lauhala bag, anger settling in all over again. *I will not be like her.* Her mother, with all her hidden emotions, unable to cope with them, had taken it out on Nohea and Ekewaka. Wena's face came to mind, when he placed his hand on her knee and asked that she not feel angry about his mother.

How can he be so calm? Nohea simply didn't understand, though she caught a word in the island wind.

Forgiveness.

Nohea immediately ignored it.

"Alchemist..." Grateful for the interruption, Nohea glanced up to see one of the king's warriors standing at the door opening. "The king has managed to free Wena. He is coming with us," he said.

"Oh. He doesn't need to," replied Nohea, sniffing. "He is free to go where he wants."

"He wanted to come with us." The warrior stepped into the hut, his thick, muscular form blocking the door completely. He had a handsome, light brown face, a tight jawline, and dark curly hair. "The king has mentioned to me that you have plans for the queen to obtain soran. He said now is a good time to do that..."

Nohea nodded and grabbed her bag full of bombs, the biggest bombs she'd built yet. She was glad the warrior came now, now that she had finished packing, and to avoid the guilt of ignoring the island's call. She *never* ignored the island's help, but she couldn't get herself to even think of forgiveness at that moment.

She was cursed, and her whole life of random physical pain, hurt, and unknown torture now ate at her heart. Edena was evil.

"He has quested me to help you, and, the sooner the better. He dines now with the queen."

"What's your name?" Nohea asked, placing the bag over one shoulder, though the warrior took it, which she gladly let him. It was a heavy bag.

"Akamu."

"Good, Akamu. Follow me."

THEY WALKED by the light of the moon, Nohea feeling awkward as she wore new sandals provided by the dark tribe. She had managed to figure out the complicated straps, just as Kiani and Wena had worn their pairs. Wearing her old brown tunic felt familiar, though she still packed the white tunics in case she needed new clothes. She pulled her hair up into a bun, so that it wouldn't get in her way.

At Nohea's request, Akamu called two more of the king's guards, and Nohea instructed them to place the bundles of food on the hauhau tree. The food Uncle Haku and Kukui collected was more than enough to satisfy the moʻo, Nohea was sure of it. Now, she passed the bundles to the guards, and they left with haste.

Then, Nohea, with Akamu following closely behind, neared the white flowing waterfall.

"Just watch your step," Nohea said, watching each of her own steps to make sure she didn't slip into the abyss below. "These bombs will go off with a timer," she added. "I've brought the hibiscus twigs so all we need to do is light them and run."

He nodded, the only thing visible in the light were the whites of his eyes. He was very tall , like the king. His muscled body sometimes seemed like it was too bulky and awkward on the small ridge, but he managed fine.

As they stepped behind the waterfall, the moonlight poured into the cave, reflecting off the moʻo's scales, again, onto the cave walls. It was beautiful, like a cave of color and light.

The dragon snored, his hot breath echoing through the cave. He was in the same position Nohea last saw him too.

She knelt down behind the moʻo and pulled the bombs from her bag. She had never made bombs this big, and she had used random ingredients, including uli, so she had no idea how it would work. The main thing, though, was that the bombs exploded loud enough to wake the moʻo.

Akamu took the bombs from her hands and placed them in the center of the cave entrance, directly behind the moʻo. The soft rushing waterfall muted their noises to the dragon.

Nohea made a little fire using hibiscus twigs and nodded to Akamu, who walked to the cave entrance, ready to run.

She lit the first bomb, then the second, the third, all the way to the fourth bomb, leaving the remaining two un-lit, because the first ones were already to go off.

She ran, barely making it to the cave entrance by Akamu. He grabbed her arm, just in case. The first bomb erupted, like the crackling of a volcano, shaking the entire cliff. Her ears popped from the noise, but she had no time to think because they needed to run in case the ridge collapsed.

The second bomb went off, another loud explosion, lighting up the whole cave, and the waterfall in front of it. Water sprayed the air, wetting Nohea and Akamu as they hurried along the ridge.

The third bomb went off, but behind it was a loud roar, so loud that it shook the ground. Rocks fell from the sides of the waterfall cliff, and both Nohea and Akamu leaped onto the safety of the mountain. Akamu helped Nohea up and they continued running.

"This way!" he exclaimed, as people rushed from their huts in utter confusion. This was the typical dinner hour, and soon, people screamed and ran, panicking.

"The moʻo is awake!" they exclaimed. Nohea looked back to see more explosions from the cave and then a long, hot stream of fire that turned the waterfall into steam. The light from the last exploding bombs lit up the large silhouette of the moʻo as he stood at the cave entrance.

He roared again.

"Let's go!" Akamu grabbed his horse, tied to a tree. The other warriors were there, already on their horses. Just as Nohea was about to look for a horse herself, she felt a strong hand reach out to her.

"Wena!" she exclaimed, taking his hand to sit behind him on a tall brown horse. Her back already ached at the memory of her first ride with Uncle Haku, but she was too distracted and excited to think about the pain.

"Hele on!" Akamu said, riding off. It was chaos, with people running around, the dragon screeching in the distance and flying into the air, his wings making the loudest *swoosh* noise Nohea ever heard.

Wena held the horse still, watching. The dragon perched himself on the top of a large koa tree, the trunk cracking under the weight. He examined the view below, his eye catching the hahau tree. He sniffed and dove for it.

Nohea's plan worked.

The dragon pounced onto the ground and bit at food on the hahau tree, breaking some of its branches. Frustrated at not having easy access to his food, he bit the trunk, uprooting the entire tree, to shake out the food the king's guards had placed in the branches earlier.

The people hid, watching. Kukui waved to Nohea, but Nohea held her breath. This was the moment that she didn't know what would happen next. Would the mo'o eat the food and be satisfied? He thrust the tree into the distance, wrinkling his nose. Then he started picking at the fallen food, as though he'd been invited to a fancy feast. Nohea caught the hopeful glances of the people, their eyes looking from the mo'o to her.

Then there was a loud cheer from Kukui, followed by cheers and claps from the rest of the people. Wena didn't wait any longer to see what happened next. He spurred their horse forward, and Nohea wrapped her arms around his waist before she took a deep breath, stunned. She couldn't believe she actually did it.

As they passed the tallest tree, Nohea saw the queen coming down the stairs, no flower crown on her head, her eyes wide, as she looked at the dragon in the middle of their beautiful wooded kingdom.

And then Queen Awa and Nohea's eyes met. Time went in slow motion, as Wena and Nohea rode past. It was a moment of understanding, anger, and hatred between Awa and Nohea.

Nohea looked away as the queen screamed. No doubt the queen would find her revenge. No doubt she already had it in her mind what she would do next.

But Nohea pressed her head against Wena's arm, avoiding his back because of his healing scars. She heard the people chanting her name, saw the green scales of the mo'o reflecting off the trees as he happily ate his food, and then that was it. The queen got what she deserved—and wanted—and that awful hahau tree was destroyed.

King Ekewaka rode past the two, saluting Nohea, and then took the lead at the front of the warriors. The men encircled the king and

Nohea, riding at full speed out of the wooded kingdom, straight through the itchy vines, and into the dark woods.

Nohea let out a breath of relief, holding onto Wena. They were going away. Away from Queen Awa. Away from her corrupt and malicious ways. Away from the moʻo. And then onto freedom, or so Nohea hoped.

CHAPTER TWENTY-SIX

"She *what?*" Olukai pounded his fist so hard on the koa tree table, it caused a crack right down the middle. It was an expensive table, but he could care less. There were more important and pressing matters at hand.

He paced the room and ran his fingers through his hair, blood pulsing through his body like fire. He'd not felt this angry or shocked in a long time.

Po stood in Olukai's large living room, his arms folded. He could feel the anger steaming off Olukai. Po was usually one to make jokes and crack a laugh, but not now. Especially since he had to bear the bad news.

Olukai paused and rubbed his forehead. "Wait... tell me again what happened." The warm smell of food cooking outside wafted through the room. Po's stomach growled as he caught a whiff of it.

He took a deep breath. "The king came with several of his warriors... and Kahiko. He had a private meeting with Nohea. We don't know everything they discussed but after that meeting, Haku found out that she agreed to go with the king." As Po spoke, Haku, followed by a young woman, entered the room.

Olukai's attention immediately went to her, every part of him distracted, his anger melting away. She was the most beautiful person he'd ever seen. The smell of fresh flowers filled the room.

With long, dark hair, warm brown eyes, and guava-pink lips, she looked like perfection. She was taller than most girls, with a slender, yet toned frame. Olukai couldn't focus on Po's words anymore. He stared at the girl. She stared at him too, standing stiff, awkward, her hands fidgeting around the handle of the spear she held. Olukai looked back to Po, but he kept gazing back at her, unable to peel his eyes away.

She wore a colorful flower crown on her head, though it looked torn and wilted. A matching flower bracelet adorned her right wrist, and she wore a white tunic, tied at both shoulders, and cut above her knees.

She, too, couldn't seem to keep her eyes off him. It felt like all time and space had frozen, leaving both of them alone in the room. It reminded him of the moment he met the great white manō. There had been so much mana pulsing between them, like lightning piercing the sky. He felt it now, staring at this young woman, his fingers feeling hot, his brain running in circles. And then, he saw it. A hint of a smile touched the corner of her lips. As soon as it appeared, she broke their eye contact and stared at the ground, biting her lower lip.

"Olukai?" Po followed Olukai's gaze. Though it wasn't a moment to be funny, Po couldn't help it. "She's single. Her name is Kiani, and she's on our side."

Heat rushed to Olukai's cheeks as he frowned at Po. Po smirked, noticing that *both* Olukai and Kiani blushed.

"She and her brother guided us to the Māku'e," Haku cut in and approached Olukai. They hugged, a welcome interruption for Olukai. Haku held Olukai at arm's length, studying his face. "You look tired, manō."

"I'm fine," Olukai said, but confusion began swelling within him. He was attracted to this girl, but still angry about Nohea choosing

Ekewaka over him. Haku released Olukai and placed a hand on Kiani's shoulder. "Kiani and Wena have been good allies to us."

The girl knelt on the ground, spear in one hand, her head down. "It is an honor to finally meet the manō." Her voice sounded warm, like the kiss of the sun, and Olukai wanted to melt in it.

What is wrong with me? he thought, and ran his fingers through his hair, trying to focus.

"I will fight for and defend the manō the rest of my days," Kiani finished.

"Please..." he motioned for her to stand. She stood, but kept her head down, her long lashes teasing him.

"I have always dreamed of meeting the manō." She spoke reverently but wouldn't look up, as though Olukai's status was too high for her to even gaze on him. "I will do whatever you ask of me."

Olukai and Po exchanged looks, as Olukai stood there, awkward, unsure of what to do or say. He finally nodded. "Mahalo. Your allegiance is appreciated.

She nodded, but kept her eyes down. "Where is your brother?" Olukai asked.

"He's with the alchemist." At that she glanced up, her voice confident. "He is not a traitor though, I assure you."

Olukai rubbed his chin, thinking.

"Nohea decided to go to the fortress," cut in Haku. "I don't understand why she was convinced."

"The king convinces everyone," Olukai sighed. "He is good with his words. Charming. Persuasive."

"My brother is with her," said Kiani. "If you intend to rescue her, I will go with you."

"She doesn't need rescuing." Olukai started pacing so he wouldn't have to stare at her anymore. Kiani was muddling his thoughts, distracting him. "The alchemist *chose* to go there, and so did your brother. We would be kidnapping her if we tried."

"Well then go talk to her," said Po. "You're the manō. She won't believe any of us. She has to meet you for herself."

The island confirmed Po's words, but Olukai pushed the voices away. *No,* he thought, his excuses, justifications, and procrastination of revealing himself resurfacing.

He shook his head. "No, no... I can't reveal myself. She would tell the king."

"But we don't know if she has betrayed us or not," pleaded Haku. Olukai shook his head again. She was on the king's side now. Why else would she willingly go to the fortress?

"We must come up with another plan," he said. Deep down, though, he wished they'd found Edena alive in the garden. Surely she would've helped him.

"Maybe we should kidnap her, and use her to threaten the king." Kiani shrugged. "Or... we can get rid of her." Olukai blinked at Kiani, surprised at her boldness. There was a kick and attitude behind her melting voice. How could she suggest something so nonchalantly?

"We can't kill her," both Po and Haku said at the same time.

"But she is a traitor," Kiani argued. "If the king wants her so badly, let's kidnap her and use her against him."

"We must give her more time," Haku replied. "Before we parted ways, she asked me to trust her."

Kiani softened. "Nohea has a good heart. Maybe you're right. Maybe we do need to trust her."

Olukai continued pacing, the anger rushing back.

"Lopaka and I brought back a group of meha," Olukai explained. "They're tasked to reproduce soran, the same task as Nohea. They said they will stall as much as they can, but they confirmed that Nohea or her mother—who is dead—"

Haku gasped, and Olukai wished he had said it more gently. "I'm sorry Haku," Olukai offered, before continuing, pacing the floor, focusing on the ground, anywhere but on Kiani. "Nohea and Edena are the only ones who can figure out how to destroy or create soran, but with Edena dead, Nohea is our only hope..."

Olukai continued to run his fingers through his hair, the frustration growing in him. Though he wanted to blame Nohea for his frustration, he wondered if it stemmed from himself: his fear of doing what he should, of revealing himself, of stepping to the plate to unite the island.

Kiani stepped in front of Olukai, stopping him in his tracks. She felt close.... Too close. Folding her arms, she said, "You need to calm down." He glanced at Po and Haku, as if to ask, *Who did you bring again?*

Po shrugged. Olukai walked around her to continue pacing.

"You are an ali'i," she said to his back. He paused.

"You have led so many this far," she continued. "And we know you can continue to lead us. We will be victorious—the line of the great white manō is courageous, like you."

He turned around to face her, his mind clearing as he felt her pure heart. Her eyes shone with deep wisdom. He smiled a bit. "You know," he said, "You're right. Let's wait."

He looked at his friends, his biggest supporters, those who honored and trusted him, even in the darkest times. He put his hand on Haku's shoulder and looked at Po and Kiani.

"My friends," he said, feeling his mother's kindness and compassion spreading through him again. "You have traveled far. Please, get some food, wash, and rest. We will speak more about this in the morning."

But Olukai couldn't sleep that night. He tossed and turned, bothered that Nohea would choose the darkness. How could she trust the king? He knew the king for many years now, going on many missions to obtain soran. Could she not see the addiction in his eyes? Or did she choose to ignore it?

Could she not see that there was something very wrong with him? While the king's plan sounded grand, it wasn't the answer at all.

Soran would destroy the entire island. Everyone would fight for it. Olukai tried to think of any positive experiences he had with soran, but they almost always ended in unnecessary deaths: deaths of Hune, mermaids, kupua, humans, plants, animals... and his own father, Sio. It never ended well.

He finally got out of bed and walked to the main room, where the balcony overlooked the ocean. The moonlight cast a white streaks on the horizon, lighting the waves enough that Olukai saw their form as they built up and crashed down.

Great white manō... he reached out with his mind. What was he to do next?

Nothing.

Olukai knew it was his own fault. He kept ignoring the island's push for him to reveal himself. *But what if people don't follow me? What if I'm not cut out to be a leader?*

Olukai leaned against the railing and closed his eyes. Had it been a dream? Had the manō truly chosen him? Or was this all a lie?

He touched the markings on his arm. No... it was all true. It was as though it happened yesterday.

Perhaps I've put too much trust in others, he thought to himself. *Maybe it's time to put more trust in myself... as a leader.*

"Couldn't sleep?"

He turned around to find Kiani standing against the side of the door. She wore a cream colored skirt and kihei, the spare clothes for his guests. Her dark hair was down, with no flowers, weapons, or grandeur, like she had earlier.

She looked beautiful in all her simplicity. He smiled and shook his head.

"I can't sleep either." She leaned on the balcony next to him, her long hair brushing against his bare shoulder. It made his skin tingle. "I'm worried about my brother."

"I don't know much about your situation, but it seems you both can take care of yourselves well," Olukai replied.

She shook her head. "It's not that. It's his heart I'm worried about. I think Nohea has really grown on him. She is his only friend, besides me." Kiani looked up at Olukai. "Nohea knows how to sign."

"Sign?"

"'Ae, for the deaf."

Haku mentioned Kiani's brother earlier, telling Olukai the whole story of how they came to be outcasts. Olukai couldn't help feeling sorry for her and Wena. But a glimmer of hope started in him as he considered Wena and Nohea's connection.

"Do you think he'll influence Nohea to change her mind?"

She shrugged. "He's never been one to force others."

Silence. The waves sounded like quiet thunder rolling along the shoreline. A salty breeze blew back both of their hair.

"Thank you for trusting me," Kiani finally said. "I promise your secret is safe with me. All my days I've heard legends of the manō. I thought they weren't real. I thought they were just that: legends."

"Me too, until it actually happened." Though his mother bore the mark of the ali'i, it had faded over time, and, as Olukai grew older, he wondered if seeing that mark had been a part of his imagination. It was far from it.

"Can I see the mark of the ali'i?" Kiani asked. He nodded and turned, holding his arm out for her to see. The torches from inside of the hut cast a warm light on their skin.

Kiani's fingers gently moved over his palm to the manō image on his wrist, then the designs that wove their way up his forearm, fading towards his elbow. Her skin was soft, yet her fingers felt icy.

"Are you cold?" He took her hands, and they gazed into one another's eyes.

Time froze for a moment, the moonlight shining on them both. Their hearts beat fast, but the only sound was the waves in the background.

Kiani slipped her hands out of his, her eyes hardening. "I'm always cold." She hugged herself and looked away.

Olukai realized his mouth was open and he cleared his throat, turning back around to lean on the railing. She joined him.

His cheeks warmed. He'd never felt his heart beating this fast before—not on any mission he'd ever gone on—at least not the way he felt just now. And when he looked at her side profile, gazing into the ocean, he could sense that she was blushing.

"You're very young," she finally said. It was an odd comment, and Olukai wondered if he should feel pleased or offended.

"So..."

She shook her head, as if realizing the rudeness of her comment. "I expected the king of the island to be older I guess."

Haku had mentioned earlier that Kiani was in her early to mid twenties, and Olukai wondered if she meant something deeper than her words. King Ekewaka only married women younger than him, as did all his counselors, and it was even expected of Olukai, Lopaka, Kahiko, and other men.

"Is there something wrong with my age?" Olukai asked, his voice tinged with offense. Kiani blushed.

"I thought you'd be older is all." A wall formed between the two, but Olukai didn't know why. They stood in silence for a while, until Kiani spoke up again. "It's beautiful out here."

"I love the ocean," Olukai nodded.

"Me too. We used to journey out here. I thought we could sail away one day, but then we learned the mermaids keep all islanders in, and all foreigners out." She tucked her hair behind her ear. "And I don't know how to sail."

"I do," Olukai smiled. "I could show you sometime. I know many mermaids, because I've delivered the soran to them before. They've let me sail around the island, even to further islands. I've seen beautiful islands—eight of them in a row."

"Eight?" Her mouth dropped.

"'Ae, and I've even sailed past the haunted island..."

"Was anyone there?" Kiani asked.

"Not that I saw." On the haunted island lived those banished from Kaimana. Because of the diseases they caught from foreigners, they became outcasts, never to walk on Kaimana island again. It was said they all died on the island, hence the name.

Kiani smiled at him. "Sounds like you've gone places."

"I'm sure a few of my tales could fill the time." He stretched his arms behind his head, smiling. Her eyes, though darkened earlier by their awkward "age" conversation, shone as she looked up at him.

"I've got time," she replied, and they both talked through the night, the melody of the water playing in the background.

CHAPTER TWENTY-SEVEN

"This is where you will do all of your work," said King Ekewaka. Nohea gasped to herself. It was the largest hut she had ever seen, with glass balls, vials, places to boil things, and all sizes of mortar and pestles. They stepped into the hut, Wena and the king ducking under the doorway because they were too tall.

"This is too much," she said, frozen at the entrance. Wena stood next to her, a look of concern on his face. During their entire travels from the Māku'e to the King's fortress, Wena stayed close. Even at night, he slept around the same campfire as Nohea, and she appreciated his protection and concern. It comforted her, especially amidst the presence of the king and his massive warriors.

"Well, we can take some things out—" the king began.

"No, no... I mean, it's perfect." Her fingers lightly brushed against the koa counter top. The king had been generous, and kind. While she hardly saw him the entire journey, he made sure that she and Wena received proper food, clothing, and warm blankets to sleep in during the night.

Then, upon their arrival at the fortress, the king showed Nohea her living quarters. She had a whole hut to herself. And not only that, but all the meals and clothes were provided.

Although the queen had offered such luxuries, this felt different. It seemed the king had been expecting Nohea. While the island breeze blew by disturbed by this, Nohea ignored it, choosing instead to be grateful for the king's goodness. Wena would live nearby in the barracks, with the other soldiers, as the king had no open guest huts at the moment. When Nohea expressed concern, Wena reassured her he would be fine.

And now, she had a lab all to herself. It was a full hut, with every tool, herb, and plant that she might need. On a counter to one side of the hut sat a row of glass balls, filled to the brim with soran.

"Will that be enough for your experiments?" asked the king.

Nohea nodded. "'Ae, it's all perfect. Thank you so much."

He then clasped his hands together, trying to conceal a frown. "I must tell you something, Nohea."

She nodded. "After we arrived yesterday, my counselor, Ano, whom you might know..."

Nohea tried to hide her disgust. She *did* know Ano, the slave master of all slave masters, the man who cared nothing for the slaves' lives. He would hurt slaves, withhold mercy while using the whip, and have slaves killed for even the slightest roll of the eyes. "He reported Edena missing from the prison a couple of days ago."

Nohea's breath hooked. After learning her mother cursed her, Nohea feared confronting her mother. Did her mother really hate her that much? And if her mother was out and about, would she come for Nohea?

"How?"

The king nodded to Akamu, whom Nohea now knew as one of the king's most trusted warriors. Akamu reached into the bag at his side and pulled out a bundle, wrapped in kapa cloth. The king opened it, revealing blue powder and burnt ti leaves.

"I didn't know what this was, until I saw what you did to awaken that mo'o," the king said. Nohea's stomach dropped, feeling like she was being scolded. She didn't do this. But, at the same time, she made bombs just like this.

The slaves... they did this. They freed Edena.

"It's not possible that you could be here, saving your mother, and there, at the Māku'e," the king said, his voice always calm. He smiled , and Nohea cringed. "But did you, by chance, share these... bombs with other people, perhaps, other slaves?"

She gulped. All eyes on her: the king, Wena, Akamu, and the other warriors standing near the door.

If she answered yes, would they investigate the slaves? Would they hurt the slaves?

She locked eyes with Wena, who only folded his arms, his gaze serious.

"We won't hurt whoever did this," the king said, reading her face. "Unfortunately, one of my counselors, along with my son, Lopaka, found Edena dead."

Nohea's legs went weak and she almost fell. She grabbed the counter's edge and Wena dipped down to take her arm. If the king suspected she helped the slaves free her mother, he didn't show any surprise. "Dead?" Nohea could hardly utter the words. She hadn't wanted anything to do with her mother after finding out about the curse but... dead? Awful guilt filled her stomach. Now she would never see her mother again. It was a confusing rush of emotions.

"What happened?" She brushed Wena's hand off her arm, standing straight and swiping hair back from her face.

"From what we assume, she died of dehydration, not drinking enough water. The strange thing, however, is that she ran to the garden, and there is plenty of water in the garden."

Nohea covered her mouth, her hands trembling. Did her mother intentionally not drink water? How could it be? Did she mean to die?

"So... did you give bombs to any of your friends in the past?" the king asked, returning to the subject of Edena's escape. His eyes, dark, menacing, and slightly annoyed, stared straight into her.

She nodded. "'Ae, in the past. I can't remember who I gave it to."

A lie. She knew exactly who she'd given bombs to: a couple of close slave friends and families, Nui included.

"Are you sure you can't remember?" The king closed up the bundle of blue powder and shredded ti leaves, and handed it to Akamu.

She shook her head. "I can't recall."

King Ekewaka simply tipped his head, then started to turn around. "If you do happen to remember anyone, please let me know."

Why? The question didn't come out of her mouth though, lingering on the tip of her tongue. Did the king want to investigate the slaves to see if Edena had any rebellious supporters?

Insead, Nohea swallowed hard. "Where is the body?"

"It has already been burned, a proper burial, even for one undeserving." King Ekewaka then chuckled. *He chuckled.* Nohea's skin crawled.

"But we must continue our work," he said. "I will find a way to undo this curse she placed on us. And you..." He tipped his head. "You will find a way to save all of us, a cure for the whole island." He didn't even look at Wena before he left, but said, "If there is anything you should need, please ask any of my warriors, nobody else."

Once he disappeared into the lonely field outside, Nohea let out a breath and rubbed her forehead, realizing that her fingers trembled. She brushed past Wena, examining the hut.

Looking under the table, she found empty glass balls and jugs. Had the king been collecting these items from the foreigners? Or was there a glass blower on the island? Her fingertips touched all the things in the hut as she tried to think.

She would never tell the king who she gave bombs to, even though he promised not to hurt anyone who used them. *But he'll keep his promise, right?* She wondered to herself. *No...* It would remain a mystery forever. Her mother was dead, and there was nothing anyone could do about it now.

Dead. She hugged her arms as she paced about, trying to process her emotions. Her mother, who hated and cursed her, was no longer a threat. And guilt sunk in, guilt for everything that had happened so far. Queen Awa probably wanted to kill Nohea. Uncle Haku didn't trust her (she couldn't blame him), but... Wena was still here. And she would be fine.

Nohea took a few deep breaths. Right now, she needed to trust herself.

She stood by the open window, noticing that on the field to the north, pineapple crowns, introduced by the foreigners and only grown by the king, covered the ground. Her heart sank.

Slaves bent over their back-breaking work, many of whom she recognized. She wanted to run out, scream and say hello... but she felt ashamed.

They would not accept her now.

Nobody would, not until they had soran in their hands. It was a sacrifice she needed to make, for her decision had been right: if she could discover how to reproduce soran, it could unify the island, save people from diseases, and open the island to the world.

Wena stepped beside her, hunching over to look out the window. He looked much better after all the trouble he'd been through, though darkness rimmed his eyes. He stared at Nohea as she squeezed her eyes shut, returning to the horrible fact of her mother. Dead. Just like that.

How many deaths had she seen? How many deaths would she continue to witness in her life?

Nohea felt the light caress of Wena's fingers on her arm and she blinked awake. He tipped his head to her, his tousled hair falling in front of his face.

Are you alright? he asked. She nodded, but felt the lie seated deep in her na'au. Something was wrong, and she didn't want to acknowledge it. Much to her dismay, she could tell that Wena felt it too.

We can leave, he signed. *If you aren't comfortable, we can leave right now.*

For a moment, her heart melted. Why was he so good to her? It was as if he understood her in a way nobody else did.

"I'm fine," she said, a little too quickly. Wena's eyebrows creased downward and Nohea, embarrassed by his all-knowing gaze, turned to the counter, feeling the thick kapa paper that rested on top of it.

Wena tapped her arm again and she sighed, not bothering to look at him. "I'm fine, alright?"

You seem... unsure, he signed.

I'm just tired, alright? she signed back, then ignored his concerned look. Though she hated to admit it, Nohea felt herself putting up an invisible wall to block out Wena's honest worries.

Instead of letting him say something else, she picked up the closest glass ball of soran, letting the light shine through the purple liquid. Her work here was important. The whole island depended on it.

NOHEA ATE meals with the king's daughters, since she was royalty, but they purposefully ignored her. And, much to Nohea's surprise, she began to understand why Edena must have despised this life. Not only were the concubines and daughters of the king petty and mean spirited, but they were outright bullies, something Nohea hadn't previously encountered in her slave life.

Api, especially, gossiped behind Nohea's back, spreading rumors that Nohea was a witch like the meha. "Nohea doesn't really know what she's doing," Api would say from her circle of gossip, loud enough that Nohea could hear. "She's tricking everyone, but in time we'll all see her to be a fraud."

Part of Nohea wanted to stand up and say something, but the other part was too depleted and didn't care enough. After a few days of this nonsense, Nohea took her food to the hut, where she enjoyed eating with Wena. Though it was highly improper for men and women to eat together, Nohea ignored the kapu rules, and Wena didn't mind either. He spent most of his day roaming the fortress, sparring with the guards or warriors, or carving spear points at the hut while Nohea did her work. But even though they spent more time together than either of them expected, Nohea still felt a strange distance, seeming to grow larger and larger each day, between them. And the worst part was she feared she created that gap herself.

A FEW DAYS into her work, Like visited. "Why are you here?" he asked as he stormed into the hut. Startled, Nohea jumped and dropped the glass vial in her hand. A brownish liquid spilled over the koa table and a shattering noise filled the room. Wena leaped to his feet, spear in hand.

"Like!" Nohea ran to embrace Like, but he limped back.

"What are you doing?" he asked. His lips pressed together, his eyes fuming with anger. He looked weak, and Nohea immediately thought about making more medicine for him. A strange realization dawned on her that she and Like were half siblings. This wasn't the reunion she expected.

"I'm finding the cure. Like, this could save you. It could probably even help Wena... no more deafness, sickness, weak bones, sore joints..." Nohea started to explain, her heart feeling like it would explode at seeing a familiar face.

Like shook his head. "This isn't like you. It's not right. What did he say to you?"

She frowned, now thinking she would rather fall through the ground than face the disappointment crossing his face.

"It's for all of us," Nohea said, trying to keep her voice upbeat. "The whole island. Soran isn't for a few islanders, it's for everyone. And it will protect against the diseases of the foreigners."

"No..." Like put his hands on her shoulder. Wena stepped closer, his tall presence both intimidating and protective. Like noticed, but kept his hands there. "This isn't right. Soran will *never* get us where we need to go. It is all about power. Soran will never help."

"Where is your evidence of that?" Nohea asked.

"The king himself! And his warriors, his unnatural warriors." He rolled his eyes. "The king is living proof too. Do you know how old he is?"

She shook her head.

"One hundred and fifty years old—that isn't normal!"

"But it's also proof of how powerful the soran is. It can lengthen a person's life span." She bit her lower lip, thinking about it, marveling at each new thing she learned about soran.

"I know you've lost many friends and family," Like said, "But death is a part of life. It's natural. Every living thing will eventually die."

Nohea frowned, brushing his hands off her shoulders. "Are you saying I'm afraid of death?"

"That's what it seems like," he said, standing taller.

"I'm *not* afraid of death." She folded her arms. "You haven't seen half of what I've seen... because you didn't grow up a slave."

Like's ears turned red. "I may not have grown as a slave, but at least I'm not running from death like a coward."

"How can you say that?" They glared at one another, then Nohea let out a sigh. "I thought you were on my side—the king's side... he's our father. He's doing the right thing."

"No he's not." Like leaned against the wall. "Nohea, he doesn't want the soran for the people. He wants it for himself, and for his warriors."

Silence, again.

Nohea threw her hands up. "Just leave. I don't want to talk to you. I'm busy." She stormed behind the counter, pretending to read her work, but she couldn't decipher anything. Her thoughts raced by, angry, frustrated, annoyed.

Like stayed put. "I know you think you're doing the right thing," he finally said. "But you should've ran when you had the chance. You shouldn't have come back."

Chills ran up Nohea's spine. "Don't tell me what to do," she said, continuing to avoid eye contact. Only when he walked out did she look up to see him hobbling away. More guilt seeped in. *I could've helped him.* How long had it been since she last gave him medicine? She let out a loud sigh as her confusion heightened. Why did she care so much about others who clearly didn't care for or support her? And why was everyone being so resistant? Sure, the king had faults, but everyone had faults. And Ekewaka was going to make them right. She was going to make things right too.

Like will regret it, she thought to herself. When he finally got a drink of soran, he'd be healed, and he'd be sorry.

Wena touched her arm. *Are you alright?* He signed the same question he asked every time he saw her.

She shook her head. "I don't understand." Pulling her hair into a bun on top of her head allowed some heat to escape off her neck. "I thought I was doing the right thing. Why is everyone being like this? Uncle Haku, Like, and who else..."

Wena glanced out the window, no doubt watching the slaves again. That used to be Nohea's life. She followed his gaze, imagining watching herself, hunched over, sweating, tired.

Do you think I'm doing the right thing? she asked Wena.

He shrugged. *I don't trust the king, but I trust you.*

A smile formed on her lips and relief flooded through her. *Thank you, my friend.*

It was about a week and a half into Nohea's new life that she crossed paths with the meha. They walked in silence through the main courtyard of the king's fortress.

One of them, with a charcoal mark across her veil, glanced at Nohea, curious. She stopped, and the rest stopped behind her, each one turning to look at Nohea.

Nohea's hair stood on end. She had never seen real meha before, and it bothered her that her mother taught her the meha's ancient language. How did Edena learn so many languages?

The woman with the charcoal mark continued forward, not a word passing between her and the others.

Nohea wondered about her mother... Was this curse truly a mark of hatred? What had her mother really been thinking?

A FEW DAYS LATER, Nohea walked to the garden with Wena, the sun setting in the distance. She paused in her tracks when she saw a familiar figure approaching: Nui.

"I heard you came back... and you are the king's daughter," Nui said. She aged in such a short amount of time, her hair turning gray and a tiredness darkening her eyes.

"How are you?" Nohea stepped forward to embrace Nui, but the woman stepped back. Yet another rejection caused a pang through Nohea's chest.

"We are not to touch the royalty—have you forgotten?"

"Nui, you are my family. Just because I have been revealed as the king's daughter doesn't change who I am..."

Nui shook her head, her shoulders tense. "Why did you come back Nohea? You were supposed to leave, become a free woman."

"I had no choice—"

"You *always* have a choice."

"Soran could have saved your husband. And if I find the solution, it will free all of the slaves. The king will change his ways... unify the entire island."

Nui glared. "You don't know that Nohea." She stormed off without another word.

Anger welled up in Nohea's chest. *You don't know that?* What did Nui know about soran or politics or the king?

Nothing. Because, as a slave, Nohea once knew nothing about it all. Nui was ignorant to this new world Nohea was in, and one day she'd be thanking Nohea for her work.

Wena placed a warm hand on Nohea's shoulder and she shook her head. Uncle Haku, Like, and Nui didn't understand any of this, not until they had soran in their hands, not until they grew an immunity and strength from it that would bless their lives and protect them from sickness.

After they had access to that resource, they'd understand.

Nohea couldn't get herself to look up at Wena, so she kept her eyes to the ground and started walking back towards the hut. But Wena gently held her arm, forcing her to meet his eyes. She wished she hadn't. He looked more concerned than before. *We can leave if you want,* he said. Again.

Please don't say that anymore, Nohea signed back, and Wena tipped his head, respecting her wishes. But Nohea wasn't sure if she did want him to obey her request. She was safe here, right? And making more soran was the best thing for Kaimana Island, right? The wind stilled, and the earth seemed eerily quiet, but Nohea ignored the signs.

CHAPTER TWENTY-EIGHT

Olukai waited, with great patience, to meet Nohea. He continued to attend the king's councils, and acted coolly about everything. But he waited for revelations about the king's plans, as well as any word of the alchemist coming up with the formula to create more soran.

But deep inside, the island kept pushing him. *Reveal yourself as the manō. It is time. Unite the island, get the help of the alchemist.*

Olukai resisted the promptings, making excuses like: it wasn't time yet, the king was too powerful, Olukai didn't know who to tell first, and he waited for Nohea to change her mind.

The king's spirits were high in his councils. He boasted proudly of how he convinced Queen Awa to free Wena, a huge factor that convinced Nohea to join his cause. He repeated ten times over his plan to unify the island, all with the help of soran.

Not once did he mention freeing slaves, or distributing the soran to save the people, but Olukai knew those were the arguments he presented to Nohea.

Olukai figured those were her tender spots, being raised as a slave herself. As he pondered on this, making his way back from the king's council, he heard a terrible howling, the noise making his skin crawl.

The meha. They had done their job of stalling time—*but for what?* The thought gnawed at him.

Olukai blinked the prompting away, wondering why the king still needed them when he had an alchemist. Perhaps he hoped to have more options, more people put to work to reproduce soran.

He hoped the meha were alright, and that they weren't hurt. He understood their sacrifices for him. Without thinking about it, he followed the noise, leading him to a remote corner of the king's fortress.

To his horror, the meha weren't howling for some ritual. They howled as some of the king's warriors whipped the women.

"Stop!" Olukai ran forward, shoving the large warriors to the side.

"Please help!" the women cried, bowing on their knees.

"That's enough!" Olukai pushed the warriors away. "Get out of here!"

They did so, surprised at Olukai's rage. He rushed towards the meha, helping them up. Blood soaked through their light brown kapa cloths.

Hopo sat in the corner, very still.

He rushed to her. "Hopo! Are you alright?" He pulled her up with his strong arms, hoping for some breath, some life.

"Ah, you..." Her voice came out raspy.

"What's going on?" Olukai reached under the veil to touch her face, and it was hot. She was alive.

Hopo coughed. "The king has not brought us here for the soran..." She rested her head against the wood wall of the fortress. "He has brought us here to remove his curse. The great woman kahuna cursed him..."

"Who?"

"The one I told you about." She waved her hand, annoyed. "The greatest sorceress, who is now dead..."

Edena. Olukai frowned. "What do you mean?"

"His golden eye... it is a curse, a mark of a great sorceress. It is too powerful for us to remove."

Olukai remembered Like talking about some curse, and the king's intense anger. "What is the curse?"

"He is connected to his daughter. When she feels pain, he feels it. When he feels pain, she feels it. Do you understand?" Hopo sighed. "If she dies, he dies. If he dies, she dies."

"That's awful..." Olukai said, then things started falling into place. "Wait... a golden eye?"

"Yes... his daughter has a golden eye. That is the daughter who shares his curse."

"Nohea." Olukai rubbed his temples. Of course! Of course Edena would curse her daughter and the king, because Nohea's father *was* the king! How had he missed that piece of information? Rumor of it had floated around, as Nohea was to eat with the royals, but Olukai hadn't really believed it. Since Ekewaka was Nohea's father, is that why she trusted him above Olukai?

"Edena left the creed of meha thinking she was a free woman, a free sorceress in the world of men, but the meha are too beautiful. That is why we hide our faces. The king saw Edena and took her for himself. She could not escape. Out of jealousy, his concubines told lies about her, and the king punished her to the life of slavery, where her daughter was born."

Olukai understood it all now. "What must I do?"

"No ordinary meha can remove the curse. You need a great kahuna, or some great source of light."

Olukai knew the answer before the meha even said the words. "The lady of the lava." *This* could be how he convinced Nohea to join him, especially since Edena was gone. He would help Nohea remove the curse.

"I will do what I must," he said.

"Wait," said Hopo, reaching out and taking Olukai's hand. "The lady of the lava does not accept guests. She only lets old friends into her home."

"Who are her old friends?"

"The black moʻo."

Olukai's jaw dropped. "A moʻo?"

Moʻo were the greedy, large, conceited dragons and geckos on the island. There were only a few moʻo as far as Olukai knew, and most of them slept under waterfalls, hiding the island's greatest, most beautiful, and valuable treasures, like golden shells, large pearls, water diamonds, and even soran.

"How do we convince a moʻo to travel with us to the lady of the lava?" Olukai asked.

"We both have crossed paths with moʻo," said Hopo. "They seem to only like the mermaids or the Hune. Perhaps if you found a mermaid, you could convince her to travel with you to the moʻo."

Olukai rubbed his temples again. This was becoming more and more complex every time he thought things might get simpler.

"Thank you Hopo, you have been so helpful."

Hopo nodded. "I wish you good luck, my friend. Perhaps we will not last very long. The king has a temper."

"Or, perhaps," said Olukai, "We will find a mermaid and get this all figured out before the king throws a tantrum."

Hopo squeezed Olukai's hand and leaned back. "Until we meet again," she said and sighed.

CHAPTER TWENTY-NINE

When Olukai told Haku, Po, and Kiani about the curse, Haku sighed. "I feel as if I never knew Edena now. It's as though she were a stranger."

"You didn't know she was a meha?" Olukai asked.

"She was very beautiful," Haku said. "It makes sense that the meha cover their faces to protect themselves. What a sad thing. They should be able to live freely too." He shook his head, as if realizing he was thinking aloud. "No, Olukai, I didn't know she was a meha."

"What mother curses their own child?" Po asked, leaning against the wall in Olukai's living space. Olukai, Kiani, and Haku sat in a circle, but Po didn't join. He ran his fingers through his hair and looked out the balcony, his eyebrows creased.

"What parents would leave their child for dead in the woods?" Kiani asked and Po nodded. "Point taken." Another thought entered Po's mind: *What parent would abandon their own child?*

"If Ekewaka were to, somehow, get killed," Olukai said, trying to stay on topic, "then Nohea would die too."

"We should try to help her," Haku said.

"Are there no other alchemists or sorcerers on the island who can figure out how to destroy soran?" Po asked. "What about the island? Can't it just *tell* us what it wants?"

"We can't tell the island what to do," Kiani said, her voice gentle. Olukai tried not to stare at her. Po nodded, "I know, but if the island —*and* Olukai's great ancestor—want soran gone, why don't they tell us *how* themselves?" Olukai could tell Po was getting impatient.

Kiani seemed to notice too, and her voice, warm and smooth, continued. "Po, I understand it's frustrating. But we'll have to be patient." She looked at Haku. "I feel the same as Haku. It feels right to help Nohea. She is a good person, and she wants to help others. Maybe she's simply confused right now."

Kiani's sympathy, mixed with her soothing voice, made Olukai feel for Nohea. She was in a tough spot.

"You should talk to her," Po said to Olukai.

"ʻAe, that is a wise idea," Haku agreed. Kiani stared at Olukai, reading him.

"You don't want to?" she asked.

"It's not that I don't want to," Olukai said. "What if she tells the king?"

"Then good, let her tell the king," Po answered, taking a fruit from the table and biting into it. "It's about time he knew anyway." All eyes fell on Olukai, and he hoped his insecurities didn't show.

Instead, he nodded. "You're right. I'll talk to her." Haku and Po smiled, but Kiani continued to study him, not convinced.

Before she could say anything, Olukai moved on. "Anyway," he said, "I can't go to the moʻo. I'm the only one of us allowed within the king's fortress, and I need to talk to Nohea."

"I will go," said Kiani, but Olukai shook his head. "I might need your help here too."

Kiani tucked her hair behind her pointed ear and Olukai had to look away. It was too easy to stare at her, or *want* to stare at her. "Why?"

"If your brother has influence over Nohea, maybe you can talk to him?"

Kiani frowned. "I trust my brother to help her do the right thing, even if it's not happening in the timing that you'd like."

"I think it's best if I go," interrupted Po. "I've..." He paused. He'd never told anyone about his experience. Only Haunani, Kamuela, and his childhood friends knew. "I've talked to a moʻo... a long time ago." His stomach tightened at the fact he told other people. He didn't *want* to go. He didn't want to see his hānai family. But if it was for the manō, and, eventually, Po's freedom, then maybe it would be worth it. A lump formed in his throat.

Kiani's jaw dropped. "You spoke to a moʻo? That's not possible."

"How?" Haku asked.

"I can't explain it all right now, but I did." Po continued, "There's a black moʻo near Hakalau village. I know exactly where he lives. I'm sure I could convince him to go with me to visit the lady of the lava."

Olukai blinked. "Well that's settled." After all the missions Po had gone on, Olukai knew Po wouldn't let him down.

"Wait," Kiani said. "Are you a mermaid?"

Po shrugged. "Not that I know of."

"Well have you met mermaids? You'll need one to talk to the moʻo." She added, "Or at least to get something shiny for the moʻo." The dragons liked their treasures, though that made no sense to Po, because they couldn't do anything with those shiny objects.

Po shook his head. "I know most of the humans on this island, not the magical creatures."

Kiani made a face. "Mermaids are dangerous. They have lured many men to their deaths. Are you sure you can resist their temptations?"

"If I can, then Po can too," Olukai said, and Po smiled, appreciating the confidence. Kiani glanced at Olukai, a sparkle in her eye. A tingling of pride erupted in Olukai's chest as he felt she was impressed with his self control.

"This is a strange turn of events," said Haku. "Po will find the black moʻo, and Olukai and Kiani will continue to work on Nohea."

"And you should return to your family," said Olukai. "You've been away from them for far too long." Haku bowed his head. "I would greatly appreciate that."

"I'll leave at the break of dawn," said Po.

"Do you want to know one more thing about the mermaids?" asked Kiani. Po and Olukai looked at her. She shrugged. "They truly are some of the most beautiful creatures you'll meet."

Olukai stared at her, wanting to say, *Actually you are the most beautiful...*

Po rolled his eyes. "I'm sure I'll be fine." He left the room, and Kiani looked at Olukai. His cheeks went red, and he hoped she couldn't read his thoughts.

"I was thinking," she said. "With all this time, I'd like to see a demonstration of your fire dancing. If you are as good as they say you are, I'd like to see it with my own eyes."

Olukai smiled. "Oh I'll show you... tomorrow." And he did.

THE NEXT MORNING, Po left on horseback to find the mermaid and dragon, while Haku went south to reunite with his family. Meanwhile, Olukai brought out his fire knives, eager to show off his skills.

Kiani sat on the beach, watching the waves.

As he approached, she glanced back at him, her eyes curious. "I'm looking forward to this," she said. "Sometimes I believe people exaggerate when they call themselves 'the best on the island.'"

"But I really am the best," Olukai argued. "Or else I wouldn't have become a trusted member of the king's council.

She smirked.

Olukai took off his kihei, revealing his tanned, muscular chest, though his scars always looked so bright against his dark skin. She blinked and casually pulled her hair back, revealing, once more, her pointed ears.

Olukai moved the fire knife in a circle, knowing full well how amazing it looked. The fire mesmerized Kiani, and she leaned forward, fascinated.

"This is the first thing you learn as a fire dancer," he said, circling the knife in one hand. Then he picked up another and twirled a knife in each hand.

Her eyes widened.

"And then you learn things like this." He tossed them into the air, catching each perfectly, and rotating them again, casting beautiful, fiery circles around him.

She smiled—a *real* smile.

"And then you can do this." He connected the knives and tossed them in the air, jumping over them, swinging them around his body, and through his legs. All without one scratch.

"That's amazing!" she said, standing up.

"Would you like to try?" Olukai asked, disconnecting the knives. She nodded.

"But without the fire..." He put out the fire with his hand, before she could open her mouth, warning him.

"It doesn't look too hard," she said, and Olukai scoffed.

"Really?"

She began twirling the knife with her hands, dropping it a few times.

"Oh... well..." she frowned.

"Can I show you?" Olukai asked and she complied. He stood behind her, wrapping his arms around her, placing his hands firmly over hers.

"Just swing it here." He took her hand and placed it on top of the other. "And then swing it again, and the hand goes back." He placed her hand again on the stick. She froze in place.

"Does that make sense?" he asked, looking down at her, their faces close. She glanced up at him, something new in her eyes. Fear. He'd seen it plenty of times, in the faces of those he fought, the faces of the king's subjects, and in himself.

"Are you alright?" he asked, letting go and facing her.

She stared at the knife. "Of course—I'm fine."

Olukai sensed another presence, and looked to the hill, as a figure approached on horse.

"Olukai!" It was Lopaka. He jumped off his horse and ran down the sandy beach. He panted, ignoring Kiani standing there. She fluffed her hair over her pointed ears, but Olukai wasn't sure if Lopaka had seen them.

"Olukai! The king needs you. The dark tribe is very angry–they want to wage a war."

Kiani and Olukai looked at one another. "Now?" asked Olukai, baffled. *The dark tribe... waging a war?*

"'Ae, come quick! The dark tribe has already gathered their armies... they want the alchemist."

"What?"

"Hurry!" Lopaka rushed back up to his horse and Olukai looked at Kiani, sorrow in his eyes.

"You must go," she said. "Hurry!"

Without thinking, he kissed her forehead and then rushed off. Only when he got on his horse and started riding away with Lopaka did he realize what he'd done. He turned around to see her sitting on the beach, with one of his fire knives in hand, examining it.

He wondered if she was blushing.

The king was furious. "I want my best soldiers prepared for battle tonight!" He looked at Olukai. "You lead the first army," and then to Kahiko. "And you lead the next!"

They nodded and bowed. "I can't believe this..." The king rubbed his forehead. "We should kill them all. It is better to kill the dark tribe than have a people who won't honor the king of the island... and *they* are the ones who waged war on me."

"I've heard that the dark tribe are excellent warriors," said Kahiko. "That deaf young man, whom the alchemist is fond of–he is from the dark tribe. I've seen him sparring with the men and throwing spears near the woods. He is an excellent shot—"

"Why are we talking about this?" The king glared at Kahiko, and Olukai smirked.

"Because, your highness," Kahiko said, trying to dig himself out of the hole. "I think it wise that you send out your finest warriors."

"We must protect the alchemist at all costs," the king said, ignoring Kahiko's comment. "I want my finest warriors around me and around her. Do *not* let anyone hurt her."

"Your wish is my command," Olukai bowed to the king.

"I'm glad I have someone that I can count on." The king rolled his eyes.

Olukai smirked at Kahiko. At least he knew that the king was still fooled by his mask.

CHAPTER THIRTY

When Nohea heard that an army of the dark tribe approached, she worked even harder, staying up late into the nights and sometimes sleeping in her lab. When she fell asleep in the lab, Wena would stay at the lab too, then wake her up, food in hand, and they'd eat together.

Nohea wasn't sure how far the army was, but she knew that she had little to no time left. If she could create more soran, perhaps she could give it to *all* the men in the king's army, not only his precious group of elite warriors, like Akamu.

Her notes, written in ancient meha language, were scattered across the room, pinned to the walls, and hanging from the ceiling. She knew she was close to finding the formula, but she also wondered if she needed to see soran in the wild.

Throughout all her muzzled thoughts, one person kept her going: Wena. Wena took good care of himself, Nohea couldn't help but notice. Each day, he'd arrive at the hut freshened up, though fresh bruises and cuts lined his body from sparring with the warriors and guards. And while he sat in the corner carving spears or sharpening his stone knives, Nohea worked on her own concoctions. The sound of the whittling or the stone grinding against stone became somewhat comforting to her. It meant she had a friend, even a protector. But while Nohea was grateful for his friendship, it felt as though neither of them progresseed... this wasn't the life for Wena, and, in many ways, it wasn't the life for Nohea. Their conversations lacked depth and simply weren't the same as they'd been when Nohea and Wena first met in the forest.

While Nohea couldn't understand why their relationship was lacking, she tried to remember her duty to the king: he trusted her with this, and he had a vision. But she also began to sense something else within herself: disgust, distrust, disrespect. And, probably the worst feeling of all was that the island had become silent.

She didn't like the king's lifestyle, surrounded by lavish things that only brought loneliness and emptiness. In her poor slave life she had felt more love and friendship than this rich princess life, where she had everything she needed.

Furthermore, she found herself worrying about the meha that marched around the fortress. Each day they had new blood stains on their clothes. Did the king treat them poorly? After all they were trying to do to rid them of the curse by Edena? Or did they self inflict their wounds?

More questions and worries flooded her head constantly: Was Uncle Haku alright? What about Po? Did Kiani find him, and where did they go? What happened with the mo'o at the Māku'e? Why did Queen Awa wage a war? For revenge or, quite possibly, to get Nohea back? Nohea wanted to discuss these questions with Wena, but they usually ended with him answering that the manō would make things right. His faith in someone he'd never seen or met continued to baffle Nohea.

Even when Nohea asked if Wena was worried for Kiani, he shook his head and said she had probably met the manō by now. Whenever he brought up the manō, Nohea didn't pursue the conversation. To her, the manō was a coward.

She pondered these things alone in her guest hut at night, her mind always a blur. Wena, Kiani, Uncle Haku, Like, the manō, the meha, King Ekewaka, Queen Awa, Kukui, Akamu, Nui.... All of their faces circled in her head, each one sharing what they believed. But she could never make sense of any of it. Who was *truly* right? The island began to prompt her but she shut it out, afraid of the answer.

And then, of course, she lay awake thinking about soran. She'd done experiment after experiment, trying to extract the ingredients from the purple liquid through smell, sight, taste, and feel. From what she gleaned so far: soran was made from plants, heat, and fermentation.

One night she tossed and turned, pondering on soran's unnatural color. There were no purple plants on the island besides taro, when it was cooked and pounded into poi, or sweet potato, but it didn't smell or have the same hue as these plants. Nohea stared at the thatched roof of her hut.

Uli. The thought came softly, yet clear as glass. That was it.

Soran was made of uli, the very ginger used to put people to sleep, used to alleviate pain, used to ease aches and relieve fevers. It made sense.

But there had to be some kind of pool that soaked in the juice of uli. With this revelation, Nohea knew she had to see the soran in the wild. The next day, she scratched her notes on paper, her head still in a daze.

On another paper, she had a different formula... the opposite of her father's desire: how to destroy soran.

After realizing that soran was made from uli, things started falling into place for Nohea. Soran had a unique reaction to fire. It seemed to jump and sizzle, like no other reaction to other elements. It sort of "blew up," which is why she frequently used uli, one of soran's ingredients, to make her bombs.

Nohea took a small leaf palette and let one drop of soran fall onto it. Then she took the torch hanging at the door frame and put it close to the drop so that it practically touched.

The drop sizzled, jumped dramatically, and fell back in an explosion of droplets. But the drops were clear. They were water.

Nohea remembered the moʻo, the large green one that burned the wooded kingdom. And, suddenly, it began to dawn on her...

The moʻo hadn't stopped the flow of soran to the pool because it was sleeping on top of the flow. It stopped the flow because of the molten heat blowing from its nostrils. It was hot enough to melt the chemicals within soran, and change it to pure water.

Nohea laughed aloud. She *knew* how to destroy soran! Her humor changed to concern. *Nobody needs to know. Nobody can know.* She hurried and looked about, wondering if anyone saw her.

The hut was empty, except for herself. She placed the torch back into its place and cleared the counter. A noise at the door grabbed her attention. A band of twelve warriors stood outside the hut, blocking every window, and surrounding the sides. Akamu even stepped inside, watching her.

"What is this all about?" Nohea asked.

"The king ordered it for your protection."

Nohea gathered her papers, stuffing them under the lab table. "Alright, that's fine..."

Akamu looked uncomfortable, and she felt as uncomfortable as he looked.

"Where's Wena?" she asked. He usually visited her by now. The warrior shrugged. "He's probably gone to fight in the battle."

"That's odd," she muttered to herself. "Well... can you tell the king I need to see an actual pool of soran for myself?"

The warrior raised an eyebrow. "This place is locked down. We will be under attack."

"I don't know how to reproduce the soran if I've never seen where it's made, or where it comes from," she replied.

Akamu bowed. "Then I will let him know right away." He left, while the rest of the warriors remained, and Nohea began to feel claustrophobic, maybe even imprisoned . The island hummed to confirm her feelings but she shook her head.

No. I'm doing the right thing. But the island seemed to be shaking its head right back at her, and Nohea hated the guilt that sank deep within her.

THE NIGHT before Nohea traveled to see a pool of soran, she ate her nightly meal with Wena. But he acted unusually uncomfortable. He hardly ate anything, and finally sat back against the wall of the hut, defeated. Nohea noticed him act restless all day, pacing the hut, coming and going frequently, and staring out the window, as if searching for something.

And though she had a sick feeling she knew the reason for Wena's restlessness, Nohea finally got herself to confront him. *Are you alright?* she signed, putting aside her food and sitting next to him so their shoulders touched. He stared at her a moment, then shook his head.

Nohea glanced at the door, where Akamu's back faced them. She would have spoken aloud, but decided to sign instead. *What's wrong?*

Wena shook his head again and looked away, the first he'd ever shown of being cross with Nohea. Fear crept into her heart and she touched his forearm. He glanced at her fingers and she pulled away. "Sorry," she muttered.

He sighed, sat up, and signed back. *I know you can feel the island...*

Nohea's heart sank. He was right. Wena was going to hate her now too, like everyone else. Swallowing hard, she looked away, only to have to stare at him as he signed to her. The warm torch light danced on his tanned skin as he spoke.

I have believed the stories of the great white manō my entire life, he signed and mouthed. *The great white shark is the ancestor of the ali'i, and everyone knows that. It's no coincidence that the shark is circling the island. It wants something done, and its descendant, the manō, will do what he's supposed to. I believe the manō is the rightful heir to the throne. Even the island confirms this truth.*

Nohea blinked. She'd never officially asked the island if the manō was the true king. There was undeniable mana when he was spoken of, and when others believed, but it seemed so... impossible. How could Ekewaka not be the king when he united the people after the foreigners destroyed so many of them?

But how can you believe in someone you've never met? Someone you don't even know exists? What if he's lying? He's even too cowardly to show his face anywhere. Nohea signed faster than she ever had before, as irritation gnawed at her.

Wena's look softened. *Sometimes you have to believe in something, even when you haven't seen it. Don't you believe the sun will rise every morning?*

Nohea nodded.

And you believe that if you put enough work into something, like how you're doing now, you'll find what you're looking for?

Nohea nodded again.

Wena shifted to face her completely, and Nohea caught a whiff of his fresh scent. *Then why is it so different to believe that the island has a true king?*

She blinked, distracted by the simplicity of his words and the attractiveness of his face. She hadn't ever sat this close to or observed him this much. A blush heated her cheeks as the corners of Wena's lips turned upward, as if he could read her thoughts.

She looked away and spoke aloud, her voice absent as her mind absorbed all the confusing emotions coursing through her. "I can't believe in others anymore. I have to believe in things I can see."

Why? Wena asked.

"Because it's easier to use logic and common sense." She met Wena's eyes. "It's how I've survived." And many slaves survived this long because of Nohea. Many of them overcame sicknesses and wounds because of Nohea. It was all because of her studying, breaking down plants, and creating new remedies. Those were all things she could see. So to follow someone who didn't show his face, who couldn't even boldly announce himself as king... Nohea frowned: then he probably wasn't a king. Furthermore, to follow someone who wanted to *destroy* such a precious resource seemed utterly selfish.

Wena tucked a piece of Nohea's hair behind her ear and she wanted to melt. He signed. *I understand you've been through a lot.* Nohea's eyes began to brim with water again and she blinked it away as fast as she could. *But you know what's right. I know you can feel it. The king will do anything to get soran, and if people start drinking soran, they'll end up destroying themselves. There will be too much power. You know this.*

He reached for her hand but Nohea pulled it away and shook her head. *No, the island is not right this time,* she signed.

Let's leave, Wena said, glancing towards the door where Akamu stood. *You know the island is right. It has always been right. Let's leave together tonight.*

She wanted to take his hand, agree, and run from this mess together... because Wena was probably right. Nohea had ignored the island, after her whole life she'd listened to it eagerly. Wena reached to stroke her cheek as a tear had escaped. Longing filled her heart.

But that longing was quickly replaced with dread. It was too late now. She was in too deep with the mess she'd made. She practically knew how to make soran and was going on an expedition with Kahiko the following day to confirm her ideas. She had made an agreement with King Ekewaka. None of it could be undone. She was stuck here. The manō would never accept her now, after she'd chosen against him.

King Ekewaka's words filled her mind once more: *We will create soran for all.* It was such a *beautiful* vision, and she wanted it so badly.

We can leave tonight, Wena said.

Nohea shook her head. *I can't—*

Of course you can. You can change your mind. It's never too late.

Nohea tried to breathe, knowing that at any moment all the tears would fall.

Come on, Wena started to take her hand but she pulled away once more. The hurt look in his eyes stung more than anything else.

I can't. It's too late and the manō has no vision.

But he'll do what is right. Soran is unnatural and you know—

Please leave. Nohea signed it in haste, fighting back the tears.

Wena's look only further softened. *Nohea, he won't hate you. Everyone makes mistakes—*

Please go. She wasn't sure if she could stand Wena any longer. He sounded like Uncle Haku, like Like, and Nui.

Nohea, please listen—

"Leave." She said it loud and clear, which made Akamu turn around. Wena's eyes, full of sadness, made Nohea wish the earth would swallow her.

"Is he bothering you?" Akamu asked.

Wena swallowed hard and nodded to Nohea, then stood and left before she could even answer Akamu's question.

Akamu eyed Wena, then looked back at Nohea. "Are you alright?" he asked.

She nodded, but she was far from alright. A sick, heavy feeling settled in her stomach. She'd never felt so alone.

CHAPTER THIRTY-ONE

"Ma, it's Po!" A scream erupted from the thatched hut atop the hill. Po couldn't see his younger sister's face clearly, but he could hear the excitement in her voice.

"It *is* Po!" Laughter sounded in the air, like a bellowing, the voice of his hānai mother, Sina.

A grin spread from cheek to cheek on Po's face as his younger hānai sister dashed down the hill to him. "You're back!" she cried over and over as she jumped and hugged him tightly. Her thick black hair nearly choked him, but she smelled like flowers, as usual.

She stepped back, squeezing his hands. "It's so good to see you!"

"And you as well Haunani," Po said, beaming.

"I returned not more than two days ago. You've come back from the fortress too, haven't you? I can feel it." Haunani wasn't like other girls. She'd never been. Though she and Po were adopted siblings, they both had an intuition, a connection to the island like so few others. Sometimes it seemed like Haunani was the only person who understood the island and understood Po.

"'Ae, did you enjoy—" Po's voice was cut off by Sina's cry from the distance.

"Get up here boy and tell your mama hello!"

Po and Haunani laughed, as she grabbed his arm and walked up the hill beside him. She grew every time he saw her. Now at seventeen, she looked much more mature. She brushed her hair back and swiped her forehead. Her heart shaped face looked tan from the sun, and a warm glow graced her cheeks.

"Mama has been talking about you lately—she wants you to get married!" Haunani giggled. "I saw Olukai again. Have you met him?" She giggled again. Po chuckled.

"He is even more handsome than the last time I saw him! And all the rumors are spreading—maybe he will ask me to marry him!" Haunani let go of Po's arm to twirl around. Every step she took looked like a dance, her expressions so clear on her face, obvious she was in love.

"Po, my boy!" Sina stood and kissed both of Po's cheeks. She was a big-boned woman with lightly tanned skin, her heart shaped face longer than Haunani's.

"Hello ma," Po hugged her back. She smelled sweaty, with hints of oily food. *Typical,* he thought, because she always slaved over preparing and cooking food. "Tua is going to be so happy to see you."

"Where is he?"

"At the yard. He's working on some new canoes for Kaleio guys."

"Ah..." Po set his bag down and wiped sweat from his forehead.

"Here, sit—drink some water. Relax. I want to hear all about your latest journey." Sina already grabbed a gourd of water and handed it to Po. Haunani stared into the distance, smiling, no doubt still daydreaming about Olukai.

Po drank. "Thanks ma—but I need to see Pa now."

"Of course—but then come right back up! I expect a good report from you!"

Po smiled. Sometimes he made up stories to pass the time with Sina. But, mostly, he made up stories to keep the truth hidden. They had no idea Olukai was the manō, or that Po was his messenger. Sina had a big mouth, gossiping with all the other women in their little village. Though he loved his hānai mother, Po didn't feel comfortable telling her anything. All she knew was that he went around the island sending messages for people. That was it.

"You better bring news of an upcoming marriage, or I'll let you know who's available in the village!" Sina teased. Po tried not to roll his eyes.

"I'll show you where—" Haunani started.

"I know where he is," Po grumbled, walking away, remembering why he hated coming home. Sina's demands really started to irritate him the older he got. Haunani followed, playing with her hands. She looked as though she was walking on clouds.

"I danced at the festival, and stayed with Aunty Moana for a week or two," Haunani chatted as they walked through the tall grass, sloping up the side of a hill. The salty ocean breeze greeted them as they stopped at the top. The ocean loomed before them, blue and mysterious. A pang hit Po's heart. How he longed to be out there.

Haunani continued. "And we spent a few evenings weaving baskets with the king's wives and daughters. They were awful. They hated me, because of the rumors. But Olukai!" She giggled then took a deep breath, twirling around and humming. "Have you met Olukai?" She asked again.

Po was quiet as he continued walking.

"Is something wrong?" Haunani grabbed his arm and stood firm. Po was stronger, taller, and bigger, so he could've dragged her forward. But he stopped, looking down towards the shore.

"Come on," he said.

"Something is wrong." Haunani's eyebrows creased. "What happened? Is it the manō—is he alright?"

Po glanced around, though he knew nobody listened. He only told Haunani the truth—about the moʻo, the manō, everything in his life. However, he never told her the full conversation with the moʻo. He never told anyone, not even the words that echoed in his recurring nightmares.

Po swallowed. "Something went wrong..." He kept his voice low, though he couldn't even get himself to say it: the alchemist was a traitor and Olukai was the manō, the true king of Kaimana Island, but he was taking *forever* to reveal himself, taking *forever* to dethrone Ekewaka.

"What do you mean? Are we in danger?" Haunani looked about too, though not a soul was in sight, only the two siblings on the hill.

"I can't tell you everything, but... I am going to need some help." Po glanced down at the seashore. The large thatched roof of the canoe house covered Tua beneath it. Po imagined Tua, his hānai father, with his large body sweating over the wa'a, slaving away the day in carving, shaving, and sanding koa wood, inch by inch.

At that moment, a young man, shorter than Po, with hair black as midnight, cut short and clean, walked from the thatched roof. His bronze skin gleamed in the sunlight, sweaty, as he carried a large, heavy beam. The young man placed it on the ground, then walked nervously, awkwardly, glancing from the beam to the inside of the hut. He stood there for a moment, looking back and forth, until he finally walked back in.

"Are you kidding me?" Po rolled his eyes, walking forward, his strides long, annoyed.

"Po!" Haunani scrambled after him.

"Tua really couldn't find an extra pair of hands?"

"Oh, you saw Kamu?" She panted to keep up. "You're being unkind. You always have been about him—"

"Unkind?" Po stopped and Haunani stepped in front of him, folding her arms. "You know what's unkind?" Po continued, "Telling on every little thing, his drunk father ratting people out too—that's unkind." Po knew the young man all too well. His name was Kamuela, a social outcast not only because of his father's standing as a king's spy, but because of his own odd behavior.

Kamuela, whom Haunani called Kamu, didn't act like the others. He fidgeted with his fingers, avoided eye contact, tripped over things, and, worst of all, tattle taled on everyone else's pranks and mischief.

"I can't tell Tua my plans while that rat is there—" Po started.

"Po, don't call him that."

"That's what he is!" Po shook his head. "What about Oni? Can't he help pa?" Oni was their younger brother, born ten years after Haunani.

"He's only six, too young."

"What about Alika, Kahale, or Ulu?" Po listed the names of his friends. "Just... anyone but *Kamuela...*" The name rolled off his tongue with disgust.

"Po, he's the only one capable of helping pa. He knows the in and outs of the wa'a unlike any other. He even invented new things to help the canoe sail better, tricks and methods to make it ride smooth. He's the best sailor and canoe maker in town."

"Ugh..." Po rubbed his forehead. *The best sailor in town?* He wanted to punch Kamuela in the face. Po should've been the best sailor in town, if Tua would've only let him go. "How long has he been helping?"

"Since your last visit." Po calculated. One and a half years.

"His father—" Po began.

"His father," Haunani interrupted, "Is still the king's personal assistant in these parts, but he's too drunk to do anything. Po, Kamu left his father's house—he was disowned." She looked sorry, but Po had no ounce of pity for the young man.

He couldn't even begin counting all the times Kamuela tagged along, only to tell Sina and Tua after, "Po peed on so-and-so's house" and "Po whistled after a girl," and "Po stole a canoe and went sailing for half the day."

Po's blood boiled. He'd always teased and mocked Kamuela, making others laugh at him too.

But, of course, Kamuela was the only one who'd been there when Po spoke to the mo'o. Po remembered falling into the cave, and the others pushed Kamuela behind him. But Kamuela never ratted about the mo'o. Perhaps he knew that Po had saved his life, so he wouldn't say it to anyone.

"Kamu lives on the outskirts by the shore." Haunani pointed to a hill in the distance. Though Po couldn't see the outskirts of their village, he knew it was the best place for an outcast.

"So pa really got desperate..." Po started until Haunani grabbed his arm again. "Po, you're being *so* unlike you. Something must have gone terribly wrong." When he didn't say anything, she added, "When you see pa, you'll know why he was desperate for help."

A pang struck Po's chest again. Had he missed something?

As their feet touched the sand, the smell of fresh koa wood and kukui nut oil, along with the constant sound of wood chipping, filled the air.

A clear voice rang through the air, mixed with the breaking of the waves.

Sweet air fills her sails,
She glides in the water like a fish,
No wave can break her wood,
She hears the song of the mermaid...

It was a song Tua always sang about the canoes. Po and Haunani rounded the corner of the large canoe hut, a covered pavilion, with two large trunks of koa wood sticking out the front.

Tua continued the melody with a whistle, hunching over one of the canoe's hulls. Kamuela's back faced them as he worked on a different slab of wood.

"Pa, Po is back!" Haunani exclaimed, her demeanor changing from concerned to delighted. Po knew she loved the reunions. She clasped her hands together as Tua looked up, his creased eyebrows releasing their tension. His back glistened in the light before he stood straight, a large grin appearing on his wide face.

"Po! My boy!" He outstretched his arms and Po fell into the thick hug of his hānai father.

But he immediately knew something was wrong. Tua let go and leaned to one side. "So good to see you son!"

"You as well." Po glanced down to see Tua's deformed left leg, like something had crushed it. It had healed, but it looked shorter and skinnier than the other leg. Tua hobbled to the back of the shop to grab his gourd of water. "Po, you know Kamu."

So Tua was calling Kamuela "Kamu" now too.

Po forced his head to turn and look at Kamuela. The young man glanced at Po, making eye contact once, but looked away, barely muttering, "Hey..." He nodded to Haunani, his fingers tapping against his legs, and he quickly turned around to continue his work.

Kamuela definitely looked older, his body now muscled, not so bony. He looked very clean though, his hair neatly trimmed and his skin smooth, though his back bore many scars, probably from years of bearing his father's abuse.

Po ignored Kamuela, putting his hand on Tua's back. "What happened to your leg pa?"

"Ahhh, nothing." Tua smiled, his wide nose shining in the light. He wiped the sweat off his face, the sawdust on his arms growing dark with the contact of the moisture.

"It got smashed in an accident," Haunani cut in.

"Where?"

"Up in the forest. The tree fell on my leg. But," Tua shrugged. "I'm glad to be alive." Haunani smiled and hugged the other side of her father. Tua looked like his heart would burst as he glanced from Haunani to Po. He placed his arms around their shoulders. "It's so good to have you back Po," he sighed.

A longing filled Po's chest. It seemed like the world lost air. He'd been away from home so long—serving, sending messages, doing anything the manō asked. He ignored these people who loved him so much, who probably thought of him often. He swallowed hard.

He hardly thought of them, only wondered where his real father was, or when he'd sail away, so ungrateful.

"How long you staying?" Tua asked, with no hint of anger in his voice, unlike Sina, who wanted Po to stay forever.

"Not long... just a couple of days." He glanced at Kamuela, wanting to tell his hānai father the mission, but not trusting the rat. "I'll tell you more later."

Haunani rolled her eyes and then sighed, breaking away from her father's arm. "Shall we dance tonight?" She spun around the canoe, telling stories with her hands, her eyes, and her smile. All of the men paused, watching her, mesmerized by the grace, the softness, and skill of her movement. Even Kamu turned around to stare for a moment.

She laughed. "Well come on!" She skipped away towards the shore, running, jumping, and cartwheeling, as she always did.

Tua squeezed Po's shoulders. "Don't worry about me boy, go along. I'll finish early today. I'll be up soon."

"Thanks pa." Po swallowed again, but a guilty sensation filled his stomach and wouldn't go away.

HAUNANI ACCOMPANIED Po as he walked about the small village. The mothers sitting outside their huts smiled, greeting Po from afar. Some of them beckoned for him to draw closer so they could kiss his cheeks and ask where he'd been, practically begging for news to gossip about. Some of them asked if he would consider their daughters in marriage, making Po's face burn red, so he hurried on. He was glad to see his friends, Alika, Kahele, and Ulu who'd taken up different trades: farming the fields, fishing, and featherwork. They agreed to take the following day off to help him fish.

All Po knew was that he had to gather as many goods as he could to please the moʻo. He remembered how famished it had been last time, and that he was lucky to make it out of the cave alive.

THAT NIGHT, Sina put on a grand supper for their little family. Salty fish, dark sweet potatoes, and mouthwatering poi sat in wood bowls. Oni and Haunani danced together, a new routine that she made up. Sina pounded the gourd on the floor of the hut, chanting the story that Haunani wanted to tell. Po and Tua watched, impressed, and then Haunani grabbed Po to do a dance she taught him years ago. He forgot most of the moves, but they had a good time. After all the fun and eating, though, Po finally had the chance to explain his plight.

"I have to get the help of the moʻo," Po said.

"You're doing what?" Sina exclaimed, her hand over her heart.

"I have to do this," Po replied. Haunani rubbed her chin, thinking. Po added, "And ma, you *cannot* tell anyone. If anyone finds out I'm going after the moʻo, they'll stop me."

"This makes no sense," Tua said, stretching his legs out on the woven mats.

"Nothing makes sense," Po laughed , still wondering to himself why Nohea joined King Ekewaka. "But this is our only chance... I can't say much, but I need your help. I need to gather as many fruits and food as I can. The moʻo is going to be very hungry when he wakes up."

Sina opened her mouth to say something but Tua raised a hand to silence her. "Our son has spoken," he said. "Po needs help. We are going to help him. Tomorrow, take one of my boats with your friends and Kamuela. He is the best spear fisher and can find the best spots."

Po tried not to roll his eyes. But he was glad his hānai parents weren't stopping him.

THAT NIGHT, he sat on the sand, listening to the waves, thinking. Tomorrow Sina would gather a bunch of fruit and roast one of their pigs in an imu. Maybe Haunani could help Po get something sweet, like honey. Tua would lend him a canoe. Alika, Kahele, and Ulu would help him spearfish. He rubbed his forehead, annoyed, *And Kamuela too I guess.*

By the end of the day, he could possibly have all the food he needed for the moʻo. But he still needed one more thing, something shiny. The moʻo had mentioned it last time, and Kiani confirmed it was needed. He racked his brain for ideas.

"What are you thinking about?" Haunani sat next to Po, holding her knees to her chest.

"Something shiny."

"What do you mean?"

"Moʻo like shiny things too. I can't just show up with food."

"How do you know that?" Of course. Po had never told Haunani the full conversation with the moʻo. It had frightened him too much, and he kept his secrets close to his heart.

"When I talked to that moʻo before, he told me exactly what their kind likes," Po confessed.

Haunani gasped. "What? And you didn't tell me?" She pushed him.

"Calm down or you won't hear a word at all—"

"You *better* tell me!"

Po laughed. "Well, he said he likes all kinds of food, and then he mentioned if I ever wanted to see him again—and get out alive—I'd need to bring something shiny."

"Hmm." Haunani rested her chin on her hand, pondering.

"Did you know that only mermaids can communicate with the moʻo?" Po asked, slightly changing the subject. "And the manō confirmed that to me too."

"Really?" Haunani looked intrigued.

"I keep thinking... about my parents." Po couldn't believe he said it aloud.

Haunani nodded. "I know you think about them. It's alright, you know. We're not offended." She chuckled and continued, "You were dying to get out of this place for the longest time."

Po sighed, guilt sinking in again. "I know."

"But hey, you did it! And now you serve the manō, the true king of this island." She smiled wide, staring into the darkness. "Anyway... what did the moʻo look like?"

"Black. Eyes like the color of the sun. Claws sharper than the teeth of the manō."

Haunani sat still, her eyes big.

Po hugged his knees. "I've been thinking... if the moʻo can only talk to a mermaid... does that mean *I'm* part mermaid?"

They sat in silence. The waves brushed against the shore, making an occasional crashing noise. A salty breeze swept Po's hair against his face.

Haunani finally spoke. "Maybe you are." A chill ran up Po's spine. He looked up at the stars, and then the moon, casting a white glow on the ocean.

"Are you glad to be back?" Haunani finally asked, moving the conversation along. Neither of them had answers to Po's heritage, so it didn't make sense to linger on it.

Po shrugged. "Yes... and no." He couldn't believe he was saying this to her. He'd never admitted that he didn't enjoy being back. But Haunani had grown older. This girl... well, she had only been a girl yesterday, but was now a young woman. Everything about her had matured, yet she still had the youthful playfulness that he'd always remember. Even Oni, their younger brother was growing fast.

"Why?" Haunani asked, still staring out into the dark ocean.

"I ... keep dreaming of the sea. I don't belong here."

"Here?"

"On land. Why didn't pa ever let me go out?"

"You know why."

"The mermaids?"

Haunani nodded. "They're dangerous. A few months ago one of the fishers spotted a mermaid, and she hissed at him." A tension grew between them, as if both realized that perhaps Tua hadn't let Po into the sea because Po himself was part mermaid.

Po scoffed. "Hissing? Sounds like an exaggeration. If it was Kamuela, I don't blame her for hissing." He laughed at his own joke but Haunani pushed him.

"Why are you so mean to Kamu?"

"Because he deserves it."

Haunani squared her shoulders. "Po, this village has treated you like family." She sounded stern, even stiff, unlike her usual, light self. "Nobody has ever treated you differently because of your skin." She paused, before adding, "Not even for your eyes and hair. Nobody has eyes like yours, the eyes of a foreigner. And yet, you treat Kamu, who is also kind of different, as an outcast."

"He deserves nothing more. It's a wonder his father didn't send him to be one of the king's slaves or petty soldiers."

"What if your father disowned you? What if he beat you every night, and treated you like nothing? What if..." She swallowed hard. "What if your mother did what his mother did?" Po knew she couldn't get herself to say it, an unspeakable, one of the most dishonorable things to do.

Kamu's mother committed suicide when he was six. People gossiped it was because she discovered Kamuela was... different. And she couldn't handle one more punch from her alcoholic husband. It all sounded so miserable.

"My father *did* disown me," Po snapped back, though he couldn't say that his father abused him. There was never a doubt that Kamuela's father beat him. When they were younger, Kamuela always showed up late to the party, with blue spots and scabs all over his bony body.

At least, now, Kamuela was free of that.

"I'm trying to help you have compassion." Haunani sighed. "I don't know why you're so hard on him. He's done nothing to you."

"Oh, he's done *plenty*."

"So you hold fault against him for things he did years ago?" She waved her hands in the air. "That is the most childish thing I've ever heard."

"Since when did you get all wiser?"

"Since when did you get all dumber?" Haunani's response came back quick and annoyed. It was so unexpected that Po laughed. She glared at him, and it only made him laugh more. He hadn't realized how much he'd missed his sister. She tried to keep her eyebrows creased, but then they broke open and she laughed too.

Through that laughter, the pang hit Po's chest again. He was missing out on so many moments like these. As they stood up and walked back to the house, he swallowed hard and rubbed his neck.

Perhaps these moments wouldn't be so rare once his job as a messenger came to rest, once the manō ruled the island again. But he didn't want to return here. He wanted little to nothing to do with his hānai family. After all the years of them keeping him on land, bossing him around... he wanted to sail away, right?

CHAPTER THIRTY-TWO

Olukai didn't forget his commitment to Kiani, Po, and Haku. He told them he'd talk to Nohea, but he couldn't find the right time. She was constantly surrounded by people, especially the king's warriors, and when Olukai stopped by the hut a few times, she wasn't there. So he continued to keep an eye out for her, and tried to find a time to speak with her, but there never seemed to be a private moment.

Kiani had disappeared after Olukai returned from the king's fortress, and he secretly worried about her. She only left behind her flower crown and a message with the servants that she "needed to return to the Māku'e and convince the people to change their plans." Part of him was grateful she was gone though, because she proved to be a huge distraction. He committed to not worry about her and, instead, focus on when he'd talk to Nohea.

Ekewaka sent out messengers throughout the island, and within a few days time, men began to show up at the fortress. Olukai greeted each one, surprising himself at how many islanders he knew. Before he started going on missions, he went through the villages of Kaimana Island, teaching the men how to dance with the fire knife.

Once they mastered that, he taught them how to fight with the knife.

"Olukai!" An older man greeted Olukai and they pressed their foreheads to one another.

"Loli." Olukai placed his hand on the man's shoulder. "What have you been up to, friend?"

The man had a weathered face, dark as clayed earth. His white hair, mustache, and beard had grown considerably long since the last time Olukai saw him.

"Ah, fishing. The usual." He gave a toothy grin. "You've grown so much. Your mother would be proud." Pain shot through Olukai's chest but he smiled.

"Mahalo, old friend."

"What have you been doing anyway?" Loli teased as he took Olukai's arm and started into the fortress.

"The same old. Going on the king's missions, getting soran, training the men..."

Loli stopped Olukai and glanced at the kapa covering his forearm. "Eh what happened there sole?"

"Just burned myself," Olukai said, putting his arm behind his back as he noticed part of the tribal design creeping out from the kapa cloth. The symbol was growing bigger and darker everyday.

Instead of letting it rest, Loli reached for Olukai's arm. Olukai was faster. "Hey old man, watch out or you'll break your back," he said.

Loli laughed. "I know what goes there."

"It's a burn, alright?" Olukai sighed and pointed into the fortress, where men set up pavilions and huts for the islanders to sleep under. "The men from Papaikou village are staying there."

Loli only shook his head. "Your mother never hid her mark, remember?"

Olukai tired of Loli's pestering. "How many from Papaikou remember her?" he asked, instead of answering the question.

A breeze blew through the fortress, and Olukai pressed the kapa cloth down, although it was held securely by braided ti leaves. The men continued to bustle by, and Olukai could hear Lopaka greeting those he knew at the gate. Lopaka knew almost as many islanders as Olukai, because he often traveled with Olukai to help train the men.

"Not many. Remember... most of the folks passed away from sickness. But," he shrugged. "You'll be surprised how many remember you. The village boys never stop talking about Olukai, the greatest fire dancer on Kaimana Island.'" He winked. "I don't know why you're hiding, son, but it's a mighty shame."

Olukai's face warmed. *A shame.* He was a shame to his mother, his family line of ali'i. Any other ali'i would have risen up to lead the people by now.

"I have nothing to prove myself," Olukai said. Another group of young men passed by, their eyes wide as they pointed at him, whispering to one another, "It's Olukai."

Loli rubbed his tongue over what remaining teeth he had. "What more do you need to prove? You've done more than your share for this island. Others will naturally feel your mana."

The incoming islanders continued to stare as they walked past Olukai and Loli. It was the sort of attention that Olukai felt self conscious about. How could everyone think so highly of him? They walked about him like he was some sort of idol, an untouchable, someone that they deeply admired. He hated being on this pedestal, and he rubbed his covered arm even more.

"Eh, Olukai," Loli said and put his hand on Olukai's shoulder. "I've known you since you were yeh high." He motioned with his hand to show how small Olukai had been. "If there's one thing I know about you, it's that you won't give up. It takes a special kind of person to be able to do what you've done."

"Thanks Loli," Olukai said, still keeping his arm away from the old man.

"These men admire you," Loli added. "Trust in your calling. Trust in the island." He pressed his forehead against Olukai's once more, then walked towards his village's hut, whistling as he went.

Olukai watched him. *Old Loli,* he thought, chuckling to himself. Loli was an old friend of Sio's, and Olukai remembered the many kava sessions the men shared together after Kehau's passing. Though not the best example to take counsel from, Loli did have *some* wisdom. *Trust in your calling. Trust in the island.*

Amidst the hustle and bustle of incoming islanders, those who came to fight King Ekewaka's unnecessary battles, Olukai tuned in to the earth around him. Though the men around continued to point fingers, saying in excited, hushed tones, "There's Olukai," he ignored them. The sky, with its warm sun shining down, the grass rustling beneath his feet, and the cool breeze against his skin, grounded Olukai.

As if approving of Olukai's desire to be one with the island, he heard the voice in the wind. *Speak with Nohea. Reveal yourself. It's time.*

CHAPTER THIRTY-THREE

Nohea said nothing to Kahiko or the other warriors as they journeyed towards a small kīpuka to the north, outside the fortress walls. It bothered her that the sorcerer came on this little expedition. She would have rather taken her chances with the warriors, and though she was familiar with many of their faces, because they guarded her hut, she was most comfortable knowing that Akamu was among them. She'd gotten used to greeting him in the morning and having him tag along, even to her guest hut, where he and the others surrounded it while she slept.

But what bothered her most was that Wena chose not to come on this expedition, though she wasn't surprised. After the confrontation, how could she expect him to ever be her friend again? He had acted with such great compassion and understanding, while she pushed him away.

Wena's words kept her awake that night, and in the morning, she knew she had to tell Wena that she hadn't changed her mind... and she probably never would. The manō was a coward, and King Ekewaka was doing a lot of good for the island, protecting it from inevitable diseases from foreigners, and strengthening every inhabitant. But Wena was nowhere to be seen, and someone mentioned seeing him leave the fortress.

"We are close," said Kahiko, disrupting her dark mood. "There used to be a moʻo here, but he is long gone now."

"Did he just... leave?" Nohea asked, refocusing on the task at hand.

Kahiko hesitated, his thick lips pursed together. "Sort of."

Nohea glanced at him. "Sort of?" They rode horses at a steady pace, fast enough to get to their destination, but slow enough to still talk and hear one another. Nohea's back hurt from riding, and Akamu, earlier, finally told her to let her hips move with the horse's movements. It sort of helped, but she kept rubbing her back, uncomfortable.

"He was a slimy creature. Lazy, greedy, serving no purpose. He had no wings, but slept there. We destroyed the moʻo many years ago. This pool has been the king's main source of soran, but it is nearly dried out. We will be lucky to find any drop of soran."

Wena's words came back to her, the ones he'd said so long ago. *The king will do anything to get soran.* How many moʻo had been killed for soran? Nohea had scared the moʻo away from Queen Awa's pool, but at least she didn't kill it.

If giant lizards were killed for the soran, how many people were killed too? She shoved the thought away.

"Does the king ever go on a journey for the soran?" she asked.

"No, he sends me or Olukai with his group of soldiers," Kahiko replied. "Sometimes we have volunteers from the kingdom who wish to help."

"Who is Olukai?"

"He is the king's second counselor—not very bright, but the best fire dancer on the island." She'd vaguely heard of him, as Like had tried learning the art of fire dancing under Olukai's tutorship. But Like was too sick and had to drop out of the sessions. She remembered Like's deep disappointment as he could only watch Lopaka and the others around his age advance in the skill.

"And you are the king's first counselor?"

"'Ae."

Nohea nodded. She'd seen many of the king's counselors sitting and walking about the fortress. They looked fat, lazy, and unproductive. She imagined Olukai to be like them. Sure, he could probably be the island's best fire dancer, but perhaps that was in his glory days.

"We approach," said Kahiko. They had been riding over black lava rock, where ferns and grass grew over most of it. The honking noises of the nēnē filled the air since they began crossing the ancient lava. 'Ōhi'a trees scattered across the rocky plains, thicker in some parts than others, their red blossoms a welcome sight amidst the blackness.

Before the group was the thickest part of the wood that Nohea saw in these parts, with some tall koa, and long ferns on the ground.

"We leave our horses here," added Kahiko. "They get spooked by the dead smell of the mo'o."

"You said it was years since you killed it though," Nohea raised her eyebrows.

"'Ae, but a mo'o never truly dies. It's legend lives on. It becomes a part of the earth, the landscape. Come, I will show you."

In a way, Nohea knew now that Kahiko was not very scary. All the rumors she'd heard of him couldn't possibly be true. He had a calm and quiet personality... but maybe the quiet ones were the dangerous ones. She kept eyeing him, watching his lips to see if he uttered hexes and spells, but he genuinely seemed normal.

He led the way through the forest. The ferns and tall grass brushed against Nohea's legs and she couldn't stop tripping on the various vines. Not even the dark wood had been this thick.

The warriors behind her also struggled. "Can we cut through this?" one finally asked. Kahiko glared back at the man. "You would do well to respect the land. We are visitors here." Nohea noted this other admirable quality about Kahiko. He truly did respect the 'aina.

A strong smell filled the air: sulphur.

"Ugh," Nohea wrinkled her nose.

"It's the steam, from the volcano," said Kahiko, and Nohea noticed the white vapors rising from random parts of the forest.

Nohea mentally noted it, especially glad to see an abundance of uli, which began proving her point even more. Ferns, ti leaves, maile, koa, and "ōhi'a also grew rich and thick in these parts.

"Here we are..." Kahiko pulled a fern away, revealing a large clearing. There was a dip in the middle of the clearing, probably where the soran had pooled up, and then eventually cleared out—or was taken out by the king's men.

"There is the mo'o." Kahiko pointed to three large, mossy rocks on the other side of the dried pool. The first rock was oval shaped, with an indent in it, like an eye. The second rock was long and thick, with some indents on the sides like legs, and the last rock curled to the side, like a tail.

"I see him," she said, and stepped forward into the clearing. With no soran left in the dried, indented pond, her sandals crunched on the grayish crumbly debris below.

At the center of the pool, she dug her hand inside, hoping for some kind of moisture. But, as she scraped with a stick, the gray debris only turned into sharp, brittle, black lava rock.

The warriors circled around the pond, standing still and watching, their big bodies looking bulky and uncomfortable. Kahiko stayed put but watched, also curious.

Nohea dropped some of the gray debris into a small vial from her bag. The debris looked and felt like gray sand but made from the dust of dried out plants.

She took a few samples of the black lava rock.

"How many pools of soran are on the island?" she asked Kahiko.

"There were many," he said. "But most of them dried out. I would say there were about twelve... and now only four."

Nohea walked around the pond. "How did they dry out?" She took samples from the surrounding trees, grass, flowers, and ferns. Nēnē pellets littered the ground. The area had to be infested with those loud geese.

"The soran doesn't reproduce very quickly," said the kahuna. "We must make our payments to the mermaids to keep our island safe." He didn't directly answer the question and Nohea knew what he meant: the king sent his servants to collect the stuff. That's how it dried out.

"So this is actually the doing of the king?" Nohea raised a brow. "He exploited nearly all the pools on the island?"

"Olukai has led many expeditions." Kahiko's thick brows furrowed. His dark hand tightened around his tall walking staff. "If you wish to know more about collecting soran, you can ask him."

A light breeze moved through the trees, sending a shiver down Nohea's spine.

Something didn't feel right. How could the king just... take all the soran?

"How much does the king give to the mermaids as payment? And how often?" she asked. Kahiko almost rolled his eyes, his nose flaring.

"Four glass balls every three months."

Four glass balls? The glass balls were almost the size of her head, and if they did *four* of those every three months? She glanced back at the dry pond. No wonder it dried out so quickly.

Just from feeling the depth of the gray debris to the brittle lava rock beneath, she imagined this must have taken years to pool as much as it did.

"And what do the mermaids do with it?"

"The mermaids' business is their own." Kahiko cleared his throat, looking into the distance. "As long as they protect the shores, keeping their side of the bargain, then it doesn't matter what they do with it."

Nohea approached the mo'o, feeling the thick moss growing over its stone hardened body.

"What was his name?"

"Palekana."

Nohea closed her eyes for a moment, paying respects to the dead. Palekana meant "safe," but this mo'o was far from safe. He'd chosen to rest by soran, something that was looking to Nohea to be more dangerous, more powerful, and more addictive than she expected.

A darkness dawned over her. Probably the most dangerous thing about the soran was its influence. It had influenced the king and so many other men, like Olukai, to kill innocent creatures...

But all of this could be avoided if she created the soran herself, and made it readily available to everyone, right?

'Ae, she confirmed to herself, glancing around.

The king visited her only a few times since they arrived. Each time he'd been so positive, reminding her that this was for *all* of the people. And, indeed, she wanted this for everyone.

Soran could have saved Kimo. It could have saved the whole ghost generation from dying.

But it couldn't save Palekana, she thought, kneeling to touch the mo'o's frozen claws.

How many others had died for the sake of soran?

It's up to me to come up with a formula for this, she told herself once more. *Then these natural springs don't matter.*

Nohea walked into the distance, completely aware of the warriors following closely behind her, some moving to walk beside her. She doubted herself to be in any danger out in the middle of nowhere, but they took every precaution.

Over the course of the journey, she observed the king's elite warriors, like Akamu. They looked supremely strong, tall, large boned, and heavily built. Their skin looked tough like pahoehoe lava rock, their dark eyes perfectly alert, and their hair growing long and healthy down their backs.

She found out, through Wena, that the king *and* his warriors, at least 30 of them, drank soran. And she mentally noted all of the physical attributes the soran gave the men. They seemed to thrive perfectly and, in some ways, unnaturally. The previous night, one of the warriors heard a strange noise in the distance, so he got up to check it out. In absolute shock, Nohea jumped up as the warrior came running back with a speed she hadn't expected for someone so big.

He was chasing a mongoose, the ugly brown ferrets introduced by the foreigners. The red-eyed creature scurried around the campfire outside Nohea's hut, but the warriors found it a sport. With great haste, they picked up the mongoose by the tail and threw it to one another.

The mongoose tried biting, but it did no damage to their hard skin. They laughed, their voices booming, much like the king's voice, and then, finally, Akamu held it with both hands, twisting the neck. A crunch sound filled the air, and he tossed the dead mongoose to the side, scolding the men for acting like children.

Even though the mongoose was the pest of the island, and the king ordered the people to kill any they saw, Nohea hated that the men made sport of it.

She drew her attention back to the ground, analyzing what natural processes created soran.

Ah yes... She found exactly what she'd expected. Steam vents had cluttered the way, filling the air with its stinky smell, and making Nohea watch every step.

As she pressed forward, the warriors circling around her, she found a deep hole. An old lava tube. The pieces in her mind came together: Steam, an old lava flow below, debris of specific plants. Soran brought life to humans because it was *made of old life,* like a cycle.

When the lava passed through the lava tubes beneath, there was a slight chance that some lava rose to the surface, not a lot though. It would burn the area, leaving ashes and dead ferns, trees, and such.

She walked back to the dry soran pool, the warriors following.

And then with all of the dead stuff, the steam from the vents below will rise, creating moisture... and it gets trapped between the dead plants and the lava rock. She dug her hand into the gray debris again. *And then it ferments... probably takes a couple of years.. And uli...*

She looked about and spotted the purple ginger.

Of course! Nohea picked off a ginger, smashing a petal in her hand, watching as it turned her hands bluish-purple, nearly the same color as soran. *The uli is what provides the nutrients in the small, fermented pool beneath the surface.*

So the soran had been created under the surface, where the heat from below, combined with the debris on top, trapped the liquid, fermenting it. That meant... *there had to be more soran.* This was one pool, but who knew how many more pools were under the surface of the island?

And it had to be easy to identify—only the spots where old lava tubes had caved in, allowing steam to poke through, debris to fall over the top, and pools of water to get stuck between those.

So how does it pool on the surface of the earth? she wondered, stepping towards an ʻōhiʻa tree. It looked old, weathered, the bark barely holding onto the sides, and stringy gray moss wrapped all around.

"Can you cut this down?" Nohea looked at the nearest warrior, Akamu.

"ʻAe." With his massive hands, he snapped the trunk in two. "Do you need this?" He held the rest of the tree, but Nohea shook her head, wanting to see the stub.

The tree hadn't snapped perfectly, leaving some shards pointing out the top. She pulled a stone knife from her bag and sawed off the shards.

I was right... The rings of the tree showed years of heavy rain. *The heavy rain and natural processes broke down the plant debris, which, in turn, soaked up the fermented water. And then it became this pool.*

And that was why the pools could only produce soran to a certain point. She pulled out her paper and began scratching notes in the ancient writing of the meha.

That's why these pools don't reproduce. But with enough uli, this could go on forever. We could recreate these pools. She already thought of all the ways to artificially make soran in her lab, or to make giant quantities, using the same natural ingredients found in the forests, burning, and then fermenting the liquid.

"Have you found something?"

Nohea shoved her notes into her bag, annoyed at Kahiko looking over her shoulder.

"Not yet. I have some ideas, but they're only theories."

"What ideas?"

"I answer to the king," she said, standing up. "Not you." She didn't trust Kahiko, and though she observed him to be calm and cool, she still couldn't let go of old prejudices. She marched past him, sure that she'd find more pools of soran in the area. The temperatures, environment, and conditions were perfect.

They'd found soran long ago, because they could *see* it, but she knew, deep down, there had to be soran under the surface, where no one could see... yet.

"Stay here... please," she said, turning around to face the warriors and Kahiko. "I can't think with all of you crowding around me."

"It's the king's orders." Kahiko's eyes narrowed at her.

"Well, I can't..." Nohea held up her hands. "If you follow me everywhere, I'll get nothing done."

"We can see her from here," Akamu said. "We don't need to stand right next to her to keep her protected." They all knew what the warrior meant, for these men could run rapidly in a short amount of time.

Kahiko pushed Akamu. "Know your place." The warrior bowed stiffly, almost unnaturally, and Kahiko turned to Nohea. "Twelve steps. That's all you get."

Twelve steps was enough for her. She counted each one, lengthening her stride to get as much distance from Kahiko and the warriors as possible.

They were a good distance from her, gratefully, so she could try to follow the lava tube and find a patch of dead, burnt plants.

As she walked past vents, the smell of sulfur filled her nose, and the steam warmed up her skin.

She caught a glimpse of a narrow hole to her left: no steam, just vines and old moss growing around it. *The soran needs heat,* she reminded herself.

She followed the old tube, hoping to find some steam. Passing nēnē, scurrying mongoose, and dozens of ʻōhiʻa trees, Nohea finally stopped, her heart beginning to beat fast. She was right. Before her was a small patch of dead plants and ashes so old that ferns grew over it. It was a distinct, circular spot on the ground, grayish, with the old moss and ferns on top.

Nohea bent over so her back faced Kahiko and the warriors, covering what she was doing.

She reached through the thick ferns, pulled away the moss, and dug her hand into the center of the dead patch. The slimy, old debris felt like mud under her hand... and then... her hand moved freely through liquid.

She brought her hand out, wanting to squirm in delight. In the sunlight poking through the trees, the liquid drops on her hand glistened purple. Nohea held back her delight as all of her ideas, formulas, and theories were confirmed.

It was an untouched pool of soran. She'd just discovered how the island made soran, and how to make it herself.

CHAPTER THIRTY-FOUR

"I want to come too," Haunani complained as Po, Alika, Kahele, and Ulu prepared one of Tua's canoes. Po glanced at his sister, rolled his eyes, and beckoned her to join. A grin spread across her face as she climbed aboard the canoe.

"No complaining," Alika teased and Haunani scoffed. "Oh shut it—if there's anyone who complains around here, it'll be you because you're *always* hungry." They all laughed.

Alika was the heaviest of the group, with thick black hair, a big belly, and bulky arms and legs. Kahele had a lean physique, with black eyes, a hooked nose, lighter skin, and long fingers. Ulu was the shortest of the group, with a nasally voice, square body, and contagious laugh.

All three of them had long hair, though Alika left his frizzy mess down, while Kahele and Ulu pulled theirs up into high buns. The friends had always been a rascal group of boys, composed of the three dark locals, and Po, the golden haired boy, though he had an equally dark tanned skin.

And, of course, Haunani trailed behind. Since being home, Po fell right into rhythm with his childhood friends, laughing, teasing, and wrestling. It almost felt like nothing had changed.

Yet, at the same time, everything had changed.

They got Tua's beautiful double hulled wa'a ready. The two long hulls were connected by a platform, with benches along the sides and back. The wa'a had two triangular shaped sails, one in the center of the platform, and one in the front.

The boys loaded up their spears, bait, and other supplies. The sun wasn't yet close to rising, so Po carried a torch as he helped load things up. He kept hoping they'd leave the shores before Kamuela showed up.

Tua limped down the sandy hill to the canoe, with Sina and Oni following closely behind. Sina held a bundle in her arms.

"Haunani is going with you?" asked Tua, glancing at her, a sparkle in his eye. She skipped to the back of the boat.

"Po said I could come!"

Tua laughed and nodded to Po. "Your mama brought some food. Don't stay out too long, eh?"

Po nodded, walking through the water to take the bundle. "Thank you ma."

"We'll take care of the sweet stuff, the honey. Oh, and we'll make sure the imu is finished by the end of the day," Sina said, frowning at Po's friends. Po cleared his throat, and Alika, Kahele, and Ulu stopped what they were doing to greet Sina with a kiss on the cheek. She looked pleased. Po knew though, if they hadn't greeted her, they would never hear the end of the gossip.

"Thank you ma," he said again, then ruffled Oni's dark black hair before handing Haunani the bundle of food from Sina.

Po got ready to push the canoe out to sea. He was especially grateful that Sina took care of the imu. It would've been a lot of work to do the fishing, find a shiny object, collect some honey, *and* cook the pig and sweet potatoes in the underground pit all by himself. He knew he'd already spent too much time traveling and making arrangements. No doubt Olukai waited, and worried, at this point.

As they pushed the canoe out to sea, Tua, Sina, and Oni watched, the water swirling up to their knees. The salty breeze blew through Po's hair. He tried to conceal a smile.

"Wait!"

Po wished they could run at this point. It was Kamuela's voice. Po didn't try to hide an annoyed groan.

"Ah! There you are! First time you late!" Tua bellowed. Kamuela held a bundle. It looked too big to be full of food for himself, and Po felt even more annoyed that Kamuela probably brought food to share.

"Sorry." Kamuela walked through the water. "I... I didn't mean to be late. A messenger of the king stopped by my hut this morning. He's..." He cleared his throat, his cheeks turning red as all eyes turned to him. "The king's fortress is under attack. They're asking for all the men to travel to the fortress as soon as possible." He avoided all eye contact and placed his bundle on the canoe.

Haunani gasped, and Sina pulled Oni against her side. They all knew that when the king called men from the villages to battle, they spared no age: boys as young as six and seniors close to the grave had to go.

"They'll come looking for us today!" Alika said, looking into the distance, his thick hair and belly taking up a great deal of space on the canoe.

"I... I directed them towards the village. We should hurry and leave, before they come to the shores," Kamuela said, now standing on the side of the canoe.

"'Ae, 'ae, go," said Tua, stepping forward to launch the boat forward. Po and his friends jumped on, and Kamuela stumbled behind them.

"Father, you can't go to battle!" Haunani said as the boys took their places, both Kahele and Ulu paddling on either side.

"Don't worry my daughter," Tua said, his face cheerful, hopeful, as always.

"Eh Kamuela!" Sina called as the boat drifted further away. "Who is attacking?"

"The Māku'e!" Kamuela said back. A chill ran up Po's spine. He let the sail down and everyone on the boat fell back as the wind propelled them forward.

"What was that all about?" Haunani complained, her hair all over her face.

"We need to hurry," came Po's quick and firm reply.

Po WAS NOT AN EXPERIENCED SAILOR, and he watched and learned, in both irritation and wonder, as the other four showed him how to do things. Haunani sat at the front of the boat, her hands on her knees, smiling into the ocean. She reminded Po so much of their father, Tua: always positive, always so pure of heart. She was probably daydreaming about Olukai, Po had no doubt, trying to distract her thoughts from Tua's obligation to join the king's battle.

Every so often, the sea water gently misted their skin, making them shiver. The wind kept going, strong and steady. The ocean began to turn bluish and light purple, the morning sun rising behind them.

As the canoe took flight, skimming across the morning water, Kamuela eventually sat at the front next to Haunani, though they exchanged no words. Alika took the steering blade at the back, and Kahele and Ulu sat on either side of the canoe at the back, getting the fishing spears and nets ready. Po stood by the center mast, feeling refreshed, excited, and yet... nervous.

He had *no* idea what was going on at the king's fortress. Was Olukai alright? And what happened with Nohea? Did she change her mind and join the manō? Why was the Māku'e attacking. Was it their revenge for Nohea leaving them?

He closed his eyes and tried to listen to the island.

Nothing. Frustrated, his hand gripped on the mast.

"*Nai'a*!" Haunani exclaimed, and even though she sat at the front of the canoe, her voice sounded quiet under the wind and waves. She clapped her hands, watching, in awe.

Po smiled at the dolphins jumping in the distance, making clicking noises, as if greeting them, saying, "Good morning!"

Haunani was obviously delighted and entertained. But Po noticed that the other guys on the boat stared at *her,* not the dolphins. Even Kamuela's eyes lingered on her face before looking out to sea. Although Po was with some of his best friends, he couldn't help thinking that *so many* things had, indeed, changed.

They were all older, and no doubt some of his friends wanted to ask Haunani's hand in marriage. And maybe even Kamuela thought he had a chance.

"Eh, you ever gonna tell us what you're up to?" Alika asked from the back, his voice booming above the wind.

"Yeah, you've been gone for how many years now, and you *still* haven't told us," Ulu commented as he braided some string and cut the end with his teeth.

"He's probably married and has five kids," Kahele teased. Po punched his shoulder and sat in the back. He hadn't intended to tell them, but deep down he hoped that the manō would soon reveal himself. And he'd need all the help he could get.

So he sat back and shared his story, though he never mentioned Olukai's true name. His good friends listened, supportive, and sometimes teasing, as always. And, in the meantime, he noticed Haunani and Kamuela conversing in the front, though, from the looks of it, Haunani didn't even have a hard time handling Kamuela's awkward personality.

THEY SAILED a good distance until Alika finally handed Ulu an anchor. Ulu jumped into the water with the large rock and Po watched him sink, until he disappeared beneath the blue. Alika, Kahele, and Ulu were pretty expert in all of this, as they started spearfishing from a young age. Meanwhile, in his own youth, Po was landlocked, learning to make the wa'a with Tua in the shop.

Kamuela, as far as Po knew, seemed to know everything. It was annoying. He and Haunani walked to the back of the boat, where Kamuela grabbed his own spear, and opened his spread of food.

"Anyone can have this," he said. Po ignored him, and Alika rolled his eyes.

"That's very kind of you," Haunani said, picking out a sweet potato, then punched Alika's shoulder as she walked past him to the front again. Alika smiled after her, and Po began to wonder if it was a bad idea to let Haunani tag along.

Ulu appeared above the surface. He smiled and nodded to the others, a signal that the spot was good. They never once said the word "fish," for fear the fish would hear them. And none of the boys ate until they got at least one fish. Po wasn't sure how much fish he needed, but he told his friends, "plenty." And he hoped to get plenty. Anything to keep the mo'o appeased, and from eating Po himself.

"We go!" Alika grabbed his spear and dove in. Kahele followed after, water splashing onto the canoe. Ulu dove back under, and Kamuela paused. He looked at Po, realizing that Po didn't have any spears. "Do you want to borrow mine?" he asked, holding his out.

Po shook his head. "No thanks, you go ahead."

Kamuela looked confused. "Do you want to borrow this?" He went to his bundle in the back, revealing a net and fishing pole.

"No, I have other things to do..."

Kamuela cleared his throat. "Are you... are you looking for a mermaid?" So Kamuela *did* remember Po speaking with the mo'o, so long ago. Although Po had communicated with the mo'o's mind, he spoke out loud too.

Po nodded. "I didn't want to tell the others that part. Didn't want to scare them."

Kamuela kept his eyes down then pointed into the distance, straight ahead of the canoe. "We're close to the island's borders, where they patrol. If you keep swimming that way, you're bound to run into one." His fingers fidgeted with his spear, his eyes always diverted.

"Thanks Kamu."

Kamuela nodded, then looked to the front of the boat at Haunani, who stared at them both, amused. Po could've sworn Kamuela's ears turned red, but he dove into the water too fast.

"That was nice," Haunani said, standing up, chewing on her purple sweet potato. The wind kept blowing her dark hair across her face, so she fixed it.

"Me or him?"

"Him, of course. He just told you where to go."

"Do you think he's met a mermaid?"

Haunani shrugged. "How am I supposed to know?" Then she looked serious as she gazed out to the wide open sea. "Are you going to be alright out there? Are you sure you want to go alone?" She squinted into the distance, no doubt looking for the large fin of the great white shark circling the island.

Po nodded. He'd been preparing for this moment. If he could speak to a moʻo, he was sure he could speak to a mermaid. And he hoped to not only find something shiny, but find some answers.

He'd brought his surfboard, and none of his friends questioned it. He figured it would be nice to rest on the board, especially if he went a distance from the canoe.

"What's your signal?" Haunani asked.

"What signal?"

"To send help, of course." The guys could be heard swimming around the boat, occasionally coming up for breaths, then disappearing back into the ocean depths.

"I don't know. I guess if I disappear for too long."

"That's a terrible signal."

"Fine, what about the call of the ʻio?"

She nodded. "I like that much better."

Po placed the surfboard into the water, off the side of the boat. Haunani let her legs dangle off the boat as she watched him, her eyes dark. "Be safe," she said.

He nodded, though he knew that those who dealt with mermaids were hardly ever safe.

. . .

As Po PADDLED OUT, the sun rose, beating hard on his bare back. All of the boys wore shorter palekoki today, making it easier for them to move around and swim. He could feel the heat on his calves and shoulders, especially. Po kept paddling in a straight direction, glancing behind him every so often to see how far he'd gone from the canoe.

The wind had died down, and there were only a few big waves to overcome. His mind kept going back to the call of war. He had to hurry. Right at that moment, Olukai could be fighting. He could be in danger or need help.

As the canoe turned to a mere speck behind him, Po sat up to rest, his legs hanging in the warm, aqua water. He thought of all the things he'd heard of mermaids, including Olukai's experiences. Olukai took soran to the mermaids a few times, and he said they were beautiful creatures, with teasing eyes and voices like honey. Olukai mentioned that the mermaids exchanged little words, their beauty and flirtatious actions speaking volumes though.

Growing up Po heard stories of the mermaids eating people, or drowning them. He figured it was meant to scare the young ones, especially himself. Tua and Sina never felt comfortable with Po going into the water. Did they fear that if he was part mermaid, he'd turn into a monster?

A glimmer nearby caught his eye. It was too colorful, like a rainbow, to be a dolphin, turtle, and certainly it couldn't have been a shark, even though the great white shark had been spotted by villagers across the island. That's how the rumors of the manō had started to spread.

With the morning sun dazzling on the water, Po could hardly see below the surface. He knew it was clear water, but the light reflection was simply too bright. Just as he was about to slide off his board, a head, then shoulders rose out of the water, staring at him with vibrant blue eyes, specks of purple and gold glimmering within them.

He stared at her, and she tipped her head; this beautiful, radiant mermaid. Her blue hair floated around her tanned shoulders. Highlights of teal, frosty blue, and light purple in her hair shone in the sunlight. She looked curious, her round face graced by pink cheeks, and full, dark lips.

"What are you doing?" she asked, her voice smooth, as Olukai described.

Po found his voice choked in his throat. He'd never seen *anyone* as beautiful as this mermaid. Nohea, Kiani, and so many other young women in his life had been beautiful, but this was a completely different level of beautiful. She was *exotic*. Heat rose to his cheeks.

She frowned, folding her arms, and Po felt the immediate tension of impatience. He slid into the water, one hand over his board.

"I was looking for you," he said, and finally managed a smile. Her eyes narrowed.

"Why? I don't see any soran on that board of yours. I assume you're not one of the king's. Or maybe you're looking for trouble." She spoke as though in a hurry. "In that case, you might as well swim away while you have the chance."

"No, I need your help." He cleared his throat, feeling rude. "I'm Po. What's your name?"

Her look softened. "Alana."

He couldn't help himself. "You're... you're very beautiful." He wished he could bury his face in the water. He ran his fingers through his hair, immediately feeling the coolness from his salty, wet hands.

Alana didn't seem pleased, but she had the same amused look as Haunani did earlier. "What do you want?" she asked.

"I spoke to a moʻo a long time ago. I need—"

"You? You spoke to a moʻo?" She laughed, and it sounded like the tinkling of glass. "No human can talk to those fat lizards, only mermaids and Hune, the magical creatures of the island."

"I know." They stared at one another, and the mermaid's face darkened, as though some thought crossed her mind, the same one Po thought of: that he had to be part mermaid. Without warning, she launched forward, wrapping her arms around his chest and dove straight into the water.

Po hadn't even a chance to catch his breath, as she forced it out of him when she grabbed him. He opened his eyes, a strangely calm sensation filling his body and mind. Her scaly body glistened when the sun hit it, and her tail—he hadn't expected it to be so beautiful. She took him down, deeper and deeper, then finally let go and faced him. He hadn't held his breath, yet he didn't *run* out of breath.

He floated in the middle of the ocean, staring at her. She looked unusually clear, as normally he couldn't see well underwater. It had been years since he swam in the ocean. And now, it felt like he was home.

The mermaid swam around him, her long blue hair trailing behind her. Her blue scales went up to her chest, forming a sort of heart-shape that covered her bust. She was a lot smaller than Po expected. He reached a hand out to touch her tail and she shivered.

"Can you hear me?" she asked, examining his body. Po felt oddly vulnerable. He nodded. Her hands skimmed across his chest, his shoulders, and his back as she continued to circle him.

"Can you speak?" She touched his lips, and Po took her hand. A confidence entered him. "'Ae." It took no effort, and he smiled.

Alana gasped. "You are part mermaid—how though? Who are your parents?"

Po looked at her hand, so thin and smooth, sparkling like glitter in the light, wishing he could take all the time in the world with this girl. And wishing he could figure out the mystery now, that he was part mermaid. This experience had to pve that his father, who he barely knew, or his mother, who he never knew, were mermaids.

Alana slipped her hand away and circled him again. "Come, we must go up for air. Your chest is flattening." She swam upward as Po looked at his chest. Indeed, his stomach sunk in, his ribs jutting out in a weird way. "You're not used to being underwater for so long," she said, her rainbow-colored tail and blue-scaled body moving gracefully.

When they reached the surface, Po sucked in air. His lungs felt odd, and he looked down, but his chest and stomach returned to their normal size. Alana swam away, her tail splashing behind her. She came back with his board.

"Who are you parents?" she asked again.

"I don't know. I don't even know their names," Po said. "My father left when I barely turned five."

Alana rubbed her chin. "Well, normally your hair signifies your tribe, but your hair is like the humans." She reached out and ran her fingers through it, coming close to him again to examine it.

"I don't have much time," Po finally said, kicking away from her. Being so close to her gave him chicken skin.

"Ah yes. The moʻo. What is it you need? Mermaids don't usually help humans, but you're only *part* human," she said, resting her arm on his board and leaning her head on it.

"I need something shiny. I don't even know where to start."

Alana smiled, the first real smile he saw on her. It made Po's stomach jump. "That's easy. The moʻo will want a pearl. They like to collect and hide their treasure in their caves. What color is this moʻo friend of yours?"

The moʻo wasn't exactly a friend... yet, but Po answered, "Black."

"Then we'll get him a black pearl." She tipped her head. "I'm assuming you don't have a pearl garden of your own?"

He shook his head. A pearl garden? She raised her chin. "Well, you're in luck because I have one."

"Really?" Po smiled. "Can I see? I mean, can I have one please?"

"What will you give me in return?" she asked, folding her arms and eyeing him curiously.

"I have nothing on me now, but I can give you my knife on the boat or some food from the island. I don't know what mermaids like." Why didn't Po think of this sooner?

"Nevermind, you don't need to repay me—"

"No, I truly want to. Maybe in the future we can meet again, and I'll bring something for you." He stammered over his words. "Right now I have to hurry..." He had wasted far too much time. "I'm a messenger, for the manō—"

"The manō?" She swam up to him again, pressing her arms against his chest. He swallowed hard as she stared into his eyes. He almost thought of stealing a kiss with her that close, but he pulled himself away. Kiani's words nagged at the back of his head. *Are you sure you can resist their temptations?*

Of course I can, Po confirmed to himself.

"You're not lying." Alana backed away, smiling, mischievous, mirroring the way he usually felt, *except* when he was with her. He felt like a melting mess around her. A wave of relief passed that at least Haunani wasn't around to see him like this. He'd never hear the end of it. "You're full of surprises." She swam around him again and ran her fingers through his hair. "Will you wait here? It might take a while for me to get the pearl."

"Can I come with you?"

"I don't think you can hold your breath that long—"

"Last time you knocked the air out of me before we even went down," he argued.

She grinned, "Fine." Then, without waiting, she dove under.

Po followed, swimming deeper into the ocean than he'd ever gone before. Despite the mermaid's beauty ahead of him, he recommitted to focusing: Olukai could be in danger. The Mākuʻe were attacking, and if Olukai had already revealed himself, Po needed to help remove Nohea's curse. Because, if Ekewaka was somehow killed, they'd lose the alchemist too.

CHAPTER THIRTY-FIVE

Night fell across the island, and Olukai, along with three of his warriors, Lopaka, Ioane, and Sefa, snuck outside the fortress walls. Usually Olukai would send his men alone, but this time, he felt he needed to see the Queen's army himself. He'd actually gone earlier that day to meet Nohea, only to find her absent. She left with a group of warriors to see a pool of soran herself. He wished he could've gone with her, instead of Kahiko.

A branch snapped in the quiet of the forest and the four young men stood perfectly still, looking around.

"A mongoose," Sefa confirmed, his voice barely a whisper. "We're clear."

Olukai nodded and motioned with all his fingers for the men to advance forward, eager to see the queen's army.

He'd met the Māku'e before, as well as Queen Awa, on one of his many missions for soran. She seemed to like him, even to the point of flirting with him. He didn't know much of her history, besides the fact that she was the only daughter and child of the king before her, so she inherited the throne when he died. Rumors said that she didn't marry because no man could equal her in grace and beauty.

But there had been nothing "special" about her to Olukai. She appeared to be more of a bitter, grumpy woman in her late thirties, drinking soran, as he now knew from Haku, and spending her days in vanity.

He remembered their first encounter, as he'd been only seventeen at the time. She kept batting her eyes at him, saying that he and his twelve warriors were welcome to stay as long as they liked. They stayed a few days, Olukai and Lopaka dining with the queen on most nights to distract her. Meanwhile the men secretly examined the wooded kingdom, discovering a well of soran behind the waterfall.

When they asked the queen about it, she expressed surprise. She couldn't hide her ignorance and Olukai realized she had no idea such a valuable liquid pooled within the confines of her own kingdom.

No doubt she started drinking the soran after their visit, though Olukai and his men managed to steal and sneak out quite a few jugs before departing. And then, as Haku mentioned too, a moʻo took residence in her waterfall, blocking the soran, causing her to create a terrible hahau tree, enslaving her people.

The image of Kiani crossed his mind, the scars on her back. Their conversations, late into the night, about her life as a wanderer, and his life as a captain, resurfacing. She had opened up to him about her life, and, in many ways, he opened up to her.

Kiani. He tried to hide a smile, though it was dark and his warriors wouldn't have seen, as they followed closely behind him. It was quite the wonder that Olukai never crossed paths with Kiani before... especially after all the places he'd traveled to, including the dark woods.

"Olukai..." Lopaka held Olukai back, and they hid in the shadows of the trees. They were getting close to Waiakea village, walking through the forest instead of taking the main road. While deep in thought, Olukai hadn't noticed shadows walking along the main road: big, hunky men, who walked so quietly, it seemed against the very nature of their size.

Olukai rubbed his forehead. He needed to focus, casting aside any worries on Kiani's whereabouts. She could take care of herself.

"Spies," Lopaka whispered. Not surprised, Olukai figured the queen would send her own men to check out the king's army too. He wondered if she came along to fight, or if she kept hidden, safe, in the deepest parts of the woods.

"I can get a perfect shot," Ioane whispered, spear in hand. Sefa, next to him, nodded, confirming he, too, could get a good shot at the spies walking in the dark. Olukai trained these two young men himself and had no doubt of their abilities. They'd been there when he made contact with the great white shark, but they never spoke of it.

Olukai shook his head. There was no way the queen's men could find the size of the king's army unless they climbed the fortress walls... which they probably wouldn't do, because guards kept watch on towers along the walls.

Olukai motioned with his hand, pointing ahead of them, a signal to keep moving forward. The other three nodded and they all continued through the forest, finally reaching the deserted Waiakea village.

In the moonlight, it looked like a ghost town. All of the people had moved within the walls of the king's fortress, or travelled in haste to other parts of the island to stay with family until the war passed. Messengers had been sent out on horses to gather as many men from the villages as possible. Olukai figured a messenger reached Po's village in Hakalau and wondered if Po was alright.

His thoughts repeated his worry for Po: *This is the longest Po has ever taken on a mission.*

The four young men crept through the empty streets, hiding behind walls, always watching their surroundings. Olukai didn't expect the queen's army to inhabit the village, or even burn it down. He expected her to keep her armies camped farther off, in case the deserted town had been used as *the* weapon. Old tales of war shared stories of deserted ghost towns infested with diseases, and when armies rampaged through them, they died from the lingering diseases, not even making it to battle.

The queen was wise to keep her distance, even if the ghost town held no disease.

Once the men passed safely through the village, finding no life in sight, they veered off the main road, back into the forest. They walked lightly so that the ferns and bushes didn't crunch and snap beneath their feet.

After walking a ways, Olukai caught a glimpse of a light in the distance—several lights. *Campfires,* Olukai thought, then motioned for his men to climb. Without hesitating, each one of them climbed the closest tree, until their heads came over the forest canopy, and they saw the queen's army spread out before them.

Olukai frowned. He had expected more soldiers. There had to be about eight or nine campfires, and nestled around each one were about ten to twelve men.

A pueo sounded in the night, and Olukai turned to see which of his warriors did the call. It was Sefa, standing a few feet away. "Ninety-eight," Sefa said loud enough that they could all hear, but quiet enough that it didn't echo.

Olukai rubbed his chin. Lopaka squinted into the night while saying, "That's the smallest army I've ever heard of. We have at least seven hundred men..."

"Let's get a closer look," Olukai said, wondering if the queen had a small army because these were "special" warriors. He'd sparred with the king's warriors, the men who drank soran. They could take on at least two normal soldiers, no problem. Not only did their tough skin act as a shield, but they didn't tire easily, like normal soldiers. The warriors ran faster, jumped higher, and moved quicker than others. Their brains worked, processed, and evaluated situations better than normal people, so they always had the upper hand.

"Are you sure?" Lopaka whispered once they all climbed down.

"I want to see their weapons, armor, and if there's a hint of any tactic," Olukai replied, then motioned for them to keep moving.

When they got closer to the army, the four kept hidden in the safety of the trees. The smell of meat cooking on the campfires filled the air. The men chatted amongst themselves, wearing white kiheis, their big, bulky bodies covering the view of the fire.

One of them stood up, holding a glass ball of something. It shone in the glow of the fire. Purple.

I knew it, Olukai thought. The queen brought such a small army because these men were, indeed, her special warriors, the ones who drank soran, the ones who were almost invincible. His army—even bigger in number than the queen's army—had much to fear, but Olukai would keep this a secret. He needed to keep his men's morale up.

"Just great," Lopaka groaned. "Soran? We're dead unless father's warriors join the battle." Olukai didn't see any reason the king wouldn't send his own special forces to battle... unless he selfishly kept his warriors to himself, and around Nohea.

Olukai didn't say anything, anger and fear growing inside him. At least seven hundred normal, untrained soldiers against almost a hundred soran-drinking warriors?

The manō does not fear, the island whispered in the wind. He gulped, knowing it wasn't true. This would be a horrible, bloody battle. And no matter how many options he ran through in his head: revealing himself as the true king of the island, trying to make a peace agreement with *both* the false king of Kaimana Island and queen of the dark tribe, or holding some kind of island council, all of it turned into an inevitable battle.

Olukai motioned for his men to make their way back, Lopaka's words ringing in his ears. *We're dead.*

CHAPTER THIRTY-SIX

The same night Nohea returned from her expedition to the soran pool, Wena appeared at the hut holding a small bundle of cloth over his left eye. Nohea glanced up and a confusing mixture of emotions overwhelmed her. As much as she wanted to treat him coldly, she also wanted to hug him. So she did neither, and, instead, asked, "What happened?"

Wena shrugged and sat on the table against the wall, leaning his head backwards. His wavy hair fell from his face, his skin shimmering with a light perspiration. He breathed deeply, purple bruises covering his tanned arms and legs, some dry blood on his knuckles.

"Were you fighting with the guards?" She approached him to examine the wounds. He nodded, clarifying, *The king's warriors.*

"You look terrible..." She held his left arm out and touched a large dark circle on his shoulder. He tensed at her touch. Wena signed, *It's my fault... I shouldn't have agreed to spar with them. I was just angry.*

"Angry?"

Was he angry at her? Wena shrugged again and sat up, his face close to Nohea's. "Let me see your eye." She placed her hand over his when he looked away, not willing to even give her a glimpse. But she carefully peeled away the cool cloth from his eye, and then cringed.

A black crescent shape had formed under Wena's discolored left eye. A thin cut from his eyelid to the eyebrow stuck together with dried blood, and all the skin around the eye swelled in colors of red and purple. "Let me get some medicine for this." Nohea whirled around, grabbing some salve from the shelf, her body tensing like it did everytime she helped a wounded slave.

Wena shook his head. *I'm fine.*

But Nohea knew it needed some attention. "Why do you spar with those guards?"

Warriors, he corrected again, but Nohea ignored him. "You know it's an unfair match. They drink soran..." She hated hearing herself say it, because one day everyone would drink soran.

And at that moment, she paused while checking his wound, the strangeness of her situation now dawning on her. She was surrounded by soran and working on a way to reproduce it, yet she never drank it. The thought of drinking it made her stomach churn. Something within her resisted soran, and a deep guilt filled her.

But why? Eventually everyone will drink it, she thought. The image of her father and his warriors filled her mind. Their huge bodies and tough skin made them almost invincible. Yet they were so... *unnatural.*

She tossed the thought aside, ignoring the island humming in agreement. Instead, Nohea focused on wiping the blood around Wena's eye. "The warriors are stronger than you. Why would you put yourself in that situation?"

You think I'm not strong? Wena raised his eyebrow then shrank back against the wall when she pushed a little too hard on his cheek.

"Sorry. No, that's not what I mean. I mean... you could get hurt, like this. Or worse..." She placed some coconut salve around his eye, then noticed he'd been staring at her the entire time.

She frowned. "Where were you today?"

He blinked, letting an eerie silence fall between them. Something was wrong. "Wena, what happened?" Nohea sat next to him, touching his shoulder. He sat up and signed. *I don't know if I can tell you.*

Please, Nohea signed back, not wanting Akamu or any of the other guards to hear their conversation. *You look worried.* And, much to her relief, it wasn't about her. But if not her, then who?

It's Kiani.

Nohea nodded, encouraging him to continue, but he shook his head. *I can't say more, but she's.... in danger.*

Nohea leaped to her feet and clasped her hands together before signing and mouthing back. *What are you waiting for? Let's go help her!*

That's the thing. We can't. It's too late.

I don't understand. Nohea grew impatient. *Wena, where is she? What happened?*

Wena's eyebrows creased as he rubbed his forehead. *I can't tell you, Nohea. I wish things could have been different.*

But she met the manō?

'Ae.

Then why is she in danger?

Wena stood, and Nohea could tell he also grew impatient with her. *I have to go,* he signed, his countenance darker than Nohea had ever felt in him.

"Wait." Nohea reached for his wrist. "Please Wena. I want to help." He looked past her, and she realized the vacancy of his thoughts. Not knowing what else to do, she wrapped her arms around his neck and embraced him. His hands immediately wrapped around her, holding her close to him. Something was horribly wrong, and Nohea's heart beat in fear.

Where was Kiani? Was she alright? What happened? All the unanswered questions left her head spinning. She held him tighter, and he returned the affection. For a moment, everything terrified Nohea: a battle was about to commence and people would die. She'd been so focused on her task, she forgot the feeling of how fragile life truly was. And how blessed she was to have Wena, one person in this whole world who loved her.

Loved her. The feeling sent warmth throughout her entire body, vibrating through the energy and seeping back into Wena, because, she realized, she loved him too. He was a dear friend, and the thought that he was in pain made her want to take it all away.

Nohea didn't know how long they stood there holding one another tight, and she didn't care. But Wena finally squeezed her close and loosened his arms as they took a step back. But neither let go: Wena's hands held on her waist, and Nohea's arms still wrapped around his neck.

I should go, Wena mouthed, not bothering to sign. Nohea nodded, trying to read his eyes, waiting for any other explanation about his sister, the manō, or his other concerns. But he didn't say anything. Instead, he leaned down to kiss her cheek, and she kissed his cheek, careful to stay clear of his tender eye.

He lingered, staring into her eyes for a moment. Then, as if he could bear his pain no longer, he let his arms fall to his side and left. Nohea slumped into her chair, more confused than ever before. Was Kiani in danger because of something Nohea did?

The thought seized her mind, and she hugged herself, horrified.

Maybe she wasn't doing all of this for the people... maybe, in a way, she was doing this for herself: to be loved. Yet, when love came to her, like this beautiful, sweet love and friendship that Wena had been offering her, she ignored it, of course, until this recent revelation. But she *had* been ignoring this beautiful relationship.

Just like Edena.

It felt like all the air had left the room. Nohea reached for her gourd of water and chugged as much as she could.

I'm not like Edena, she said, but no matter how many times she said it, the island chastised her denial. Finally, Nohea stormed out for some fresh air, with Akamu and a few other guards following closely behind her.

CHAPTER THIRTY-SEVEN

Po lay on his back, staring at the hut ceiling, his fingers playing with the smooth pearl. His friends got five fish each, and Kamuela got eight—the biggest fish too. It bugged Po, but he decided to be gracious about it, as Kamuela's haul alone was sure to please the moʻo.

They returned in the late afternoon, and while Alika, Kahele, and Ulu had to return to their families, Kamu, Haunani, and Po cleaned and cooked the fish. They wrapped the cooked fish in ti leaves, ready for Po to take to the moʻo the next day. Both Haunani and Kamuela volunteered to help carry the food, and Kahele got permission to join too.

It was too late to go to the moʻo that night, but Po was much too tired anyway. He rubbed his eyes, hoping that the nightmare wouldn't come when he fell asleep.

He hoped to dream about the mermaid. He couldn't stop thinking about her eyes, her smile. Kiani had mentioned the lure and temptation of mermaids. Perhaps Alana had toyed with him. His heart melted, and he thought, whatever Alana did, it had worked.

Whenever the manō becomes king of the island, Po thought, *I'm going to build a canoe and sail away... and see Alana again.* He tried not to smile in the darkness, but he couldn't help it. Because a part of him wondered if she liked him too. All teasings and flirtings with other girls, including Nohea, had all but disappeared for Po when Alana *hinted*, in the tiniest way, her interest. He sighed at the memory.

Once they swam to Alana's pearl garden, where rows and rows of oysters sat in organized rows, she gently touched a large white oyster, which opened, revealing a giant black pearl. She took out the pearl, rubbing the outer shell again, and it vibrated in delight, like a dog being scratched behind its ear.

Alana smiled at Po and began swimming back to the surface. By the time they reached the board, Po couldn't see the canoe in the distance. He didn't know how far they'd gone, but he knew it would take a while to get back.

When Alana handed him the pearl, she stared at his face, studying, waiting for a reaction. He thanked her profusely, and she finally smiled in delight. When he told her he should get back, she hesitated. "It's kind of far and you seem tired," she said. "Can I escort you back?"

So he paddled back, while she swam alongside him, asking random questions, like where he'd been on the island, whom he met, what he ate, and so forth. He figured she was curious, as she probably never spoke to humans before. When the canoe came back into view, she rested her arms on the front of his board and stared at him.

"This is where we part," she said, adding, "You know, mermaids aren't really supposed to talk to humans so I hope you don't go telling everyone about this."

He grinned, as he still laid on his stomach, resting his chin on his fists, the pearl safely closed in his palm. "I won't say a word." They stared into one another's eyes.

"I better go," she said.

"Wait." Po heard himself say. "On the island, we give each other a kiss on the cheek..." He was sure his ears turned red as a crab. "It's a way of saying hello, and goodbye."

"Oh," she smiled slyly. "Well then are you going to kiss me?"

He leaned forward and kissed her wet, warm, salty cheek. Then he pulled back, smiling. Her cheeks had flushed. "Well, good luck with that moʻo..." She slid off the board and bent her head to one side, observing him. The sly smile disappeared, and a look of sentiment filled her face.

"Truly, good luck Po," she said. She swam forward to touch his arm, *that* moment of contact meaning so much more than luck. It made his skin crawl, and then she dove under, the last sight of her being the rainbow fin. He watched her until the blue water covered her completely, like a blanket.

He didn't dare share the story with Haunani until they sat around the campfire, cooking the fish on the shore. Kamuela had been there, but for once, Po didn't care if Kamu heard the story. Perhaps Kamuela's acts of kindness in offering his spear and food, as well as spearing the most fish, had softened Po's heart. Of course Po left out the parts about Alana flirting, but Haunani smiled wickedly the entire time he shared the story.

As the night wore on, Po touched the place where Alana had touched his arm. He couldn't wait to see her again. But tomorrow, he had a moʻo to meet.

THE MORNING DRAGGED ON. Kahele arrived, eager to help, but Sina was in one of her moods, bossing everyone around, sweating over everything, and making it more chaotic than it needed to be. Tua and Kamu made a stretcher, and Haunani and Sina wrapped food in big bundles of kapa to carry on their backs.

King Ekewaka's messenger had come to Tua's home the previous day, while Po and the others were at sea. Po had little to no worry about it, but Kahele said his parents wanted him to leave as soon as he finished helping Po. Even Tua gathered things to leave.

Although he hated to admit it, Po knew that many of the villagers still obeyed the king—they never questioned politics, blindly obeyed. And, in some ways, the villagers didn't seem affected by King Ekewaka at all, besides paying taxes. Haku had visited Hakalau village many times, and the people embraced his message that there was one true ali'i left. Tua and Sina knew Haku too, and though they liked his message, they never spoke of it. Po hoped that when Olukai became king, the people would embrace their true ali'i. Until then, however, they still obeyed Ekewaka.

"Alright I think that's it!" Sina said, wiping her hands on her skirt. "Po! Get over here—you and Kahele are carrying this." She pointed to the stretcher, then handed the bundles to Haunani and Kamu. Po took the front two bamboo poles of the stretcher, and Kahele took the back. It was heavier than Po thought, as a huge cooked pig, along with the imu goods, like sweet potato and breadfruit, filled it up in a big mound, but he didn't mind.

Po set it back down to double check the pouch at his side. When his fingers wrapped around the large black pearl, he hid a smile.

"You better be careful," Sina said, her voice firm as she kissed everyone's cheeks, her hands sweaty and the oil from her face rubbing on their skin. None of them dared make a move to swipe it off, gross as it was, for fear they might make her more angry.

"Off you go!" she said. Tua and Oni, who stood on the side the entire time, out of Sina's way and wrath, waved goodbye.

"Good luck!" Tua said, holding up his thumb and pinky to Po. Po smiled and nodded.

Once the four descended into the thick woods, the view of Sina, Tua, and Oni long gone, Po placed the stretcher down and wiped his face. The others followed.

"Ma can be so bossy sometimes!" Haunani huffed.

"Just like you," Po teased. She glared at him. Kahele laughed and she glared at him too.

"Are you nervous?" she asked as they picked up their huge loads.

"Not really… I feel really calm." Po took a breath. "I think this is going to work."

"*Think?* Or know? Cause I sure hope you *know.*" Haunani sounded like her younger self, years before, trudging behind the group, talking too much.

"You're right… I know it will work."

As they walked on, Po's arms grew weary from the heavy load, yet he verbally reviewed the plan with the others: He'd climb down the cave with both bundles. Then Haunani, Kamu, and Kahele could use woven ropes to lower the stretcher down as well.

"And then we run—yes, we know," Haunani said, breathing heavily. "This is the fourth time we've gone over the plan."

Sweat dripped down Po's forehead, and when he looked back at the other three, their faces looked equally red and muggy. The forest grew thicker by the minute.

"It doesn't feel like it was this far last time," Haunani said after they'd been walking for a few hours.

"Oh, it was far…" Po set the stretcher down and the four sat in a circle for a rest.

"This manō…" Kamuela said, his hands playing with the string on his gourd, "Does he need more messengers?"

Over the campfire the previous night, Po had briefly explained to Kamuela that he was a messenger for the heir of the great white shark. Po fought to keep his eyes from rolling. Of course Kamuela would want to join the manō, and then Po would have to see him all the time. As much improvement in their relationship as they made, it was definitely not enough for Po to openly support and help Kamuela.

"No, he doesn't need anymore—he already has me." It was a lie. Olukai really needed all the help he could get, and another messenger would be helpful… anyone but Kamuela though…

"But he needs warriors?" Kahele asked, then took a chug from his gourd and swiped his mouth.

"'Ae…"

"What if we gathered all the men, as if going to the fortress," said Kamuela, still fidgeting, avoiding eye contact, "And then we join the manō. Is that... Is that possible?"

"'Ae, I'd rather join the manō than that tax-loving king," said Kahele.

"Can girls join?" Haunani piped in.

Po sighed. "'Ae, 'ae... You *all* can join." He hated to admit it, but he forced himself to say it. "That's not a bad idea, Kamuela. Maybe our village can start the army of the manō."

"'Ae!" Kahele and Haunani exclaimed. Kamuela looked into the distance and nodded.

"Where should we go then?" asked Kahele. "My ma expects me to leave after I help you." Kahele's parents didn't know Po served the manō, but they did like Po. Po was surprised when Kahele's parents granted him permission to join. But Po realized that it was probably because Kahele had a younger sister, and his parents probably hoped Po would marry her. At least, that's what Po figured. Alika and Ulu didn't have any younger sisters so they'd already left to join the king.

Po tried to think. Where could he send his friends, who would march and gather more troops to join the manō along their journey? "On the eastern shores. There's a bay, it's called Huna bay."

"Secret bay?" Haunani asked, thinking about it. "I've heard of it. The girls from Kea'au village spoke of it." She brightened up. "I think Olukai lives not far from there."

Indeed, Olukai lived quite close to the bay, not more than an hour's walk.

"I'm sure we can find it," Kahele said.

"We can catch up to the other villagers heading towards the fortress," Haunani said, "And gather whatever men we can on the way."

"Ma and pa wouldn't let you go," Po cut in, not wanting to get her hopes up. She wasn't a particular young woman of importance, like Nohea or Kiani. She was not a warrior either, only a dancer. He didn't want to put her in danger, unnecessary danger. Plus the idea of her being alone with a bunch of men, without his protection, made him nervous. Even if they were good men or his friends, Po still didn't feel comfortable with the idea.

She frowned. "It's not fair that pa has to fight. I would rather go in his place, and I would rather serve and help the manō." She looked around at the three young men, but none of them offered support. She sighed and rolled her eyes. "I want to go, alright? I'm sure I can be of use! Why can all of you fight for the true ali'i, and I can't?"

"I know it's not... it's not fair," Kamuela cut in, and this time, Po could see the tips of Kamuela's ears turning red. "But Po is right. It's not safe for a woman, like you, to travel with a group of men... it's not appropriate either." He avoided her gaze, staring at the ground. Haunani looked shocked that he'd spoken against her, like after all the years of defending him, he now betrayed her.

"Just you all wait and see," she muttered, drawing her knees to her chest. Po looked at her, sympathetic.

"I'm sorry Haunani..." But she didn't glance at him, staring only at her gourd of water.

Kahele stood up, to break up the awkward tension. "We should keep going," he said. "We're almost there."

THEY CARRIED the bundles for an hour longer, and then, finally, the smell of sulfur filled the air. Kahele pointed into the distance, where mounds of lava rock had fallen on one another. The old black rock donned heaps of moss and ferns, and then, when Po looked towards the biggest mound, he saw the black hole in the ground. The cave.

"Made it," Po said. Haunani grabbed his arm to hug him before he descended.

"Good luck," she whispered. Kamuela and Kahele both nodded to Po, and he started the climb down. Last time he'd fallen in, receiving only a few cuts and scrapes, luckily. Kamuela hadn't been so lucky though. Po remembered the huge, bloody gash on Kamu's knee, but he ignored the thought.

When Po's feet touched the ground, he marveled at how much taller he was now than the last time he fell in. Everything now looked so much smaller, including the cave entrance. Already he felt the warmth coming from the cave, a guarantee that the mo'o still slept within. He nodded at the three heads, peeking in from above.

Kamuela and Kahele lowered the bundles using ropes, and then they carefully lowered the stretcher. They did it in such a profound silence that the only noise Po heard from them were the ropes grinding against the sides of the lava rock.

When the stretcher hit the ground, Po nodded to those above. Kahele saluted him and disappeared. Haunani bit her lower lip, hesitant to leave. Po waved. She looked like she might cry, and it reminded him so much of her younger self.

He nodded again, but she stood there, frozen. Then Kamuela touched her arm and she finally nodded back, moving away from the cave.

Po let out a sigh: the hard part was over. Now the *harder* part.

He opened the food from the ti leaf wrappings, the smell of fish, pig, sweet potato, and fruit filling his nose. It made his mouth water. He reached into his pouch, closing his hand around the giant pearl. Then he lit his torch and took a breath.

Time to wake the mo'o.

He'd done this before, and it felt odd to do it again. Walking in, his feet crunched on things but he didn't look down this time. He touched the black glittery wall—that was not a wall, he knew now.

The warm air coming from the cave paused for a moment. Po stepped back, watching, as the big black eyelid opened, revealing a large, yellow eye.

It took a moment to adjust, and then focus on him. Swallowing hard, Po took another step back.

Hello again, Po reached out with his mind. *Are you hungry? I brought you real food this time...*

He heard the mo'o lick its lips, a drooly sound, and then it reached out its claws, stretching like a cat. Po's hair stood on end.

Well, well, said the moʻo to Po's mind, its voice deep, like Po always remembered it. *We meet again.*

Then the moʻo stepped into the light, revealing its gigantic, black body. His legs were the size of Po around, his claws a pearly white, and his head the size of a small whale, if not bigger. His body, especially, filled up the entire cave. Po kept wondering how the moʻo fit in there—it seemed so uncomfortable, squished, and claustrophobic.

When the moʻo stepped into the light, the scales reflected like glitter on the walls.

Please, eat, Po motioned to the food. A smile from the moʻo revealed shiny white teeth.

Something tells me this is not a gift, but an exchange—am I wrong? The moʻo hovered over the food, sniffing, smiling with those sharp razor-like teeth.

You are not wrong—I do need your help. Po hesitated, and the dragon let out an internal sigh, impatient to get started.

Will you be joining this feast? He poked the whole breadfruit with one claw and popped it into his mouth, licking his lips over and over again. *That was salted just right—I'm going to assume you didn't make all of this.* The dragon looked amused.

Po sat beside the moʻo, reaching for some food himself. *No, of course not. My hānai mother helped.*

It felt odd to sit side by side, a moʻo and a man, eating food together. But, at the same time, Po realized how hungry he'd been—he hadn't eaten much that morning, too nervous to get this done with.

Now, as they sat together, a sense of calm overcame him. *This will work out,* he kept thinking over and over, knowing that as each minute passed, Olukai could be at battle with the Mākuʻe. Po might be able to convince the moʻo to help beyond a visit to the lava lady.

Mmm... Exquisite. The moʻo commented on nearly everything he ate, choosing to bite the pig in pieces, crunching on the bones, which grossed Po out. He avoided the pig and, instead, ate fish and poi, licking his own fingers.

So what is the exchange about? the moʻo asked as they ate.

I must visit the Lady of the Lava, and the only way to do that is by bringing an old friend. Po swallowed hard, hoping.

Ah yes, I have not seen her for many years now. A wise, fiery sorceress that one, Why are you seeking her? As the dragon ate more, his energy felt more pleasant, and his tone less irritated, more willing.

I have a friend who's been cursed. The only one who can help her is the lady of the lava.

A curse, you say? What sort? Is he diseased—I will not carry a diseased human.

She. She was cursed by her mother, so that whatever pain her father feels, she feels. And vice versa.

Sounds like the curse of a meha to me, not the work of the lava lady.

They ate in silence, both pondering. *We have no other options,* Po finally said.

What's your name anyways? The moʻo asked instead after swallowing some fruits. The fact that Po could hear it going down the dragon's throat made Po cringe.

Po, short for Pōmaika'i. You?

'Ele, short for Ele'ele. You know, usually you get to know a person before you eat, especially their name. You are a strange human...

Po smiled. He'd forgotten all the pleasantries because of his nervousness. But now he felt like they were bonding over this food. They ate in silence until 'Ele licked up all the bits and crumbs off the stretcher and every ti leaf wrapping, his thin red tongue watering. He rested his head on his hands, pleased, a smug look on his lips, his eyes half open.

I would agree to help you, said 'Ele, *but you forgot one thing.*

Po tried to conceal his own smirk. *What is that?*

Perhaps you forgot our exchange from long ago, but I would like something shiny. A treasure.

Po reached into his pouch, enclosing the pearl in his palm. *Actually, I didn't forget. I brought this for you.* He held out the large pearl, and 'Ele's eyes widened. *That is the biggest I've ever seen...*

Po rolled it to ʻEle, who used his claw to move it around, amazement in his eyes. *You must be some kind of special mermaid to have this...* He looked at Po. *Because you are a mermaid... otherwise you couldn't talk to me.*

The realization, once again, sent a shiver down Po's back. After his encounter with Alana, talking in the water, holding his breath for extended periods of time, and, of course, mind-conversing with the moʻo, there was no doubt of his mermaid heritage. But how? Was his father part mermaid? Or his mother? He wished he knew all the answers.

Po didn't think it right to tell the moʻo that it came from Alana's garden. He figured ʻEle had the large pearl, he liked it, and that's all that mattered. Maybe one day, when he trusted the moʻo more, he'd tell the truth—that Po wasn't a special mermaid, but Alana definitely was.

Well, you've brought everything to appease me, said ʻEle. *It's probably about time I got some fresh air anyways.* Po tried to keep his chest from swelling with hope and pride.

ʻEle stretched, like a cat, again. *Now would you close your eyes so you don't see where I put this?* His claw played with the pearl.

Of course. I'll even turn around. And Po did, facing the cave wall, while ʻEle moved around in the background.

Done. Alright, when do we go to the lady?

Po looked up at the sky. After walking several hours, and resting a few times, with his sister and friends, then sitting to eat with the moʻo for another few hours, it had to be late afternoon.

Can we go now?

If that is your wish.

It is... but before we go to the lady, I have to get my friend.

Where is she?

The king's fortress.

ʻEle wrinkled his nose, a strange movement for a moʻo. *You mean Ekewaka?*

ʻAe. Is there a problem?

I'd rather not... He dug his claw into the black lava rock, bored.

Why? Po folded his arms.

I don't know if you've heard but... that king has killed many mo'o.

He won't kill you, I won't allow it. I will do my best to keep you safe.

'Ele laughed. *You? You're a weak human—*

I can take that pearl back now. Po started for the cave and the dragon backed into it. This was taking too long, and Po felt his options slipping away, his kindness and patience turning to threatening.

No, it's mine now! You don't know where I put it!

Of course I know where you put it. I could hear you moving around in there. He pushed the mo'o's head aside, much to both of their surprise.

I could eat you up in one bite! 'Ele threatened, though he didn't sound one bit convincing.

Fine. Eat me. You'll never get pearls that size ever again. They stood face to face, annoyed.

'Ele sighed. *Fine. We can stop by the fortress to get your friend, but I refuse to go in the daylight. We go when the sun sets, and I can hide in the darkness of night.*

Po crossed his arms, wanting to protest, wanting to find out if Olukai needed help on the battlefield. But he had no other option. *Fine.*

Fine. The mo'o crossed his arms too.

But I'm going to wait outside of this cave. It's too cramped. Po started climbing out of the cave opening and was surprised to find the mo'o climbing behind him.

When he stepped onto the mossy forest floor, he stretched. They still had a few hours until sunset. Po leaned against a tree so he could keep an eye on the dragon. 'Ele looked much larger, and more beautiful when he wasn't cramped in the cave. He stretched his wings and rested his head on his hands again, also taking a rest. Po wondered when was the last time ʻEle ate, as he looked neither weak nor terribly muscular.

For some reason, watching the moʻo made Po feel like he didn't belong. ʻEle was comfortable in his own skin, and a longing filled Po's heart. ʻEle knew who he was. And Po didn't.

How long have you been friends with the lava lady? Po asked.

Many, many decades. I have not left these confines since that false king started roaming the island, looking for soran.

Po shifted, uncomfortable, then asked, *How many moʻo are left anyways?*

At least five of us. We are a quiet type, preferring to not bother others, or be bothered.

So what is your purpose? Po folded his arms. The moʻo seemed lazy and bored.

To serve when needed, ʻEle replied. *To protect certain villages and families who honor us.* He grinned. *What is your purpose?*

Po let his head rest against the tree and shrugged. "I wish I knew," he said aloud, and the moʻo shifted.

You don't seem to know where you belong, he began, then added, *Sometimes you can lose sight of the good around you, especially if you focus too much on what's ahead.*

ʻEle spoke in riddles. Again. His deep rumble of a voice echoed in Po's head as he questioned why he always wanted to sail away. Was it really because Po wanted to sail, or was it because he wanted to run from something?

CHAPTER THIRTY-EIGHT

"A messenger of the queen wishes to speak with you," said one of the soldiers from the fortress gate. His face looked red, Olukai guessed because the man ran as fast as he could.

"Is he accompanied?"

"She, sir. The messenger is a woman, and she is accompanied by what looks like a kahuna." The soldier cleared his throat, adding, "And by three guards."

Olukai rubbed his chin. He stood outside the captain's large hut, his personal hut, overlooking a map of the island. He wondered. A female messenger? With a kahuna? It was a strange thing indeed. Usually the messenger was a man of high ranking, an orator, smooth talker, loyal to the throne. It wasn't that a woman couldn't do the role of a messenger, but it seemed odd to Olukai, especially since it was a dangerous thing to send a woman into an enemy camp.

"Let them in," he said. The soldier bowed and ran off towards the fortress walls, a good distance from where the army kept camp within. Behind the army was another little camp, where the villagers set up. He knew they waited eagerly to return to their homes.

In the distance, the gates opened. Olukai didn't fear the queen's army rushing or charging in. With all of the men ready at the gates, along with the men on top of the walls on towers, they would be unwise to do such a thing. Though, deep down, Olukai still worried for the safety of his men. The image of the queen's army, drunk with soran, filled his mind.

The king's men looked at the newcomers with disgust. As the queen's little group got closer, a brief panic hit Olukai. He *knew* the messenger, her long dark hair flowing down the sides, her tanned, tall body, and warm brown eyes. She carried a yellow hibiscus plant, a symbol of peace, and the kahuna walked at her side.

Po had trusted Kiani, as did Haku, so Olukai trusted her too. But what if she had played them all? She was very beautiful, after all. Dozens of thoughts ran through his head: did the queen know he was the manō? Had Kiani and her brother been traitors all this time?

He saw Lopaka's jaw open, recognizing Kiani too. "Isn't that the —" Lopaka began to say, as he'd seen Kiani on the shores near Olukai's home.

Olukai cleared his throat. Lopaka would make him explain later, and what would he say? Would he *finally* tell one of his best friends that he was the manō?

As they got closer, Kiani met Olukai's eyes, then she quickly looked down. Something about her felt heavy, unnatural. He searched her to understand, but she avoided eye contact. Though her hair had been gently oiled, and her skin looked clean, he wondered if it was a facade. Her eyes looked unusually puffy and red, her lips swollen, and she walked awkwardly, like something was wrong with her leg.

The kahuna looked old, with dark brown skin. His round, wrinkled face had an odd look to it, and his thick nose took up most of his face. Hair, white as snow, ran down his back. He, Kiani, and the three, towering guards wore white skirts and kiheis. Thick green leis donned their necks, wrists, ankles, and necks. They all wore sandals made of soft koa wood, with straps of silky braided koa fibers.

The little company stopped before Olukai and his tent. Meanwhile, a crowd of the king's soldiers followed the group of Māku'e, surrounding them, and now watching with contempt.

"You are in the presence of Olukai, the king's personal counselor and alaka'i," said Lopaka, always the one to introduce Olukai or be his own spokesperson. "Speak now. What message from the queen?"

Kiani looked up, though she acted incredibly stiff. "I am Kiani, the queen's personal messenger. This is Noa, the queen's personal kahuna. We come with a proposal from the queen." It sounded like she had something in her throat, for her voice came out hoarse, even forced. She glanced from Lopaka to Olukai, her eyes pleading.

"What is the proposal?" Olukai stepped forward, and Kiani swallowed hard.

"If King Ekewaka will give up his prisoner, Nohea the alchemist, to Queen Awa, she will retreat her armies with a vow of peace." A grumble rustled from the crowd of soldiers.

"And if not?" Olukai took another step, and Kiani's lip trembled.

"She will kill every last person in this fortress, including the king... including you."

The soldiers around scoffed, holding up their weapons, throwing out verbal threats. Kiani held the hibiscus plant firmly, eyes straight ahead, and Olukai held up his hand to silence his men.

"Order!" Lopaka barked.

"I wish to speak to the messenger alone," said Olukai. Kiani flinched, and the three tall, bulky guards looked at the kahuna. Kiani's shoulders relaxed, and she let out a breath.

"Go," said the kahuna. Olukai stepped into the hut and folded his arms, his back to the door, waiting.

He heard the rustle of the heavy kapa flap, and a pause. Then arms encircled him, a warm body pressing against his back. "Olukai..." Kiani barely breathed. He turned around, surprised.

"What are you doing?" He held her shoulders, pushing her away from him.

"I am so sorry Olukai... I am so sorry..." She balled her hands into fists and pushed them against her eyes, trying to keep from crying. They both spoke softly, as the hut offered little privacy, and Olukai worried some soldiers might be prying around, trying to hear.

He pulled her hands away from her red eyes but she avoided looking at him as she spoke. "I was on my way back from the Māku'e when the queen's warriors captured me. The kahuna, Noa... it's a curse..." She whispered her words so fast, Olukai had to discern the meaning as she pulled back the greenery on her right wrist, revealing ugly scabs and a black mark. Olukai gaped. He'd never seen an actual hex on a person. "He can only control me when I'm next to him..."

Olukai processed it all. He had vaguely heard of and seen the work of kahuna before. They usually had the ugly jobs of offering people as religious sacrifices, burning dead bodies, and doing strange things to help cure others. He'd heard of ancient kahuna doing spells, like curses and hexes, but not in their time. Most kahuna were symbolic now. Although, Kiani was now proof that the kahuna could actually hex people and control them. He released her hands and wiped her tears.

She rubbed her eyes. "I promise I am on your side." Her entire body trembled. "I convinced the people that the queen left behind. My cousin is a warrior and will bring another army to help you against the queen... the Māku'e... they are good..."

Another army? Olukai's mind processed it all—Kiani *had* gone for help. But could he really trust her?

"Does the queen know?" he asked, taking her shoulders. Kiani covered her mouth, her fingers trembling, and nodded, the tears welling up in her eyes again. "I'm so sorry Olukai... so... sorry... When they cursed me, they forced me to talk... I couldn't..." She tried to breathe so her tears wouldn't be that obvious when she walked out, but she broke into quiet sobs.

He rubbed her shoulders. "It's alright. It's not your fault." The queen would find out about Olukai's true identity some day. It made Olukai wonder if he could speak with the queen before an unnecessary battle, and come to some terms of peace.

"That's why she sent me." Kiani took a deep breath, though her whole body still shook and tears ran down her cheeks. "She knows that we—" She blushed, not finishing, and Olukai caught the rest of Kiani's words, lingering in the air. *She knows that we have feelings for each other*. He wiped another tear and stroked her cheek. "She knew you'd want to talk in private," Kiani said, running her hands through her hair. "She... she plans on killing me if her men have to go to battle, if you don't give her the alchemist."

Olukai's stomach flopped. Kiani continued. "You *have* to protect Nohea. Please don't... don't think about me. The island led Wena to me—he told me Nohea knows how to make and destroy soran. She didn't tell him how to destroy it, but she knows."

Somehow Olukai and Kiani's hands found one another, their fingers intertwining. Kiani squeezed his hand, and horror crossed her face. "This isn't me."

Olukai couldn't help his head from pounding with confusion. "What do you mean?" Her hands felt so good in his. She blushed. "It's the kahuna... they're using me against you. You *have* to protect Nohea. She is good, just confused." She looked toward the heavy kapa door, her eyes nervous. "Wena snuck into the queen's camp to find me. We said our goodbyes."

Olukai couldn't believe this. Wena and Kiani, siblings, said their goodbyes already? Wena was going to let his sister die? A darkness crossed his mind—it was because they believed in him, the manō. And they wanted to restore balance to the island. They would make any sacrifice for it.

"Don't come for me, Olukai." Her brown eyes pleaded again. "Promise me you won't, *please*... You must protect Nohea. You *must* get her away from here..."

She managed to pull her hands free of his. "You must protect yourself too—you are the true ali'i. If the queen gets Nohea, she *will* torture her for answers... or she will use the kahuna to force her to speak. You must get her far away from this place." Kiani kept repeating herself, then, much to Olukai's surprise, she wrapped her arms around his neck and embraced him. He pressed her against himself, holding her tight, never wanting to let go.

It felt like his heart was literally being torn. What was real and not real anymore? Kiani's rapid breaths slowed down in his arms, and he realized: This embrace was real. This was Kiani's goodbye. He held her tighter, only releasing her when she gently pushed him away.

"Do you promise me?" She asked, staring up at him, begging. "Please Olukai. Promise you won't come after me."

He stared at her, blank. She started shaking again. "The kahuna —he's pulling me back..." Olukai grabbed her against himself, hating that the kahuna could control her.

"I can't promise you," he said, and her head dropped against his chest.

"You must... please..." She spoke so softly, he could barely hear her. His heart pounded too loudly in his ears, drowning out her voice. Anger, confusion, and longing coursed through his veins, like the currents in the sea.

"Why don't I go out there and kill that kahuna?" Olukai asked, his hands disappearing through her hair as she looked up at him. "You'll be safe here, with me, where you belong."

Tears began streaming down her face again, and her eyes looked truly sorry. "Olukai..." She stroked his cheek. *That* was real. He could sense the mana in what was really Kiani, and what wasn't. "We're not meant to be." The pain that shot through his chest felt different than the loss of his mother. It was a rejection, but why? Did Kiani want to reject him or she was really trying to say goodbye?

She pulled away from him. "I... I have to go... I'm so, *so* sorry Olukai..." Then she turned, stiffly, and walked out. Olukai shook himself, following. The men were waiting.

"We were not able to come to an agreement," he announced, his heart heavy, and his hatred directing itself towards the kahuna. "We will go to battle in the morning, following our usual customs."

The old kahuna smiled, tipped his head, and turned around.

Kiani's eyes begged Olukai again, the last glimpse he saw of her face before she turned around. The three giants followed behind her, blocking the view of her completely. The soldiers cheered on Olukai, then scoffed at the company of Māku'e, threw out curses, and spit at their feet.

"Alright! Back to work!" Lopaka yelled. "All of you! We've got a battle to prepare for. Captains get your men organized! You know the drill!" The soldiers scurried around. Lopaka turned to Olukai.

"What happened?" His eyes fumed with anger, and rightly so. Olukai had kept his secrets from Lopaka far too long. If the queen knew, maybe it was time his closest friends knew too. Maybe even his twelve warriors.

I have to protect Nohea...

"You knew her before. I saw her at the beach with my own eyes," Lopaka said. "That was not a coincidence—are you committing treason Olukai?" Lopaka spoke softer, though with the same amount of anger. "Are you on the queen's side?"

Olukai noticed the yellow hibiscus on the table. Kiani must have set it down before walking into the tent, before wrapping her arms around him from behind, something probably orchestrated by that sick kahuna, meant to toy with Olukai's emotions.

"Do you trust me?" Olukai asked instead, the bright yellow color of the flower beginning to haunt him.

"I've trusted you all these years, as a brother. And now I'm wondering if I was blind." Lopaka ran his fingers through his hair, annoyed. "What is going on?"

Olukai took a breath, pushing aside all his emotions. This was a moment he'd thought about, and perhaps Lopaka would turn on him now... perhaps this was it. The secret was out, as Queen Awa knew already. Soon King Ekewaka would know, and he'd send his warriors to kill Olukai.

It was time.

He had to trust Lopaka's loyalty and have confidence in himself. Olukai glanced around, noticing a few of his trusted twelve warriors standing nearby. He called them. "Sefa, Ioane, Kehua." They stood around him, although Olukai knew they anticipated his words.

He unwrapped his right forearm, revealing the tribal manō symbol. For a moment, Lopaka stood there, stunned. He frowned. Then folded his arms, thinking about it, conflict in his eyes: should he choose his father, or his brother in arms?

A smile crossed his face and he punched Olukai's shoulder. "Why didn't you tell me sooner?"

Sefa, Ioane, and Kehua only smiled. They'd been there when Olukai touched the great white shark. Ioane folded his arms. "So does this mean you're telling everyone, *finally*?"

Olukai nodded. "'Ae."

Lopaka leaned in. "I've never told this to anyone but... I learned a few years ago that my father is not the line of the great white manō. Our ʻaumakua is a bird, and bears no markings of an aliʻi."

Olukai's eyebrows raised. Lopaka sighed, like a load had lifted off his shoulders. "I secretly hoped..." He laughed at himself. "I secretly hoped the true heir of the manō would come back." He reached out to punch Olukai again, but Olukai blocked.

"The blessed rumors are true," Lopaka said. "The manō has returned."

It meant that Lopaka was *not* next in line to rule Kaimana Island. Lopaka had never wanted it, Olukai knew. Olukai observed Lopaka, unsure of his friend's reaction. Lopaka stared into the distance, and, much to Olukai's surprise, he asked, "What can I do to help?"

This time, relief flooded through Olukai. He placed a hand on his friend's shoulder. "Tell me where the alchemist is now... we need to get her out of here."

"And what about the battle?" Ioane asked.

"Gather the men in an hour for an announcement," Olukai said. "I'll get Nohea first." He patted Lopaka's shoulder hard. "Then get yourselves ready. Lopaka and Ioane, you're coming with me to pay the queen a visit. Let's see if we can stop this war before it happens."

CHAPTER THIRTY-NINE

Wena didn't visit Nohea after their sweet embrace, but she didn't have time to look for him either. Her frustrations grew within her, conflicting emotions, confusion, guilt, and, worst of all, a feeling that she and the island were *not* on good terms. She continued to wonder if she was the cause of Kiani's situation and didn't blame Wena if he never visited her again because of it. Though she knew he cared for her, maybe time apart was best. The loneliness finally started sinking in.

Edena was lonely. The thought nagged at her, and she hated it. Why was it so hard to follow through with her vision?

With the Māku'e nearby, readying for battle, the whole fortress was in commotion: soldiers marching about, slaves cleaning up after them.

As she worked, trying to ignore her stormy thoughts, Akamu moved aside and King Ekewaka entered the hut. Nohea had gotten used to Akamu's back at the door, so anytime he moved, she noticed right away.

Nohea stopped mixing and covered her notes with a blank paper.

It wasn't that she didn't trust the king... she didn't like people to overlook her process. Or so she told herself.

"How goes the soran, my daughter?" he asked, placing a bowl of fruit on the table between them. Nohea bowed her head. She still didn't like being called his daughter.

"It goes well."

"Have you discovered the formula?" He smiled down at her, then glanced at her plants, papers, and the boiling cauldron in the corner.

Nohea hesitated. "No... not yet. I think I am onto something, but I'm not exactly sure."

The king's golden eye glistened in the midday sun. "As you know," he started, folding his arms. "I am very grateful for your work. You have been here everyday, diligently studying and..." he waved at the table full of ingredients, finding the words, "experimenting."

Nohea nodded and swallowed. Why did she feel so uneasy around the king today? She had felt so confident with him, but perhaps all her emotions had worn her out.

"But I have terrible news... two things, actually." He looked down and paced slowly across the room. "The dark tribe is at the borders of Waiakea Village. They gave me two options: come to battle... or hand you over, and they will return peacefully."

Nohea swallowed hard. The king wouldn't turn her in, would he? Instead, she asked, "Are the villagers safe?"

The king nodded. "The people of both villages outside the fortress have deserted. We have men coming from every corner of the island to aid in battle. I am sending my best alakaʻi to lead an army against this darkness."

"Are you sending your warriors?"

"No, they will stay here to protect you." He stopped pacing and leaned against the table. "So you will have no worry—you are safe here. I will not let the queen kidnap you. My best guards will stay."

Nohea felt a sense of guilt... she had caused the queen's anger in the first place. But she had no intention of turning herself in either.

Queen Awa had every intention of keeping soran for herself, whereas King Ekewaka wanted to immunize the entire island.

"Thank you."

The king tipped his head. "'Ae... and the other thing is... " he pointed to his golden eye. "The meha finally revealed that the only way to remove the curse is..." He sighed and stood up straight, looking to the sky, his hands pressed against one another.

"What is it?" Nohea looked up to the ceiling, but she knew he was probably thinking, not looking up.

"They said the golden eye must be removed."

Panic. "Removed?" Nohea's hand went immediately to her right golden eye.

"'Ae..." The king rubbed his face. "I begged them, asked for another solution, but that was all they could say."

Nohea's body went numb. Her eye? *Removed?* She stepped back, leaning against another table behind her. "You mean... " She couldn't even finish her sentence, blinking hard.

The king nodded. "I have tried to think of an easier way, but this truly is Edena's last act of hatred towards us both." He rubbed his face again. "I have lost sleep over this. I did not know how to even tell you." He truly looked sad.

Nohea imagined the pain, and then the loss of an eye. Just the thought of seeing through one eye made her head spin.

The king rested against one of the pillars of the hut. "You do not have to agree to removing the eye, but I do ask it of you... for your own safety. If things go wrong... if the queen's army wins... she *will* kill me. And if she kills me..."

"I will be killed too," finished Nohea, understanding their danger. Her throat felt suddenly parched and she rubbed her eyes.

"This is the last thing I would ever wish upon you," he repeated. "My heart weeps even asking it of you now..." He placed his hand over his heart.

"But it is for the better," Nohea said, trying to stand with confidence, but inside felt hollow. "It must be done... if not for me, then for the future of the island."

"'Ae, because you are the only one who knows how to replicate the soran."

"Well, almost..."

"I know you are the one." He pressed his hands together. "Will you go forward with the removal of your eye?"

A choked swallow. "'Ae."

The king bent his head. "I have arranged for an older, more experienced kahuna to perform the removal."

"Who is it?"

"It is an old man, almost ancient. He lives in the garden within the fortress."

"Oh. Old Nono?"

"'Ae.. you have met him before?"

"No, but..." Nohea bit her tongue, about to say she'd been in the gardens. She'd heard of Nono from the other slaves, but she didn't want the king knowing that she'd roamed the gardens before. She didn't want to deny the slaves that privilege now...

Even though she planned on them being free soon. The confusion boiled over in her head.

"Let us do it tonight," said the king. "Nono is also a chanter. He will cast spells of good fortune and healing upon us."

"And the armies?"

"What about the armies?"

"When do they march to battle?"

"'Tomorrow. My alaka'i will lead them." The king bowed. "But I must leave you to your work. Kahiko will come by later to escort you to the ancient kahuna."

"Where is Wena?" Nohea blurted before he turned to leave.

"I hate to be the bearer of bad news," the king started, and Nohea felt her heart racing. What did they do to him? "But he was a traitor." A traitor? Nohea opened her mouth to interrupt, but listened instead.

"He was actually a spy of the queen. He left in the night to tell Queen Awa about how many men we have, and our plans of defense. One of my warriors caught him coming from the queen's camp—"

"He's not a spy!" Nohea couldn't believe what she heard. "Your warrior is lying. Wena is not a spy. The queen wanted to kill him—his parents wanted to kill him! He has no care for the Māku'e."

The king shook his head. "I so wish that was the case, my daughter, but... he fooled all of us."

"Where is he?" Nohea felt the deep frown on her face.

"He is in prison—but do not worry. We will set him free if he proves to be on our side. He may come to battle with us."

Nohea pulled at her long hair. "He is innocent. Please let him go."

The king bowed his head. "I must talk to my counselors before doing so, but I will consider your words. Your words have greater weight than theirs." He took a breath. "I must be leaving you."

Nohea couldn't believe Wena was in prison again. It seemed that the entire time they were together, she had done something so he ended up in prison: at the dark kingdom, and now here. Unless he *really* was spying for the queen. Which she highly doubted. He had no allegiance to them.

The image of Kiani flashed through her mind. Maybe, just *maybe,* he'd been talking to his sister and they thought she was a spy? She rubbed her head as a secret thought crept up. Was the king lying?

She shook her head. *I need to trust the king on this,* she thought. *I'm sure he will set Wena free. Everything will be made right.*

"I will see you tonight," said the king. "When we remove our curse."

"Wait..." Nohea put out her hand, and the king paused before leaving the hut. She had one more burning question, something she longed to know, in case there was something that revealed another solution to the curse.

"When Edena told you about the curse," she started, "Did she mention the tribe she came from? The meha you have here... are they the same tribe?"

The king lowered his head. "I do not know. That is something I never considered, as the meha have always looked the same to me. I will have one of my counselors inspect this."

He glanced around and then sighed. "When I did speak to Edena before leaving for the dark forest, she said she wished us both dead. She wished us both to never live another year." He held his arms together. "But we will prove her wrong."

Nohea shivered. "Thank you for telling me." The king bowed and exited the hut, and Akamu stepped into the door frame.

Nohea sat on the stool, crossing her legs and resting her chin in her hands. Her stomach still churned at the idea of getting her eye cut out, but she couldn't shake off the story.

Her mother had never seemed crazy. Edena always acted so calm, composed, unamused. Did she lose her mind? Was Kimo's death the last straw for her as a slave? Or maybe she felt she had no other purpose after teaching everything from the books to Nohea?

Nohea crouched on the ground to pull her notes, written in meha, from the cubby holes built into the side of the hut. The notes looked like archaic markings, the charcoal all smearing around. Did her mother hate her so much that she taught her this language? Did her mother hate her so much that she taught Nohea every bit of information from the books in the king's library? Or how to break down the composition of plants and liquids?

All of those things looked like acts of love, but were they?

Nohea touched her right cheek. Her eye had been golden ever since she could remember... and it was her mother's doing.

So, perhaps her mother did hate her from the day she was born.

I must do what I can, thought Nohea, *and I must have this removed.*

Though, deep in her heart, she wished it weren't so. And as she looked about the room, hugging her arms, she wished Wena was there. She could use some counsel.

Or a friend.

But she was all alone, the only other person was Akamu, his back to her, as usual. She shivered. It would be a most painful and gruesome night, but she couldn't see any way out of it.

CHAPTER FORTY

As Olukai, Lopaka, and his warriors made their plans, Like appeared, red faced, and said, "Father is going to remove his golden eye... and Nohea's." Like probably had nobody else to tell, but Olukai was grateful for the message, and he ran to Nohea's hut. He had to get her out, *now*. The words of Kiani rang through his mind, as well as the tender feelings Haku displayed for his niece: *She is good*.

He reached the hut, a large bamboo framed home, with open windows, woven mats on the sides, and a thatched roof. At least twelve warriors stood around it, and one blocked the entryway.

It was Akamu. "Sir," he said, bowing to Olukai.

"I must speak to the alchemist."

"Only those on the king's orders may speak to her," he replied. "I'm sorry sir."

"I am on the king's orders—"

"You are not, sir. He tells me who is himself."

"I just came from the king—" Olukai lied, feeling his anger rising. This had never happened before. His entire service to the king he had been able to roam and speak freely with whoever he wanted.

"No, sir." Akamu's hands tightened on the spear he held.

"Let me in." Olukai held up his hands, showing he had no weapons. The kapa cloth covered his forearm again.

"The king will not be happy to hear if—" began Akamu, but a voice interrupted him.

"Let him in!" It was the alchemist, her voice sounding surprisingly young. For some reason, Olukai thought her to be older.

Akamu turned. "Wha—what?"

"I said, let him in." The girl stood behind the tall warrior, much shorter than Olukai expected.

Akamu bowed, "'Ae..." He moved aside and Olukai stepped in, looking down at Nohea.

"Who are you?" she asked. Olukai stared at her for a moment. Po hadn't lied. Nohea was quite beautiful. She had large eyes, one light brown, one golden. Her hair fell in chunky waves, a light brown, down her sides. Her nose angled up , dainty. With light brown skin and pink plumeria-colored lips, Nohea looked like a princess—which, as the king's daughter, she was. She placed her hand on her soft pointed chin, studying him.

"I am Olukai, the king's first counselor."

She looked amused. "Kahiko said you were the second." Nohea walked behind her table, crumbling up some plants with her hands and placing them into a pile on the other end of the table. A soft breeze blew through the hut, sometimes picking up the crumbs with it, and creating a pile on the ground too.

"I was expecting you to be a little more..." she paused, a small smile on her full, pink lips.

"What?" Olukai folded his arms.

"Just... bigger." She imagined the fat counselors, like Ano.

"If you're wondering, I don't drink soran, and I don't live in the fortress. I am not like the king's other counselors *or* his warriors." It came out quicker than Olukai expected.

She raised an eyebrow and Olukai took a breath. All the emotions from the day made him feel like an overfilled gourd. He remembered his first interaction with Kiani, *You need to calm down—you are an alakaʻi.*

Nohea crushed more leaves in her hands. "Then what brings you here?" She looked tired, and as heavy with confusion and feelings as Olukai.

"I wanted nothing more than to meet the famed alchemist. After all, I *am* the one protecting you. I will lead the king's armies into battle tomorrow."

"Oh, so you are an alakaʻi." Nohea paused and looked up at him, observing. She thought him handsome. His chiseled jaw, long dark hair, and brown eyes were his striking features. He bore many scars on his arms and chest, painfully reminding her of Wena.

"I am." They stood in silence for a moment, staring at one another. Then Nohea got back to work, crumbling her plants.

"How are the experiments?" Olukai asked.

"Well."

"And the journey? That was your first time seeing soran in the wild?"

She continued crushing the things, her eyes meeting his. "It went well. You are the traveler, aren't you? Kahiko said you were the one who led most of the missions to find soran."

"ʻAe..."

"Then you know how to find soran?"

"ʻAe."

"But you do not know how to make it?"

Olukai shook his head. "I was not blessed with the ways of the meha."

"The meha?" Nohea paused and Olukai almost covered his mouth. "What do you mean?"

"I mean..."

"I am an alchemist," Nohea said, her eyebrows creasing, "Not a meha."

"ʻAe, you are... but your mother..." Olukai cut himself short. For some reason, he thought Ekewaka had told her this, but from the look on her face, she didn't know.

Nohea tipped her head. "Is there something you know?"

Olukai shook his head, trying to act smooth, though this wasn't the conversation he imagined. "Of course. Well, I simply wanted to meet you. We appreciate your service, Nohea. Good night."

"Wait!" Nohea ran all the way around the table. "You came to tell me about my mother, didn't you?" She stepped closer to him and then her eyes narrowed. "Is she a meha? Which tribe?" The king said that Edena learned the ways of the meha, but that very fact made Nohea wonder if Edena might be a meha herself.

Olukai nodded. "She was a very powerful meha." He placed his hand over his chin, thinking. "It's not my place to tell you what to do, and I really don't know much but... I do not think your curse was meant to harm you—"

"How can you say that?" Nohea stood in front of him. He was at least two heads taller than her. Though she hardly knew Olukai, it felt somewhat relieving to have someone—anyone—to talk about the situation. After all, she agreed to have her eye removed. Did Olukai know of another way? "If the king dies, I die," Nohea said. "If he feels pain, I do too... and vice versa. How is that not a curse?"

"How well did you know Edena?" Olukai asked.

"My whole life—"

"But what about her life before you? Did you know anything about that?"

"Do you?" Nohea tipped her head to the side again.

"Perhaps..." Olukai shook his head. "But it is not my place to tell. I really must go."

"Wait, please." She grabbed his arm, the one covered by kapa. Desperation filled her grasp, and Olukai felt her loneliness, her pain.

They weren't so different. He paused, though Nohea didn't let go of him. "Please, will you tell me? I would like to know... I... I don't want to lose an eye..." She finally spilled the truth and wiped her eyes in the hopes that Olukai wouldn't see the water pooling.

"But you trust the king's judgment?"

Silence.

"I... I must do what I can. It is for our own safety."

"Your mother was a meha," said Olukai. "She left her tribe. The meha are beautiful women, which is why they hide their faces." He spoke softly and close to Nohea so the warriors couldn't hear. "She had a hānai family—"

"Uncle Haku," Nohea whispered softly to herself, but Olukai heard it.

"But the king lusted after her, and forced her to marry him. The concubines were jealous—they plotted against her, did terrible things to her..." Nohea made a face, knowing exactly what that felt like. Olukai noticed but continued. "The king didn't want to lose Edena. To please his jealous wives, he forced her into the ranks of slavery, giving her the simplest task of caring for his library."

Nohea stepped back. She'd heard two different versions of her mother's story: the version from the king and the version from Olukai, the king's first—or second?—counselor.

"I do not think she meant to curse you," Olukai said again. "And I do not think the curse is removed by taking out your eyes. A curse isn't always physical—it's in the energy."

"What are you saying?"

"I'm saying, I don't think you should go to the old man tonight."

Nohea blinked, relief flooding through her. This stranger came out of nowhere to give her counsel, and it never felt so good. She liked this Olukai. But the relief was replaced with doubt.

"I have no choice," she said. "I cannot be connected to the king like this until he or I die..." Her guard was down now, completely, and she kept wiping her eyes and sniffing.

"You always have a choice," Olukai corrected.

"And I've made my choice." Nohea's heart raced. "I've made my choice to come here. This is the only way to free the slaves, the only way."

"Do you think it could have saved those close to you?" Olukai asked.

"It could save *everyone.*" Nohea rubbed her eyes then glared up at him. "You haven't come here to meet me... you've come here to persuade me against the king's wishes."

She stood face to face with him, saying quietly, "You *don't actually* serve the king."

Olukai hoped Akamu hadn't heard it—especially with the warriors's superhuman abilities due to soran. Olukai folded his arms. "*You* don't serve the king... you keep your secrets close to your chest, still deciding if you should reveal them... like your mother. She had no friends—if she did, perhaps she would've changed the course of the future. But, no. She chose her path, and you are choosing yours."

This *certainly* was not the conversation he imagined having with Nohea. He thought it would be simple: come to the lab, introduce himself, show her the mark on his arm, and walk away together. But now that seemed silly. The lab was surrounded by the king's warriors, and Nohea was so conflicted, she wasn't thinking straight.

"Nohea," he said after taking a slow, deep breath. "I know this is hard for you, all of this."

She melted under his kind voice. Though she appreciated Wena, it was sometimes hard not to hear his voice. Olukai had a soothing, calm voice, and she could feel the mana in it.

"Do you want to take a walk?" he asked, offering his arm. She blinked.

"Kahiko is coming to get me soon."

"It'll be quick," he said and winked. She tipped her head, studying him again. Her eyes locked on the kapa cloth covering his forearm, and much to Olukai's surprise, she reached for it. He didn't stop her, letting her untie one of the ti leaf cords and pull back the kapa.

She paused when the tribal design of the shark came into view. Her fingers traced the pattern, similar to the way Kiani had done. Olukai waited.

Her shoulders sank and she rubbed her forehead, as though trying to think. "I can't get out of here," she said, soft enough that he could hear. Her eyes pleaded with him. He covered his forearm with the kapa cloth again and held out his arm. "Let's take a walk," he said once more.

She understood his meaning. He was going to get her out of here. But she was frozen in place. *The manō is here. Olukai is the manō,* she thought over and over to herself. The island hummed beneath her feet. This was her chance to escape, to leave.

But what about Ekewaka? Would the manō kill her to kill the king? Fear crept into her chest and she stepped back. "No, I don't want to," she said.

Olukai sighed, and Akamu turned around. "Is he bothering you?" Akamu asked. Nohea held her arms and stepped back, her eyes locked on his forearm. *Olukai is the manō. I should go with him.* But he wasn't going to make soran for all. He was going to destroy it. How would that help the island?

"Nohea?" Akamu asked, standing behind Olukai. Instead of waiting for her answer, Olukai turned to leave. She was lost, hopelessly lost. He could see it in her eyes. She wanted to go with him, yet was probably manipulated by the king. She also didn't know him, so how could he expect her to follow him?

He stepped past Akamu into the cool night air, defeat overwhelming his senses. Maybe Po was right. They needed to find other options.

"Wait!"

Hope rose in his chest. He'd gone a good distance in a few strides and Nohea ran after him.

"I have a friend," she said, hugging herself again. "His name is Wena. The king said he's in prison because he is a traitor. But he's not. You and I..." she paused, and Olukai's heart sank. "We are not very much friends, but since you are the alakaʻi, I ask that you find a way to free my friend."

"You think the king will kill him if I don't?"

"I don't know what to think anymore." Her voice choked a bit. She frowned. "That is all. Goodbye." She hurried back to her hut.

Olukai nodded. *She's torn.* He could tell. She wanted to reproduce the soran, find the cure, but she didn't know who to trust, and apparently she couldn't even trust the manō. Maybe he wasn't much closer to earning her trust than the king was. *But she trusts Wena,* he thought as he walked through the fortress. He would get Wena's help then.

"Olukai." He recognized the voice before seeing the face.

"Kahiko." Olukai smirked, folding his arms, as the old kahuna approached, torch in hand. The sun had set.

"The king is pleased with your response to the messenger today," said Kahiko. Olukai shrugged.

"Where are you off to?" he asked, as Kahiko rarely spent time in this part of the fortress.

"Ah, well... as you may have heard by now, the king and the alchemist must undergo a procedure. I am to escort the alchemist to the garden."

Olukai tipped his head to the side. "Good luck."

Kahiko stared at Olukai, as if examining him. A moment of self consciousness washed over Olukai, as he now realized that some of Olukai's warriors *and* Nohea knew he was the manō. Did Kahiko know?

Then bitterness crept in. Kahiko, a kahuna, like Noa, did nothing for the people. The kahuna hurt, manipulated, and tortured people. Olukai walked past Kahiko, furious, not even bothering to say goodbye.

And then his worries turned to the next tasks at hand: reveal himself as the manō to all of his army, meet with the queen, and possibly rescue Kiani.

As for Nohea... He sighed aloud, hating that he had to resort to the next plan of action. It felt so much like Ekewaka: force. Olukai sent a silent call out to the island, asking about Po. Wherever Po was,

Olukai needed his help to kidnap Nohea. Because Olukai saw, in the corner of her hut, a fresh mixture of soran.

Nohea really was an accomplished alchemist, and if she knew how to make it, then she probably knew how to destroy it too. They couldn't waste anymore time looking for other alchemists, witches, or sorcerers. Nohea knew the answer, so they needed her, no matter the cost.

CHAPTER FORTY-ONE

"My 'aumakua is the great white manō," the king said to Nohea as they walked together to the garden. She glanced at him, wondering if she really believed that. Kahiko had come to get her, and now walked behind her and the king. Nono stood in the distance of the garden, a lonely black figure against a raging bonfire.

"Have you ever seen the great white manō?" Nohea asked.

"No, but the blood of that great ali'i flows through my veins, and yours. The great white manō is the protector of our family line. He protects me, as well as you."

Nohea was about to say something about the rumor of the manō, but her teeth started chattering, a direct result of her anxiety. The sun had set a few hours ago, and ever since Olukai left the hut, Nohea felt nothing but anger... and sadness. Olukai was probably right. He seemed like an honest man, so why didn't she listen to him?

How could her mother do this to her? How could she curse her with a golden eye and the only way to remove it being to remove the eye? It was such a dark and wicked thought, but Nohea knew it would feel worse in real life.

She couldn't keep herself from trembling, bracing for the pain.

The fact that Edena was a meha, also meant that meha blood ran through Nohea. It was no wonder these things came naturally to her. It made her question things too, like when the old kupua grabbed her with his roots and said, "Our kind used to be friends." And if Nohea was a meha, was there a way that she could possibly remove the curse herself?

Though Nohea wracked her brain for ideas, nothing came. She didn't know spells or "magic," like the meha. She only knew "science" and alchemy, things she could see.

Nono approached the group, hobbling over, his back hunched over as he looked up at them. He had a long white beard, a wrinkled face, and a toothy smile.

The slaves called Nono the mad man, because he would wander around aimlessly, muttering things to himself. He was once a great kahuna, much like Kahiko. But his old age and strange ways distanced him from normal society. Now he lived in the deep parts of the king's garden.

"Your highness." His face practically touched the ground, as he already stooped so low. "Everything is ready." He moved aside, extending his hands to some seats made of tree trunks, inviting them to sit.

A group of five warriors had joined the king and Nohea, and they stood in a circle, a distance from the bonfire, keeping watch.

An owl hooted in the distance, and Nohea looked up, but she didn't see it. She missed her old owl friend, and a pang struck her chest. *What am I doing?* Her mind raced over and over, as she remembered her old self, so full of independence. And now what was she?

"I will chant and then begin the process," said Nono. "Wash your hands first." Next to the tree trunks they sat on, there were two brown bowls of water. Nohea rinsed her hands and then her face. She could hear the river nearby, where Nono probably got the water.

The owl hooted again and Nohea squinted above them. It was

too dark to see anything in the tree canopy above. The birds always warned of things, but... how could she get out of this? She felt that she no longer had a choice. This had to be done. Nono heard it too, as she caught him looking up. But then he cleared his throat.

"Your highness," said Nono, bowing. "Who will go first?"

The king and alchemist looked at one another. "I can go first," Nohea said, her voice barely audible.

"So be it," the king said, sitting perfectly straight and still. Nohea figured that was his way of handling his nervousness.

"It will not take long," Nono said, holding a small brown bowl of water and a ti leaf in the other hand. "I do not plan on removing your whole eye, just the golden part."

Nohea blinked hard.

Nono began chanting. His old, wavy voice rang through the forest trees, a haunting melody. It made the leaves above shiver, and the mossy ground grow cold around their feet.

As Nono circled around Nohea and the king, he dipped the ti leaf in water and sprinkled it on them.

Let this pass... He chanted towards the end. *Let this pass...*

When he finished, he placed both items by the fire, then got on both knees and touched the ground with his face.He then looked up to the heavens, muttering strange words.

Next, he picked up a small searing knife that sat at the bonfire's edge. It had been specially placed there.

Nohea gulped.

Nono stood and turned towards her, his eyes glistening in the light of the fire. He motioned to a woven mat on the ground.

"Lie down."

Nohea's body moved of its own accord. Nono knelt next to her. With his left hand, he held her eyelid open.

He muttered some words and Nohea began trembling, watching the knife close in on her eye, feeling the heat hovering above her cheek. The last thing she remembered was the fiery heat. Screaming.

Strong arms grabbing her wrists and legs to pin her down. And then everything went dark.

CHAPTER FORTY-TWO

Olukai stood at the edge of the garden, listening and watching. He could see the light of the bonfire coming out the tops of the trees in the distance, but he was too far, and the garden was too thick to see anything.

With one hand, he spun his knife in circles, nervous.

A girl's scream erupted from the forest—not a long scream, but short bursts. Olukai nearly dropped his knife as he stood straight and stared.

His skin crawled.

The screaming lasted no longer than a minute or two.

She better be alive, he thought. Then he headed towards the king's prison. He had to get Wena.

A few minutes later, another cry erupted from the forest, like a roar.

The king... Olukai couldn't imagine what the two were feeling, but he felt awful about the whole ordeal. He had allowed Nohea to recognize him as the true ali'i, but perhaps she didn't want to listen to the island. Or maybe his worst fears were true: he wasn't good enough to be king, and Nohea saw that. *Where's Po?* Olukai hoped nothing happened to the messenger, as the thought of the mo'o swallowing the messenger whole was a possibility.

As he walked about the fortress, he noticed some of the king's warriors lounging about. "Why are you all here?" He paused, looking at a group of at least twelve of the king's tall warriors.

"We're waiting sir… king's orders."

Olukai rubbed his chin and then continued on. *That's odd,* he thought. No doubt the king took warriors with him to Nono, but that was plenty to protect him *and* the alchemist while Olukai went to battle.

Wena was not hard to find, as he was in one of the beehive-shaped prison huts, made of black lava rock, with only one window for light and air.

"I'm here for Wena," Olukai said to the prison guard. It was obvious which of the men drank soran, and which didn't. The soran drinkers always stood taller and bulkier than any other, and their skin looked—and felt—harder than wood.

Nobody questioned Olukai and the guard opened the thick door to one of the huts. Wena stepped out, the same height as Olukai. The manō immediately saw the resemblance between Kiani and Wena: both lightly tanned, with a few freckles across the cheeks, and a soft pointed nose. Wena had sunkissed hair, different from his sister's dark hair. Olukai was surprised that Wena's hair was cut short, hanging loosely above his ears—nobody on the island would willingly cut their hair.

"I'm Olukai." Olukai placed his hand over his chest. Wena bowed and signed, mouthing, *Wena.*

"Nohea has requested your freedom. I'm taking you to the camp grounds with me, understood?"

Wena tipped his head then motioned with his hand like he was writing.

"'Ae, follow me," said Olukai and they walked to a large sand pit, where the men would take off their shoes to spar and wrestle. Olukai motioned to the sand and Wena knelt down, drawing in it.

There was no written language of the people, besides petroglyphs, but Olukai had learned to read the strange language of the foreigners, and he could speak it too—not very well, but well enough that he could probably communicate should the foreigners come to their island. He learned the language many years ago, when he started working for the king, from an old foreigner teacher. The white man passed away, so not very many people had the opportunity to learn the foreigners' words.

Wena wrote a name, and Olukai's eyebrow raised when he realized Wena wrote in the language of the foreigners, their strange letters forming words.

Nohea.

"She's gone with the king... They are removing their golden eyes."

Wena's eyes went wide. *Safe?*

"'Ae... There is not much we can do for her..." Olukai met Wena's eyes. "The alchemist may change her mind, but... in the meantime, we must do what we can to unite the island." Olukai paused, then added. "I met your sister... "

Wena's brows creased. His amber colored eyes seemed to light on fire, though it was only the reflection of the nearby torches. No words needed to express their common understanding: Wena had already said his goodbyes to his sister. But Olukai didn't want to give up hope, even if Kiani didn't want him.

Wena drew a picture in the sand of a shark and pointed to Olukai.

Olukai nodded and brushed out the drawing with his hand. "Nobody knows. I trusted your sister and therefore trust you." He leaned in closer, though Wena drew back and Olukai realized it was because Wena was reading his lips. It would make no difference if Olukai whispered or spoke loudly—Wena only needed to see Olukai's lips to understand.

"You will come with me to battle, but I still think we can rescue your sister..."

Wena nodded.

"And you will help me."

Wena crossed his arms over his chest, a sign of trust, a sign of commitment. Olukai nodded and stood. Wena came across as a wise person, someone reliable, and trustworthy. Not only were Wena's eyes full of wisdom, but he bore many scars, proof of his prowess in wars, and that he'd seen tough times too. The scars covered parts of his face, his arms, and across his chest.

Olukai had seen so much of the island, and, for some reason, felt like Wena had too... though a completely different experience because Olukai sought soran for Ekewaka, and Wena sought... something else.

Freedom. Acceptance. The words came to Olukai's mind. Kiani had been so eager to join the cause. She believed in Olukai, and now here stood Wena, crossing his arms over his chest, wanting to help too. Kiani and Wena craved the same things, and believed Olukai would help them achieve those feelings.

It gave Olukai a sense of hope. For this long he'd been hiding his identity, but the fact that people wanted to serve and help him made his heart swell with gratitude. Just as he led Wena to the camp, the ground beneath trembled, and Olukai stopped.

Po is safe.

The island spoke.

Relief flooded through Olukai.

Where is he? He stood still, listening to the wind, the ground beneath, and the island.

Close... It didn't feel like Po was close enough for Olukai to talk to him, but that meant Po was alright. Wena observed Olukai. He signed something, but Olukai didn't understand and Wena shook his head, as if to say, "Nevermind." Olukai wished he could understand. He motioned for Wena to follow.

If Po was close, no doubt he got the help of the moʻo. And if he got the help of the moʻo, he probably would look for Nohea first. It was the most logical thing to do. But Olukai deeply wished to have a brief talk with Po, to make plans. He wished Haku was there too, as the two messengers were his closest counselors and friends.

I have to trust Po, he thought. And in the meantime, he had to figure out the next step. He went over his speech in his mind as he approached the camp.

Already, the group was assembling, led by each of Olukai's twelve warriors. Ioane saluted Olukai and motioned to the captain's hut, where Olukai would address his men.

Olukai's heart rate rose. This was it. Lopaka and Like stood by Olukai's hut, the one he'd been in with Kiani earlier that day. The torches lit up the area around them, and Lopaka held a smaller torch over the map, reading it.

The hibiscus still sat there, and, making Olukai want to leave and rescue Kiani this minute.

"Who's this?" Lopaka asked, when he looked up from the map. The men's voices, as they gathered round, made it almost impossible to hear anything.

"Wena, Kiani's brother."

Wena and Lopaka clasped hands and clapped one another's backs. Wena looked at Like, who shrank under all the tall men around him. A few more of Olukai's twelve warriors approached the hut, ready to listen to the announcement.

"Doubt is spreading amongst the king's army," said Lopaka, forcing the others leaders, except Wena, to lean in to hear. "Only a third of the men arrived from villages around the island. A rumor has spread that most of the village men march to Huna bay, waiting for the manō to lead them."

How? Olukai desperately wished Po was around. Po could verify the information, or even lead this rumored group of troops to fight the queen and her army of soran warriors.

"But we've received fresh troops from the villages everyday," Olukai said.

Lopaka nodded. "'Ae, we have... but have you seen how small the groups are? Look, some men are approaching now."

Indeed, a small group of about ten village men approached the circle of torches. Leading them was a dark man with a wide nose, thick lips, and a square shaped face. His bulky body revealed years of labor, and he limped along. The group that followed him consisted of young men, anywhere between the ages of ten to their mid twenties.

The leader of this pack opened his arms, a warm smile on his face. Though Olukai didn't recognize the man, he gave him a hug.

"Where have you come from?" asked Olukai, standing back, looking down at the older man.

"Hakalau Village."

Olukai remembered Po returned to Hakalau village, his hometown. "What are your names?" Olukai asked.

"I'm Tua, this is Alika, Ulu..." Tua kept speaking, but Olukai felt that he remembered this name. He couldn't point out where he'd heard it exactly. He knew many families from the island, so perhaps he met Tua at some point on his journey.

"We are honored to serve the king," said Tua, bowing his head.

"And the king is honored to have you join," said Olukai then motioned to the large group of men gathered around the hut. "If you'll join the men now, we're about to have an announcement."

"Thank you," Tua paused. "Are you, by chance, Olukai?"

Olukai nodded, "'Ae, why?"

Tua smiled. "My daughter. She is the greatest dancer in the island—she has a liking for you." He winked and turned to leave.

Of course! Olukai knew Haunani, Po's hānai sister, meaning Tua was Po's hānai father. He couldn't help himself. "Po—where is he?"

Tua frowned, worry crossing his face. "He..." The young men behind him looked equally as uncomfortable, avoiding eye contact. And Olukai realized they might know Po as serving the manō. If they reported him anywhere besides serving the king at the moment, it meant treason.

Olukai cleared his throat. "Nevermind, I'll ask you after. Please, join us for the announcement." At that, Ioane blew a conch shell, the sound vibrating through the air. The men immediately silenced and turned their attention to the alaka'i and captain, Olukai.

Lopaka introduced Olukai, as he always did. "Please listen as Olukai has something very important to share." He stepped back and Olukai stepped forward, feeling small under all the gazes of the army.

"My men, my brothers, my friends," Olukai started. "Tonight you have gathered to fight the battle for King Ekewaka, but I am here to tell you he is not your king."

Rustles of surprise sounded through the army.

Olukai unwrapped the ti cords from his arm and the kapa cloth fell. The symbol had now reached his elbow and started up his bicep. He raised his arm into the air, causing a ripple of gasps throughout the army.

"I am the manō, a descendant of the great ali'i who once ruled Kaimana Island—" Before he could continue, the men clapped and cheered. His spirits rose.

"You will no longer fight for a false king. Fight for the manō! Fight for the true ali'i of Kaimana Island!" Olukai cried. At that, the army erupted into cheers and claps. All of the "cheehoos" made Olukai's skin crawl.

When the men quieted down, Olukai continued. "The queen wishes to battle, but I will avoid it if possible. Tonight, get your rest, prepare, but pray for mercy, both from Queen Awa and King Ekewaka. We will not spill blood if we can avoid it." The men clapped at this.

Lopaka cut in. "Fight for the manō!" The men cheered and the next thing Olukai knew, he was bombarded by soldiers who wanted to hug him, clap his back or hand, or simply thank him.

Olukai's twelve warriors established order again, by leading their troops back to their respective camps. Tua lingered behind and placed his hand on Olukai's shoulder. "'Po flew over us this night... he *is* very much safe."

Olukai smiled. Relief. Happiness. Po would rescue Nohea and take her to the lady of the lava. And now, Olukai needed to see if there was any way he could make peace with Queen Awa and King Ekewaka. This war was unnecessary, and hopefully they had the wisdom to agree with him.

CHAPTER FORTY-THREE

Nohea stared at the treetops, the moon now shining brightly. She watched as the owl circled, covering and uncovering the moonlight. He seemed restless, until he finally perched on a tree and hooted a few times.

"Sit up," Nono said, as his hand pressed a cold clean kapa cloth to Nohea's face. His old hands trembled with the weight of helping Nohea sit. Nohea leaned against the trunk, and the king leaned against his tree trunk.

Nohea and Ekewaka both held their eyes, their bodies trembling under the pain.

"It is finished," said Nono.

"The curse should be removed," said the king, his voice hoarse. He turned towards Nohea. "Give your hand to Nono."

She held out her free hand to the old man, then gasped when he sliced a shark tooth knife right through her palm. She cried out at the initial shock of the torn flesh, then winced as the pain started tingling through her palm.

The king screamed, then stood up, roaring at the sky. "Nooooo!"

Nohea wanted to scream herself. They *both* felt her pain, meaning one thing: The curse was not removed.

"How can this be?" The king paced around the fire, pressing his hand against his eye. She wondered if the soran helped eased the pain in his eye, sparing her his pain, though he had to feel hers. "No! Those witches lied! We must kill them!" He kicked Nono's water bowl into the fire and violently pushed Nono aside.

"It should have worked," Nono whispered.

"Kill them, all of those filthy meha!" the king yelled at his men, then glanced at Nohea. Their eyes met and Nohea felt it: pure anger, disgust, and hatred.

The moment went by in slow motion, the energy passing between them of pain. Nohea knew it was a moment of weakness, when his heart opened up, revealing his true emotions.

He would kill me if he had the chance. The thought went through her head, but she brushed it away. No. He needed her. He needed her knowledge because nobody else on the island understood soran the way she did.

But he'd kill me the second this curse is gone, and the second he doesn't need me anymore. The truth sent a pang through Nohea's chest. Yes, that part was true.

The king's hand dropped and he marched past her, breathing heavily, his nostrils flared. "Get over here," he yelled to his warriors, and all of them, including Kahiko, hurried behind him, leaving Nono and Nohea alone in the dark woods.

This was the first time none of Ekewaka's warriors lingered around Nohea, but she didn't think about it too much, as her body convulsed.

The old sorcerer looked down at Nohea. "I do not have the remedies like yours," he said. "You know much more than I do." He took her hand, the blood dripping down her forearm and drying. He placed a clean kapa cloth in her palm and she closed it, the palm stinging.

"You must return to your hut." His old eyes looked sad. "I can do no more for you."

Nohea's eyes welled up in tears, her head pounding. She cried more from the physical pain than the hurt of feeling unwanted, useless, and rejected, feelings she'd dealt with her entire life from Edena. It didn't come as much of a surprise that Ekewaka hated her too, though her heart kept hurting with every breath, deep down wishing that it wasn't so. She thought she meant something to him, and she did. But as soon as she accomplished her task, he wouldn't need her. He didn't even want her. Ekewaka and Edena were not so different, after all.

Nono helped her stand, then stayed by his warm fire, cleaning the mess, as she hobbled through the garden. Tears blinded her view of the ground. She hadn't cried in so long. Where was Wena when she wanted his arms, his support, his protection? Where was her slave family? Where were her friends? Did she even have friends?

And where was the manō? Olukai had come to help her himself, but she rejected him. She once thought he was a coward, but he was far from it. He didn't want soran or power. He simply wanted to help.

So how did it come to this? How did Nohea step into this, quite literally and figuratively, with both eyes open? She knew the pain would be this bad, and she had been warned that *this might not work...* but she made her choice. And now she suffered the consequences.

Nohea tripped and fell into a bush. Ferns brushed her side as she caught herself, extending her free hand. Landing on the large cut across her palm made her wince aloud.

Nohea curled into the fetal position, her knees tucked close to her chin.

Why am I here? Nohea wondered, and all the emotions she hid previously now came out. She sobbed uncontrollably, shaking, with blood and tears streaming down her face. It all felt awful—physically, mentally, emotionally. Every bit of her body felt shriveled, defeated.

Nohea didn't know how long she lay there in the dark, weeping. All she could think of was how foolish she'd been.

Wena was right. Like was right. Uncle Haku was right. Olukai was right. They were *all* right. The king wasn't out to help everyone —he was only out to help himself.

And Nohea had suffered terribly by believing he'd been out to help her.

He didn't want the curse gone for *their* sake. He wanted it gone for *his* sake. Now she was blind in one eye, as was he... and they were *still* cursed.

He didn't even want soran for everyone. He wanted it for himself.

She felt a sudden hatred for the king. How dare he manipulate her. How dare he even *think* to take advantage of her... and why? Had she been craving acceptance, and wanted to please him? Was it because she truly didn't believe in the manō, or she wanted acceptance from someone with authority?

His blood ran through hers, and she hated it. She hated being related to him, sharing the same lineage.

My family is shameful, she thought. *My mother with her secrets, my father with his lies.*

She controlled her sobs, took deep breaths, and lay still for a moment. A cool breeze gently made its way through the garden. A few insects chirped in the background, and the stars dazzled across the night sky.

"Get up."

Nohea wiped her face. She sat up, finding that a man stood a few footsteps away. There was a strange glow about his body, though Nohea couldn't tell if it was the moon light shining on his back, or an odd countenance.

He was not very tall, probably about her height, she estimated. She couldn't tell exactly the color of his skin, though he must have been dark. He had a long, rectangular face, with thick, grim lips, a wide nose, and almond-shaped eyes with wrinkles gracing the corners.

In a way, he looked familiar, felt familiar, but she couldn't recall where or if she'd ever met him before.

He wore a white kihei and palekoki, his feet bare. Tattoos covered his right shoulder, little triangles and various shapes that formed the image of a pueo.

"You knew better," said the man, his voice deep. He had straight white teeth.

"Who are you?" Nohea asked, sniffing and wiping her face, blood and tears smearing everywhere. Her hair and tunic were plastered to her sweaty body.

"My name is Lono."

"Have we met?"

"'Ae. Many times. I have warned you before of danger. You have always listened. But not this time... You have made your choice, and I respect that. But you are now in grave danger."

"You've helped me?" Nohea stood up slowly, walking to his side so he turned. His eyes were a bright golden color like the setting sun. She slowly took in a breath. "I know you."

The dark brown color of his skin, the symbol of the pueo on his shoulder, the mysterious eyes. "My 'aumakua..." It dawned on her that moment.

Not very many people met their 'aumakua in human form. It was rare, and sacred. Nohea dropped to her knees.

"Thank you, ancestor, for watching over me."

Lono knelt before her, resting one arm on his knee. He took her injured hand and examined it. "Nono is not skilled like yourself. Your wounds need tending, proper tending. I will bring help to you."

She bowed her head, then looked up. "I made a terrible mistake," she said, tears coming to her eyes, the pang hitting her chest again. "Olukai tried to help me, but I turned him away. He probably thinks me a traitor..."

"You are not a traitor. It's what's in your heart that matters." Her ancestor's eyes softened, and she realized that the light around his countenance was not the moonlight. He was glowing. "You have learned the true heart of your father, and now you must make things right."

Nohea nodded. "I will."

"Find the manō, and give him your help. You know the answer to destroy soran... You can end the lust of it, once and for all."

"What about the king?"

"Ekewaka is of my line, and he will be put in his place."

Nohea marveled. "Are you his father?"

"His grandfather." Lono smiled. "I know you have seen much of what he can do, how cruel and cunning he can be to the most innocent people, like yourself. He is capable of great evil." Lono closed her fingers, with the kapa, over the torn fleshy palm. "But just because you are his blood doesn't mean you will be like him."

Lono stood, raising Nohea with him. He pointed into the darkness. The canopy of branches above opened, and moonlight poured onto the path, lighting her way out of the garden, out of this mess.

"Find the manō, cleanse the island of soran, and do not lose hope." Her great grandfather's words resonated deep in her heart, creating a warmth that she hadn't felt in so long. A richness of love, comfort, and peace surrounded her body, like a hug.

She nodded, appreciating the moonlit path before her. "Where can I find the manō?" Nohea looked back at Lono, but he was gone. She scanned the treetops, the woods, and the ground. But he had vanished.

She held her forehead. Was it a dream?

The wind rustled through the bushy ferns nearby and Nohea shivered.

No, it hadn't been a dream. Her ancestor had visited her. But she needed to hurry and find Olukai. She was ready to help him.

CHAPTER FORTY-FOUR

Po and 'Ele circled a distance from the king's fortress. 'Ele's wings stroked the air with great power, yet remained quiet as the night. The mo'o kept them covered by the clouds, avoiding any angle that might cross paths with the large moon, for fear they might be seen.

Have you decided yet? the mo'o asked.

I'm still not sure where she is. They had stopped at Olukai's home and, while 'Ele concealed himself in the grove of palm trees, Po ran in. Lala had been there, cooking. She said Olukai was at the fortress already, leading the king's army to battle.

So Po and 'Ele flew over the army, but Po couldn't find a safe place to land, and still had no idea how to find Olukai. He found Tua along the path, as 'Ele's nose picked up the scent of the islanders from Hakalau village. It had been good to let his hānai father know he was safe.

But now they circled over the nearby fields, trying to decide where to find Olukai or, more importantly, the alchemist.

'Ele's words from earlier continued to affect Po. He worried selfishly about the future, about *his* future. He served Olukai, yes, but with the intention that after all of this, he'd sail away. He always looked far ahead, wondering about when he would be able to do what he wanted, instead of being here. Present.

Kiani's words of wisdom resurfaced: *You can't sail away from your problems, you know. It's better to face the storm head on.*

And the thing was, Po didn't have to face the storm alone. He had friends: Olukai, Haku, Haunani, Kiani, and so many others. Why couldn't he appreciate those around him now? It sent a pang through his chest that he'd been so selfish for too long, so bitter for too long.

I'm coming Nohea, he thought, realizing that this was his purpose *now.* Maybe the purpose would change in each new season, but right now he had to help Olukai. Po had spent too long waiting for the future, wanting to get out here. But he had to be here, first.

'Ae, the dragon said, cutting off Po's thoughts. For a second, Po wondered if the dragon read his thoughts.

What is it? Po asked.

An owl. He wishes for us to follow.

A small, dark brown owl, with long wings and a white underside, flew in front of them. It's brown face looked back, making sure they followed.

Where is it taking us?

Where else? To your friend, the alchemist.

Po smiled, grateful. Things would work out as they should. He trusted his friends, and he was here. Present. There was no time to pine bitterly for the future, only time to be here, in the present.

CHAPTER FORTY-FIVE

As the exciting news of the true ali'i ran through the camp of Olukai's army, he prepared to visit the enemy. He did worry about speaking with Ekewaka, but felt more concerned about Queen Awa. Ekewaka's army easily accepted Olukai as the king—they saw the mark and felt the mana. It was right that Olukai was king, and the island confirmed it, so they would hesitate to obey Ekewaka's orders if he happened to come around.

Furthermore, Ekewaka was in pain at the moment after having part of his eye removed. Olukai felt it best to focus on the enemy army wanting to battle in the morning.

As he tied his kihei over his shoulder, his eye caught hold of the shark symbol. It had now spread up to his shoulder in a matter of hours. Perhaps embracing himself encouraged it to be visible.

"Olukai." Lopaka stood at the door of the hut as Olukai hung his knife at his side. "My father is here, in the camp. He's... not very happy."

Olukai frowned and brushed past Lopaka, wondering how this would go down.

The sound of "boos" and commotion filled the air as Olukai

approached several groups of his army. In the midst of them, Ekewaka's voice rang through the night.

"*I* am the true king of the island! Not just anyone could rise up to reunite the island or cast out the foreigners!"

"The island is more divided than ever before!" Someone shouted.

"You fools, he is a liar!" Ekewaka screamed.

Olukai broke through the circle and a silence fell over the crowd. Ekewaka, along with a few of his warriors and Kahiko, stood in the middle of the circle. The false king's face reddened at the very sight of Olukai. A bloody patch covered his eye, secured in place with a braided ti leaf cord. "You imposter!" he screamed and spat on the ground. The men gasped while others murmured quiet threats. Olukai realized his army was ready to defend him if they needed to.

"I'm an imposter?" Olukai asked, and the army laughed. Ekewaka's face reddened even more, his veins popping out of his neck. He pointed his finger.

"You coward. You served me for years—" he glanced around at the army. "This man is not innocent! He went on many missions to obtain soran. He killed many people and animals to do that!"

Olukai scoffed. "Really? Is that all you have? I killed no one. Come on, Ekewaka. It's alright to admit you aren't the king of the island." He paced. "You have done much good for this island, and you should be commended and appreciated for that." The army mumbled in agreement, and, for a moment, the king relaxed. "You are an excellent alaka'i," Olukai added. "But now I ask that you step down honorably." He tipped his head. Olukai truly meant no disrespect to Ekewaka. It did take a special person to rise up and unite the people after the foreigners devastated the island.

"I will visit the queen tonight," Olukai said, "And try to stop this war. You know, as well as I do, that with so few islanders left, it's best to spare innocent lives."

Ekewaka only glared.

Olukai continued. "We have to destroy soran, Ekewaka."

The old king's face soured and his fists clenched.

"It's the only way to have any sort of peace on Kaimana island." Olukai reached out his hand. "Let's unite to do what the island asks of us, what our ancestors ask of us."

Ekewaka looked from Olukai's face to his hand. At first he processed the information, and the sensibility and honesty of Olukai's words. Then, his eyebrows creased, his teeth clenched, and he lashed out with a knife to Olukai's hand. The army exclaimed in surprise and stepped back.

Olukai dodged the attack, grabbing his own knife that hung at his side.

"You liar!" Ekewaka said, jumping forward to deliver blow after blow. Olukai blocked, stepping back each time, his demeanor calm. Ekewaka had never been a good warrior. He was too sloppy, lazy, and preferred to put his warriors through the training instead of himself. As long as he had the warriors at his side, he was protected, and while he did have warriors at his side, none of them jumped in.

"Soran *is* the key to prosperity and health on Kaimana island!" Ekewaka exclaimed, continuing to deliver his blows. "It will protect the people and open the way for trade and learning. You selfish coward!"

Olukai still didn't attack. He wanted the king to get out his anger. Though Ekewaka had his faults, he was still an excellent leader, and very dedicated. Olukai could use his help, and, furthermore, Olukai didn't want to kill Ekewaka. He didn't want to kill anyone.

"Please," Olukai said as he blocked another hit. "Join our cause. You are an honorable alakaʻi, just distracted by this evil island drink."

"I am not distracted!" The king let down another blow so hard that Olukai rolled out of the way and kicked Ekewaka's back. He twisted the knife in his hand, waiting for Ekewaka to gain his composure. The army snickered and laughed at Ekewaka's fall, which only made the old king angrier. He ran to Olukai, slashing, but Olukai simply blocked. The clanging of knives rang through the air and when Olukai finally had enough of the king's tantrum, he delivered a blow to Ekewaka's knife, tripped the old king, grabbed the knife handle straight out of Ekewaka's hand, and held both knives to the fallen king's throat.

The army exploded in cheers and claps at this display of Olukai's skill.

"Ekewaka, please," Olukai said. "Enough of this. Will you join our cause or not?" Either way, Olukai still had no intention of killing Ekewaka. Even if the old king didn't agree with Olukai, he would let him depart in peace.

Purple faced with fear, Ekewaka glanced back towards Kahiko and the warriors. The black-tattooed warriors ran straight towards Olukai, causing him to free Ekewaka. The army crowded in, ready to defend Olukai, and a brawl ensued. Ekewaka slipped away, running free of the commotion. Olukai started following, but a warrior grabbed his kihei and yanked him back. The armies ran to his aid.

"You'll be sorry for this," Ekewaka yelled to Olukai as he, Kahiko, and his warriors fled with intense speed. The army started pursuing them, but Olukai ordered for them to stop.

Lopaka, who had been watching the entire time too, repeated Olukai's words. "Order! Stop!"

"My role as king is not to force anyone," Olukai said to the men. "It is to unite us to a common cause. Ekewaka will always be appreciated for what he's done for our island." He sighed. "If you see the false king, let him go in peace."

The army looked at one another, stunned at Olukai's compassion. He rubbed his forehead and nodded at Lopaka and Ioane. It was time to visit the queen, and Oluka hoped his compassion hadn't run out.

"So you're really not worried about my father?" Lopaka asked as they took the path towards the queen's camp.

"Of course I'm worried," Olukai said. "But he has nobody to back him up."

"What about his warriors?" Ioane asked. Olukai thought about the warriors and Kahiko, who stood off to the side, watching. They continued to follow Ekewaka, even though they knew he wasn't a true ali'i.

"The only reason his warriors might continue to follow him is soran. But it won't be long before soran runs out, and they fight amongst themselves."

Lopaka sighed. "I wish he'd admit he was wrong."

"Did he know he was wrong from the start?" Olukai asked.

"Of course he did—"

"But he did a great thing for the island," Ioane said. "Nobody knew what to do when the ali'i were killed by the diseases. If he hadn't risen as an alaka'i, who knows where the island would be now?"

"Which is why I still admire the man," Olukai said. "He did an honorable thing."

"But maybe it doesn't matter where one started," Lopaka said. "Maybe what matters is where they are now."

"And it's too bad he's addicted to soran," Ioane finished. They stopped talking after that, each of them wrapped in their own thoughts. Olukai focused on the task at hand: convince Queen Awa to stop this nonsense. This war was unnecessary, and soran needed to be destroyed. If she were a true alaka'i, she would listen to the promptings of the island and agree with him. But if not, well... Olukai hoped they could come to some agreement, anything besides war.

THE QUEEN's army did the same thing Olukai's men had done when Kiani, the kahuna, and warriors arrived at the fortress. The men scoffed, spit on the ground, and made verbal threats. But Olukai and the others ignored them. Ioane held a red hibiscus plant in a coconut shell bowl to signify they didn't come here to fight, but to talk.

The men were led to a large tent made of the finest white kapa. It was so tall, the warriors didn't have to bend down to step inside. A warrior stood at the entrance and folded his arms.

"Your weapons," he said. Unlike the king's warriors, who bore tattoos to signify their status, these warriors had no defining features besides their stature and white clothes. Many of them walked around with only skirts, revealing the muscles and bulk of their upper bodies.

Olukai removed the knife from his side, so Lopaka and Ioane followed. Once the warrior took all their weapons, he opened the flap door of the tent and an overwhelming smell of flowers flowed out.

Queen Awa sat on her bamboo throne at the center of the tent, surrounded by warriors. There had to be at least twelve warriors beside her, or circling the tent. To her right sat the kahuna, Noa, on a smaller chair. To her left sat Kiani, though her eyes were vacant and when she met Olukai's eyes, it felt like she wasn't actually looking at him. It made Olukai's skin crawl. What had they done to her?

She sat cross legged, with flowers covering her neck, chest, wrists, ankles, and even around her waist. Olukai tried to read her, but she only looked at the queen, as if uninterested by the visitors.

"Olukai, the man who calls himself the true king of Kaimana Island," Queen Awa laughed. She reached out and stroked Kiani's cheek. Kiani remained unmoved, though Olukai did notice a hint of anger cross her eyes. "Did you come to rescue your love?"

Heat rushed to Olukai's cheeks. "I've come to make peace," he said. "This war is useless, and you know it."

"This war is long overdue," Awa replied, resting her head in her hand, as if bored. "It's about time we wiped out you puny humans. You, who think you're so special and so intelligent." She slammed her fist on the armrest of her chair. "No, it's the Māku'e who are superior. The Māku'e deserve to survive and outlive anyone else on the island."

"What?" Olukai hadn't expected this. So the queen did want soran, but she was also horribly racist. Ioane made a face, and Lopaka frowned, exclaiming, "That's outrageous."

Awa smiled and sat back. "So nothing you say will stop this battle. It is inevitable. Once we wipe out all the puny men in your army, we'll get the alchemist and raid the rest of the island—the Hune in their caves, the humans in their villages, and all the strange people in between."

Olukai still didn't know what to say to this, but he regained his composure when the island sent him a feeling of peace. His body grounded again after this shocking news. He had to stop this murderous queen.

"Awa, you know that isn't right." He stepped forward and the warriors made a move for him. He ignored them. "If you listen to the island, you know soran is bad. It will cause our people—who once were united—to fight against one another. It will turn brother against brother, sister against sister. It's already started, but we can stop that right now."

Awa laughed. "You're so sentimental Olukai. I told you once, and I'll tell you again. There's no stopping this war." She glanced at Kiani, who grew paler by the moment. "Unless..." A wicked smile crossed the queen's face. "When I sent my messenger, I did present an offer, and I renew that offer now. If you bring me the alchemist, you can have Kiani, and we will stop this war before it even begins."

Now Kiani stiffened, and Olukai knew that was truly her doing, not the kahuna. Both Ioane and Lopaka made faces. It was a horrible deal, and they all knew it. Not only would the queen take advantage of Nohea, but she'd be able to make more soran and *still* wipe out the rest of the islanders.

Tears streamed down Kiani's face, but she didn't move. It broke Olukai's heart. He could hear her voice from earlier: *You have to protect Nohea—please don't... don't think about me.*

But how could he not think of her, when she sat right there, so close he could get to her in a matter of steps? He hated that he couldn't save her.

At that moment, the earth shook, a clear sign to Olukai of what he needed to do.

"Earthquake!" Noa exclaimed, but it lasted a few seconds.

Olukai took the hibiscus from Ioane's hand and tossed it on the ground at the queen's feet. "If you didn't get the message from the island loud and clear," he said. "Then so be it. We fight at dawn."

The queen looked surprised, but only for a moment. She smiled again, calm. "Good. Be sure to watch the stars tonight. It will be your last." She reached out and wiped Kiani's tears. "And take a good look at your love. She won't be around much longer."

Olukai did meet Kiani's eyes and, for the first time in their brief relationship, there was nothing but pure trust in them. Kiani trusted him, and he trusted her. Things would work out as they should, though he loathed to leave her there.

He turned and left, sorry that the battle had to take place. Kaimana Island had spoken loud and clear, and he would listen.

CHAPTER FORTY-SIX

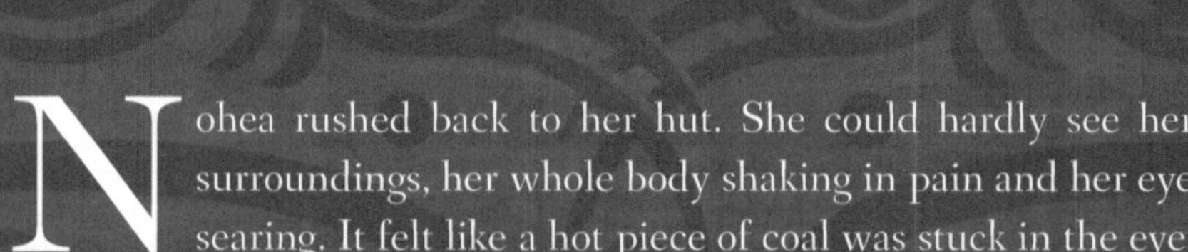

Nohea rushed back to her hut. She could hardly see her surroundings, her whole body shaking in pain and her eye searing. It felt like a hot piece of coal was stuck in the eye, and the more she pressed against the eyelid, the more it burned.

A group of warriors finally eased around her as she walked to her lab hut. It was as though Ekewaka forgot she needed protection and sent them to find her.

Nohea thought about what herbs and balms she might be able to use. Nohea knew most of her remedies would ease the pain, but not disinfect the wound. She needed to use alcohol for that, which she didn't have.

But the king might have... She almost turned back to find him, but changed her mind, as her next plan of action was to get out of here.

The warriors stood uncomfortably close.

When she entered the hut, she dug her free hand into the cubbies, pulling out herbs and branches, clippings and tree barks. She let them fall to the ground.

Where did I put my balm? It was the stuff that she put on her raw legs after the skirmish with the kupua, the old spirit in the forest. It seemed so long ago, and her heart ached at the thought of leaving her uncle.

I'll find you Olukai. And I'm coming Uncle Haku, she thought.

She reached into the back of a cubby and found the gourd, as she'd stuffed it there to keep it hidden. Some of her old notes were back there too. But her formula, the one that *actually* worked, was hidden under a bunch of ferns in the cubby under the table. Her hands shook as a kapa cloth soaked red on her palm.

"Do you need help?" Akamu watched her, pity filling his eyes. With trembling fingers, she handed him the gourd, not having to wait long as he twisted the top off with ease.

"Mahalo Akamu." She didn't dare release the pressure from her eye, so she placed the gourd on the table, stuck her dirty hand in, and slathered the balm on her palm, rubbing her palm against her thigh to cover the entire hand. Blood smeared everywhere, but she didn't care because of the relief.

Nohea knew it was a bad idea to put the balm in her eye though —her eye needed to be disinfected. So she sat there a moment, trying to breathe, the pain making her head pound like she'd been slammed down by the waves—or what she imagined the ocean to feel like.

"Akamu," she started to say, wondering if he would escort her to see the army, when, in reality, she wanted to get to Olukai.

"'Ae?"

The ground shook and Nohea gasped as things fell off the tables and cubbies. Akamu ran out. She heard the men outside running to the south end of the hut, to her left, and she stood up.

Was the queen attacking? Was this a surprise?

As these questions coursed through her head and she ran to the hut entrance, she heard a roar, so deafening and loud, it shook the whole house, shattering glass vials and sending things flying. She covered her ears, still stepping towards the door, seeing a warrior flying to the ground. He got back up, looked at her, and yelled, "Stay inside!"

He ran towards the south end of the hut, spear in hand. As he did so, there was a terrifying crunch and crash noise.

Nohea's eyes widened as she saw a large, scaly hand with white claws rip the entire south wall of the hut open.

A large yellow eye peeked inside, looking straight at her.

Then the creature's face slid back and she could see clearly, from the light of the torches in and out of the hut, a magnificent black moʻo.

His scales reflected from the torch lights, his long black neck curved into a beautiful face, with glittery small wings on either of his cheekbones. White spikes lined the back of his neck and on top of him sat...

She squinted, then a smile formed on her lips. "Po!" She exclaimed and began to rush towards him, but Akamu grabbed her, holding her arms.

Po smiled at her, his white teeth glowing in the torchlight.

"Attack!" The warriors had gotten up after the dragon's roar, and they ran forward.

"Stay back!" Akamu said, but he hesitated as they watched the chaos.

The men were like ants against a bumble bee. The black dragon swiped a warrior away with his thick claw, grabbed one with his mouth and spit him to the side, and then he breathed fire. He purposely breathed it away so it wouldn't burn Nohea, but would harm the men. The men burned, and Nohea's heart pumped, knowing this was her exact experiment.

She needed something hot enough to burn soran, turning it to mere water.

And the fire had worked, though, the horror of watching the men burn made her squeeze her eyes shut. They seemed invincible for the first few seconds as the fire raged on them. They even continued running towards the dragon.

And then, in the blink of an eye, one of them burst apart. Nohea gasped and stepped back into Akamu, remembering how the soran had danced and split when the flames hit it. The soran had burned, leaving the liquid. But in the human body, where soran coursed through the bloodstream...

This shook Akamu too, and he pulled her away.

"No, let me go!" she said, realizing that Po was her way out of here. The dragon terrified her, but this was it. As much as Nohea had appreciated Akamu and his kindness and wariness of her, right now she didn't need him. First of all, he held *both* of her arms, leaving her eye with a bloody kapa cloth hanging onto it. Secondly, Akamu didn't deserve her anger. He had been so kind, and was only obeying the king, just as she had. Nohea kicked, but nothing worked because he was bigger and stronger.

The other warriors had been defeated by the moʻo, and now the dragon looked intently at her and Akamu. The moʻo had no regard for the nearby huts, his tail lashing out in a hungry way as he bounded straight for Akamu.

Akamu looked around, seeing that all the other warriors had been killed. "Get out of here," he whispered into Nohea's ear and let her go. The moʻo stopped mid-walk, watching this. Akamu put up his hands, as if to surrender, "Please, have mercy."

Nohea didn't even bother to see what happened to him, though she wondered if he had been on her side all along. The confusion made her head hurt even more. Po lifted her onto the moʻo, as if she were light as a feather. She put her arms around his waist and held on tight as the dragon slithered back, preparing to fly.

"Attack!" A voice came from around the huts, and some warriors on horseback approached, charging past Akamu, launching spears straight at the moʻo. The dragon roared. Some of the men fell backwards from the force, while the horses neighed and stood on their hind legs. It was enough time for the dragon to push from its legs and launch into the sky. Nohea's stomach flipped as they flew upside down for a moment, swirling away.

The spears kept coming towards them. Nohea marvelled at the

men's strength—how was it possible for them to throw that far and high? Surely it was the work of soran.

Another spear hit the dragon on the side and Po yanked it out, launching it back at the men.

The dragon veered from side to side. "Hang on!" Po said to Nohea, but she was already doing so. The men on horseback followed beneath them, going through the king's fields, towards one of the forests surrounding the area. They fell behind, as the horses moved much slower than the dragon. However, much to Nohea's surprise, their spears still reached the dragon.

Nohea had no idea where they were going, but her shoulders relaxed when she saw the brown pueo flying beside the dragon. He nodded to her and then flew ahead, leading the way.

"This is ʻEleʻele, ʻEle for short," Po said. His hair was pulled back into a bun on his head, and he wore black again. It felt like years ago she'd met Po, but it had only been a few months.

"He said he's been poisoned." Po had to speak over the wind rushing past them, though he blocked most of it from Nohea. She buried her head in his black kihei, especially her right eye, because she was too scared to hold onto him with one hand.

Po groaned and reached for another spear that hit the moʻo. "Their spears are poisoned!" He tossed it to the ground. Nohea held him tighter as they swayed from side to side, even flying upside down at some points.

"Watch out!" Nohea said, but it was too late. Another spear struck the dragon.

Nohea squeezed her one eye shut but when she opened it again, she let out a scream. They were barely above the treetops, going at a slow pace, and it looked like they might tumble to the ground.

"We're going down," Po said, turning to grab Nohea. "Cover your head—" but Nohea hardly heard the rest as he pulled her close to him and jumped off the dragon. The dragon went headfirst into a field of lava rock, scattering ʻōhiʻa trees growing about it. There was a steeply sloped hill next to the field, covered with moss and ferns.

Po lost grip of Nohea and they both rolled onto the lava. Nohea let out an "oof" and lay still, her body burning from the scuffs and scrapes. "Nohea!" Po knelt next to her. "Are you alright?" She didn't move, but sobbed.

"It hurts Po."

"We gotta go sis, I'm sorry. I know you're hurting." When she didn't move, Po scooped her up, his own skin scraped and bloody from jumping off the moʻo, and ran towards ʻEle.

The lava field was quiet, though the warriors would catch up soon enough.

"No, no, no...." Po sounded frantic as he knelt by ʻEle's head. Nohea wiped her face and took deep breaths, trying to reground herself.

"At least get yourself out of here," Po said aloud, and she realized he spoke to the moʻo. How? Her head pounded so hard she wasn't sure she could comprehend anything else that night.

It broke Nohea's heart to see Po's eyes water in the moonlight. Then it dawned on her that he was communicating with the dragon... with his mind. She put her hand on his back.

The dragon limped up, his massive body breathing heavily beside the two. A wet pool lied in the spot he stood.

"I see them!" The king's warriors approached the lava field, encircling them faster than Nohea realized. She backed up against the dragon. Po got his spear ready.

"Give her up!" said the leader, his voice deep.

"Come and get her!" Po stood, spear extended.

The men threw spears and one of them went straight for Nohea. All time froze as the dragon let out a roar and whipped the spear with its tail. Then he stepped in front of Nohea and Po, to act as their shield. The spears pierced ʻEle and Nohea winced at the unnatural cracking sound of his scales.

The dragon roared fire, and Po rushed forward to fight a warrior. Nohea ducked by the dragon's rear legs, knowing that his tail would keep others away.

A few men went for the dragon's mouth, throwing a net with weight so the dragon's face was pinned to the ground.

"Po!" Nohea didn't know what to do. She pulled at the net but it was so heavy, made of some foreign material, probably a relic of the king's.

A warrior rushed forward, screamed a war cry, and pierced his spear straight into the mo'os neck.

"No, stop!" Nohea screamed.

Po fell back, stunned, and the man he fought jumped on the opportunity, punching Po's face.

The dragon lay still, and Nohea knew this was it. They'd take her back to the king, Po would be killed. All was lost.

The warriors ran to grab her, but, as they did, something happened.

The earth shook, making every person fall to the ground. Then, a spout of red, orange, and black flew into the air. Intense heat suffocated the air.

Lava.

Other spouts of lava flew into the air, making cracks in a circle around the dragon, Po, and Nohea, separating them from their enemies.

The warriors stood back, unsure of what to do. Nohea held onto Po, terrified by the lava flying into the air, though, miraculously, none of the drops fell on them.

Then the spout started to die, leaving an opening between the two runaways and the warriors.

"Get them!" said one of the warriors and began running forward, but when he did, the ground cracked before him, like brittle petals, and he fell in, lava exploding out.

Nohea and Po stepped back, bumping into the dragon's body.

Small lava fountains spouted from the ground around the warriors, and they scattered like ants.

"You would do well to run," said a voice, dark, soothing, and calm. It echoed through the lava itself. Nohea pointed to the steep hillside where stood a woman, her thick long black hair cascading down her back. She wore a red tunic, with an orange kihei on her shoulder. Her eyes looked like fire, and her arms were outstretched.

Po glanced at the fallen moʻo then took Nohea's arm and started running, avoiding the lava spouts. The warriors would not follow them, for everywhere the warriors ran, lava spouted out. It was like a game. They had nowhere to run but back from whence they came, the lava following them.

Nohea panted as they ran. Every step felt like pulling weights. She finally sat on the ground, her legs unwilling to take another step. Po knelt in front of her.

"We're almost there," he said. But she had witnessed too much that night. The pain was unbearable.

She closed her eyes and everything went dark.

CHAPTER FORTY-SEVEN

"The alchemist is gone!" The warrior was out of breath. Olukai recognized this warrior, the one who stood at the door of Nohea's hut.

Olukai's stomach flipped—a moment of hope, then concern. "What happened?"

"She flew away on top of a moʻo... with a golden-haired man."

Olukai didn't even conceal his smile. Lopaka stood next to him, as well as the leaders of sections of the army. Olukai and his leaders had reviewed their plans again, as none of them could sleep anyways. Lopaka clapped his hand against his fist, smiling, and then clapped Like's back, nearly sending him head first onto the table. Wena, in the corner, with his arms folded, leaned forward, his eyes intent on Akamu. The other leaders, Olukai's closest warriors, looked at one another, muttering their surprise at the appearance of a moʻo.

"They're gone?" Olukai asked, hoping for a solid confirmation.

"ʻAe, but a part of the king's warriors went after them. They flew north."

Olukai crossed his arms, praying they got away from the king's warriors. Though no horse could possibly outrun a mo'o, Olukai still worried. Those warriors could throw spears miles into the distance.

"Does the king—er, Ekewaka know?" A sense of awkwardness filled Olukai anytime he referenced Ekewaka.

"I came to you first," said Akamu, bowing on one knee. "The true king." Olukai frowned . How did Akamu know, unless...

"I hope you don't mind..." Akamu added, looking up. "I overheard your conversation with the alchemist. Many of the warriors have been suspicious of you for a while and that..." He pointed to the mark on Olukai's arm, now unwrapped. "That confirms my own suspicion." Olukai reached out his hand so he and Akamu could embrace with a hard clap to the back.

All were welcome in his army, his side, his kingdom. The idea made Olukai's head spin. This was real, and it was happening. Fast.

Akamu loomed over the rest of them, an obvious result of his drinking soran, and, for the first time, Olukai wondered if any of the king's warriors actually wanted to drink soran. Many of them turned into addicts of the stuff, but what of those who had to do it out of obligation? He had to trust Akamu on this one. After all, he brought the news of Nohea to Olukai first, or so he said.

"Where is my father?" Lopaka asked.

"He's at his hut with at least half of his warriors. The others are chasing the alchemist."

"Do you know his plans?" Lopaka asked.

"Why is that important?" Olukai cut in.

Lopaka shrugged. "He usually has at least thirty warriors at his side. What if..." He paused, but Olukai raised an eyebrow so Lopaka continued. "What if he joins his thirty warriors with the queen?"

Olukai rubbed his chin. "I see no reason why he would do that."

"For soran, of course," Lopaka laughed.

"Sir, can I make a suggestion?" Ioane piped in. Olukai nodded.

"What if we sent this warrior to report to Ekewaka? Maybe he can report back how many warriors guard the king. If he has many warriors, we will fight two battles in the morning... or tonight."

Olukai's head already hurt from such a long day. His body wanted rest, but his mind refused. *Everyone knows I'm the manō, Kiani is going to die, Nohea and Po are flying away to safety—or so I hope...*

He wiped his forehead. "'Ae. Akamu?" He looked to the warrior for approval, to which the warrior bowed his head.

"It would be my honor."

"But you have to pretend you're on *his* side, you know," Like cut in again. "Or else he might kill you..."

"'Ae, I understand," Akamu replied smoothly. "What do you expect Ekewaka to do anyways?"

Olukai shrugged. "I do not wish to cause any more bloodshed. Should anyone choose to join the manō, I will gladly accept them."

Lopaka scoffed. "Even Kahiko? That old man has been such a pain. Remember that one time—"

Before Lopaka could go any further, Olukai gave a dismissive wave of his hand. "I know, I know... He has his weaknesses, as do we all. If Ekewaka—and even Kahiko—swear loyalty to the true heir, like so many of the good men here, we will welcome them. If not... well, we can figure that out after the time of war."

He secretly wished Po had been there. He would've lightened the mood, made things less tense. He always had something to say when Olukai didn't.

"Alaka'i, you know your stations. You are dismissed," he said to the young men around the table, then nodded to Akamu. Four of his warriors and Wena stayed, the new personal guards of Olukai. Before leaving, Lopaka said, "You look tired Olukai. You should get some rest. Your warriors will keep watch. And if anything happens, we'll alarm you right away."

Olukai nodded in gratitude, then stepped into his tent. He laid on the soft bundles of kapa cloths, but sleep didn't overcome him, only the perpetual worry that Nohea and Po would get captured, he would witness the innocent deaths of too many, and that his men didn't stand a chance. And the worst thought of all—how could he ever live with himself? Kiani was going to be killed.

And there was nothing—*nothing*—he could do about it. But he had to trust the island. She trusted it, and that made their relationship stronger. He sighed, tossing and turning the rest of the night.

In the dark morning hours, Olukai walked about the camps, spoke with the villagers-turned-soldiers, consulted with his alaka'i, and made sure the youngest boys and oldest men took the safest positions: at the back of the army or on the walls to sling rocks at the enemy.

Akamu didn't come back by the time Olukai opened the gates and led his men out to battle on the fields. He hoped nothing happened to the warrior, but he had no time to think of it. He led his armies, as the manō, to fight the soran-drinking warriors of the Māku'e, led by an addicted, selfish queen.

The sun didn't yet touch the sky as Olukai, on horseback, led the men out. Wena and Lopaka rode on either side of Olukai and the soldiers marched behind. The soldiers wore more oil than any armor, as they only wore skirts, and the front lines carried spears and leiomanō. When the men came into close combat, as they expected, the oil made it harder for the enemies to grab hold of them.

Olukai glanced at Lopaka. The previous night he heard Lopaka and Like fighting, as usual, Lopaka saying that Like was too weak to go to battle, and he'd only get himself killed. Olukai didn't see Like anywhere so he assumed Like did, indeed, stay behind. Lopaka pulled his dark hair into a bun, and he looked serious as ever.

On the other side of Olukai, Wena's eyes sunk in, tired. He probably hurt from the loss of Kiani. When Olukai saw Wena that morning, they both exchanged sad glances, an understanding, acknowledgement, and loathing acceptance that Kiani might get killed that day.

When they reached the field between the nearest village and the king's fortress, Olukai halted his men, listening. The march of heavy footsteps sounded in the distance, and now light finally began to paint the sky, though the sun still did not show it's face over the horizon. A cool breeze made Olukai shiver.

A dark line of men appeared on the other side of the field, and then they stopped. Olukai squinted to see the leader of the queen's army, a thick, tall warrior on horseback. Olukai didn't expect the queen to ride at the front of battle herself—it was far too dangerous. But he did expect a large leader.

He nodded to Lopaka, and they both rode forward. It was custom, in an effort to avoid battle at the last minute, to send a few warriors to spar to the death. It sometimes satisfied the bloodlust of both armies, and the two enemies could work something out in peace while the armies dispersed.

Olukai had a feeling that this would be anything *but* normal. The queen had made it very clear to him the previous night, but he still wanted to try to avoid war.

The large enemy captain and a warrior rode to the middle of the field and they stopped before Olukai and Lopaka. The queen chose a handsome, burly man to lead her troops. He looked about the same size as Ekewaka: tall, brawny, with a big head and voluminous hair.

The man on the horse next to him, equally as large, though with a shaved head, said, "Captain Kuhe of her majesty, Queen Awa, sovereign ruler of the Māku'e and the dark forest."

"Olukai, the true heir of the great white manō," Lopaka said, "King of all Kaimana island." It sounded like Lopaka tried to hold back a proud smile through his words. The chilly morning air hung in a profound silence for a moment, letting Lopaka's words sink in. *The true heir... King of all Kaimana island...*

"So you are the manō," Captain Kuhe finally said, his voice guttural. He glanced at Olukai's arm to confirm it then smirked. "The queen gives you one last chance to make a choice: surrender the alchemist now, or die in battle."

"She will not even follow the customs of a formal spar to avoid bloodshed?" Olukai asked. He had little reason to hope for it, but now he knew people—*innocent people*—would die that day.

"There are no war customs on the island," Kuhe scoffed. "They were all destroyed when the foreigners spoiled our people." His nose flared. "Speak your decision."

"Will the queen not speak to me herself again?" Olukai asked. "I would rather spare the lives of your men than kill them."

"Ha!" The captain spit on the ground. "You mean you wish to save the lives of *your* men. We all know the warriors will kill them. They will break your limbs and crush your bones. Your army will not survive the morning."

Disgusted, Olukai frowned. "The soran is unnatural—it is not meant for humans. The island wishes it to be destroyed."

"I am not here to argue—you are stalling. Hand over the alchemist or we go to battle."

"The alchemist is gone."

A surprised silence. Then, "What do you mean?"

"She is no longer in the fortress. Even I do not know where she is," Olukai said—a half truth. He figured Po took her to the lava lady, but nobody confirmed that. And besides, the king's warriors had followed, so the two could be anywhere on the island at this point.

"You're lying." Captain Kuhe glared at Olukai, trying to read him.

Olukai shrugged. "Why would I lie? Ekewaka is no longer king of his own men, the alchemist is gone, and now I will restore the true line of the great ali'i to the throne of the island. Surely the queen would choose to side with me now—it is inevitable that I must unite the entire island. That includes the Māku'e."

"The queen refuses to join the manō—"

"Even if she has proof?" Olukai held out his arm, revealing the mark. At every minute, the sky grew lighter and lighter.

"She will not destroy soran. She will have it reproduced, share it with the Māku'e, and we will thrive, while the rest of the island grows old, kills one another, accepts the filthy foreigners, and dies."

Olukai tried to calm his frustration. Queen Awa and King Ekewaka probably would've joined one another as allies, as they *both* shared the same vision with their people: soran would solve all their problems. Except, it wouldn't.

Once people got a hold of it, they wouldn't be able to stop drinking. And no matter how much they reproduced the liquid, it would consume them.

"Then we will go to battle," Olukai said, loosening his fingers on the horse's mane, not wanting to cause it harm. He hadn't realized he'd been squeezing the loose hairs, and he rubbed the horse's neck, his eyes still intent on the captain.

Kuhe laughed. "Once we wipe you and your little army, we will find the alchemist."

Olukai shrugged, unaffected. "That's what you think." He turned his horse while saying, "Til we meet on the battlefield." Kuhe's nostrils flared, as though annoyed at his inability to bug Olukai.

"Say goodbye to your little girlfriend then!" He yelled after Olukai's back. Olukai kept calm, though his heart hurt. "The queen *will* kill her the minute she hears the battle cries!"

It meant that Kiani was still alive. If only for a moment more.

Olukai wished he could turn around, fight the captain, break through the armies, and rescue Kiani. He wished it with all his heart. Yet, as the alaka'i and the ali'i, he had to lead his men. They fought for him. They fought to destroy the evil island drink of soran. They fought for the balance and life of the island.

He looked at Lopaka and nodded. They spurred their horses to Olukai's army, calling out shouts, cheers, and beginning the ancient war chant. The men chanted in unison, some doing the ancient haka.

The time to battle for Kaimana island had finally arrived.

CHAPTER FORTY-EIGHT

When Nohea opened her eyes, she gazed up at large bunches of gray moss hanging from thick, intertwined ʻōhiʻa branches above her.

She lay in a soft bunch of furry ferns, the birds chirping cheerfully in the distance, with the sound of soft water moving in the background. She held up her hands, all washed up, the left one wrapped in white kapa cloth.

Nohea still wore her dirty tunic, but the blood had been wiped completely off her arms, neck, and face.

She gently touched her eye, covered by a soft, folded white patch, held on by a vine wrapped around her head.

Nohea sighed and slowly sat up, her long hair falling behind her. Soft voices sounded from the other branchy room, and the waft of sweet potatoes and fish filled her nose.

Where am I? she thought as she held her throbbing head. The room and bed she laid in was made completely of ʻōhiʻa branches and ferns, but everything was surprisingly comfortable.

A honeycreeper chirped nearby, startling Nohea. She stood up, shaking. How long had she been sleeping? What happened?

To her right was a sort of table, made from the same intertwined ʻōhiʻa branches. But she marvelled because on top of it was a medium sized mirror.

She'd never seen a mirror before, only heard of them. Walking slowly to it, Nohea was almost afraid to see herself. Her heart thumped as she stood before a girl: not very tall, with slim wrists and a square torso, tanned skin, and some light freckles across her nose.

She licked her dry lips and stared right at the white patch. What did her eye look like? Was it ruined? How was it not bleeding anymore?

Nohea touched her sun-kissed brown hair, moving it to the right side of her face, hoping it would cover the ugly eye.

She had never quite felt beautiful, but now she felt outright ugly. While she never thought she had much options in marrying, it now felt there was not a single chance that someone could love such a hideous figure. Nobody could love her with a ruined eye. Every person who saw her would believe her to be cursed, unfavored, and, therefore, the root of every bad thing happening. Every young man, including Wena, wouldn't want her.

Well, she thought, *Wena probably doesn't want me anyways now.* Not after she failed to appreciate his goodness.

Why am I thinking about this? There were more pressing matters at hand right now, and she needed to find Po.

"Nohea."

As if on cue, he stood in the door frame, his sea-blue eyes tired. Po wore his black tunic, which looked scraped and torn in places from their fall off the dragon, but his skin was clean and fresh. He rushed to her and they hugged.

It felt good, and Nohea didn't know how long they embraced. Even though she'd only known Po for a short time, her heart warmed at his companionship. She had a second chance to make things right, and Po was on her side.

He held her shoulders, examining her face. "Are you alright?" His breath hooked. "I thought you were gone..."

"I'm fine." She placed her right hand on his left forearm. "My head just hurts."

His face looked sorry. She wondered what he'd gone through to get a dragon, and then what happened after she blacked out.

We have much catching up to do, she thought, but didn't have the energy to say it.

"I'm sure it hurts. Come. There's someone you need to meet. She can help you."

He took her hand and led her through the strange branch doorway. It opened up into a large clearing, the soft mossy grass underfoot, and more ʻōhiʻa trees spreading their branches high above. It was like a home made completely of ʻōhiʻa trees and branches.

Nohea had been in one room, but there were several hut-like "rooms" that surrounded the center clearing. A river rushed by the branchy room Nohea had rested in. A soft, cool breeze drifted past the two as they walked to one of the five different rooms.

"She saved our lives," Po said, looking back to Nohea.

Nohea remembered the woman, her hands outstretched, her burning eyes.

They stood at the doorway of another branchy hut, a fire burning inside, the smoke rising out of a perfect circle at the top. Soft mats made of banana leaves sat round the fire, along with three leaf plates of food. At the head of the fire sat the woman, her skin smooth as a pearl yet dark as wood, a long face, with full red lips. She had a wide nose, and her large eyes, fringed with long lashes, shone a bright hazel color.

She stoked at the fire, the glow reflecting in her eyes. A thin, round haku lei sat on her forehead, made of red feathers. Her thick black hair, complimented by a few strands of silver, fell down her back, while wisps of hair frizzed out the sides. A big-boned woman, with toned arms and long fingers, her appearance intimidated Nohea.

She looked up. "I've been expecting you." Her voice was soft, yet there was a darkness to it, ancient sounding almost, with a depth of years and experience.

Po bowed, so Nohea followed. She knelt on one knee, feeling a stirring in her soul that this woman knew more than Nohea ever would. Nohea bowed.

"Rise." The woman motioned to the two. "Sit. Eat."

The two sat on the mats at the woman's right hand, and both waited patiently as the woman dipped two fingers into a coconut bowl of purple poi. She placed it in her mouth and then smiled with satisfaction.

Only after the woman began eating did Po and Nohea start eating. It was only proper to wait for the hostess before digging in.

Nohea hadn't realized how hungry she'd been. She'd never tasted salted fish so juicy and tender, nor sweet potatoes so perfectly cooked.

The woman kept filling their plates with coconut pudding, poi, even bananas, a forbidden food to women.

Nohea caught Po's eye and he smiled as he took a bite of the fish.

"This is delicious," Nohea said between bites, and the woman tipped her head. Although she had many questions, Nohea was grateful they ate first.

The woman ate little food, more amused and entertained by the two, than interested in her plate.

As the three finished eating, the woman handed them a large bowl of fresh cut mango.

"I am the lady of the lava," she said.

Nohea swallowed and nodded. By now she knew in her heart the true identity of the powerful woman. She glanced at Po, who nodded too.

"What is your name?" Nohea asked and the woman's eyes darkened.

"I do not have a name, nor a family." A sharpness entered the lady's voice, and Nohea felt herself shrinking under the gaze. The woman moved on, sitting perfectly proper, and looking into the fire.

"I have been asked to help you," she tipped her head to Nohea. "Your eye..."

"Can you remove the curse?" Nohea asked, feeling her spirits rise. The food had given her a great amount of energy, even though her head and eye still throbbed. It now felt like a million grains of sand had entered beneath her eyelid, and everytime her eyes moved, her wounded eye scraped across the sand, burning, and hurting.

"I have my ways with the world," said the lady. "But I cannot remove your curse."

Nohea's shoulders sank.

"I can only heal your wound," she said. "That is all."

Nohea bowed. "Even that I would appreciate."

"She usually requires payment," Po said. "But since we came with her old friend, she considers us a friend."

"Though I highly doubt my true friends would endanger a moʻo and let it get hurt so brutally." The lady looked grim and sighed. Then she stood up and began looking through some cubbies in the wall, made from the branches of the ʻōhiʻa trees.

"ʻEle is..." Nohea looked at Po and he nodded.

"He didn't make it." He glanced at the fire and used his fingers to brush his long golden hair back.

"I hope you know he was one of the last of his kind." The woman's back was still turned towards them, her hair so full, it looked like a wavy black bush covering her shoulders, arms, and back. Guilt washed over the two, even though it wasn't completely their fault.

"Ah yes..." The lady knelt before Nohea, holding a coconut bowl of a white salve. It smelled fragrant, like coconut milk and flowers.

Being so close to the lady, Nohea felt a strangeness in her own bones, as though she knelt before a mysterious spirit, a wanderer.

It's because she's a witch and a powerful sorceress, Nohea told herself, recalling that she felt this way around the meha, but she still couldn't shake it off.

"I only ask one thing of you."

"What is it?"

"Do you believe that there is one true aliʻi left?"

Nohea nodded. "I do... there is no way it could be my father. After seeing who my father truly is, I believe it."

The woman glared. "Well you better. Your bloodline is good for nothing."

Nohea felt her heart sink, but Po's hand slid to her shoulder, as if reminding that Nohea's life was not worthless.

Nohea almost opened her mouth to say something, but thought better of it. Perhaps her bloodline was worthless now, simply a bunch of traitors to the people of the island. But it didn't have to be like that. Nohea felt, deep down, a new hope. Lono had reminded her that she could help. And she could change.

She had been so blinded by her father, thinking he was a good king, that he'd never do anything wrong... but she was wrong. And now she could make things right, not only helping the manō destroy soran and create an island of peace, but she could restore honor to her family.

I can be the one to make things right in my family, she thought, or *be the person that* they *so desperately needed to look up to.*

"Hold still." The woman carefully took the bandage off Nohea's eye, and Po scooted even closer to Nohea's side to watch too. He clenched his teeth when the bandage came off, and Nohea blinked, feeling the rough eyelid scraping. A strange odor filled Nohea's nose and she wrinkled it.

"You smell the infection," said the lady. She dipped her tanned fingers into the salve and wiped it on Nohea's eye. Nohea's immediate reaction was to blink but the woman held Nohea's eyes open wide, with her other hand, to place the remaining salve directly on the eye.

Nohea flinched and almost pushed the lady's hands away. The salve burned, not what she had expected. It smelled so good.

She winced and began trembling, her whole body affected by the wound.

"Hold still." The woman's voice turned low. Po moved behind Nohea, holding her arms down, steadying her, and she felt grateful.

The woman put her hand over the fire, the salve dripping down, but her hand didn't burn. She began chanting, a low, smooth ʻoli.

It seemed as though the fire burned slower, dancing with her chant. The woman placed her hand back on Nohea's eye, but it was so hot, Nohea tried to move. Po held her steady. Time moved by too slowly, the woman singing an ancient chant, her stinging hot hand on the wounded eye.

Amidst all the fear she felt, the strange smell coming from her eye, the burning of the woman's hand, it felt good to have a friend. Nohea was glad Po had found her, and that he was helping her even though she'd turned her back on him, her uncle, the manō, and many others in the past.

The chant continued, and Nohea jumped, startled when she heard a distant drum. The woman continued singing, her melody haunting, as she looked up to the open sky, where the smoke wafted out of the hut.

She finally took her hand off Nohea's eye and outstretched her arms to the heavens. Something hot dripped down Nohea's cheek, from the wound.

Let the heavens bless the nearly dead, the heritage-less, the cursed blood.... The woman finished chanting.

Then she looked directly into Nohea's eyes, though Nohea could only see out of her left eye.

"You once were a sight as majestic as the sea," said the woman. "Hence your name... but now you must have burning, instead of beauty."

Nohea felt her cheeks, indeed, burn, as she blushed. She bowed her head, knowing that this was her fate now. She had never felt beautiful anyways, so why try now?

Po squeezed her arm, as if to say, *That's not true*. Her heart lifted .

"Come, child," said the woman, standing up. "The infection has left your eye, but we must finish cleaning it."

"And bandaging it," Po added. He helped her up and they followed the woman out of the hot, stuffy hut and into the clearing.

The woman went into another hut, the opening masked by heavy, twiggy gray moss. She moved the moss aside, motioned for Nohea and Po to wait, and went into the darkness beyond.

"Are you alright?" Po asked.

Nohea wiped whatever dripped from her eye. Blood. She shuddered. "I think so. It doesn't hurt as badly now."

Yet, she still couldn't get rid of the prickly feeling in her eye, like there was still something bothering it.

It dawned on her: her father must still be hurting. He didn't have very many healers to go to for help... his eye could possibly still be infected. He could still be hurting.

Or the soran will heal him, she thought. Soran could heal his wound, though she didn't know how quickly it worked.

"Here." The woman handed Nohea a clean, folded kapa cloth. Then she opened a large gourd in the other hand.

"This will wash away any impurities. It will not remove the curse, but it will help."

"What is it?" Po asked as he and Nohea tried to look into the gourd, seeing nothing.

"Water," the woman said, "From the highest mountain on the island, where the earth turns white...there is a lake."

Nohea smiled, recalling Kiani and Wena teaching her about the place. "Mauna Ki'eki'e," Nohea said.

The woman nodded. "Kneel, and I will pour this over your eye. Do your best to keep your eye open, but do not touch your eye."

Nohea nodded and knelt on the soft moss in the clearing. Po knelt next to her, ready to help should she fall over or try to use her hands.

The woman lifted the large, smooth gourd and tipped it over Nohea's face.

Nohea had the inclination to close her eyes, as anyone would when something came straight down on their face. But she focused, knowing this would help.

The water poured over her eye, cold as ice. She shivered and put her head down, rubbing her face.

"Good enough," said the woman, putting the gourd down. As Nohea wiped the water off her cheeks, the woman picked a vine from the long gray moss that covered the hidden room. Through her blurry vision, Nohea thought the woman's black hair looked strangely similar to the gray moss: thick, frizzy, full, and long.

The woman took the clean cloth from Nohea's hand and placed it over the eye, then she tied the long strand of moss around Nohea's head to keep it in place.

"You will not touch it for the next few days—or even weeks," said the lady. "Now come, we must talk... because your friend is in danger and you will not stay here much longer."

CHAPTER FORTY-NINE

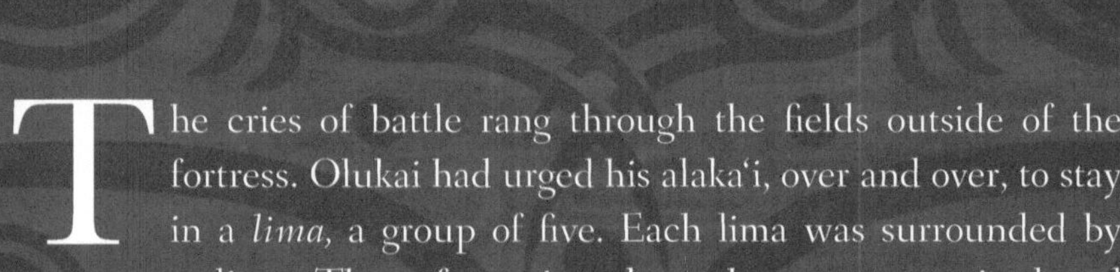

The cries of battle rang through the fields outside of the fortress. Olukai had urged his alaka'i, over and over, to stay in a *lima,* a group of five. Each lima was surrounded by seven more lima. These formations kept the army organized and provided the best way to fight the enemy.

When the queen's army approached the lima, the first row attacked with their long, wooden pikes. The second line would attack with their spears and clubs. The ones in the back threw spears, or used slings to fling stones. The lima was an ancient way of fighting, but for good reason. It worked.

Olukai's twelve leaders fought and led their men well, but the soldiers (mostly infantrymen who lacked training from Ekewaka) and the island villagers (men of trades and arts) were being wiped out, like waves breaking the shore lines. Wave after wave of men fell as the queen's warriors advanced.

One, Olukai counted those he saw fall. *Twelve. Twenty-one. Thirty...* He stopped counting, and his anger rose.

It wasn't fair that the queen's army drank soran. If his own soldiers did that, they'd have a fair battle. The soran-drinking warriors, indeed, caused terrible destruction, smashing skulls, tearing limbs. It was such an awful sight, that no words could adequately describe the horror. Every inch of Olukai's body pulsed with adrenaline, which kept him going through the fray.

By midday, his men tired, and many groups of lima joined with each other. It was at that moment, Olukai called the retreat. They had planned for a retreat, though they hoped it was unnecessary.

"Fallback!" Lopaka yelled, barely recognizable with the mud and fleshy debris all over his body. Olukai caught Wena in the corner of his eye. Wena stooped to pick up a fallen soldier, though still alive. He swung the man over one shoulder, and then another man on the other, and ran towards the fortress gate.

"Olukai!" Lopaka pointed to the gate as it opened, though there seemed to be some confusion with the men atop the fortress walls. Instead of facing the queen's army, hot on the tired soldier's heels, they faced the inside of the gate, slinging rocks and launching spears.

What are they doing? thought Olukai. *They should be launching those spears at the queen's warriors.*

The sound of a conch shell blew and Olukai's hairs stuck on end. It was the conch shell that Kahiko used to blow, signifying an assembly or gathering to the villagers.

Ekewaka.

The men retreating towards the gate were met by another army, Ekewaka's army. Ekewaka's warriors stood at the gates, blocking the way into the fortress. Some of them threw rocks or spears at Olukai's men on top of the walls.

Panic washed over Olukai.

The men on top... Those were the old *and* the young, as young as eight or nine years old, boys that shouldn't have even been there. Olukai had strategically placed them there to keep them safe. But now he regretted his decision and watched as they fell, one by one.

Though small in number, from what Olukai could see, Ekewaka's army consisted of his personal warriors, the giants, men with black tattoos, who had probably drunk soran longer than the queen's army. They loomed over the exhausted soldiers running towards the gates.

"Olukai!" Lopaka's voice again, urging a decision. The manō's army was surrounded—by Queen Awa's army on one side, and Ekewaka's army on the other. It had been a smart decision of King Ekewaka to wait until the army was tired, ready to retreat. Then he could block their safety, the fortress, their only place to catch a breath.

The old king and vicious queen would massacre Olukai's dwindling, fatigued army. Olukai wanted to curse. How could this happen? How could he be so outnumbered when he was the true king of the island? Is this how the island intended it to end? Or had he just failed?

His eye caught hold of the green forest nearby, the same one he'd run through only a few nights earlier to spy on the queen's army. And he did the only thing he could think of.

"Retreat to the forest!" he called. The men immediately veered towards the trees. Olukai and Lopaka stayed behind to fight off and stall the warriors.

Olukai had never blocked so many blows, inflicted so many wounds, and *killed* so many men. He'd done terrible things on his missions for Ekewaka, but nothing like this.

"Fallback to the forest!" Lopaka repeated over and over, his voice hoarse.

Olukai saw old Tua limping along, and he rushed past him, hoping to stall enough of the queen's warriors that they wouldn't chase and stab the old man in the back. Wena joined Olukai, and for a brief moment, Olukai wondered where Wena had placed the wounded men. They had medics in the fortress, but not in the forest. He wished he thought of a retreat in the forest. They could've hidden a surprise ambush, or had medical help in the deep woods. How had he been so unprepared?

"Forward!" Captain Kuhe's voice echoed through the field.

"Spare none!" The ferns, vines, and bushes grew so thick, many soldiers and warriors, from both armies, stumbled through.

Olukai and Wena both fought different warriors. Wena moved with confidence, unafraid. Olukai, likewise, stepped as a dancer—with grace, precision, and purpose. As they worked to hold off the queen's warriors, whose morale raised as they saw the manō's army retreating, another conch shell blew.

All fighting paused for a moment.

"Fallback!" It was Captain Kuhe again, and the other bald man who'd been next to him earlier that day. "Fallback!"

Why? Olukai wondered. Then it dawned on him. They must have seen Ekewaka's army. Perhaps they didn't know what to do, and they certainly didn't want to get in the middle of it. By pursuing Olukai's army, Ekewaka could chase and slaughter the queen's army from behind.

In a way, then, Olukai felt a sense of relief that the warriors wouldn't follow. His men could get a much needed break. But he worried about the men at the gates, the boys and seniors he placed on top of the walls for "safety," though they now occupied the most dangerous spots, closest to Ekewaka.

"To the forest!" Lopaka kept yelling, rushing to aid fleeing soldiers, though the warriors turned around and ran out of the forest. As Olukai watched them disappear, he hoped—against hope—that the king and queen's army would not join forces.

But he had a feeling, deep inside, they definitely would become allies. After all, they both lusted after soran, and the manō did not.

CHAPTER FIFTY

The lady of the lava led Nohea and Po to a different part of the wooded home, a section where the river ran in a circle around a small mossy island. Mats sat on the island, surrounding an unmade campfire.

The woman motioned for them to sit.

"Now tell me your story, child," she said to Nohea once they sat and filled coconut bowls of water from the soft river running around them.

The sun had set by then, and the stars shone through the trees, the birds sleeping in the treetops above.

"What do you mean?" Nohea asked.

"Tell me about where you are from, how you know what you know. I wish to hear it from your mouth, not his." She pointed at Po.

Under the stars, Po shifted, uncomfortable.

"My name is Nohea," she started. "I was born a slave to Edena. She taught me everything I know: how to break down plants and understand their properties, how to understand the making of liquids, how to understand the source of problems with wounds, and what medicines to make that could help."

The woman nodded as Nohea spoke. "She was killed recently because she burned the books in the king's library. I ran away, with help from my uncle and Po."

The woman glanced at the unmade campfire and Nohea now noticed a small coal start burning. "Continue," the woman commanded, her voice low, unearthly.

Nohea did so, her eyes now intent on the campfire before them, the coal burning brighter and brighter as she spoke. "We got separated and my uncle and I found ourselves in the dark woods. Two siblings helped us—a brother and sister. They were exiles from the dark tribe, but they took us to Queen Awa. We made a deal. If I found a way to get her soran source to flow again, then she would let us free and spare the lives of the outcasts."

"Did you find out the secret of soran?" A little flame began to burn from the hot coal. The woman poked it with a long stick then leaned on the stick to look at Nohea.

"I did not. Well, I did, but not when I was with the Māku'e. I made bombs to wake up the mo'o and scare him out of the cave."

A smile formed at the corners of the lady's lips.

"By that point, my father, the king, had found me. We also made a deal... I believed he was right, and my uncle's stories about the *manō* weren't true. I thought if I helped my father, we would make the island better, have soran for everyone but..." Her voice trailed off.

Silence. Then the woman spoke up. "But what?"

"There is no good that comes from soran. I've thought of the many ways it could be good, but in the end, men are weak. They only seek power for themselves. Soran is a way to be more powerful than others. It has the potential to be used for a good cause, but based on all I've seen... it's only going to cause destruction."

Nohea noticed Po was staring at her, and when she met his eyes, he nodded. It was as though a secret message passed between the two: Nohea had done the right thing, and Po was proud of her.

Other coals in the fire began burning brighter, and Nohea finally started feeling the warmth from it.

"When you went to the fortress, did you discover the formula?" The lady stoked the fire and more flames grew.

Nohea nodded, and Po leaned forward. "So you really did?" he asked, his blue eyes wide.

"'Ae. I know the formula, how long it takes to make it, the perfect conditions... I know exactly how to do it. I started an official experiment but then my father said we needed to remove this curse. And now I'm blind in one eye." Nohea rolled her eyes and winced when the right one hurt.

The woman folded her arms, lowering her chin. "I do not know how you can discover such things," she said. "But I do see the wisdom in your eyes, and that you are not lying. Does the king know the secret?"

Nohea shook her head, then bit her lip. "He doesn't know it... yet." Po frowned as Nohea met his eyes. "My papers are still in that hut. I should have burned them as soon as I changed my mind. I was thinking about the salve for my hand and—"

"It's alright," Po interrupted. "We'll have to go back though. It needs to be destroyed."

"I know."

"I have lived many years," said the woman. "I have guided many lives, helped others find a home, befriended the many creatures of the island, but I have never met one like you." She studied Nohea for an uncomfortable minute, then continued. "You have figured out your path, or at least the next step."

"I know that those papers must be destroyed," said Nohea. "But the king must be too. He's too powerful, invincible. He's been drinking soran for centuries. The only way to kill him would be to kill me." She glanced at Po, who shook his head.

"That's madness."

"It's not. It's the truth."

"She has a point," the woman said to Po and he threw his hands up, but before he could say anything, the lady spoke first. "But you do not need to sacrifice yourself. Your mother was a powerful sorceress, more so than myself. She knew the darkness and light of the island better than anyone else."

"She was evil to do this to me," Nohea cut in.

"She was wise. It was the only way to preserve your life. Perhaps one day you will understand." The woman leaned over the fire and her hair fell down her sides, covering her dark arms. "Go to your mother's tribe, an ancient tribe of meha in the southern slopes of the great white mauna. They hide in the thick forests there, and they move swiftly as not to be found. They are learned in the same ancient, deep magic as your mother. They should be able to help."

For the first time that evening, Nohea felt a flicker in her heart. Even Po lightened up a bit.

"You will learn more about your mother," said the woman. "And more about yourself. Perhaps you will learn things you don't like."

"I am so tired of my heritage," Nohea sighed at the lady's words. She looked up at the stars, thinking of her ʻaumakua, Lono, and remembered the wisdom he shared with her. She would honor that good side of her family, and start a new legacy, one that her future descendants would be proud of.

If I have descendants. The whispered thought made her cringe, remembering how ugly she felt and looked now.

"Every person has darkness and light in them," the woman said. "Every family has darkness and light in it too. It's not about the blood that runs through you. It's about what you choose to do."

The woman stoked the fire again. "You both have been rescued and helped by one of my oldest friends on the island, ʻEle. He was a great moʻo, a protector of the people... until the people became greedy. Then the foreigners started coming, and the moʻo hid."

Nohea heard this story before, the tales parents told their children as they dozed off to sleep.

"But there was a time when the island was full of goodness and love. Every plant, bird, animal, drip of water, and every human acknowledged that if they took care of one another and the earth, then it would take care of them."

Po hugged his knees and stared at the fire.

"It isn't about uniting the island—that's not why the great white manō called a distant descendant. It's about restoring balance. There must always be a mutual respect and love between the humans and the life of the land. It is pono."

Nohea understood. Everything became so clear. Not only did she have to destroy the paper that contained the formula to soran, but she really did need to find a way to destroy every bit of soran. The manō needed her help.

"We have to go," she said, "Before the king finds that formula." And they needed to find more moʻo, the kind that breathed fire. She began to stand up but Po grabbed her arm.

"Wait! We don't know everything yet."

"He has been patiently waiting his turn," the woman said to Nohea. Nohea glanced at Po. *His turn?*

She sat back down. "What is it?"

Po stared at the woman, a longing in his eyes. Not a romantic longing, but a sadness that Nohea hadn't seen in him before. She saw him grieve the moʻo, but this was different.

"You have a mind that understands the moʻo," said the woman. "That is unusual, and unlike anything I've known, for only those of mermaid or Hune blood can speak to the dragons of old. But the island has revealed its secrets to me."

The fire now burned brightly.

"The Haunted island. Po, you must go there and meet your family." The woman tipped her chin to Po and a strength entered him. He breathed faster.

"But the island is haunted," Nohea cut in.

"You will find answers there." The lady ignored Nohea. "Make haste. The manō needs help now. The queen and her people will not give up the fight, nor will the two self-proclaimed kings of the island. Blood will be spilt, but the island must be cleansed."

"How are we going to destroy *all* the soran?" Nohea asked, even though she had some ideas.

The woman frowned, almost annoyed. "You will know what to do." She stood up, wagging a finger at Po. "And he will help you."

Nohea nodded. She had hoped for a solid answer, solid direction, like the woman gave to Po. But Nohea knew the answer: they needed the help of more moʻo. If they could get one, or even two moʻo to blow their hot fire on the pools, they could destroy the soran off the island.

Though, that didn't prevent more soran pools from forming, as uli grew in abundance. And that bothered Nohea. She had much to think about and figure out.

"You will not stay any longer." The woman handed them both dark golden capes, hidden in a corner of the room. "You may have these, a gift from myself."

Both Po and Nohea bowed. "We cannot repay you for your kindness—" Po began but she cut him off.

"You will never be able to. My friend is dead because of you." Both Nohea and Po cringed at that. "But I will not hold it against you if you restore balance to the island. Do *exactly* what it asks, even if it scares you."

The two nodded, eyebrows creased in concern. Nohea wrapped the cloak around her and couldn't help holding it closely around her arms, loving how light and warm it felt.

"What is this?"

"The silk webs of the happy-face spider. It takes years to make these."

Nohea's jaw dropped but she simply bowed her head, honored. She couldn't even imagine how to begin weaving something with only the hair-like threads of spider webs.

She and Po made their way to the clearing, where Po handed Nohea her sandals. He moved in haste.

"How are we going to get into the fortress?" she muttered. "If we had the moʻo we could burn the hut to pieces... I don't need any of my papers in there." She pointed to her head. "All I need is here."

The woman stood a distance from them, watching.

"If the legends are true," Po said. "There is a shapeshifter nearby. The manō has met him a long time ago—"

"That man is a pig," the woman interjected, and both looked up from tying their sandals.

"The manō?" Po asked, confused.

"The shapeshifter." Her nose flared . "He is a coward and a pig."

"He's probably our only way into the fortress," said Po. "There are no mo'o in this area, or horses. If we can find the shapeshifter, he can turn into a mo'o—"

"His shape shifting has become limited," the woman interjected. She rolled her eyes. "Since you are set on the shapeshifter, I will not deny you information. He lives north of these parts." She folded her arms, fire in her eyes. "Some call him Kama."

"Yes, that's him," Po nodded at Nohea. "Kama. We have to hurry. He's our only way into the fortress."

They bowed again to the woman. "Thank you again for your kindness and hospitality," said Po, and Nohea quickly added, "And for saving our lives back there." She wanted to add everything else, but when she met the woman's eyes, she knew the woman understood.

"Hurry, go," said the woman. The two nodded and began to rush off. But it wasn't long before the woman called to them. "And don't forget to listen to the island... or I will find you." Her eyes glowed from a distance. Nohea and Po nodded, then ran off, afraid that if they stayed any longer, their good graces with the lady of the lava would come to an abrupt end.

CHAPTER FIFTY-ONE

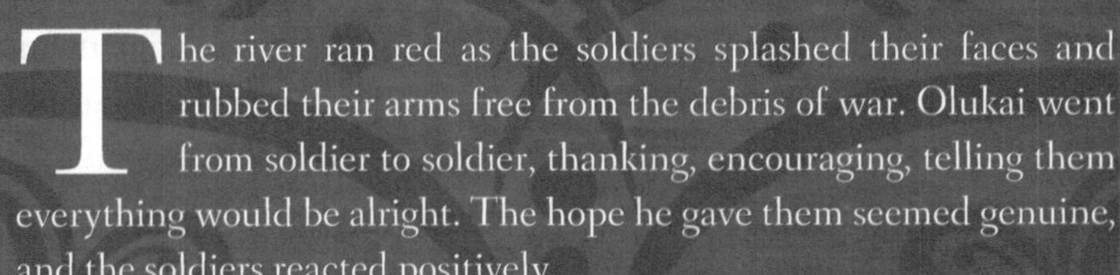

The river ran red as the soldiers splashed their faces and rubbed their arms free from the debris of war. Olukai went from soldier to soldier, thanking, encouraging, telling them everything would be alright. The hope he gave them seemed genuine, and the soldiers reacted positively.

Their morale dropped when many groups of lima started falling and then when Olukai called for retreat, but now, having rested, they spoke softly to one another, and looked to Olukai with hope.

The men helped one another dress wounds by ripping parts of their skirts and kihei. Lopaka went from one alakaʻi to the next, hearing their reports on losses, wounds, and those left behind.

Olukai walked upstream, needing a moment to himself. How could this happen? The great white manō chose him, the last in his line. Had he just let his great ancestor down, and let the island down too? After all, he felt like they were *losing*... losing against the queen *and* king with their soran drunk soldiers.

It will be fine, he reassured himself, washing blood off his arms. Yet, his fingers trembled as he thought about all the lives lost this day:

so many innocent villagers turned soldiers. So many of Ekewaka's, now Olukai's, ill trained, unprepared soldiers. And Kiani.

They were all gone. Dead. And all for the support and loyalty to the true heir of the island, the manō. Olukai shuddered.

I can't do this, he thought. *I'm a fraud.* As the river washed the blood off his arms, the mark of the manō appeared once more: a beautiful great white shark, with tribal symbols and waves surrounding it. It now covered his entire forearm and ran up his shoulder, as if it had waited this long for him to finally own his *kuleana,* his personal responsibility, his true identity. He sighed.

How could he give so many men hope when he felt hopeless himself? He had no reinforcements, not even a place of refuge, no medics in sight, and hungry, fatigued, worn out men. Just men, not bulky giants infused with soran. For every one of the queen's warriors killed, there had to be *at least* four of his own men killed.

He tried to think about how many warriors he saw pursuing them into the forest, but it was hard to tell. After splashing cold water on his face, Olukai paused as his face reflected into the pool of water in his hands.

Scratches, bruises, and dripping blood covered his face, though he could hardly focus. He took deep breaths, trying to stop his hands from shaking. They never shook, though he couldn't blame himself. The scene from that morning would haunt him for the rest of his life.

Olukai reached his thoughts out to the ocean, skimming past the shore, diving under a wave. The sounds of the underwater world filled his mind. *Great white manō...*

He looked about the ocean in his mind, searching, calling. Imagining the ocean brought a sense of calm to him. There was no great white shark—at least not reaching out to him. Just the great wide sea. Emptiness.

I failed my ancestors, he thought, letting water run through his fingers and then rubbing his forehead. He sat back with his face in his hands. He couldn't face anyone. Not now. Not ever. He had failed every single islander, his ancestors, and the island. Queen Awa would kill everyone, if Ekewaka and his band of thirty warriors or more didn't do it first.

"Olukai." A chill ran up his spine as he recognized the voice. He looked around, but nobody was there. He frowned, and the island prompted him.

Be still.

Olukai took a deep breath and closed his eyes. A vision played before him, one from his youth:

A woman found a young boy coughing on the shores. He almost drowned, pulled by the current. He swam for hours, following the waves, getting closer and closer to the shore until, finally, his feet touched the sand. The woman knelt beside him, stroking his hair. She was beautiful, just like he always remembered her. Her dark brown skin looked warm like the color of morning sand, her green eyes gentle. Dark, thick hair ran down her sides, and the black mark of the manō lined her wrist, going up her elbow, covering her shoulder, and barely reaching her neck.

"My son," she said, helping the young Olukai sit up. He was in shock, knowing that he could've drowned.

"Ma," the young boy said and hugged her. "I was a fool."

"We all make mistakes," she said, holding him tight. "And now you are here. You are stronger than you think."

"No I'm not."

"Olukai." She gently pushed him away, holding his shoulders and looking into his eyes. "You are an ali'i. You have always been one."

"But I'm not. I don't even have friends."

She placed a kiss on the young boy's forehead. "My dear son, you have more support than you think. Continue to listen and have courage."

A rustle in the bushes brought Olukai back, away from the vision. He stood, bewildered.

"Olukai, sorry to interrupt."

Olukai blinked as Lopaka approached, realizing he had seen a vision, a gift from the island to remind Olukai of his place. And he couldn't forget it. He looked at his bloody hands and felt a new strength within. He would live up to his role as ali'i, even if he died trying.

"What news Lopaka?" he asked.

"We lost four alaka'i—"

Olukai looked away, a lump in his throat. Four of his good friends, warriors, the men he trained and took with him along so many missions, gone. Just like that.

"Keoni, Aoloa, Hani, and Kaholo."

Olukai could see their faces clearly, and he took a slow, deep breath.

"Many of the alaka'i are down to at least twenty men each. We've lost more than half our army, and I'm not sure about those at the fortress..." Lopaka paused. "We can assume they didn't make it. And if they didn't, we are less than two hundred men..."

"Thank you for the report Lopaka," Olukai said before Lopaka could continue. He didn't need to know their odds of triumphing against the warriors.

"I sent some spies out to see the whereabouts of the king and queen's armies. I've instructed the men to set up camp. It's too dark to return to battle."

Olukai rubbed his chin, thinking.

"You look tired," added Lopaka. "You should come join the men. Some have already foraged food for the night."

Olukai agreed. He had to boost the men's morale, and he eagerly waited to hear news from the spies. What were the king and queen up to now? Did the men at the fortress get slaughtered—or did the king spare them?

When Olukai and Lopaka joined the others, they spoke softly. Four men kept watch around the camp, and every soldier was on edge. Olukai felt their concern: they were too exposed, out in the open. The warriors could encircle them at any point, and they'd all fall.

As the night wore on, some men slept, but most, like Olukai, lied awake. His thoughts raced, his head pounded. But his heart hurt the most. *We've lost more than half our army...* Lopaka's words echoed over and over, until Olukai could bear no more, and he took a turn on watch duty, trying to remember his mother's wise words: *Continue to listen, and have courage.*

Before the sun arose, the spies, Ioane and Sefa, finally arrived. They spoke privately to Olukai and Lopaka, so the other men wouldn't hear.

"The king and queen have joined forces," Ioane said. A pang struck Olukai's chest, but he nodded. "The gates to the fortress are closed, and our men they've taken prisoners."

Olukai let out a sigh of relief about all those old and young men he placed on the walls. Being taken prisoner was better than being killed, or so Olukai hoped.

"The king's men camp within the gates, and the queen camps where they've been. It looks like they will wait for us to come from the forest to fight."

Olukai nodded. They had to go out and fight. There was no other way around this.

"What of the wounded?" Lopaka asked.

Ioane shook his head and gulped. "The queen's warriors went through the field and killed any who were found breathing."

Olukai rubbed his forehead. "Anything else?"

"'Ae. The king has at least thirty warriors. Akamu is part of them."

Olukai didn't quite know what to think of Akamu, his first thought being, *traitor*. But Akamu had seemed pretty honest and convincing.

"What else?" Lopaka asked when Olukai said nothing.

"The queen still has at least fifty strong warriors, maybe more."

Olukai grimaced. He and his army were back to their starting point: with the king and queen combining forces there were at least a hundred of the soran-drinking warriors. And now, Olukai had less than half his army. To make matters worse, each of his men looked deeply fatigued. Many were wounded, and others had little to no strength left to even get up. They lied there, resting, having lost so much blood, and were on the verge of accepting death.

With his soldiers and army now completely weak, taking his men to battle would be marching them to their deaths. He knew it. Lopaka knew it. And Ioane and Sefa knew it.

"We would go to battle if you asked us to," Ioane said, his dark eyes thoughtful.

Sefa nodded. "'Ae, our allegiance is to the manō, the true king of the island."

"You wouldn't lead us to our deaths, would you?" Lopaka asked, cutting off the others. He didn't look one bit confident, the only one of the group who bluntly called out the truth.

Olukai sighed. "I wouldn't ask it of any of you. We should ask the men. Take a vote. We can either go to battle and fight to the end, or surrender."

"The manō would not surrender!" Ioane said, as if ashamed that Olukai had even thought of the option. And Olukai felt ashamed that he offered the suggestion, but it wasn't fair to his men to lead them to their deaths. "It would dishonor us," Ioane continued. "We would lose our mana as warriors. We would rather die serving the true king and saving the island, than bow to a fake king."

Olukai sighed. He listened to the island, and sought out the great white *manō* in his mind.

Nothing.

"We have no other choice," he finally said. "I will not let these islanders die in vain. Maybe in surrendering we have a better choice."

"They will treat us as slaves," Sefa said. "I would rather die a free man than become a slave to those soran-drinking fools."

"I admire your courage," said Olukai. "But an ali'i listens to his men too. Come. Let us talk to the men."

His heart ached as Ioane and Sefa looked away, disappointed.

The two alaka'i hurried off to get their men's attention, and soon, the entire camp surrounded Olukai.

The cool forest breeze wafted through the area, carrying the strong scent of the sweaty men, and the thick smell of iron.

"My men," Olukai said. "You have fought well. You have been warriors—*true* warriors, not the kind as the king and queen have, but true warriors for your courage, determination, and strength. I cannot thank you enough, and I cannot ask more of you."

The men watched, serious. Tua and the boys he brought looked eager, hopeful even. Wena stood off to the side, arms folded.

Olukai sighed, hating to bear the bad news. "Ekewaka and Awa have joined forces."

A stir ran through the crowd and the men murmured. Olukai continued. "There are at least a hundred of them... and we have less than half of what we started with."

He felt the pangs that shook each man, and he wished he could take it all away. "As your alaka'i and your ali'i, it is my duty to listen to your voices, and make a decision on what is best for all of us, the island, and that would honor the people and our ancestors."

The men nodded to one another. It was fair. It was right for him to listen to their opinions. "We will take a vote. All in favor of a surrender, say 'ae."

Shock filled Olukai. He looked about, and only met silence. The faces of the men and young men, hardened and made older in such a short amount of time, stared back at him. Dark, determined, fierce.

"All those who will march to battle, say 'ae."

The chorus rang out loud and clear. "'Ae!" said the men. Wena nodded. Though they looked exhausted, wounded, and near the point of death, it would have dishonored their families, the island, their own mana, and the great white shark, the fiercest predator in all of Kaimana, to surrender, Olukai knew it.

He glanced at Lopaka, whose eyes were wide in shock. Then he nodded and said, "'Ae."

"We meet them at the fields again, before the sun rises," Olukai said, and the remaining eight alaka'i sprung into action. "Keoni's men join me!" said Ioane, hollering orders. "Into formation!"

It didn't take long for Olukai to take his place at the head of the army and march out of the forest to their enemies. And, perhaps, to their deaths.

CHAPTER FIFTY-TWO

Nohea and Po walked for, what felt like, miles. The stars and moon overhead lit the way through the thick ferns. Their sandals grew soggier with each step and a cold wind chilled their skin.

"Shh..." Po stopped and Nohea bumped into him. Her body felt tired, but the tingling pain from her head and sore eye trumped the bodily fatigue. As they traipsed, Po reviewed the last day to her: after she blacked out, the warriors continued to run for their lives. The lady of the lava rescued Po, Nohea, and 'Ele using whatever powers she had to control lava. 'Ele didn't make it, and the lava lady buried him deep within the island. Po carried Nohea in his arms to the woman's home.

"You slept the entire night and most of the day," he continued, but Nohea felt like she hadn't rested one bit. She stumbled over her legs, sometimes holding onto Po's dark golden cape for support. They walked in silence for a while, until Nohea spoke up.

"You seemed uncomfortable at the lady's house, especially around that fire," Nohea said.

Po didn't reply, so Nohea continued. "Is there... something you want to talk about? Maybe... about visiting your family at the Haunted island?"

"No, I'd rather not. Thanks."

The quiet between them grew uncomfortable, but Po didn't care. It was the dream that bothered him, his recurring nightmare. He considered sharing it with the lady, but he didn't want to anger her. After all, the moʻo clearly said, *the island must perish, or the humans will perish...*

He considered sharing it with Nohea, but decided to keep the dark vision to himself.

A rustle from above made Po pause in the dark.

"What is it?" Nohea, who felt like she slept walked, whispered. She grabbed his arm again, now awake. He wiped his eyes and looked up.

"A hawk."

Nohea couldn't see it. She stepped to the side and her foot slipped on a slippery branch.

"Ouch!" She grabbed her raw ankle.

"Careful!" Po took a look at the chafed skin. He shook his head. "Maybe this is useless.... It's late. We're never going to find him—we don't even know what markers to look for."

Nohea wiped the blood from her ankle onto the nearby ferns.

"The lava lady called him a pig. What do pigs like to eat?"

"I don't think she meant that literally." Po folded his arms and looked about. "We should head back. Maybe we can sneak into the fortress ourselves and burn the hut..."

"It will take too long," Nohea interrupted. "First of all, it will take us *forever* to get back. Second, we don't even know where we are."

Po moved strands of hair out of his face, thinking. "The lady of the lava didn't sound too happy when we said we were visiting Kama, huh?"

Nohea wiped her muddy legs off with some nearby leaves. "I don't understand her, to be honest." She shivered, remembering the strange dancing fire, the burning eyes of the woman, and her mysterious dark voice.

"Yes, but it sounded like she *knew* him before..." Po rubbed his chin.

"So you're saying?" Nohea stood and dusted herself off. The heat from her raw ankle cooled with the light drizzle of rain.

"I'm saying that maybe he won't be so friendly to us because of her. We should go back."

A shuffle in the fern bush nearby brought the two close together. Nohea reached for a stick off the ground. Some defense was better than none. Po stood in front of her.

"Come on, let's check it out," he said.

"Check it out?" Nohea sighed aloud as she followed him towards the direction of the noise.

They entered a small clearing, the roots of the ʻōhiʻa trees so thick that Nohea and Po's sandals slipped as they walked.

"Who's there?" Po asked.

Silence. The two stepped forward again, their breathing the only sound in the clearing.

Po brushed the ferns aside with his knife.

A sudden noise erupted from the bush, a scream that made their hair stand on end. It screeched through the night air, so loud, high, and deafening, Nohea covered her ears. And then a large, black boar ran out of the bush, darting right between Po and Nohea, separating them. It was so large, it stood up to Po's waist.

Nohea let out a startled yelp as the boar charged to the other side of the clearing and disappeared into the bushes, rustling every leaf, branch, and twig as it ran into the darkness.

"Was that him—" Nohea began to ask, but then a few more smaller pigs ran from the ferns, past the two, and into the other side of the clearing.

A sudden rush of noise sounded in the distance. Ferns rustled, the mossy ground making squishy noises.

"They're coming back—" Po grabbed Nohea and began running.

The grunting of the pigs sounded behind them. Adrenaline made them run faster than before.

As Nohea stumbled to keep up, holding tightly to Po's hand, she felt a sudden weight knock into her right side. Her tight grip on Po's hand broke, and she pounded to the ground, falling down a nearby hill.

"Po!" she yelled, but tumbled downhill, coughing, and trying to catch herself.

"Nohea!" she heard, but he sounded so far away.

When she lay still at the bottom, a figure jumped on top of her.

"Get off of me!" she screamed, terror rising in her stomach. A hand covered her mouth, and, in the light of the moon, she saw an outline of a man on her. He had so much hair, it fell all over his back, his arms, and on the ground next to her. It looked like there was another head on his shoulder, and when he turned his face, she saw that the "other head" was a boar pelt across his back.

"What's your name?" he asked, his voice dark, deep, and raspy.

"Get off me!" she screamed when he released his hand. He laughed, throwing his head back and standing up. He grabbed her arm and stood her too.

Standing a few heads taller than her, he leaned over, his body so wide and bulky, he was probably three times her size across. He grabbed her chin, examining her face in the waning light. She trembled as she looked into his black eyes.

"You're Kama," she managed to say, her teeth beginning to chatter.

"And you're a meha," he glared, then his look softened. "A very beautiful one..." His skin was darker and smoother than koa wood, with black tribal tattoos covering his entire chest and arms. He had a handsome, strong face, though mischievous.

He held her so close to him, she could smell the coconut oil on his skin, and the bristles of the boar on his shoulders brushed her cheek.

"What happened to your eye?" he asked, reaching for the patch but she slapped his hand down.

"Whoa calm down!" he laughed. "Why are you here?" Then he suddenly dropped her, as he plummeted to the ground. Nohea scurried away, surprised to see Po and Kama on the ground, wrestling.

Po was strong, but Kama was bigger. He pinned Po to the ground and punched.

"Stop!" Nohea screamed, running to the frenzy. A family of black boars circled the area, and Kama stood, satisfied. He cracked his neck and smiled, his white teeth gleaming in the moonlight. His canine teeth grew longer and sharper than the rest. Now, Nohea could also see Kama had a well-groomed mustache and beard.

Nohea helped Po up as he held his eye. "You're Kama?" he asked, baffled. The large man clapped his hands and then held them out.

"Want to go again?" he asked, then threw back his head and laughed so loudly, it echoed through the woods.

"How do you know my name anyway?" Kama asked, running his hand through his long, long hair.

"The lady of the lava told us," Nohea said, feeling bad for Po's bruised eye. She didn't have any of her bags on her, which meant no salves, no clean cloths, not even a gourd of cold water for Po's eye.

Kama made a face. The pigs in the circle grunted loudly. "And what did she say?" He glared at the ground.

"She said..." Nohea glanced at Po, who nodded to her. "You're the most charming person she's met."

"Don't lie to me!" He grabbed Nohea by her neck, and Po leaped forward to help, but his punches and kicks were nothing to the large man.

Nohea tried to breathe. She kicked her legs.

"What did she say?" he yelled. "Tell me!"

"You're a..." Nohea choked. "You're a pig."

He dropped her and chuckled, the temper immediately gone. "That's better." He pushed Po away without the slightest effort.

"Why are you two here?" he asked, circling them. Nohea knelt by Po as he rubbed his head.

"We need your help," Nohea replied.

"My help?" Kama laughed out loud again. His obnoxious head-throwing laugh began to annoy Nohea.

"And what can Kama do for you?" He did a sweeping bow, mocking them.

"Maybe we don't need your help," Po muttered under his breath and Nohea sighed .

"We need you to shapeshift so we can get into King Ekewaka's fortress."

The man scowled, fixing the black pelt on his back. "And why would a meha want to get into that place of evil?"

It made Nohea slightly uncomfortable to be called a meha. Yes, her mother was a meha, but nobody had ever called Nohea one. *I guess it's in my blood though,* she thought mournfully.

"I'm an alchemist." Nohea sighed. "I've been asked to help restore balance to the island. If you don't help us, the king will continue to use soran for his own gain and power."

"There's nothing wrong with power." He snorted. "Can't you tell I'm all about power? Look at me." He grinned and stood before them, the light shining on every oiled muscle, every tattoo, and his charming face.

Nohea did everything to keep from rolling her eyes, though she didn't dare look at Po for fear he'd be making a face and that would anger the shapeshifter.

"We'll give you whatever you want," she said. "Just help us get into the fortress."

"Whatever I want?" Kama folded his arms and smirked at Nohea. She felt her cheeks burn red, feelings of vulnerability rushing to her. Po stepped in front of her and Kama wrinkled his nose.

"Don't ever touch Nohea again," Po warned.

"Fine," he said. "Give me your cloaks."

"But these were from the lady of the lava," Nohea quietly protested.

"Then no deal." Kama turned around to leave.

"What about soran?" Po asked. Kama paused.

“I know what you intend to do,” he said, barely a whisper. “You intend to ‘restore balance’ by destroying all the soran.” He almost glared and Nohea wondered if Kama drank soran. He was of an unnaturally large size, so could it be? “I see it in your eyes, I hear the island whispering that is your purpose.”

Nohea avoided his gaze. Po stood firm.

“Soran once kept me alive for many years,” Kama said, confirming Nohea’s suspicions. He clenched his hand and then loosened it, as if studying the muscles and bone structure. “But I have not tasted it for a very long time.”

“There are huge glass balls of soran in my lab,” Nohea cut in. “If you take us safely to the lab, you can have all of it.”

“How many?”

Nohea tried to recall. “At least five.”

“And I want your cloaks too.”

Po spoke before Nohea could. “You can have them,” he said.

The man grinned, showing all of his white teeth. He rubbed his hands together. “So when do we leave?”

CHAPTER FIFTY-THREE

The battle started long before sunrise again. The king and queen's men stood at the field, facing the forest, waiting. As Olukai led his men out of the trees, Captain Kuhe called out. "Ready to surrender?"

Olukai held up his knife. "Never." He pointed his knife forward, yelling, "Charge!"

His alaka'i repeated the call, and they moved swiftly towards the enemy. Ekewaka nor Kahiko stood among the ranks of the warriors. Apparently Kuhe had taken the role of ordering the king and queen's men around.

"Charge!" Captain Kuhe yelled, and his men cheered in response, running forward.

The immediate noise of collision—flesh against blades, bones crushing, and muffled cries—filled the air. The morning waned on, the bodies grappling against one another, every one of the manō's soldiers fighting to defend their groups of lima.

Hours went by, the sky heavy with clouds, and a light mist of rain filled the air. Sweat, rain drops, mud, and blood gleamed off every soldier and warrior.

Ekewaka's warriors jumped into the various groups, but they had no advantage, as the lima's tight formation allowed the soldiers to circle those brave enough to jump into the fray.

But even as one of the king or queen's warriors fell, Olukai could count too many of his own men falling. They struggled to hold their ground against the warriors.

Olukai came face to face, finally, with Captain Kuhe. Kuhe's face dripped with carnage, and Olukai had no doubt his own face reflected that. He hated it—he hated this image of himself, and he hated that they had to fight the soran addicts. If only the people hadn't started drinking that in the first place.

If only he, Olukai himself, hadn't so boldly introduced soran to Queen Awa. As Kuhe struck first, and Olukai blocked, he remembered his mother's words.

"We all make mistakes. And now you are here. You are stronger than you think."

Olukai noticed his own self-infliction—not everything was his fault. He had done stupid things in the past, but now, he had a duty, a kuleana to his people, to this island, and to his ancestors. And he would make right the wrongs he did of getting soran for the false king.

He kicked Kuhe's stomach and waited, bored. Kuhe lunged forward and attacked. Again and again, Olukai blocked Kuhe's blows, twisting his own knife in his hand, wishing he'd lit his knife on fire. Kuhe went for Olukai's neck, but Olukai ducked and swung his knife up, cutting off Kuhe's arm.

The captain growled, screamed, and retreated. Olukai expected Kuhe to retreat, and he didn't follow. His men needed him here: in the front of battle, holding off as many warriors as he could. Wena and Lopaka fought not far from him. It seemed Wena had taken it upon himself to defend the old soldiers, as he constantly moved from place to place, assisting older islanders in their battles.

Suddenly, five of Ekewaka's bulky warriors surged forward, and one of them flung Olukai to the side, as if he were a mere rock that needed to be kicked off the road. Olukai fell at the edge of his army. To his horror, he watched as many of the tight groups of lima broke, the king's warriors rushing through, smashing individual soldiers, something easier when the men weren't in a tight formation.

Terror filled the eyes of Olukai's men. They looked about for him, for an order. "Keep fighting!" Olukai yelled, and Lopaka repeated the call. But Olukai's men started to edge back, some looking to the forest as a retreat again. Ekewaka's men ran through the army, crushing the soldiers like ants.

Olukai's heart sank. This was it. They were all going to die. He pushed himself off the ground, though he immediately knew something within him was wrong. His lungs ached with each breath. He grabbed his ribs, but it only furthered the pain. No doubt one of the bones within had broken.

"Kill them! Kill them!"

Olukai recognized the voice. At the back of the army, Ekewaka and Kahiko sat on top of their horses. The sun barely touched the horizon, and clouds covered the sky, hiding what light the morning sun did give off.

Ekewaka screamed, raising his hands, cheering, his face red, veins popping out of his neck. A clean white patch now covered his eye, but he still looked huge, intimidating, and angry.

Olukai called out, though his chest screamed in protest. "Back into line! Back into line!"

Lopaka caught Olukai's words and yelled the same thing as he fought a warrior. "Back into line men—get back into line!" An arm hoisted up Olukai, and he coughed in pain. With one arm across Wena's shoulder, Olukai marveled that Wena always seemed to be in the right place at the right time.

The soldiers, in confusion, regrouped, but in one tight circle, allowing the warriors to surround them. The king and queen's warriors paused for a moment, which gave the soldiers a few brief seconds to gather.

"You are surrounded!" Ekewaka laughed from a distance. He

always had a loud voice. "Surrender yourselves now—give your loyalty to the *true* king of the island!"

The warriors inched closer, and the men held out their spears, knives, and clubs, ready.

"Never!" It was Tua's voice.

"Never!" Lopaka echoed, openly defying his father.

"For the manō!" Sefa yelled, and the others joined. Olukai knew this was their last stand, their last acts of bravery. Deep pride entered his heart. His men had fought well, been courageous to the very end.

Just as Olukai's army was about to charge, a conch shell rang out from the forest. Every person stopped in mid step. All eyes turned to the trees, the same trees from whence Olukai's army came earlier.

Figures stepped from the trees, at least fifty men, young men. And one young woman, a big bag slung over her shoulder. She looked familiar, but, in the chaos and darkness of the early morning, Olukai couldn't remember where he'd seen her.

At the head of them was...

Olukai squinted, the cloud cover making it hard to distinguish details.

Haku? An instant boost filled him up.

"Haku!" he exclaimed, and the men around him lightened up, realizing that the manō recognized at least one man coming from the forest.

"For the manō!" Haku exclaimed, raising his knife. The army behind him shouted the same, and then they charged. An immediate gust of morale rippled through Olukai's soldiers like wildfire. They cheered, hollered, and celebrated.

The warriors, unsure to turn towards the forest, or attack the circle, stood still for a few seconds.

"Charge!" Olukai exclaimed before they had any time to think about it. And then both the army led by Haku, and the army led by Olukai, surrounded the startled warriors.

CHAPTER FIFTY-FOUR

"You can... transform into a pig?" Nohea asked, both disgusted and intrigued. She didn't trust Kama one bit, but she knew this was their only chance of getting in. The night slowly turned into morning, though the heavy clouds made it difficult to tell.

"Ae, I'll transform into a pig, and you both can ride on my back."

Po wrinkled his nose. Kama held up his hands. "Hey, it's the fastest way to get there. Horses are too slow, and mo'o... well, no can do the mo'o. I don't dare try."

"Why not?" Nohea asked.

"You ask a lot of questions, don't you?" He snorted. "The island has only bestowed this shapeshifting gift to me for the... *normal* animals."

"How does one become a shapeshifter?" Nohea asked, and felt Po grab her arm, impatient to get going.

"It is a blessing from the island," Kama said and bowed his head, as if acknowledging the island itself. He fixed the skin on his back again. "So you're telling me that when we get to the outskirts of the fortress, I will transform into a man named Kahiko?"

The two nodded.

"But you must show me this man—I can't shapeshift into someone I've never seen."

Nohea looked at Po. "Kahiko wasn't there when we went to Nono. He's not with Olukai either."

"So where is he?" Po asked.

Nohea shrugged. "I imagine he's at my lab—he's probably trying to read my notes right now as we speak."

"And if he's not?"

"Then let's draw out one of the warriors into the woods behind the hut, have Kama transform into the warrior and somehow get us in."

Po nodded. "And if that doesn't work?"

Nohea scowled and folded her arms. "Then we improvise, alright?"

"I like it." Both Po and Nohea gasped, as Kama leaned over them, eavesdropping.

"You promise you'll help us get into the lab—" Po started.

"In return for all the soran and those cloaks," Kama finished, nodding. "What do you want, like a contract written in stone? Isn't my word enough?"

Nohea and Po made eye contact, both of them uneasy, and Nohea raised her eyebrows. "Let's go," she said.

Kama faced the moonlight, taking a deep breath, and then outstretched his arms.

The next scene frightened Nohea, as she had never seen anything so unnatural, so *different.* Kama's silhouette in the moonlight hunched over, his back growing tall, his nose extending, and bristles coming out of his once-smooth skin.

His arms and legs shortened and his hands turned into hooves. Sharp white tusks came from his nose, sticking up and outward. His eyes, once black, turned blood red.

When the transformation was complete, he stood before them, a large boar, as tall as Po. He snorted and let out a loud cry. Nohea covered her ears.

Kama looked at them and motioned, with his head, to his back.

Nohea grit her teeth.

"No games," Po warned as he swung his leg over, grabbing the bristles to sit on the pig. It wasn't very comfortable, as the sharp bristles brushed against his legs.

Po helped Nohea up, and gave her a warning look. "Don't let go of me, no matter what—not until we get to the fortress, alright?" He said it quietly and she nodded, wrapping her arms around him. This felt so brotherly, and she appreciated his concern.

"A deal is a deal—" Po began to say to Kama but the boar squealed, lifting its head into the air. The other boars squealed, and then Kama began running.

They rode with such great speed, the wind rushed into their faces, forcing tears down Nohea and Po's cheeks.

Po looked back at Nohea and she nodded, leaning into him.

This is it, she thought. They were going back to the fortress, to burn the papers and forever destroy the formula to make soran.

IT DIDN'T TAKE VERY long to get to the fortress. They made their way through the thick forest, over the long plains of old lava fields, and soon, they looked on the outskirts of the gated community. The noise of battle rang from the other side of the fortress: men hollering, wood clashing against wood, and other echoes that Nohea didn't want to guess at.

Nohea and Po quickly got off Kama, holding hands in case Kama tried anything.

"That was fast, wasn't it?" Kama said behind them. He'd already changed back into his normal form. Po tried not to roll his eyes, and Nohea stepped closer to Po.

"How do we get in?" asked Kama.

"There's one of the entrances," Po pointed to the gated way in the distance. They were hidden in the forest, far enough away so the guards couldn't see or hear them.

"There's a man up there... black hair, dark eyes..."

Both young people looked back at Kama. He had the face of a hawk, and the body of a human. Nohea covered her mouth to keep from screaming, and Po jumped .

"Don't act so shocked," Kama laughed, smiling. "Describe your man to me," he said to Nohea.

"He's not my—"

"Who cares? Just tell me what the old guy looks like."

"Black hair. Black eyes. Dark skin. Wide nose..." She tried to picture Kahiko in her head. "He has black tattoos on his back and neck. He carries a wood staff and ti leaf. He—"

"Like this?"

She turned round and gasped. There stood Kahiko.

"He's not at your lab," Kama said to her, his voice still the same. He pointed to the main entrance gate, which was locked. "He's there."

"Well that's even better," Po said, though, as he squinted into the light rain, he added. "I don't see him."

"Because you don't have hawk eyes, do you?" Kama ruffled Po's hair and Po glared.

"Can you sound like Kahiko?" Nohea asked.

"Describe his voice to me?" Kama smiled at her a lot, and Po rolled his eyes.

"Dark, deep... kind of old."

"How's this?"

"Lower."

"Better?"

"Close enough."

Kama, in Kahiko's form, winked at her. She looked away, completely uncomfortable.

"Now how do we get in?" Kama asked.

"Let's go through the south entrance, " Po said, remembering the night he and Haku waited for Olukai. Over the years of traveling the island, Po made a mental map. He imagined the fortress in his mind. "It's the closest to the lab..."

The three moved silently through the bushes. Kama left the other boars behind, because they were too loud.

"They can distract the guards here if needed," said Kama.

When they reached the south gate, it was sealed shut. Two guards stood on top of the gates, watching.

"If I get in," said Kama, "How will you two get in?"

"You can distract the guards, linger by the gate, and we can sneak in," Po said.

"I knew there was something in there," Kama smirked and reached to ruffle Po's hair again, but Po blocked Kama's hand. The shapeshifter chuckled and winked at Nohea again.

"Ready?" he asked. She nodded.

As Kama, in Kahiko's form, walked boldly up to the gate, Nohea and Po ran to the side of the tall fortress walls. They pressed against it, moving towards the gate, where Kahiko walked.

"Who goes there?" One of the guards called down.

"It is I, Kahiko."

To Nohea, Kama sounded too proud. She waved her hands, trying to motion to turn it down, but Kama paid her no attention.

"Kahiko? What are you doing out so late?"

"I went out searching for the girl, and I must report to the king."

Silence.

Then, "Open the gate!"

Easy! Nohea thought, smiling at Po. He nodded, but didn't smile, focused on the task at hand. They moved closer to the gate, until Kama stood only a few steps away from them. The gate, made of bamboo and koa trunks, groaned as it opened.

"Hurry in," Nohea and Po heard one of the guards say. "The king does not wish any of the gates to be opened long—"

"'Ae, I know. And thank you both for being so vigilant."

Kama walked into the gate, and Nohea watched his shadow as he grabbed the two men's shoulders and turned them around, walking towards the light.

She peeked around the corner, their backs turned towards the two. She nodded to Po and they slipped in, hiding behind the door for a moment, before sneaking behind the nearest hut.

"Tell me what news of the war?" Kama asked.

The men looked at one another, suspicious. "You should know," one of them said. "You were just there."

"But I wondered if you saw any commotion here."

The guards looked unsure, but Kama didn't flinch in the least. "Nevermind, close the gates."

He walked past them, head up.

Still too proud looking for Kahiko, thought Nohea, but she felt grateful that he didn't flinch under the pressure.

Kama walked in front of the huts. When he was a distance from the guards, he slipped into the shadows with Po and Nohea.

"Not bad, huh?" He grinned at Nohea.

"Let's focus, alright?" Po moved past Kama and walked next to the tall walls of the fortress, in the darkness. A small forest soon appeared, the same forest that was behind Nohea's lab.

"We're close," Nohea said.

From the darkness of the trees, they soon saw the light of the lab. At least six guards stood around it, Akamu being the one at the door frame. The hut looked a mess, with half of it broken to pieces from the moʻo.

The men still stood sharp, spears in hand, watching, waiting. Nohea wondered why the king had guards at her hut when she was obviously gone. And there was a war going on. Didn't he want all his warriors on the battlefield?

Unless... An icky thought crawled up Nohea's skin. *Unless the king has it guarded because he knows we're coming back.* Her eye throbbed at the mere idea.

"I'll draw the guards away," said Kama. "You two can head in."

He touched Nohea's cheek and she stepped back. "Your cloaks now, please?"

"The deal's not over," Po resisted.

"But it will be soon. Give them to me now... Or we wait here til the morning sun comes over the horizon."

Po rolled his eyes and removed the cloak. Nohea did too. Kama snatched them, his eyes full of greed. Then he did something that neither Po or Nohea expected. He took a deep breath into them. A look of relief crossed his face. He folded them up and placed them into Kahiko's side bag hanging on his shoulder. "Alright, see you inside soon."

Both Nohea and Po nodded, feeling colder without the gold cloaks. Kama ran through the forest, breaking free to hide behind some nearby huts, then disappeared.

They waited. Po whispered to Nohea. "You burn the papers first. If you can't burn them in time, just run. I'll hold off the warriors and set fire to the hut if I need to."

Nohea's heart pumped as she nodded.

Kama's voice, his Kahiko improvisation, rang through the night air. "The king has given me orders to send you to the battlegrounds. We will need more help than we thought."

The other warriors' heads turned, curious to see what was going on with the warriors at the door frame. Nohea watched Akamu amongst them, and deep down she felt relieved that he was fine. He let her go last time, instead of putting up a fight. Surely it was a huge risk.

As Kama distracted the guards, it gave Nohea and Po an opportunity to run to the nearest huts, blackened out. The warriors didn't even notice.

"The king has ordered us to stay here—unless he, himself, comes to tell us otherwise," Akamu said.

"But you know the king is not well. He is still recovering. He has sent me—You *will* go to the battlegrounds," Kama demanded.

Akamu hesitated, then, "Very well." He called the men. "Come on boys, we are needed elsewhere."

Nohea's jaw dropped, and she saw Po smiling for the first time that night. This was going smoother than she ever imagined.

The men lined up and then they marched together. Kama watched from the door frame, then stepped into the hut. Nohea and Po followed.

Kama hummed as he collected the large glass balls of soran. Nohea rushed to the cubby under the table, tossing out the ferns, and reaching her hand into the back.

Nothing. She threw things out of the other cubbies.

Po helped her, but only branches, leaves, and flowers fell to the ground. No papers or any notes. Nothing.

Nohea grabbed her head in frustration. "Where are they?" she asked, ready to cry.

But he was already lighting fire to the walls with a torch. "We don't have time," he said. "The king probably has those papers by now."

And Nohea's heart sank. She failed.

CHAPTER FIFTY-FIVE

The sun finally shone through a break in the heavy clouds. No doubt it would rain soon, making the battlefield more muddy, bloody, and slippery. Haku brought at least fifty men with him. Where he gathered them, Olukai had no idea. But he was grateful. Grateful that Haku listened to the island and returned, grateful for all the young men, and a few older men, who heeded the call.

He saw no sign of the girl again, and hoped she didn't get killed in the fray.

As the hours wore on, Olukai realized that even with Haku's help, the men were still tired. Though their morale had been boosted, it now wavered.

The queen's warriors never seemed to tire. They pressed on and on, laughing and mocking the soldiers as they fought. The whole war appeared to be a game to them.

The king's warriors, however, held grim expressions. They attacked with such fury, and they never looked happy about anything. Olukai didn't see Akamu amongst the king's warriors and wondered if the king ended up killing the warrior.

But his thoughts only served to distract him from the present scene of horror and the burning, painful sensation in his chest. Over and over, he tried to get the men into groups, but each time the men attempted to band up, one of Ekewaka's warriors jumped into the fray, crushing some soldiers and breaking the group as quickly as it started.

So Olukai went from soldier to soldier, encouraging, offering hope and help. When he reached Haku, the two embraced, though it was brief, as they fought, back to back, the enemies.

"The island called me!" Haku said. "I found this little army on the road—going towards Huna bay! Po gave them the idea!" Haku blocked a warrior's club and grabbed a spear from the ground.

"It's so good to hear Po's name!" Olukai said, grabbing Haku's spear and launching it towards his attacker. The man fell down, and Olukai leaned on Haku.

"Olukai!" It was Lopaka. The soldiers were getting slaughtered, including the new army. Lopaka rushed to Olukai. "Even with the reinforcements, we must call a retreat."

The men kept glancing towards Olukai, waiting for the call. Indeed, they looked exhausted. He couldn't keep pushing them.

Haku emphasized Lopaka's words. "I think he's right. Our numbers are too small, and our men are too tired."

Olukai glanced towards the fortress, but the gates were shut tight. He wished they could go there.

"Retreat!" he finally called, his heart heavy. He couldn't lose anymore men. After the morale boost and reinforcement, this battle would always be unfair, unless Olukai had hundreds more men. And not men, warriors, like the specialized ones trained by the king and queen.

The men began running towards the trees, and the warriors looked to their leaders for instructions. The bald man, the one who had introduced Captain Kuhe the day before, yelled, "Follow them! Kill them all—the queen wants no survivors!"

Olukai squinted to see Ekewaka and Kahiko on their horses in the distance, still watching the battle but not participating. A light rain began to pour, and Haku grabbed Olukai's arm.

"Come on!" he said. Olukai still stared at the old king and Kahiko. They turned around and began riding away. Some of the king's warriors followed, and a few others stood on the battlefield, blank.

One of the queen's warriors raised his club to hit Olukai, but Wena jumped in to block it. He glanced at Olukai, curious, as if to ask, *What are you staring at? Let's get moving!*

Olukai stepped back, his head pounding, watching as Wena fought off the warrior, watching the soldiers run into the forest. He saw the girl, the big bundle on her back, a wounded soldier with his arm over her shoulders.

Too many times that day and night he figured would be their last. And now, he watched the retreat, the men with exhaustion and fear in their eyes, fleeing. How many islanders had died? And for what?

Have courage. His mother's voice rang in his ears.

Wena grabbed Olukai's arm to move him along, but Olukai wouldn't budge. He'd fight these warriors—all of them—til he died. He wanted to get as much distance as possible between his men and these murderers.

Wena read Olukai's face and then stood next to him, spear in one hand, and knife in the other. Lopaka joined too, their last stand.

The queen's warriors charged, while the king's warriors lagged behind, looking confused, even ashamed.

Wena launched his spear, getting the first kill. Lopaka leaped into the air, delivering a swift death to another warrior. Olukai swung a knife in each hand, creating a beautiful circle in the air. He had been the best fire dancer and fighter on the island, and now he would die doing the skill he'd worked so hard to master.

The three young men fought together, the warrior bodies forming a circle around them. They lasted a good while, but the fatigue and over-exertion caused them to make mistakes, to not react as quickly, and to have poorer form.

Wena got tossed to the side. His head hit a tree and he fell, unconscious or dead, Olukai didn't know. Lopaka, distracted for a brief moment, received a swift blow to his face. Olukai threw a spear at the skull of Lopaka's contender. The man fell dead.

Two warriors gained up on Olukai, one of them reaching for one of Olukai's knives with his bare hands. He hurled the knife at Olukai but Olukai dodged. The other rammed his body into Olukai's chest and he fell to the ground, shocked by the impact. His already broken chest area shot a pain up Olukai's throat that he screamed and coughed up blood.

"Olukai!" Lopaka tried to run to help, but the warrior he fought grabbed his hair and slammed him to the ground.

The queen's warriors laughed as they tried to stomp on Olukai's head. He dodged and rolled over, grabbing the nearest weapon on the ground, a broken spear. He threw it straight into the warrior's eye. The man reeled back, cursing and screaming.

Two more warriors came to "smash" Olukai. One of them grabbed Olukai's leg and threw Olukai to a tree. Olukai heard a "crack" and coughed more blood into the ground.

This is it, he thought as the warriors approached, all with knives, spears, and clubs. Another warrior had Lopaka's neck in his grasp. Lopaka struggled to break free.

This is how we die.

The warriors circled Olukai. They smiled, amused.

At that moment, another conch shell blew... but it sounded different from any shell Olukai had heard before. It sounded much lower, deeper, *darker*. It couldn't have been Ekewaka or Awa's call.

All warriors and soldiers paused, glancing to the east, where the noise came from.

"The Māku'e!" The queen's warriors exclaimed, and when Olukai squinted to see the army appearing, he saw a line of many soldiers, on horseback. They carried the white flag, and a woman led them, her long black hair blowing in the wind. He didn't recognize her, but her eyes looked fierce, and she was adorned with a colorful flower lei, crown, and wristbands.

The queen's warriors seemed to forget all about Lopaka and Olukai, as they turned around and stared. Every person wondered the same thing: *Whose side are they on?*

"Māku'e, fight for the manō!" The woman held up her fisted hand. "Attack!" The Māku'e cheered and charged forward. The rumbling of the horses' hooves sounded like thunder. Olukai ran to help Lopaka up and they watched, amazed, as the Māku'e launched spears with perfect aim, sliced their enemies with no fear, and crushed the large warriors.

Wena slowly stood, rubbing his head, and regrouped with Lopaka and Olukai. His eyes widened.

"There's hundreds of them!" Lopaka cheered. He and Olukai looked back to see their own retreating soldiers pause. "Victory is ours!" Lopaka yelled.

"With what strength you have left," Olukai called to his retreating men. "Fight for the manō! Fight for the island!" The three young men ran forward, and the queen's warriors turned around, shocked. They had focused on the charging Māku'e, they forgot about the retreating army behind him.

Two warriors gained up on Wena, and as Olukai ran to help him, a girl on a white horse cut him off. With a speed and grace he'd never witnessed in his life, she back flipped off her horse while launching a spear into one of the warriors' heads. Wena looked at her as she landed next to him, and, in a strange way, Olukai thought he was seeing double. The girl and Wena looked similar, both tall, lean, with amber colored eyes and sun-kissed hair.

"Where's the manō?" A woman's voice brought his attention back to his surroundings. He caught a glimpse of the bald man, one of the queen's leaders, dead on the ground. Without direction, the queen's warriors did their best, but the Māku'e swarmed around them, their horses giving them height and speed.

Olukai's soldiers cheered and ran back from the retreat.

This *is it!* He thought over and over. It was so obvious—victory truly was theirs.

"Manō!" The voice of the woman sounded again. It was the leader of the Māku'e, who slashed at a warrior as she approached Olukai. Two men followed her, one of them with an extra horse. "You are victorious!" She exclaimed, flashing a smile. She then nodded to the soldier who brought the extra horse. "Take a horse—the true king should have one."

Olukai took it, grateful. "Who are you?" he asked, as he got onto the horse. She bowed her head. "Kukui. Kiani is my cousin—she came to gather us for battle. We marched as fast as we could."

"And I will be forever grateful," Olukai said.

Kukui nodded, looking about. The king's warriors knelt on the ground, surrendering. From what Olukai could see, Akamu was not amongst them. The queen's warriors put up a fight, but only a few remained, surrounded by the fearsome Māku'e.

Olukai.

Olukai looked about, but no person had called his name. The wind breathed into his ear again. *Follow the king...*

The island had spoken. He looked at Kukui. "The king is fleeing —I must go."

She nodded. "What are your orders?"

"Sweep the queen's camp, take the remaining men prisoners, get the wounded to the medics, free the men within the fortress." He spoke with such haste, he wasn't even sure Kukui could understand. But she nodded. "Trust my alaka'i—I must go now."

"Good luck manō," she said, but he hardly heard it as he urged the horse at its fastest speed, rain now pouring all around. He had to follow the king and Kahiko. Something told him they were up to no good.

CHAPTER FIFTY-SIX

"Let's get out of here." Po dropped the torch to the corner of the hut and grabbed Nohea's hand to start running.

"I thought you might come back." The voice made Nohea's hair stand on end.

She turned around to see her father, the king, along with Kahiko. The king stood in the doorway, his warriors standing behind him, Akamu included.

Kama made a face. "Ooh..." he said. The king looked at him, and Kama transformed from Kahiko to his regular self.

The king nodded to Akamu, who handed Kama a big bundle wrapped in kapa cloth. Nohea frowned. More soran.

Kama had known all along. Nohea didn't know the details of how he knew the king, or how they struck up this deal, but she realized he had probably lied earlier. He pretended to see Kahiko at the gate but he wasn't really there. Kama somehow knew Ekewaka and Kahiko from before.

"You liar," she said.

"I didn't lie," he laughed. "I brought you to the lab safely." He saluted her with his hand, though offered no explanation of how he had already been on the king's side. "And I'll be off. Thanks for the cloaks." He walked out of the lab, transforming into a large hawk, the bag swinging from his wings as he flew away.

Po and Nohea stood up against a table. Her hand touched a branch: uli.

"You came back for these, didn't you?" The king held the papers. He looked terrible, a white patch on his eye, his other eye sunken in exhaustion. Though, Nohea had no doubt that she reflected his fatigue. Seeing his white patch made Nohea's eye tingle.

"The notes are useless," she said. "Only I can interpret them."

"No, I figured it out." The king shuffled through the papers. "The meha can read them... and you are the daughter of a meha, a wicked witch sorceress who hated you." He made a face. "*You* are a meha."

A lump formed in Nohea's throat. Meanwhile, Po scanned the room for anything. His eye caught hold on the thatched roof. It was already starting to burn.

"My offer still stands," Ekewaka said calmly. "Leave this boy and the wild dreams of a foolish, cowardly ali'i. *We* are the descendants of the honorable, the great white shark. Join me." His dark eye looked sad. "We can change the course of the island, restore balance."

Nohea listened, remembering how she felt the first time he told her this. She had felt like there was a purpose, like she finally had a place, and she belonged.

"Let's create more soran," he continued. "Give it to all the people —we will *all* be immune to the diseases of foreigners. We can live longer, live healthier, and prosper. You must remember the vision..."

Nohea stared, feeling the longing in her heart again. She had wanted that so badly. Po glanced at her. "He's lying," he said, then looked at the king. "You've lied for too long—you have never been the line of the manō. And you will not give soran to the people. You will keep it for yourself."

"Soran causes only greed," Nohea managed to say.

"Come, daughter," the king continued, his voice gentle, tender even. "The man who calls himself the manō, and his men, are dying even now. Let us give our people strength and immunity. Let us change the future of Kaimana Island."

Nohea stood there, blank. She reached out to the island around her, feeling the hum beneath her feet, hearing the voices in the wind. Her whole life she had listened, until she ignored it to hear Ekewaka's voice. The lure came back.

It's for the people, the future, and the island... Ekewaka's voice rang in her head. And she truly, *truly* wanted that.

No. The island spoke clearly to her.

Grabbing strength from her ancestors and the voice of the island, Nohea shook her head, meeting his eyes. "You keep telling yourself that," she said.

Then she threw the uli powder and branches into the air in front of her and Po, catching on to her cue, grabbed the torch he'd dropped earlier. He lit the bundle she'd thrown on fire.

It exploded, blue sparks flying about the room, lighting the roof on fire too.

Nohea reached her hand into the cubby hole and grabbed some homemade bombs. She always had them around in case. Po threw them at the king and the warriors, the whole hut a frenzied mess of blue powder, sparks, fire, and smoke.

"Get them!" The king coughed through the powder. Kahiko stood still next to the king, his eyes focused. Nohea coughed too, still connected to her father.

The warriors surrounded the two, and Nohea knew they were outnumbered. Po threw more bombs, causing a blinding mass of blue, and a few warriors fell to the ground, inundated with the sleepy scent.

But more came charging, and Po fought them off with his shark-toothed paddle.

The king grabbed Nohea's arm to drag her out but she resisted, grabbing the nearest torch and holding it to his face. He screamed, and Nohea did too, feeling the burn herself.

He yanked the torch from her hand and threw it to the ground, grabbing, once more, her hand and dragging her out of the hut.

She could hear Po in combat with the warriors behind them, the hut a burning mass of flames. The papers were in the king's other hand. She needed to burn them. But his hand was firm on her wrist—there was no escape, as much as she tried to get free.

Then she thought of something. She pushed on her eye, screaming from the pain. The king let go of her, grabbing his own eye.

He roared. "Are you mad—"

Nohea ran back towards the hut, grabbing the torch he'd tossed out of her hand. Her eye stung, like a million pieces of sand had blasted into it.

He chased after her, but she held the torch out, as if to fight him with it. He laughed. "What are you going to do?" The king raised his hands, mocking.

"Your friend will die soon, and you will be alone—"

"She's not alone." A figure rose from behind the king, spilling some kind of oil on him. Both Nohea and Ekewaka jumped. A tall young man shoved the surprised king to the ground.

The young man's eyes seemed to glow, with the fierceness of an animal—the shark. Though he was covered in mud, blood, and water, Nohea could see the mark of the shark on his arm, spiraling up to his shoulder.

Ekewaka spit, showing his disgust. Then he lunged towards Olukai and they rolled on the ground, wrestling. Both were tall and strong, though the king was broader and more muscled. Ekewaka managed to pin Olukai to the ground, getting ready to punch. "Fire!" Olukai yelled to Nohea as he dodged and hit the king's forehead with his skull.

Both scrambled off the ground and Olukai stood in front of Nohea as she handed him the torch.

"You've betrayed me!" The veins protruded from the king's forehead and neck. Nohea felt the pain in his heart. She wanted to do something, help him, make it right.

But she couldn't.

"You were never the line of the great white manō," said Olukai. "You were a good alaka'i—a great one. But you've fallen."

"You defile the blood!" The king lunged at Olukai, but the manō simply dodged and put the torch to the king's skin. It lit on fire and Nohea screamed, her back and arms burning.

The king roared, falling to his knees, trying to get the fire out. He fell to the ground, defeated. Olukai held Nohea steady as she winced and shook violently.

She felt the deep heartache, the pit in the stomach, and the burning of her back and arms, where Olukai had thrown the oil on the king. Olukai grabbed the papers from the king's hand and burned them with the torch.

Nohea's heart ached for the king, as he lay on his side, in a fetal position, helpless. A great moaning came from the depths of his stomach. It was a sadness neither Olukai or Nohea had expected.

"You betrayed me." He spoke to both of them. For a moment, his black eyes watered, sweat dripping down his face and neck, his back and arms beginning to smell of burnt flesh. "You betrayed me..." He moaned again then let out a wail of pain, his veins throbbing. Nohea could barely keep her eyes open, because it hurt her too.

"Leave him," she spoke softly to Olukai, but he paused, something in him stirring. Nohea could see he felt pity for the king too.

Ekewaka looked at them both, his eyes large and weak, protruding. His eyebrows creased, as his lips turned downward and he trembled. "You betrayed me!" He screamed, the words directed at them both He reached his hand out. "I will kill you!"

"Come on—" Olukai put an arm around Nohea's shoulders and moved towards the frenzy of fighting warriors and Po. Kahiko, who still stood by the door, focusing on the fighters who sparred with Po, then noticed the commotion behind him and froze.

He and Olukai made eye contact and Olukai hesitated, as if considering whether or not he should kill the sorcerer. Just as he decided he might, Nohea grabbed his arm and said, "Leave him —let's go!"

Kahiko rushed to the king's aid, throwing kapa cloths on to stop the burning. The warriors left the fight with Po to help the king too.

"You will pay for this!" The king's haunting voice raged. Every part of Nohea's body burned, and the pathetic image of her father, crumpled on the ground, hurt her heart. She did feel sorry for him, for the great man he once was, and the wicked man he turned into.

The warriors carried and hurried Ekewaka away, and the three watched. Akamu looked back at them, open cuts across his bare chest and back. Something in his eyes looked sad, and Nohea longed to help him, but he served the king.

"Are you sure we should let them go?" Po asked.

Olukai nodded. "We will have mercy. He won't come back..."

Nohea let out a loud sigh and then Olukai and Po reached out to keep her steady. "Po, it's so good to see you!" Olukai exclaimed and grabbed them both into a hug. "And you too Nohea. I thought we'd lost you."

Nohea burst into tears. She didn't know why she cried. She didn't understand, but so many feelings, fears, and worries exploded out of her. She also felt extreme pain, knowing her father's skin raged from the fire and that he felt betrayed, but extreme relief overwhelmed it all. Olukai laughed, and she sobbed more. Here she was, safe, finally, with the manō and the messenger. Olukai's sweaty hair stuck to her face and neck but she didn't care. She couldn't stop crying.

Olukai gently rubbed her back. "You're safe now." Then he let them both go and Po laughed, patting Nohea's shoulder. And then she saw, Po was full of emotion too: relief, exhaustion, happiness, yet still anxious.

"Let's get back to the battlefield," said Olukai. He led them in the direction that the warriors and Kahiko took Ekewaka.

"Where are we go—" Nohea started asking as she wiped her eyes and nose.

"Horses," Olukai answered before she even finished.

"Did we win the battle?" Po asked, scooping his shoulder under Nohea's arm to speed her up. Rain began pouring again. Olukai walked ahead of them, fast, his body smothered in gore, mud, and sweat.

"'Ae, but we need to get back. Now." He didn't want to leave his men unattended for too long, even though he trusted Kukui, Lopaka, and Haku. And, deep down, he wondered what Kukui and the Māku'e would find when they swept the queen's camp. Would they capture Queen Awa?

And, more importantly, would they find Kiani... dead, or, maybe, alive?

CHAPTER FIFTY-SEVEN

Olukai rode as fast as he could. Po and Nohea trailed behind, their horse going slower as it carried two people. Olukai could see his soldiers and alaka'i moving about, the fortress gates open, and the Māku'e helping carry wounded men. The rain continued to pour, making it harder to see into the distance.

He steered to the left, towards the queen's camp. Hundreds of bodies littered the ground, and the smell of iron stenched the air. He hated battle. He hated war. He was glad it was over... for now.

"Manō!" Kukui rode her horse towards them, then turned it so they rode side by side. He slowed down, catching his breath. "Every one of the queen's warriors are dead," she said, breathless from trying to catch up with him. "None surrendered. At least ten of the king's men have surrendered."

"The queen—where is she?" Olukai felt anger rising within.

"Gone! No sign of her kahuna either."

"Does the queen have prisoners?"

"'Ae, my cousin—"

"Where is she?" Olukai spurred his horse, looking back at Kukui for answers.

"She's..." Kukui started, then pointed to the largest tent that Olukai had visited with Lopaka and Ioane. A few soldiers stood around the area, and, from a distance, Olukai could see Haku, Wena, and the young woman with the pack on her back going towards the tent.

Olukai didn't wait for Kukui. He hurried forward, afraid that Kukui meant to say, "She's dead."

The rain pelted, mixing with all the debris on his skin and causing streaks across his body. Kukui didn't follow him but urged her horse towards Po and Nohea, who struggled to keep up with Olukai.

Before his horse even slowed, Olukai jumped off and ran to the makeshift hut. He rushed in, seeing Wena kneeling over his sister. Pale as sea foam, her lips purple, and her eyes closed, Kiani looked lifeless. Her hand limped when Wena took it, checking her pulse.

The young woman who had come with Haku earlier, took the bundle off her back and began rummaging through.

Haku looked down, "Hold off Haunani... she's probably gone."

Haunani? Olukai recognized the name. Po's hānai sister—how could he forget? The greatest hula dancer on the island. But he didn't have the time for pleasantries.

He rushed to Kiani and scooped her into his arms. Wena nodded.

"She's alive?" Olukai asked, heart pumping. Wena confirmed with a tip of his head, but he didn't smile, maybe because she was waning. Haunani gasped and continued looking through her bag.

Wena motioned to a glass ball at Kiani's feet, and Olukai wanted to curse the queen. In the glass ball was a purple liquid. It would save Kiani's life, they all knew it.

"How about some salve? Juice?" Haunani asked, pointing out all the items in her bag.

Haku shook his head and waved a hand at her, as if to say, *Not now*. It was too obvious that nothing but soran would revive Kiani, yet, they all stared at it, unwilling to use it.

Soran itself had caused this battle, and Olukai vowed to destroy it, not use it. He loathed it. He loathed the situation, the queen, and the kahuna. This was their last act of spite, to barely kill Kiani, and leave one last option.

"You all are going to let her die?" Haunani asked, amazed, frustrated even.

"Only soran can cure her now." Haku sighed. "The kahuna are powerful." He knelt and pointed out Kiani's cut wrist to Haunani. "She has been cursed. The kahuna has most likely sucked nearly all life from her."

"So you won't use the soran?" Haunani looked from Haku to Wena, and finally to Olukai. Her brown eyes looked fierce, and the tips of her ears turned red when she met Olukai's eyes. She looked away.

Olukai rubbed Kiani's shoulder, wishing she would wake up, but she felt cold in his arms. Wena took his sister's hand and bowed his head, as if waiting. Waiting for her last hā, waiting to say goodbye, to let her rest forever.

Haku bowed his head as well, and Olukai let out a sigh. Would he use the soran to revive Kiani? Every part of his being said *no*. But his heart strings tugged at him. Wouldn't he use it for someone he loved? But wasn't that the same excuse that the queen and king used? He hated himself for not using the soran. He would never forgive himself if he used it, or if he didn't use it.

"I can't believe all of you," Haunani huffed, standing up and grabbing the ball of soran. She leaned over Kiani and poured the soran into her mouth. Nobody stopped Haunani.

Kiani coughed, spitting up blood and the purple liquid. It was the first movement she made that entire time. Haunani put the glass ball aside, pleased.

Kiani's color returned almost immediately, though her lips remained a dull purple. Her lashes fluttered, and Olukai's heart pounded. She looked up at him, confused. Then she glanced around, seeing Haunani, Haku, and then Wena. Her chest rose up and down as she took short breaths.

"Wha—what happened?" Her voice sounded raspy as she sat herself up, leaning against Olukai's chest. He wanted to hold her forever.

"I saved your life," Haunani said, and Haku let out a laugh.

"'Ae, she did."

Kiani looked amazed. "Thank you..." She glanced up at Olukai, blushing, as she pulled herself from his arms. Then she saw Wena and they hugged.

At that moment, the tent flaps opened and Kukui entered, followed by Nohea and Po.

"Uncle Haku!" Nohea exclaimed at the same time Haunani screamed, "Po!"

Nohea hugged Uncle Haku fiercely, while Haunani rushed into Po's arms. Nohea found herself crying again. Uncle Haku kissed her head and held her close.

"I'm so glad you're safe," he kept saying over and over. He let her go so she could wipe her eyes and nose. Nohea smiled at Po, his arm around Haunani's shoulder. Then she turned and met Wena's eyes as he knelt on the ground, next to his sister.

All previous anger melted away.

"Wena?"

He stood up and wrapped his arms around her. She cried into his chest, her snot and tears making it hard to see and breathe, but she didn't care. She was too overjoyed to know that her friends and family were safe this far.

"Isn't this so sweet?" Kukui smiled, amused, her arms folded, as she looked about the company. She reached to help Kiani stand up on shaky legs. The two young women embraced, and Kukui let Kiani lean on her.

Kukui cleared her throat. "If I may be so bold to interrupt, the alakaʻi wait for orders from the manō."

All eyes turned to Olukai, who knelt on the ground, alone. He stood and cleared his throat, avoiding Kiani's gaze. Nohea noticed it, but she kept her thoughts to herself.

He let out a sigh. "'Ae, thank you Kukui. I will come now." Then he met every person's eyes. "It's *so good* to see all of you."

"'Ae," said Po, smiling with relief. Uncle Haku squeezed Nohea's shoulders and she dared to glance at Wena, who was staring at her, though it was hard to recognize him beneath all the blood, mud, and sweat. He looked as exhausted as she felt.

"Where's pa?" Po asked Haunani.

Her eyes widened. "I haven't seen him but I'm too afraid to look."

"'Ae, we must find all our wounded, and give our dead a proper burial," said Olukai. "Wena, can you tend to Nohea and Kiani? Haku, I'd like you to stay with Nohea as well... as added protection. Po and Kukui, come with me." He sounded like a true alaka'i. He then focused on Haunani, whose cheeks turned a deep red. "Are you a medic?" he asked her.

She cleared her throat. "I never learned the ways, but I brought as many medical supplies and food as I could..."

"Good, please join the medics in the fortress."

Haunani nodded, and left the tent, followed by Po. "Maybe we can find pa before you have to go with the manō?" Haunani asked. Po nodded and they ran to the field of bodies, hoping Tua was not among them.

Haku and Nohea stepped out of the hut, his arm still around her shoulders. Her whole body continued to tremble, still in pain from her father's pain and the burns across his body.

Wena came from the hut too, standing next to Nohea. When she looked at him, deep gratitude filled her heart. He had been a true friend and loyal to the island and the manō. She smiled at him, but he seemed distracted.

Kukui helped Kiani walk, and Olukai stayed next to them. He wanted to help Kiani, but awkwardness filled him instead. Everytime he glanced at her, she avoided eye contact. Kukui looked from Kiani to Olukai and frowned at the tension between them, but said nothing as they emerged from the tent.

"Should I escort Nohea somewhere else?" asked Haku. "This

doesn't seem like the best place to rest and recover... and surely we should take Kiani out of here."

Olukai nodded, "'Ae, you can take them to my home. I plan on sending the soldiers to their homes across Kaimana, and then we can figure out the deal with soran." He smiled and winked at Nohea, as if to remind that she, the alchemist, knew all the answers. Nohea nodded. She didn't know *all* the answers, but she had a really good start.

Haku hugged Olukai, and, as he clapped Olukai's back, Olukai coughed blood. Nohea jumped.

"Are you alright?" she asked, rushing to him, examining his chest.

"I'm fine," he said, brushing her hand away.

She frowned. "You better get yourself checked by the medics."

Olukai tried to smile, casting a hopeful glance one more time at Kiani. But she kept her eyes to the ground.

"I'll be fine," he said to Nohea and tipped his head before walking off.

As Nohea watched him walking away, her heart hurt for him. He was a leader. He had to be strong, and lead, even when he was tired. *There is the manō,* she thought, *the true king of Kaimana Island.*

Po and Haunani walked across the field, examining the bodies and then helping wounded soldiers to the fortress. When they stepped into the gates, they were surprised to find plenty of able men assisting the medics. Po found out these were the men whom Olukai placed at the top of the fortress walls. Many of them were too young or too old to fight in battle.

Po also noticed many of the young men's heads turn when Haunani walked by. She broke into a run.

"Kamuela!" she exclaimed and hugged him, much to his and Po's surprise. A kapa cloth covered Kamuela's arm, and he mumbled a hello to Haunani. She kissed his cheek then grabbed his face, noticing a large gash across his right cheek. "Are you alright?" she gasped.

"I'm fine," he looked uncomfortable, yet, at the same time, a small smile formed on his lips.

"Are you alright?" he asked, avoiding her eyes.

"'Ae—and Po is alright too!"

Kamuela nodded to Po. Much to both of their surprise, again, Po clapped Kamuela's shoulder and said, "It's good to see you, friend."

Kamuela relaxed.

"Oh and Alika, Kahele, and Ulu!" Haunani ran to the other boys and hugged them each too. They all beamed in pride, showing her their wounds. Kamuela and Po stood off to the side, watching. "Have you seen Tua?" Po asked.

Kamuela cleared his throat and shook his head. "I saw him once in battle..."

"And?"

"And that's it."

"Come on Po," said Haunani, grabbing Po's arm. "Let's keep looking." Po felt all four of the young men's eyes lingering on Haunani until they disappeared into a crowd of soldiers.

"Po!" It was Olukai. He held his ribs with his right hand. "We're having a meeting—you coming?"

Haunani's hand dropped from Po's arm.

"'Ae," Po answered, though he felt sorry to leave Haunani. Olukai disappeared into the group of soldiers again, and Po intended to follow, but he paused.

"I'll find him," Haunani said, barely smiling now.

A song filled the air, about the wa'a:

Sweet air fills her sails,
She glides in the water like a fish,
No wave can break her wood,
She hears the song of the mermaid...

Haunani and Po looked towards the sound of the singing, and Haunani's eyes welled up in tears.

"Pa!" He stood a distance from them, leaning on a crutch. A young man stood next to pa, also on a crutch, an assisting medic.

Haunani and Po ran into Tua's arms, and he kept singing, while Haunani sobbed.

After all the dead men he'd seen in the field, Po knew it was a miracle Tua had survived. He'd been one of the lucky few to get through the whole ordeal. Many men would not return to their homes. Many women had become widows, many children had become fatherless. Po knew he was incredibly lucky to still have a father, even a hānai father.

For the first time, he felt a deep gratitude, love, and admiration for his hānai father. He'd held so much resentment, always asking, why didn't Tua let him become a sailor? Or even a spear diver or fisher?

And now, it all made sense, it all had a reason. If Tua hadn't been so adamant on keeping Po from the sea, Po would've never been here, helping the manō, rescuing Nohea, and acting as the manō's personal messenger. He would've never met the moʻo or even the lady of the lava, who told him where to find his real parents.

If Tua had let Po into the ocean, Po would've never done what he'd done. He would've sailed away forever, never met Olukai, never met Nohea, and so many of his new friends.

"Thank you pa," he said as Tua held his two children back to see their faces. And Tua smiled, knowing exactly what Po meant.

CHAPTER FIFTY-EIGHT

The king of Kaimana Island paced back and forth in his living room. He was worried about Nohea. She lay in the guest bedroom, sick with a fever. Lala did all she could to help Nohea, but Lala was not a nurse. In fact, Olukai swept the fortress, looking for any healers, kahuna, or nurses, but there were none. All who volunteered to be medics were not trained in any ways of healing. It was something Olukai committed to take care of once he got the government organized.

Po rested well, as he'd been badly beaten by his skirmishes with the king's warriors. Bruises and scratches covered his entire face and body. Before he went to rest, Po told Olukai everything that Po and Nohea had experienced: from the black mo'o, to the lady of the lava, and the shapeshifter Kama.

Olukai could see the tiredness in the messenger's eyes.

After having a meeting with Kukui, Po, Haku, Lopaka, and his other alaka'i, Olukai ordered the soldiers and islanders to return to their villages once they recovered. He expressed gratitude to as many of them as he could, and held a beautiful funeral and memorial service to honor the fallen.

Then he retired to his home and finally fell asleep. A medic said he had a broken rib and sustained damage to his lung, so Olukai needed to rest.

But he never found the time, too busy meeting with people, talking with others, and mourning with those who lost loved ones. Four days had passed, and Olukai kept returning to the fortress to say goodbye to the soldiers and islanders. Ekewaka was nowhere to be seen, nor Queen Awa and her kahuna.

He decided not to worry about them, for they held little sway over the people. He doubted Ekewaka could get his own brother to join forces, as everyone knew of Ekewaka and Makana's eternal hatred for one another. If anything, Olukai hoped that Ekewaka and his men would live in exile the rest of their days, though the sight of Akamu's sad eyes did bother Olukai often.

"Sir!" One of Olukai's older servants rushed up the stairs, panting. It was a strange thing for Olukai to finally be at home, instead of walking around the fortress, helping out as much as he could. And it felt like years since he slept in his own bed. "An army approaches."

Olukai's stomach sank. "How far?"

"Over the northern ridge."

That was close. Too close.

"We have no time to prepare," Olukai said, rubbing his chin. "Get the horses ready. We must flee to the fortress."

"I don't think that will be necessary."

Olukai looked to his right, on the balcony. A figure stepped into the light from the shadows, her dark eyes glimmering.

"Kukui?"

"My army will stand watch over your home, and we will serve as your personal guard if you wish it." She folded her arms. "Well?"

It felt like a thousand pounds fell from Olukai's shoulders. He took a deep breath. "I... I don't know what to say. Thank you."

The corner of her lip creased upward. "You're welcome. When you set up your government, we should like to have a good standing with you."

He nodded. "Of course. I see no reason why the Mākuʻe deserve any less."

Kukui plucked a strawberry guava from the fruit bowl on his table. "How is Kiani doing?" She bit into it and chewed.

Kiani.... Everytime he heard her name, deep longing filled his heart. He checked in on her a few times over the last two days, finding her fast asleep. All he wanted to do was talk to Kiani. He wanted her to feel well, and to figure out all the crazy emotions they'd been through. What was real, and what was contrived by the kahuna?

"She seems to be doing fine," Olukai said.

"And Wena?"

Wena kept watch of the house, returning only for meals or to check in on Kiani or Nohea, though Olukai sensed a wariness between Wena and Nohea. Wena also barely slept at all, and he paced about Olukai's home. Though Olukai urged Wena to rest, he had a feeling that Wena wouldn't rest until he knew Nohea's fever went away or that his sister was well.

Meanwhile, Haku found things to do, like helping the servants and staying by Nohea's side as much as he could.

"Wena is... a little restless. But, otherwise he's fine."

Kukui finished chewing and swallowed. "I worry about my cousins." She gazed out to the ocean. "Sometimes I'm ashamed I didn't go after them." Then she sighed before Olukai could say anything. "I found something out, something from a young man who wishes to be a kahuna."

"Who?"

"His name is Makoa. He trained under Noa, Queen Awa's kahuna. He was an apprentice."

Olukai motioned for Kukui to sit on the mats, and he leaned in. Kukui had proved herself a powerful ally, and Olukai appreciated all and any information she found out for him. He had long pondered on the queen's kahuna and his strange ability to control Kiani. He'd seen nothing like it.

He even wondered about Kahiko's abilities. Ever since Ekewaka's warriors surrendered, they sat in prison, each one pleading their loyalty to the manō. They acted crazy, and it bothered him. He figured it was the soran that made them so crazy. They probably wanted to get out because they wanted to get more of the drink.

Yet, there was something missing, Akamu's sad eyes came to mind. Olukai truly felt sorry for him.

"Makoa said Noa cursed Kiani, that is for sure. He collected her blood to do some sort of hex and as long as he has her blood in a small vial of his, he can control her."

"I'm confused."

Kukui, older and wiser than Olukai, tried to keep from rolling her eyes. "It means he can *still* control her if he's within a certain distance." She winked. "I think it's no secret you have feelings for Kiani."

Olukai blushed, but he couldn't deny it. Even though Kiani had told him, over and over, that they weren't meant to be, he still couldn't get himself to move on. Even when there were other amazing, talented, beautiful young women, like Nohea, or even Haunani, Olukai still couldn't help himself from being drawn to Kiani. He tensed but his uncomfortable behavior only made Kukui smile.

She continued. "I know for one thing, she won't stoop to marrying someone younger than her."

Olukai gaped. Was that what this was all about? It sounded so silly.

"And I know she will keep her distance from you because of the curse. If that kahuna were ever to get near her, he could make her do whatever he wanted."

Kukui's words confirmed two things for Olukai: Kiani still rejected him, prejudiced because of his age. And Kiani wanted to stay away from him for his own safety.

So in the end she doesn't want me. It hurt. He swallowed hard.

"How do we break the curse?" he asked.

Kukui eyed him before answering. "Destroy those vials. Or

destroy the kahuna." Kukui shrugged and so many of her gestures reminded him of Kiani. She reached for another guava fruit and Haku entered at that moment. He awkwardly bowed, as if to excuse himself but Olukai motioned for him to sit.

"But would you like to know something else that's interesting?" Kukui asked. Olukai nodded, grateful for her inspections of all the things he had no time to do. "Ekewaka's warriors, the ones in prison, they have the *same* cuts on their arms as Kiani, though the hex mark looks a little different."

"You're saying..." Olukai's eyes grew wide. He understood now. "Kahiko did the same thing to Ekewaka's warriors." It all made sense. *That* was why Ekewaka always took Kahiko with him, not Olukai. The warriors did whatever Kahiko commanded them to, even those who didn't want to, like Akamu.

It was only when Akamu was a good distance from Kahiko that he had his freedom. But, of course, the night Olukai sent Akamu back to investigate the king's whereabouts, the warrior could not return. Kahiko held a firm grasp on him. It was a wonder to Olukai that he never noticed the hex marks on the warrior's wrists. For all the times he'd sparred and fought with the warriors, he couldn't believe this detail had slipped.

"If Kahiko were ever to come close to those warriors," Kukui said, "They would turn on you."

"So we can't set them free until we find Kahiko—"

"And destroy those vials of blood or destroy him," Kukui finished. She glanced at Haku. "Sorry if this is confusing—I can fill you in later." He shook his head, pondering.

Olukai felt sorry for the king's warriors, remembering them standing confused on the battlefield as soon as Kahiko rode away. Guilt sank into his stomach. He'd judged the warriors these many years for drinking soran, but little did Olukai know it was all forced. They probably hated the stuff.

"Why haven't the warriors said anything? One of them rebelled—

Akamu. But he never mentioned the curse," Olukai wondered aloud. "And then Kiani told me right away that she was cursed."

"The kahuna can control what they can and can't say." Kukui played with her high ponytail and added, "Makoa said it is an old, evil curse. It was once buried with a powerful kahuna, never to be spoken again, but I guess it was uncovered."

"The queen's army—were they controlled by the kahuna Noa?"

Kukui shook her head. "Unfortunately not. They were convinced by the queen that theirs was the right cause. I mean, she gave them plenty of soran to drink—it was her secret army that the rest of us knew nothing about." A look of disgust filled her face. "If anything, the queen has groomed them to do her bidding."

Olukai glanced at the direction of Kiani's room, deciding that he would do all he could to help her, but he needed to keep his heart guarded.

Kukui changed the subject. "The island expects you to set up your government. I know you have many curses to break for your friends, but you also have a duty to the people. After all, they defended you."

"And I have a duty to the island," Olukai added. "To destroy soran."

"We will be ready to help when you need it," Haku cut in. Olukai already knew the next steps: Nohea had yet to reveal how to destroy soran, and then Nohea and Po had a duty to find her tribe of meha and remove the curse, her connection to Ekewaka. Po deserved to meet his parents, as the lady of the lava told him their exact location. Just the previous night, Olukai released Po from his service as a messenger. It was bittersweet, excitement filling Po at his freedom, then a lack of purpose. "I'll still help," Po had said. "We have to destroy soran, and I'm here for that."

Olukai looked out to the ocean. It was his first duty to actually destroy the soran, as Po supported. Only then would the island rest, balanced and content.

. . .

Nohea stood on the shore, the warm water rushing past her ankles. As soon as she felt well enough, she wanted to see the ocean, feel it, experience it. She went alone, as Haku had left briefly to visit his family and bring them back to Kea'au village. A sense of peace had overcome everyone, Nohea noticed.

Uncle Haku spoke excitedly about bringing his family back to their home. Kukui spoke endlessly of the Māku'e's willingness to protect the manō at all costs. Several old leaders from the island visited Olukai's home to discuss politics and share their support. Po was eager to help Nohea remove her curse, and meet his parents on the Haunted Island. A new enthusiasm filled the air, the suffocating stiffness of King Ekewaka's rule finally evaporating. Even Olukai breathed easier, with an army that had his back, and especially with Nohea safe.

She told him everything she knew about soran, and, much to her surprise, he agreed that they needed to burn every last bit of uli. It was the main source for soran, so there seemed no point in keeping it around. Though, Nohea worried that even if they burned every bit of soran and uli, the uli might come back, the same way 'ōhi'a trees rose from ashes.

Olukai said he'd ponder on it too, though a quiet thought passed Nohea's mind that it would be impossible to find every bit of uli. If anything, the whole island needed to burn as cleansing, but she didn't say it aloud.

The waves crashed in the distance, sending white mist into the sky. Nohea still looked pale, purple bags under her eyes, a new patch on her eye. Her hair was pulled into a high bun on top of her head. But the ocean... how could she live so many years without experiencing it? Now, with the manō as king, there would be no slaves, no soran. The island would be balanced, and the people would live freely. She could visit the ocean whenever she wanted.

Nohea closed her eyes and soaked it all in. The island filled her heart with warmth, goodness, and peace. Things would work out.

Soon enough, she would remove the curse from her mother, ending the connection with her father. She hugged herself, grateful.

Many of the older men urged Olukai to plan for a coronation after the time of mourning passed. So many had died, that it only felt appropriate to wait before having any kind of celebration. Deep down, Nohea admired Olukai. With so much pressure on his shoulders, he did a surprisingly good job of staying calm.

A light brown pueo flew over the ocean in the distance and Nohea smiled, bowing her head, grateful.

"Enjoying the view?" Olukai approached, looking handsome and stoic, as always. She shivered and nodded, smiling wide. Olukai had cleaned up well, looking rested, yet, somehow, older than the young man she met a few days ago. He wore a cream-colored kihei, which he took off and placed around her shoulders. It was still warm from his own body.

"I love it out here," she said. "The ocean... I can't believe I never got to experience this."

"I love it too." Olukai stood beside her, his hands clasped behind his back, staring out to sea. "You can live out here, you know—" He laughed. "I mean, you can live anywhere on the island. I hope to establish districts and then leaders over the districts. We'll take care of the mermaids, open the bays for foreigners..." Nohea rubbed her forehead, a blankness in her eyes, her mind obviously distracted.

Olukai longed to share all his visions with someone else, all the things he could see happening to Kaimana Island to make it better for everyone, but Nohea looked tired, her eyes vacant.

He didn't blame Nohea for not showing interest. She was still recovering, after all. He cleared his throat. "I'm glad to see you're feeling better."

"Me too. It's..." Nohea swallowed hard. "It's hard feeling what my father feels all the time. I'll be grateful to get rid of the curse."

"And I'm sure he will be glad to be rid of it too," Olukai smiled grimly. He then looked down at her, serious. "Are you concerned about your father? He could be anywhere on this island..."

"Sometimes." She shook her head. "But I doubt he could do anything to me. He looked so..."

"Helpless?" Olukai finished, when Nohea struggled to find the word. She could see the image of her father so clearly, his pathetic body in a fetal position, burning. His words rang in her ears: *You betrayed me! I will kill you!* She remembered the pain, not only physically, but emotionally and mentally.

He had done so much evil in one lifetime, and he pushed violently against the guilt, shame, and horror of it all: keeping slaves, creating cursed soran-drinking warriors, forcing a woman to marry him, killing people for soran, and doing whatever he could to keep his addiction. She should've been angry at him for all he did to her, but... in the end, she only felt sorry for him.

"'Ae." She spoke softly.

"After all these years," Olukai said, "I've accepted that we all have fears, including Ekewaka, including myself."

Nohea glanced up at him. "No—not you?"

"'Ae... I don't know why it took me so long to reveal myself as the ali'i of Kaimana island. I mean, as soon as I did, the island flocked to me. I could have spared so much suffering if I had done something sooner." Even Olukai spoke softly now. The image of his mother filled his mind. She was a true ali'i, and he wanted to follow in her footsteps.

"But you changed." Nohea pulled the kihei around her closer as a salty breeze passed.

"'Ae. We always have a choice." They stood there, both pondering.

"You're awake!"

Nohea jumped, turning to see Po and Haunani rushing towards them. "Does that mean you're ready to go?" Po asked, laughing. Po's healthy color had returned to him, though his skin showed many purple-green bruises and cuts. He wore a one-shoulder tunic, his arms revealing the fights he'd been through. His golden hair, cleaned and washed, was now cut short. Since he wasn't the messenger anymore, he wanted a fresh start.

Haunani rolled her eyes. "Give her a break." She smiled at Olukai and then examined Nohea, looking her up and down, almost judging, calculating. Nohea didn't like it, nor understand it. She'd heard rumors that the island girls—the not-slave people—were quick to judge others based on appearance. She figured this occurred now. Or, Haunani acted suspicious because Nohea wore Olukai's kihei around her shoulders.

"Actually, I am ready to go soon," Nohea said, sighing. "I think the sooner we leave, the sooner we can meet your parents and get rid of this curse."

"And the sooner we can destroy soran," Olukai finished, looking out to sea. Po stood next to Nohea, and Haunani stood on the other side, leaning forward to stare at Olukai.

"I've always loved this view," Po said. "One day I'll be out there sailing. I'll wave to you all, don't worry."

"Or maybe we'll all be sailing too," Olukai laughed, though he realized it wasn't actually a joke. Maybe all the islanders would one day have to sail away. The four of them stood there, enjoying the view of the blue water.

"What changed your mind?" Olukai asked Nohea. She knew what he meant: she left her father to join the manō.

She shrugged. "I guess I had to lose my vision in order to see the truth." She met Olukai, then Po's eyes. They had been right all along. The island had whispered it to her, but she didn't listen. She had turned to the darkness.

But no longer.

Her strange eye would always serve as a reminder to *listen* and make better choices. She was a new person now, with a determination to make things right on the island. "We will destroy the soran," she said to Olukai, and he understood her meaning, as both of them began to realize that maybe destroying soran meant destroying *or* leaving the only place they knew. "We have to, for the future of Kaimana island."

Po raised his eyebrows, studying them both. "That was deep."

For the first time that day, Nohea laughed. Olukai, confused, laughed as well. Soon, all four were laughing, a moment of lightness amidst the heaviness that lay ahead: removing Nohea's curse, meeting Po's parents, finding the old kahunas to break the curses that ailed the warriors and Kiani, and destroying soran once and for all.

As the four looked to one another, friends, brothers and sisters of the island, they knew it would be done. The manō had risen, now the true king of Kaimana Island. The messenger had done his duties, and now deserved to learn his true identity. And the alchemist had chosen.

Nohea smiled at the two young men, her heart swelling with a deepness she hadn't felt in a long time. They each had a long road ahead but, for this moment, this peaceful break on the shores of the blue ocean, with her two trusted island brothers, and, quite possibly, a new friend, she was safe.

The End.

COMING SOON

The adventure continues in Kaimana Island Book Two:

Wrath of the Moʻo

A NOTE FROM THE AUTHOR

Did you know that almost 100 million sharks are killed each year? That's a startling statistic, and one that should concern us. As apex predators, sharks help maintain a delicately balanced marine ecosystem. They're also linked with carbon cycles, ocean cleaning, and much more. Unfortunately, sharks have been demonized in the media for years, as well as killed for things like shark fin soup.

As I've swam with sharks myself, done my own research, and been inspired by shark activists like Ocean Ramsey, I can see why this beautiful species is so important. They are misunderstood creatures and we can do better to protect them. While shark attacks do and have occurred, if you educate yourself on what to do, as well as what not to do, in a shark encounter, you'll feel better prepared. Sharks truly are incredible creatures.

I hope this book has played a small role in portraying sharks in a better light. I imagine my ancestors honoring sharks, not only as 'aumakua, but as ocean caretakers. We can do the same. If you want to get involved in shark conservation, it's never too late to start today. Mahalo!

-Lei

GLOSSARY

This book uses many words from the Hawaiian language. The following glossary contains some of the most commonly used words throughout the book. The *kahakō* is a macron symbol over vowels. It signifies an elongation of the vowel, such as in *hānai, nēnē,* or *hā*. The *'okina* is a glottal stop, in the form of a single apostrophe symbol, used to denote a short break, such as in *a'a, nai'a,* or *mo'o.*

A'a - Broken, sharp, rough lava rock

'Ae - Yes

Alaka'i - Leader, Guide

Ali'i - Chief, Ruler, Aristocrat, King

'Aumakua - Ancestors that take the form of an animal; family members would feed and care for their 'aumakua, and, in return, the 'aumakua warns and guides in dreams, visions, or revelations. 'Aumakua stands for one guardian ancestor, and 'aumākua is the plural form.

Hā - Breath, exhale, breathe

Hānai - Adopted

Heiau - Place of worship, made of stone platforms

Hele - Go, walk, move

Ho'okipa - To entertain, visit, hospitality

Hula - to dance, Hawaiian dance

Imu - Underground oven used to cook food

'Io - Hawk

Kai - Sea, near the sea, seaside

Kalo - Also known as taro; a staple plant used by Hawaiians for food. The root is used to make poi, and the leaves, also known as luau leaves, are used to make laulau or luau stew.

Kalua - Baked in the underground oven (imu), mostly used to describe "kalua pig," which is pork cooked in the ground.

Kapa - Also known as tapa. A type of cloth made from the bark of wauke

Kawa - Usually pronounced *ka-va*, a drink made from the root of the kawa plant

Kipuka - the lush forests growing in the middle of old lava fields

Kukui - A tree that grows *kukui* nuts. The nuts are usually made into lei or used for their oil.

Kuleana - Responsibility

Kupua - Old spirits that could take the form of whatever they wanted, sometimes leaf bodies, flower bodies, bird bodies, or tree bodies

Kupuna - Grandparents, ancestors, old folks

Lauhala - Leaves of the hala tree, used mostly to weave

Lehua - Flower of the 'ōhi'a tree

Leimanō - Wooden weapon with shark teeth around the edges of the blade

Lū'au - Hawaiian feast, also referred to the taro top baked with coconut cream and chicken (or squid)

Mahalo - An expression meaning 'thank you'

Maile - Endemic shrub that is stripped to make fragrant maile lei

Māku'e - Dark brown or any dark color

Mana - Energy, vibe, power

Manō - Shark

Mauna - Mountain

Mo'o - Legendary giant lizards (geckos)

Nai'a - Dolphin

Nēnē - Native Hawaiian goose

'Ōhi'a - Endemic plant that grows in the form of trees and shrubs all throughout the Hawaiian islands

'Oli - Chant that is not danced to

Pahoehoe - smooth, unbroken, type of lava

Palekoki - skirt

Pākīpika - Pacific

Paniana - Banyan trees

Pilikia - Trouble

Poi - A purple, starchy food made from cooked taro (also known as kalo) roots

Pono - Balance, righteousness

Pueo - Owl

Ti - Long glossy leaves used in many ways, including roofing for homes, skirts for dancing hula, wrapping food, making lei, etc.

Wa'a - Canoe

PRONUNCIATION GUIDE

This is a brief pronunciation guide to help you learn the character and place names in this book.

Alana - ah-lah-nah
Alika - ah-lee-kah
Akamu - ah-kah-moo
Api - ah-pee
Ano - ah-noh
Awa - ah-vah
Edena - eh-deh-nah
Ekewaka - eh-kay-wah-kah
'Ele'ele - eh-lay-eh-lay
Ioane - ee-oh-ah-nay
Hea - hey-ah
Haku - hah-koo
Haunani - how-nah-nee
Hopo - hoh-poh
Kaimana - Kae-mah-nah
Kahele - kah-he-lay
Kahiko - kah-hee-koh

Kama - kah-mah
Kamuela - kah-moo-eh-lah
Kawena - kah-ve-nah
Kawika - kah-vee-kah
Kehau - kay-hau
Keoni - kay-oh-nee
Kiani - kee-ah-nee
Kimo - kee-moh
Kukui - koo-koo-ee
Lala - lah-lah
Lapa'au - lah-pah-au
Likeke - lee-keh-keh
Loli - loh-lee
Lopaka - loh-pah-kah
Lono - loh-noh
Maka - mah-kah
Makana - mah-kah-nee
Manō - mah-noh
Nohea - No-hey-ah
Nono - noh-noh
Nui - noo-ee
Olukai - oh-loo-kae
Onekaha - oh-neh-kah-ha
Oni - oh-nee
Po - poh
Pua - poo-ah
Sefa- seh-fah
Sina - see-nah
Sio - see-oh
Tua - too-ah
Wena - weh-nah
Ulu - oo-loo

ACKNOWLEDGMENTS

First and foremost, *mahalo ke Akua*. All thanks be to God. Although this book is not based on a Christian religion, I hope my readers will be able to identify lessons and themes that will bring them closer to God and Jesus Christ. God is good.

Thank you to my husband, Jordan. I say it all the time but it's so true: I couldn't do any of this without you. Thank you for being my constant support, reading my books, and helping me find the pictures I needed for my front cover when I decided to change it ten days before launch. 😂 I love you so much!

A huge mahalo to my sister, Kamele, for being one of my first readers and biggest cheerleaders of *Kaimana Island*. Your enthusiasm, interest, and support has meant so much during this process. Honestly, I don't think this book would've happened without you!

Thank you to my nieces, Mel, Eva, and Sadie, for your examples. I write with you in mind. Nani, thanks for the picture of the shark you gifted me, as it inspired the shark design for this book!

Thank you to Mikayla, my dear friend, for starting the beta reading process on this. I'm so grateful for your friendship, patience, and support along the way.

Finally, mahalo to the rest of my family and friends who have sincerely expressed interest and support of me and my book. I'm grateful for you!

ABOUT THE AUTHOR

From the Big Island of Hawaii, Leialoha Humpherys loves God, her husband, and good food, of course! She graduated with a Bachelors degree in English from the University of Hawaii at Hilo. Her debut novel, *Aloha State of Mind,* came out in 2021 and she plans to keep publishing more self help books, along with young adult fiction and fairy tale retellings. Her work features Hawaiian culture, language, and folklore with plans to incorporate other aspects from her Chinese and Filipino heritage. Leialoha enjoys the ocean, painting, and drinking smoothies. She currently lives with her husband in the small town of Santaquin, Utah.

Email: leialohahumpherys@gmail.com
Website: www.naturallyaloha.com
Instagram: @ladyleialoha
Pinterest: @naturallyaloha

Made in United States
Troutdale, OR
04/30/2024

19551830R00300